talking to God

JOHN F. MCDONALD was born in Carlow and later moved to London. He now lives in Hertfordshire. His diverse career has included a variety of activities — from barman to analyst in the City of London. His writing career took off in 1980 with the stage play *Otherwise Kill Me*, which was produced in London and subsequently translated into French and staged in Paris. Television scriptwriting followed and his work won awards from Channel 4 and Holmes Associates of London. Since then he has continued to write for a variety of media. *Talking to God* is his second novel; his first, *Tribe*, was published by Wolfhound Press in 1999 and he has just finished his third novel.

Also by John F. McDonald

tribe

'McDonald's insight into this very different world allows the reader to sample life from the other side of the tracks ... [*Tribe*] is notable as much for its language as for its examination of things past, and things to come.'

Belfast Telegraph

'Intense prose conveys a world largely ignored in fiction and, in truth, mainstream culture ... *Tribe* is refreshing in subject matter — its hard contemporary pace satisfies. It's a compelling if not unnerving novel about an oft-neglected theme.'

Irish Post

'rich, thick ... and magically poetic ...'

Sunday Independent

'McDonald is an explorer of courage and a writer of immense talent.'

The Irish Times

talking to God

John F. McDonald

WOLFHOUND PRESS

Published in 2001 by
Wolfhound Press Ltd
68 Mountjoy Square
Dublin 1, Ireland
Tel: (353-1) 874 0354
Fax: (353-1) 872 0207

Wolfhound Press receives financial assistance from The Arts Council/An Chomhairle Ealaíon, Dublin, Ireland.

British Library Cataloguing in Publication Data
A catalogue record for this book is available from the British Library.

ISBN 0-86327-856-6

10 9 8 7 6 5 4 3 2 1

Cover Image: Slide File
Typesetting and book design: Wolfhound Press
Printed in Scotland by Omnia Books

for

John and Paul

Author's Note

Even in the twenty-first century, relatively little is known about schizophrenia. While modern psychiatric methods are improving all the time, and genetic research may eventually provide some answers, we are still very much in the dark ages when it comes to understanding, diagnosing and treating this condition. What is known is that schizophrenia affects one in every hundred people throughout the world — it has no respect for class, status, nationality, colour or creed. It is an illness largely neglected by the media, and its devastating effects engulf millions of people every day.

Schizophrenia is not a single condition, but rather a wide group of conditions that are referred to collectively under that title. Few schizophrenics experience exactly the same symptoms, which can range from mild to chronic; and in some sufferers the disease is never detected at all. Thus the experiences of Francis Page, the main character in this book, will not be the experiences of everybody who has had, or may have, the condition. They are authentic nonetheless.

Talking to God *allows the reader through a door — into the mind of a fictitious schizophrenic. The book portrays many strange landscapes that are alien to most individuals, but which are a very real part of the human condition.*

chapter one

chapter one

chapter one

Francis Page was kept in a state of semi-consciousness in Pentonville Prison until arrangements could be made to move him to Broadmoor Secure Psychiatric Hospital in Berkshire. Charges already formalised and a trial pending for the murder of one and serious assault of two more prison screws. Medicated again with something. Ritanserin or amitriptyline or zotepine or olanzapine or phenothiazine or chlorpromazine or sertindole or ziprasidone or MAO1 or MDL100907? And nobody allowed to visit except his solicitor who shouted at him and said he was fucking mad with only eighteen fucking months to go and now he'd never see the fucking outside again. But Francis didn't care. Too far down on the drugs to give a shit about any fucking thing.

Pieces of lost time floated past in the black-hole singularity where there were no certainties. Only probabilities.

Can't stay in here. PROMETHAZINE. The future is out there. Outside the Universe. HALOPERIDOL. In *Amitabha*. Something missing. Something gone! Forever. RISPERIDONE. Words. Meaningless. Repetitive. Grainy and discontinuous. Can't see the whole picture. No windows in the wall. Black inside. Not white. No light. Can't see. No pictures. Everything distorted and compromised. CLOZAPINE. Bizarre and sinister. Can't get back out! From the collective mythological unconscious. Can't. Fourth dimension of evil. Badness. STELAZINE. Can't come back out! Abandoned. Betrayed. Denied. BENZHEXOL. Can't hide from the unbearableness of illusory reality. Not in here! Not in here! Can't escape the urge to escape. Always there. All the time. Can't look at the stars to escape any more. Heaven is closed to communication with God. Look! Don't look! Tell me what I know! Tell me what I don't know! I'm going down! I'm going down! Can't come back out! I can't! Never come back out! To fly with Jesus. Fly with Procla. Fly with Longinus. Fly with Charinus and Leucius. Fly. Fly. I can't! Can't! Can't! Down. Down.

Down.

Nobody came to Francis after that. For a very long time. How long he didn't know. Didn't know what year it was. Or what season of what year. Or what month or day of what season of what year. Except that one minute it was snowing and the next minute the sun was shining and the next minute it was raining and then it was dark early and light late and now it was exactly the opposite. Nobody visited neither. Nobody allowed to visit. Except for once. When he'd been in Broadmoor a long time. Maybe six months. Maybe six years. Hatchet Harry Kane came. Francis thought it was Hatchet Harry. Although he couldn't be sure. It might have been somebody else. A psychiatrist? Things were said. Faraway things at the back of his consciousness. Subconsciousness. He could recall the words with great difficulty. Killing. Was one of them. Trial. Toilet. They were two others. Time? Maybe not. And sex ... sexsex ... something like that. All a blumble to Francis now. All a mumble. All a stumbling crumbling fumbling bumble. In his brain. In the parts I must play and the cues I must take when old men lecture me, bureaucrats hector me, mountains frown at me, lovers laugh at me, the white waves call me to folly and the desert calls me to doom and the beggar refuses my gift and my children curse me.

'I'm afraid you *are* schizophrenic, Francis.'

'Am I, doctor?'

'Yes. But there's a lot we can do these days.'

'Is there?'

'Yes. A lot we can do.'

'Is there?'

'Many things.'

'What can you do, doctor?'

'Drugs. Many drugs. New drugs ... as well as old drugs.'

Francis wondered if the doctor had a God. And who that God was. He didn't really hear the words explaining that the way in which his brain selected ideas and pieced them together was being profoundly affected by the schizophrenia. He was more concerned about the doctor's God.

'That's why you have difficulty in thinking straight.'

'Is that why, doctor?'

'Let me try to explain ... schizophrenia comes from the Greek ... *schizos* meaning split, and *phrenos* meaning mind. Not to be confused, of course, with multiple personality disorder. Which many people do ... confuse it with, that is.'

Words buzzed around in the anaesthetic air — about schizophrenia being a whole group of illnesses — a spectrum of disorders — psychological states — some psychotic — some not. Francis saw the doctor's God. A medicine man. A medicine God. With cures for everything. Analysing. Diagnosing. Telling him the disease usually manifested itself in younger people — but could be episodic — coming and going — on and off. A word God. Absurd God.

'Was it my mother, doctor?'

'No, no ... we don't blame the parents any more.'

'Did my mother give it to me?'

'Some schizophrenia genes have been isolated ... and targeted proteins and enzymes may soon lead to new procedures. But for the moment, we must do our best with what we have.'

'Did I give it to her? Did it seep out of me in her womb?'

'Of course not ... schizophrenia affects a lot of people, Francis, in a lot of ways. For a variety of reasons. We're not really sure about the cause ... there may be many.'

Heard the words. Absurds. Sounds. Saying he may feel misunderstood. Frightened. Alienated. Frustrated. A sickness of the ego. Words like synthesis and perspective — spatial relationships. Anxiety — aggression.

'Not all those who hear voices are schizophrenic, Francis ... and not all schizophrenics hear voices. Ha ha ha ha.'

Francis heard the light laughter. The sound was yellow. Bellow. Ing. Reminded him of other sounds he'd heard. When? Maybe a long ago time. Transparent sounds. Silent sounds. Creeping up on him from behind sounds.

'Will I get better?'

'You'll never be completely well, Francis, but with structured daily routines, along with proper reality testing, supervised group therapy, vitamin controlled diet and, of course, the right medication ... we'll endeavour to reduce the psychotic periods and make life as easy for you as possible.'

'Can I go home?'

'No, Francis ... you can never go home. Not after what you did. Consider this place to be your home from now on.'

'It's not home here ...'

'I'm afraid it is.'

Over the passing months, Francis had many sessions with passing psychiatrists. Each had their own prognosis on his current psychological diathesis and their own hypothesis on his course of treatment and their own interpretation of his condition — or group of conditions. Some talked of primary delusions and some of ego disintegration and some of paranoid delusions and some of cognitive epistemology and some of other things like visions and normality and violence and to Francis all of them sounded suspicious and weird and wired. Crazy themselves. From spending too much time with crazy people.

That's when he thought at all. But they never mentioned depo-medication or sick side effects or terrible torments. Or maybe they did. Behind their hands. When he wasn't listening. And he appeared calm on the outside. And didn't know that the neuroleptics were palliative and not curative and could do long-term damage. Like hyperlipidemia and heartfailure and functionalhyperglycaemia and perniciousanaemia and butterflyrash and osteoarthritis and uricacid and other things as well. Could do? Would do. But he was a mental murderer. A killer.

So?

They discussed depressive delusions and their faces frowned and hands made little expressions of desperation. Others told him there was too much dopamine in his brain — which he understood was a neurotransmitter for messages before a surge of adrenaline. Or serotonin — which was another neurotransmitter involved in sleep and mood and even appetite. And histamine — which had an effect over emotions and could cause bad behaviour. Histamine low. Copper high. Imbalances of zinc and zymogen. And B3 and niacin and nicotinic acid and vitamin C to control homocysteine levels which were harmful to his nerve cells.

Francis couldn't see their faces most of the time and their disembodied voices reminded him of the Alien and the Animal and the Scientist and all the others he had heard. In another life. Long ago. Or maybe yesterday. Talking talking talking talking. About things. Like wheat gluten and opoids and exorphins were bad if you were born in wintertime and prostaglandin and prolactin and melatonin were good if your body could produce them and, if not, they had to be supplemented. Eicosanoids! And the drugs.

Always the drugs.

Francis tried to tell them about the Voices. What they said to him and how he learned a lot of things from them. Until they gave him the drugs. Now the Voices didn't come at all. But the psychiatrists didn't care and said the Voices knew fuck-all and he wasn't to listen to them and it was best if they never came back. Because they were only driving him madder than he already was. Francis told them about Alienchrist and his female friend Animalkhan. And others who hadn't spoken to him since he left Angeline. Or she left him.

Which?

And many mad geniuses and the visionaries who were everybody who ever lived. And ever would. And Scientistein of the Speedoflight and the drugdealers and some others he couldn't remember and Eyeless and Earless and motherfuckers and midgets and *Jeanne* of Dreams and others. Others.

Others!

And they told him things he never knew before. About Space and Life and Time and tiny little atoms and huge philosophies and Death and Madness and the meaning of everything and sometimes he could see it and sometimes he couldn't. And when he did, a light shone at the back of his brain and he could smell the essence of the Universe. And when he couldn't, he felt something sad. Like a loss. Like the death of a child. Francis knew it all meant something. Even if the doctors didn't. Something to it all. Sublime. Supreme. Profound. Pristine. The psychiatrists couldn't see it. He could!

When he was off the tablets.

Francis Page - Parson

They always let him come up for air before a court appearance. So he wouldn't look like a complete fucking cabbage in the dock. A cauliflower. So the judgeslag could see he was responsible for his actions. It was during those relatively drug-free intervals that Francis caught little glimpses of God. And he understood the state of mortality and the concept of infinity and saw beyond himself. Beyond the nut-house. Beyond London and even New York. Beyond the world and the solar system and the galaxy and the Universe. He flew away over the wall and he lovehated those little times while he could. But the purity was too piercing to be sustained for long. The keenness of all his six senses hurt him and then he wanted to go back down under. Where everything was dull and dozy and safe and sound. And he'd rest for a while from the colours and sounds and smells and knowing of all things.

Hatchet Harry didn't come again. If he'd come in the first place. More months or years went by and a trial date set for September. Murder. Or manslaughter due to diminished responsibility if his solicitors could get the charge reduced. Because he wasn't a killer. No. Not that. Many other things. But not that. Terms like 'personality disorder' and 'psychotic disorder' were used. The courts liked them. But they meant fuck-all to anyone except the legal profession and were used to put sick people into prison instead of hospital. Because the politicians didn't want to spend the money. On a section of society that was politically moribund. No mileage. Nothing to be gained from the windowlickers. Spend the cash somewhere else. Somewhere visible. High profile. Hailfellowellmet. Photopportunegenic.

Francis kept to himself in Broadmoor. Much as he'd done in Pentonville. Getting sloppy and dirty and odd looking but mostly too lethargic to care. Sat alone in his cell-room a lot looking out through the barred window and often wanted to kill himself but never enough impetus to do anything about it. At times like that he wished he had the Voices to encourage him. Get him going. Give him the energy and the will to do away with himself. It wasn't that he hadn't the will — just the will-power. Times like that. Times of depression. Times of being down under. The Voices didn't come. Weren't able to get through the dense mind-fog of tranqs. The tranq-teichopsia! And anyway — Francis didn't want no trouble. Even though it was all irrelevant now about remission, and time off for good behaviour, and possible parole, and any thought of seeing the fucking outside again. For a very long time. If ever. The significance of this didn't really register. Only half relevant to Francis at that time. In a way, he felt safer in Broadmoor. In another way he didn't want to feel safer. Wanted the security of the sedatives and also the adrenaline rush of the outside. Sometimes he believed he could settle for the first only to realise later that he missed the second. Missed Fiona's visits and seeing Agnes D'Argensola and remembered now and then the name Glendora. Though he had difficulty putting a face to it. Face gone. Shot away? She drowned. Didn't she? Or maybe it was someone else. Altogether.

And that was ok. Until one evening outside some specialist's office when he was coming up he heard these voices discussing Francis Page. A name he recognised. As his own. Voices that could only belong to the conspiracy cunts. Creeping about all over everyone. Searching their pockets. For bits of information they could use against him. Same shitbags who'd done things against him before. In Amsterdam and Heathrow Airport and other places as well.

'So ... any indications of relapse?'

'Page? Not so far. It's softly, softly.'

'A reducing regime for now?'

'Up until trial time, yes. We want him to be able to stand up.'

Stand up. And be counted. Out. Of the real world. Whose world? Inner world. Outer world. Francis wondered what was real. Reality? Whose reality? Id and ego were one and same now. In the new world. Reality.

'Well ... we'll just keep our fingers crossed. Monitor the situation.'

'What about visitors? Several people have been trying to get in.'

'No! Not a good idea.'

'He was all right with Kane.'

'Wasn't in the real world then. If they saw him now they'd only cause problems ... or try to.'

'What about the daughter?'

Daughter? The word meant something. More than other words. An image. Filling some primal need. An image of himself. On which to construct a new ego. Something that was an extension of himself, yet other than himself.

'Not the daughter. She caused that whole thing in Pentonville.'

'We can't be sure what really triggered him ...'

'She's an addict, isn't she?'

'Ironic, isn't it?'

'What?'

'Page smuggles the stuff and his daughter gets addicted to it.'

'Poetic justice?'

Francis didn't wait to hear any more. Stresstrigger! Heeaarrtt! Beeaatt! Heeaarrttbeat! Heart! Beat! Heartbeat! Heartbeat! Heartbeat! Office suddenly a Charybdis of white coats and flying clipboards. Two consultants caught in a savage rush of punches and kicks and clouts of chairs and computer terminals crashing in pieces to the floor. One of the bastards managed to press the panic button and keep the desk between himself and an obscenity-screaming Francis until help arrived. The other wasn't so quick and left lying on the floor with blood pumping from his head and face. Francis was subdued quickly this time. Because the panic squad in Broadmoor was better trained in these situations than the screws in Pentonville. And there was no crowd of hysterical visitors blocking the door like before. And he was still half-comatosed by the tranqs. Even though they were letting him come up.

Gradually. Soon handcuffed and hypodermiced and a hood pulled over his biting head.

Francis saw the Fenrir in the darkness that followed. Whose jaws touched heaven and earth and swallowed Odin. And the flesh-eating horses of Diomedes. Who ate the carcass of their master. And Francesca da Rimini. Who was put to death for adultery. And the Fair Rosamond. Who lived at Labyrinthus and was poisoned by Queen Eleanor — *hic jacet in tumba Rosa mundi, non Rosa munda*; Who that talking? Who? Who that? Then it was all quiet. Black and quiet. And Francis fell deeper and deeper down the well. Falling. Falling. Waiting for the water to break his bloody neck.

chapter two

chapte r two

chapte r two

I hear him talking at me again. Fuck off and leave me alone! He's saying, listen Chela ... Not when I'm working! He's saying I got to ... Not when I'm working. I can't talk when I'm fucking working! But he keeps on at me ... telling me I'm *yogin* ... And I'm saying I can't talk to you now! But he says I got to! You got to! You got to! For Christ's sake ... He's telling me I'm just like him, Chela ... *Yidam. Chö nyi*. But I don't fucking care if he's God or not. Not God. Jesus then ... what's the difference? I ask him again to please fuck off and talk to someone else? He asks who? And I say a priest or someone. He's saying eternal life, Chela. Eternal life! You're of this world, I ain't ... John, 8: 23. I ask him who he really is and he says he told me, Chela ... I'm Jesus ... Iesous ... Yeshu ... Isa ... Alien. Says he was one of the guys ... the twenty-eight *Nabis*. I don't know what the fuck he wants with me! He says he wants me to follow him, Chela. Do what he did. I say you got yourself crucified. Because it was the *only* way, man. The only way? Because there's no beginning and no end ... like God. I don't believe in God! He says sure you do

Chela, everybody does. They all believe in God now just like they all believed in God then. All the dudes ... Pharisee, Sadducee, Samaritan, Essene, Roman, Hellenist, Hasmonean, Herodian, Sanhedrin, Levite, Sicarii, Zealot ... all believed. All still believe. But He ain't my papa. I ain't His beautiful boy. I say I have to sort some of these wankers out ... I can't can't can't fucking talk! Not when I'm fucking working. He says I can be *Rasul*, like he was ... and Moses. I tell him I'll read the bible! And I ask him again to fuck off or he'll get me sacked. Chela, Chela, Chela ... you can be *arhat*, man ... clearlight ... *yggdrasil*. Go away!

And freedom is at the other side of fear.

Flashing lights above the entrance to the Pink Peacock nightclub winked their welcome to the punters passing by in the death dark street. Come on in! Drink and dive-bomb and dance till you drop. Come in! Francis Page stood in the glare of the crimson entrance. Dressed all in black — *El desconocido Diablo*. Black boots, black bomber jacket and black shirt. Beside him, Agnes D'Argensola and Matthew Moore eyed up the queue. And it's yes sir — you shithead; and madam — you mare. Come in! Come in! Young clientele mostly cautious and courteous, not wanting to tangle with the doormen. Or woman. Francis a fearsome scarface with a reputation for taking no shit from absolutely anyone. *Un Satan en aliéné*. While he took a different view. Saw himself more as a minder. A shepherd. A sheepdog. Keeping his little flock in ordered formation outside the nightclub. A benign benefactor to his young charges. Even if now and then a lesson had to be learned. The hard way.

'Who were you talking to, Francis?'

'When?'

'There now.'

'Nobody!'

'I heard you ...'

'I wasn't fucking talking to anyone!'

'C'mon, I heard you!'

'You didn't fucking hear me, Matthew. You heard nothing! You must be hearing fucking things!'

'Leave Francis alone, Matthew!'

'Sorry I'm fucking sure, Agnes!'

'*Estúpido irlandés!*'

Body searches carried out at the door for concealed weapons and illegal substances which the bouncers quickly confiscated and later sold on or kept for their own use. Francis and Matthew frisked the men and Agnes looked after the ladies.

'Watch out, these little prats here have a few too many in them.'

Always some fulloflager fools who fancied their chances of getting into the Pink Peacock despite the house rule of no pissheads allowed. The bouncers were well used to them. A less salubrious part of Paddington and the club had a good name for fights and drugs and girls on the game. That's why they used Francis — management saw him as an experienced serious-situation diffuser. A deterrent to damage and disorder. By his very reputation. Someone who could size up a potentially dangerous situation and deal with it appropriately. When required. With as little impact on the honest peaceloving and paying public as possible. Francis saw himself more as a fightstopper. Even if he had to start one to do it.

'Where d'you boys think you're going?'

'Inside ...'

'Do I look a complete cunt?'

'You said it.'

Francis didn't like this young brat's attitude. A threatening face. Knew something. Too much. More than was good for him. And his father should have kicked the shit out of him several times and saved the rest of the world a lot of trouble.

'I see we have a hardman here, Matthew ...'

'Looks like it.'

'I'll give you boys one last chance to fuck off.'

'Why can't we go in?'

'Because we say so.'

'Who the fuck do youse think you are?'

'The management.'

The bouncers held their ground in front of the crew of little fuck-faces. But the boys were confident and full of charlie.

'You have to have a fucking reason ...'

'I don't like the size of your ears.'

'Bastards!'

'No need for that kind of swearing in front of the lady, sonny.'

'What lady?'

Francis could feel his heart beginning to beat a bit faster. Why wouldn't this boy just go away? Blood to the brain. Agnes stepped in front of him.

'All you *niños* are drunk, are you not?'

'No we're not!'

'You must be shot up then ...'

'Not that neither!'

'Then you must be *retrasados mentales*, the way you're staggering all over the place.'

'What did she call us? Who the fuck do youse think you are?'

'Not back to that again ...'

Francis irritable now. Jumpy. Suspicious. Jangly. Harder to concentrate. Stresstrigger! Heartbeat-panic-violence. Tried to control it. Didn't want the violence. Wasn't the place for it. Real doormen don't get provoked. Stay cool! He took the lippy boy to one side and explained in very certain terms what was about to happen if he and his mates didn't fuck off. That very minute. The brat answered back. Full of booze and himself. Not realising the seriousness of the danger he was in. The mortal peril of the impending situation. Francis saw Konrad. Saw several people he knew and didn't like. Saw faces of hatred. Society. The Demon. Wanted to fling the young fucker down onto the ground. To boot him around the road like a fucking football until he howled and his friends had to help him away. Until blood and teeth dribbled from his wordless mouth and the vomit came up his throat and choked him. And a river of gore flowed down Bishop's Bridge Road. But he didn't. Stopped. Stoodstill.

Matthew Moore came across and the boy began to get a sense of the situation. Some basic instinct made its way through the fog of alcohol and told him to go. Now. He motioned to his mates and they sloped away down Eastbourne Terrace towards Bayswater. Francis stood back — facing the queue to see if there were any more members of MI5. Or 6. His head twitched from side to side and mouth opened and closed in silent curses. Watch out! Watch out! They'd be fucking after him now. The young people in the queue looked away and didn't meet his eyes for fear of incurring the barelyunderthesurface gutgrowling of the big bouncer.

'A quiet word is as good as a kick in the head sometimes ...'

'I suppose you're right, Francis.'

'Francis always knows what he is doing, Matthew.'

'Although ... sometimes a slap can put manners on them as well.'

'You'd only get yourself done for it. Little wankers go off crying to the cops ... their mammies and daddies get their solicitors onto you ...'

Francis listened to Matthew Moore and wondered who he was. Really was. Maybe Matthew was thinking the same. About him. Francis Page. Who he was. Who was he? Who his God was. Who was his God. Matthew's? Was there something between what was signified and the sign itself? But he never let on what he was thinking.

'Things are different all right these days, Matthew ... not like when we had the right to rough them up a bit. All part of the job. Just doing my job. Doing the job.'

'I would be your witness in any court, Francis.'

Agnes moved her body up close to him. He moved away. Francis sometimes had difficulty distinguishing her from the symbol of her. She was a mobile body set in an immobile space. Sometimes.

'I know you would, Agnes. There, see? No need for silence in court.'

'What are you talking about now ...?'

'Can be too soft. Can't be too soft. Otherwise they'll all think they can do it.'

Who this Chela?

Matthew Moore shook his head and walked back to the door. Agnes D'Argensola smiled and flashed white teeth through her black lipstick. Swung her small handbag with the housebrick inside. Just in case the occasion called for it. The Bolivian eye she fixed on Francis was more than mere admiration for the forty-two-year-old who stood in the club entrance like some dark lethal Laestrygon with a black frown and a mumbling mouth and a distant look in his eye. She moved close again to feel the warmth of his big body. He immediately pulled away and walked nervously up and down the queue.

The doormen allowed a regulated number of bodies to pass inside every now and then. Favouring a few and refusing others who were less to their tastes. Like some lords of land and water.

He won't go away. Keeps talking at me. Saying the glorious unity of being one ... all being perfected into one ... John, 17: 22. I don't know what it fucking means. I don't know what the fucking thing means. Busy, busy. I'm too busy. It means Father, Son and Holy Spirit ... meself, youself and soulself. Son of God, Son of Man. All the samesung self-thing. Don't you see it? No! Don't you want to see, Chela? No! Look! I can't! He's saying unless I become *tsul trim* I can never enter ... Enter? Enter. I ask him who the fuck he really is? You know who I am, man. I'm Alien. Kinda like ... as you hear the *vana* and can't tell where it comes from or where it'll go ... likewise. I say please ... I'm trying to fucking work here. I told you I'm please trying to work. And he's telling me I gotta beware of the serpent within, Chela. It's more than any external danger. You have a duty to yourself, man. You're. Self. No no no no I haven't! I owe myself nothing! Nothing! No. Fucking. Thing. If you alter the I-ness you'll create a new creature. The you that emerges will no longer be you. It'll be stranger. It'll be other. Why don't you go heal the sick or something? Would you listen if I did? No!

Francis noticed the clubbers in the queue looking at him in a peculiar fashion. All turned away from his eyes when he looked back. Shrugged his shoulders and pretended he was talking into a microphone attached to his jacket lapel. John Nightingale emerged from the interior of the Pink Peacock at that moment. And a chill covered Francis. Shook his body. Trembled his deepsoul. *Odi et amo*. Not because he was afraid of Nightingale. But because Nightingale was afraid of him. Francis. Afraid in a fascinated way. A way which drew him like a moth to the candle conflagration.

John Nightingale was an American with some sort of college degree and Francis' South African father told him never to trust those who thought they knew too much. Not that Francis gave a fuck now about anything his father said in dayspast. But the other man looked aloof with long blond hair like a woman and was young and loud and bloodbetter than any of these crazy lowclass cunts. Smiled like a woman. Walked like a woman. Was a woman. Maybe that's why Francis didn't like him. Maybe it was something else. It could be he saw himself twenty years earlier. Just a difference of birthplace and sexual preference. But the same arrogance. The same swagger. The same sureness. And the fear? Still sometimes arrogant and swaggering. But now not so sure. And the fear. Nightingale always rubbed Francis up the wrong way. Maybe it was deliberate. Maybe it was. Affinity? No. How could it be that? Nothing in common. Nothing so condom. Hankie. Pankie. Yankee cunt.

'Francis Page! You're some guy ... a real *nil desperandum* dude. But now you gotta take a break.'

It wasn't what the American said upset Francis — it was the way he said it. Not even the way he said it — the way he meant it. He attempted to move inside the club — Nightingale stood in his way.

'Don't push ... me.'

'Now you sound like Sly Stallone. You a Stallone, Francis Page? You a stallione?'

Why did he do this kind of shit? He knew it upset Francis and Francis couldn't understand. Did he have a fucking death wish? Or was his God telling him to do it? His Yankee God. Hankiepankie God.

'Get out of Francis' way, *puto marica*!'

'Wow, if it ain't miss steel-girdle herself. How the hell are you tonight, Agnes?'

'Not the better for seeing your queerface, Nightingale.'

'Ain't you beaten up any little boys yet? I hear it's the only thing gives you an orgasm.'

'Long as I'm not depending on you.'

Francis didn't wait for any more. He pushed John Nightingale to one side and went into the club. He could hear the laughter following. And the question *mens sana in corpore sano*? And he knew what it meant. Even though he didn't.

Francis' heart began to flutter. Like a flute. Against his efforts to stop it. Agnes came in with him. Prevented him from losing what was left of his temper and turning round to smack the sack of educatedwomanshit on his smirking snout. That was the way Francis usually handled things — when he was provoked — even if he didn't want to. There was no other way. Was there no other way? Only one way. The direct way. But real doormen don't get sidetracked. Stay calm! Even if Nightingale made him feel like killing. And he didn't need to become involved in a bout of verbals with a man he considered his intellectual superior. That would be suicide.

Francis considered most people to be of superior intellect. That was his father's fault — and his crazy mother's. No. Didn't mean that. Yes. Did! Loved his mother. His known and unknown mother — whose memory nowadays he couldn't recognise in situations independent of himself. She was silver. She loved him too but wasn't able to cope with the craziness. His skunk of a father should have stuck by them. But he fucked off, the lousy South African bloody fucking seashit. He was the reason Francis was so fucking thick. Could have stayed around and sorted things out. Now every bastard was cleverer. Every fucking shitarsed prick from Watford to fucking Wimbledon. Especially this university womaniron was smarter — had more words — knew it! Strange words. The prick knew it! He fuckingwell knew!

Francis made his way inside the club and crossed to the bar. Ordered a Jack Daniels and soda. Took the drink and sat alone in a dark corner. Let his heart stop. These verbal stand-offs always depressed him. The same with Angeline. He inevitably backed down and it filled him full of rage. Took everything to stay in control. He could easily get homicidal at times like this. But he wasn't a killer. Many things but no killer! Bad things maybe but never killing. Always been a bit volatile and managed for the most part to keep it under control.

But lately there was a new edginess. Something strange inside him. And he worried about the conversations in his head. Newthing. Nevertherebeforething. That he could remember. Started with Alien talking but now there were a couple of others as well. He knew they were real and he knew they couldn't be. They were all dead people. But they were still alive somehow — otherwise they wouldn't be talking to him. There was some mistake somewhere. He didn't like it. Some bastards somewhere were doing something — why were they talking to him? Francis tried to make sense of it. Maybe it was the world's way of getting back at him for being such a stupid prick all his life. Maybe not all but mostof. Wished he'd worked harder at school. Had a good brain. All the teachers said it. And could have gone for a legitimate job or even become a politician or a plumber or something that made sense. Now. But crazy Annie put a stop to all that. All the namecalling and fighting and the teachers saying how he was now such a little monster after being such a clever boy and expelling him even though he wanted to learn. He wanted to learn! The fucking inchargers and interferers! The fucking fucking fucking intellectuals! Now he could barely read and write and felt inadequate in his dealings with smart people. John Nightingale was a smartman. Had words that he used like a weapon. Francis sometimes wanted to mutilate him. Agnes D'Argensola came and sat with her Bolivian junglesmell by his side.

'Do not take notice of that *bastardo*, Francis. He thinks he is *testículos de perro*, but he is only *culo de perro*!'

'I'm not bothered about that dogshit! Why doesn't he leave me alone?'

'He is after you.'

'After me?'

'As I am.'

'Not right, Agnes! He wants to be like me ... to be the big man.'

'He will never be!'

'He can if he can! He can have it. I don't want it any more.'

Francis tried to make some sense of the scene all around him. Tried to work out what had happened to him. What had happened to his life? What was happening? What was happening to the years? He found it easy to remember some things some of the time. Sometimes he could remember everything and sometimes nothing. Flashes of the past. So real he was almost living them over again. Other times he could see images dimly through a word-haze. Ghosts in the gloom — menacing and threatening. He was glad these images were blurred.

Didn't want to see them clearly. What the future held. What was coming round the corner. He still had the Jaguar, his house and a few shillings in the bank — from the good days. If that's what they were.

But even Francis was clever enough to know he couldn't carry on in this profession much longer. There were no pensions in the door game! Had to make your money while you were in. There was nothing on the outside. Other bastards had done well. But Francis hadn't yet found that golden opportunity — the pot of raingold that would set him up for the rest of his life. And there were more of them like Nightingale — loads of the bastards! All wanting to take over his shoes. Stand in his footsteps. All in some sort of fucking conspiracy against him. All wanting to depose the rightful king. To be the man who took the place of Francis Page. He needed to get out now, while he was still a bit of a legend in his own lifetime. Seen others stay on too long. Become laughing stocks — telling stories for drinks in pubs around the city. Young pricks taking the piss and others taking pity. Agnes slipped her hand into his and gave his fingers a reassuring squeeze. No response. Francis was nervous around women — except for Glendora. There was something about females. All the females in his life had let him down or threatened him in some way. Didn't trust them. Women.

Maybe *that* was the thing with Nightingale?

Agnes was a good-looking girl, but he knew if he gave her an inch she'd take his life and soul. No good! No good! No good! He believed she was only excited by the danger. He had a reputation of mad bad and dangerous to be with and that turned some women on. Francis didn't know why. But he wasn't like that any more and knew he was getting past his shelf date. What then? Would any of them want him then? What the fuck then? They sat there in silence for a while watching the pantomime parade before them. Agnes not removing her hand from his as the myriad lives moved abound them in the half-reality of the club. Grotesque. Threatening. Mocking. A sea of bobbing bodies and a thousand little dramas and comedies being played out against the backdrop of pounding music and swingling beamlight. Francis didn't like being inside the nightclub. The noise was too loud and the colours too vivid and the smell of the crowd too overpowering. Preferred to be outside, where it was dark and cool and controllable.

He's back again! Saying forget about black pigeons, Chela! Whatever that means. He says the essence is much more important, man. I ask him again to please go away and fucking leave me alone. But he won't. He says he's Yshwa. One minute he's Jesus, then he's Alien. And I don't care who he is. I am I. As a man I can't explain clearly, as the spirit of truth I'll live in you ... John, 16: 25. I tell him I'm really really really trying to fucking work here. And it's hard enough without interruptions. But he doesn't care. Calls me Chela and says the threadbare armour of a rational mind can easily be breached by *samadhi*. Man. Telling me I'll regret it if I don't listen. I can't! Why? No time. I want him to leave me alone. He won't. Says he could come back again but the hokey *sems* who yell Christianity would crucify him over again. That's why we gotta talk, Chela. And my word is Love. And I'm just trying to live. Love has nothing to do with it. Even though it might have. Once ... sometime ... pastime. Can't remember. No! They're trying to kill me. Why d'you think they're trying to kill you? I know they are. How? You told me. I did? I say I know what his game is. My game is goodness.

Him and the others ... trying to confuse me. I'm trying to enlighten you, Chela ... How would you like it if I kept invading your head and talking to you when you were fucking busy with something? Would you? Would you? Like it. He's asking if it's that bad for me? But I don't understand the context of the question. Is my meaning a *maya*, grinding out guilt and unreality? Go away! Answer my question! An internalexternal horror? An unremitting strangeness? Grotesque? Angelic? I know nothing! He says he'll teach me, man. Because there is another life ... John 14 :1. Love or hate? Kill or be fucking killed? I know all about that. He's asking if I believe that's all there is? That's all! There's much more. Black and white, death and evil exist for the flesh but not for the spirit ... Matthew 13: 33. I say it's really all just a big fucking joke, isn't it? He asks if I believe God has a sense of humour? I believe life is an unfair fucking thing and I need someone to blame. Don't blame God. I *do* blame God.

Agnes was pulling gently on his sleeve. He looked at her darkskin face through the vivid haze of the kaleidoscope night as she hypostasized before his eyes. Francis pretended to be clearing his throat as he rose from his seat and made his way through the sultry club. His vision and concentration focused as he reached the door and stepped out again into the friendly night.

chapter three

chapte r three

chapte r three

Francis Page was back on the inside of the Pink Peacock nightclub by 2.20 a.m. Doorwork done and time for the house lights to go up and the bar grilles to come down. The madmusic turned itself finally off for the night and left a shattering silence behind. Punters who could still stand upright tilted towards the exits. And the bouncers did their rounds — urging the slackers to drink up please and grabbing glasses from pissed-up paws. Those who couldn't make it under their own steam were helped to the door and those who point-blank refused to go were dragged there. Young girls lay on the floor of the ladies' lavatory, too pissed on Pernod or down on diamonds to be able to walk. Looking at their underwear in the mirrored walls. Agnes D'Argensola took no pity. Hauled out by the hair to where the men took over and threw them into the street — on top of their unconscious consorts. Likely lads looking for a fight after too much Rolling Rock or Sol or sulphates. Given a quiet word first and a knee in the bollocks or a fist in the kidneys if that didn't work. Before being flung outside.

Where they could sort it out with their peers. Police cars patrolled the area, picking up the more obnoxious of the cunts and all the cells full for the rest of the night with puking youths pissing down the air-vents because the duty officers couldn't be bothered to open the cell doors and let them use the lavatory.

Once the Peacock was cleared, the bouncers joined George Dimitrov at the bar for a drink. George was club manager and came originally from Leningrad before it went back to being St Petersburg. Some said he had *Mafiozniki* connections and was sent to London by them to look for ways of expanding their operations. It was a cosmopolitan place all right, the Pink Peacock nightclub in Paddington. With all the Latins and lighteyes and lunatics.

'Is there no end to it all, Francis?'

'Life is a joke that's just begun, that's what I always say, George.'

'Indeed you do, Francis. So you do. Very optimistic it is too.'

'Just like you, George. Wish they were all as easy as tonight though.'

'Agnes had a few pillheads in the ladies'.'

'Couple of *estúpidas colegialas* on dennis-the-menace. Nothing to worry you boys about.'

'Oh, you are a very useful woman, Agnes.'

'Tell that to Francis.'

Agnes D'Argensola moved down the bar and sat beside Francis Page, resting her Altiplano arm on his shoulder. Matthew Moore chatted to the bar staff while John Nightingale drank back a mineral water quickly and picked up his blondehairflying coat.

'You broads may have nothing to do tomorrow, but there's sure more to life than this joint.'

'Like arsebanditry?'

'Don't go knocking something you ain't tried, Matthew Moore. *Sua cuique voluptas*. Or maybe you have ... with Francis Page there?'

The American was going the right way — the wrong way — the right way about getting a short sharp shock. Fucking smartman! Francis wanted to answer him. Use some smart words to put him down. But the Universe was losing its spatial structure and being replaced by something subjective and unstable. So what came out of his mouth wasn't what he intended.

'I'll fuck you, Nightingale!'

'There ... *veritas vos liberabit*!'

Another bout of facing off with the fucking Yankee as George Dimitrov got his big Russian head between Francis and John Nightingale. The American laughing and Francis fighting his emotions. Told himself he wouldn't be the first to face down. But he was. Because all this eye-contact stuff was a load of shit. Meant nothing. And he knew that many physical ailments had psychiatric symptoms. Annie told him. So who gave a fuck? Nightingale's laughter subsided to a smile and he said catch you guys Saturday as he sauntered out of the club. Francis was glad to see the back end of the bollocks. One of these fucking days. He knew. He knew. Agnes pulled him back to the bar where he stared at the shadows in the glass surface of the counter. The suggestiveness gleambeamed back at him. And he could remember as a boy looking at his own reflection in mirrors. For long periods of time. Looking in. And not being able to recognise who was looking out. Himself but not himself. Trying to touch the image — but the mirror-glass got in the way. Then he saw himself cry — though he himself wasn't crying at all.

'Why do you have that homosexual *agitador* here, George?'

'Not down to me, Agnes. I am told who to take on.'

'You are the *mánayer* ...'

'I am indeed, but Percy Shillinger owns the place.'

'What's his connection with Nightingale? And what's with this Latin bollix?'

'It is better for a man in my position to keep his mouth shut, Matthew.'

Despite his reticence, George Dimitrov told the others that John Nightingale came from some dull place called Hartford, Connecticut which was really a sort of conservative high-rent suburb of New York. Where rich people could cheat on their taxes. He came from a military family who could trace their roots right back to the revolutionary war. Went to Yale where he studied the classics but fell in with some New Haven undesirables outside the Ivy League idyll. His father sent him to West Point to knock that kind of crap out of him but he got some general's back up.

'Probably touched his arse.'

'Or wouldn't.'

Agnes and Matthew wanted to know more. But Francis wasn't really interested. It didn't matter where the man came from. He was still a strangething. A dangerousthing. But he sat back and listened to the others with an affectedness dissociated from an intelligence that was intact and not intact at the same time.

George was gabbing on not like a man who was afraid to open his mouth — about Nightingale sodomising some rich boy and getting slung out of the army. Then his family disowned him so he hung around the Christopher Street area of Greenwich Village for a while before making his way to London.

'But how did he get into this game?'

'That is all I am prepared to say, Matthew.'

'Maybe Shillinger is queer?'

'No, no ... he has his girls ...'

'Just because he runs a string of *putas*, does not mean he samples the goods.'

'I tell you both, it is nothing to do with me. And I would not be going around saying too much stuff like that neither.'

'Agnes can say whatever she likes ... and so can Matthew.'

'*Gracias*, Francis, *majete*.'

'All right ... have it your own way. But do not be telling it to me.'

Matthew Moore drifted off soon after, saying he had a young woman waiting. George let the bar staff out and started his rounds — locking all the doors and turning off the lights. Francis stared into his drink. The glass seemed to be alive — and the drink inside it as well. And laughing at him. He looked up and the other drinks on the bar were doing the same. So were the bottles and the stools and the tables. Talking to him — all at the same time so he couldn't understand what they were saying. Just a jumble of words growing louder until it was all shouting and screaming.

'How are you going to get home, Agnes?'

George Dimitrov's voice brought a sudden silence. Everything still again.

'I will call a taxicab.'

'Francis can drive you. Will you not, Francis?'

'I don't know ...'

'It is only over in Southwark ... on your way home.'

'Look, George ... I can see the snow-white feathers falling ...'

'What?'

'Like pieces of torn paper ...'

'What are you talking about, Francis?'

George Dimitrov looked at Agnes D'Argensola and rolled his eyes upwards. Her responsive frown told him to take his own advice and keep his mouth shut.

'Ok! All right! I'll take her.'

'Very good man yourself!'

The streets of London were mainly deserted as the Jaguar stalked its way east along the Marylebone Road. Francis was quiet. Thinking. About the big deal he was waiting for. It had to come soon. Maybe a run of luck on the horses or a miracle down at the Cosa Nostra Casino in Gloucester Place. Or save some rich punter's life and be rewarded with a small fortune. Or find a priceless piece of jewellery on the floor of the men's lavatory in one of the clubs. Might be lucky with the lottery numbers or get a job minding some big shot. All pie in the fuckingapplesky. Couldn't be counted on. And there was always the drugs. That's how most of the bastards made their stash. That's where the big cash was, despite all the chit and fucking chat about it. Selling the snow and charlie and wash. Flogging the smack and junk and diamonds and doves. To make the kind of money Francis wanted, it would have to be hard stuff. Nothing in dope or grass these days and happy faces were two a fucking penny. New things coming on the market all the time — like flatliners and fiends and all kinds of other shit. No knowing where it would end. Dealing or smuggling. Or both! Where the big money was. The place to be. A dangerous game — but that wasn't what worried Francis. There was something else. You could trust no fucker. He heard the bastards on the television — saw them smiling with their skeleton skulls. Just waiting to catch him out and he had to be careful. It wasn't just the normal risks — he skinned the odd spliff and snorted the odd line himself every now and then. Sniffed the billy sometimes to keep him on his feet and chewed a bit of blot at parties. It was just the junk he didn't like. Had no time for junk or junkies. Wasn't scared or any fucking thing like that — just didn't trust the noncey stories and didn't like ugly money. Agnes had fallen asleep with her black hair spread out across his shoulder. Francis knew she liked him but he wasn't able to like her back. Not that he had anything against her. Just couldn't like her back. That's all.

Sometimes he could remember being born. Not all the time, but sometimes. Other times he could remember fuck all. People and places he had known just disappeared temporarily from his mind. Gone somewhere — not necessarily destroyed completely. But gone somewhere more remote than the ordinary past. Francis drove the car along the Embankment and across Blackfriars Bridge into Southwark.

He's saying that heaven and hell are just different points of the same view. Alien. Again? Sure thing, man. Samsara and Nirvana are one, Chela? I ask him where he's coming from? Where does he get from to pester me all the time like this? He says he's from the planet Gyr which orbits round the sun-star Gamma-Ben. I say I thought he was the Son of God? I had to tell them something! What else could I have said? What else would the softintheheads have understood? I reckon he'll tell me next his fucking spaceship crashlanded in Bethlehem in the year dot? Of course not, Chela! I was implanted, man. Mary of Judah was abducted and I was implanted. Fuck off! Please. For sure! Jesus Christ! That's what they called me ... my people wanted to see if the human line could be genetically improved. Enlightenment bred into the darkness, so to speak. *Dharmakaya*. The Son of Man came into the world so men should understand the life which is implanted in them ... Mark, 12: 2. He's saying now they weren't the first. Who? Them. I want to know why his aliens didn't just come down and exterminate us? He says because they're civilised, Chela! We just wanted you guys to open up your minds ... stop behaving like savages. You humans will be out there in the Universe some day, we don't want you going around annihilating everything just because you don't understand it. Love. That's what he says he's trying to teach me ... to bring truth he neither shouts nor is his voice raised and he won't break a straw or put out the smallest light and all hope of men is in his teaching ... Matthew, 4: 20. That's what I'm trying to explain, man. That's what I gotta understand. And what does he mean, they weren't the first? He says his race ain't the only masqueraders. Enoch the Ethiopian was from the Galaxy of ÇGhxsty and Juliana of Norwich from the Ñšøμ†æ Nebula. You mean there's half-breed aliens running about all over the place? He says not us, Chela ... we discontinued the experiment. Why? Because you guys crucified me! But then ... you don't believe Alien, do you Chela? Only Hollywood and Hell. Not until I see for myself. See for yourself! Spaceships! He says you don't need a spaceship to travel in the Universe. You do! It's just a matter of knowing. Yourself. What you are. Only those who understand the enlightenment can become like God ... John, 1: 12. I don't understand. He knows I don't. That's why he's here to teach me. Love is my word. *Chö nyi* is my word, man. Just close your eyes and look inside. You gotta know the inner Space to know the outer Space. Then you can find everything you're looking for, Chela.

Death is the meaning!

Agnes D'Argensola stirred and woke, rubbing her eyes as the car came to a halt outside her flat near St George's Circus, at the southern end of Blackfriars Road. She smiled brightwhite teeth at Francis and leaned over to kiss him on the cheek. He pulled away.

'Sorry ... I must have dozed.'

'Don't worry about it. Does the colour of the sky look different to you?'

'It is dark, Francis. It's night.'

'That's what I mean.'

'Want to come in?'

'Better not ... it's late. You're tired.'

Agnes' eyes fired up for a moment. Then grew soft again.

'Why do you not like me, Francis?'

'I'm married, Agnes ...'

'Only in name. It's not a real marriage.'

'What *is* a real marriage?'

'One where love lives ... but, I don't want to marry you, Francis.'

Agnes let her arms go round his neck. She kissed his ear and allowed her tongue to lick at the corner of his mouth. Her hand crept down between his legs. Francis didn't pull away. But he didn't respond either. Agnes persisted for a while then sat back frustrated in her seat.

'*Tipo raro*! What is the matter with you, Francis?'

'Nothing.'

'What is the matter with me?'

'Nothing.'

'Do you not find me attractive?'

'Of course I do ... anyone would ...'

'Why do you not fuck me then?'

'Look Agnes ... fuck wouldn't be, sort of like ... part of it ...'

He tried to say some words that would make her understand — that she shouldn't blame him because he couldn't say them. It was too smooth. Too impersonal. She wanted to understand him. It wasn't that she didn't. It was that she couldn't. And that wasn't his fault. Even if it was.

'You are not making sense.'

'I've got a lot of problems at the moment ...'

'I would not be a problem.'

'You're young. I'm old ... older. Too old. Angeline has a lover ...'

'What? All the more reason ...'

'I feel exhausted sometimes, Agnes. Not just inside ... I can feel it outside my body, lying on me like a stack of bricks.'

'It's that black bitch, is it not?'

'Don't call her a bitch!'

His tone told her enough was enough. Silence fell down between them in the car. Like a smoothshiny wall. That could never be climbed over.

'Ok Francis ... I can take the hint.'

'Sometimes the younger are older and the older are younger ... fuck Angeline!'

'*Jesús Cristo* ... what are you talking about?'

Agnes jumped from the car and slammed the door behind her. Chinasupaystamped away across the pavement to the front door of her flat. Then looked back at the car once she had the key in the lock. Already moving away from the kerb. Agnes stood watching the Jaguar until it turned the corner. Then slipped inside and closed the door. Francis sighed deeply as he drove back across the bridge and up through the East End. The sky seemed luminescent — a kind of deep velvet colour. He felt sorry for Agnes even though he knew he shouldn't. She would have to trust him. He knew what he was doing.

It took just over ten minutes to get home to the Leytonstone Road in Stratford. Francis parked the car on the driveway in front of his garage. Looked at his watch. 4.23 a.m. He sat behind the wheel for a few minutes. His babies would be in bed. They were used to his unsociable hours. Angeline never got used to it — nor did she ever manage to accept how Francis made his living.

They met fourteen years ago. Francis was twenty-eight and Angeline twenty-three. She was in the beauty business and he had the world at his feet. Or so he thought. In reality he was only an approximation of the man he believed himself to be. Angeline worked for Revlon as a beautician and was a very glamorous woman. They met at a club where he was minding and started going out together. Her family were Irish Catholic noseintheair arseholes and didn't trust him. Even though he and Angeline were in love. Backthen. For such a short time. He loved her not for the obvious reasons but for her sureness. She was always sure. Knew where to go. Where she was going. Never doubted herself for a minute. Not like him. He liked that. Was drawn to it. This knowingwhereyouaregoing thing. But she made one mistake in her life. And that was taking up with him. Francis Page. Or that's what she said even though she loved him. She loved him and still she said it. Without laughing. Like it was true. Why? Three months after they met she was pregnant with Fiona. Francis knew she never forgave him for that. Even though she didn't say it. Like she said about making the mistake. That's how he knew it was true. It stopped her going where she wanted to. Finished her career and gave them a child that neither of them really wanted. Knew what to do with. The noseintheairers wouldn't hear of abortion and insisted on a full church wedding. The fucking hypocrites. For appearances' sake. In a way it was ironic. She married him even though she made that one mistake in her life. Or so she said. And he married her even though he knew she'd never forgive him.

The glamour went out of their relationship with his unsociable hours and her failure to adapt to early motherhood and dull domesticity — though she had to in the end.

Little bubbles of memory rose and burst on the roof of Francis' head. He wanted to sit there forever, never having to go any further. Never having to go inside the house again and never having to compromise to the situation again. Three years after Fiona was born, Francis and Angeline got it together for another brief period and she fell pregnant with Sinéad. Angeline had a hysterectomy after that and the earth never moved for either of them again. Once the girls grew older, Angeline got back into the beauty business. Now she was a cosmetics buyer for Yves St Laurent and travelled all over the country, and abroad as well. She earned more money than Francis and was, for the most part, her own woman. They stayed together partly for the sake of the noseintheairers but mostly because neither of them was willing to give up their share of the girls. But they were only hanging on by their fingernails. She was. He was ok most of the time, except when she got into her betterthanyou mood. No love? Lovehate. Maybe Alien could talk to her as well and it would all work again. Maybe not.

Francis closed the car door quietly and didn't turn any lights on inside the house. Took off his shoes before climbing the stairs and checking on the girls. Then slid into the twin bed on his side of the room. Angeline was in the other one and was turned away from him. She remained in that position. Whether she was awake or asleep Francis didn't know. Neither did he think he cared. Any more. But really he did.

Sometimes I just don't need it. Chela ... Go away, for fuck's sake! Come with me and I'll tell you everything ... John, 1: 38. I don't want to know everything. He says I gotta know about Nir ... about Eden ... about Dodona ...? I'm tired. I don't want to talk to him any more. He's asking if I see that Being necessarily transcends and eludes ordinary objective thought? I don't see anything. My eyes are closed and I'm trying to sleep. The Kingdom of God ain't in any definite time or place, it's like lightning, here, there and everywhere ... Luke, 16: 23. He says I know there's gotta be more than meets the eye, Chela ... why d'you fight it? Not to you there isn't ... you don't exist! Don't I? No, so do me a favour and let me get to sleep! If I don't exist, how can I leave you? I need to get some rest. Wait, Chela ... come to me out of your shadowy world of unreality. The Kingdom of God is within you, man ... Matthew, 13: 15. Leave your anger and your little life of comparative values and come to the absoluteness of *tat tvam asi*. Let me sleep, for Christ's sake! Saying he could stop by my dream and I'd see the *bindu* of mindstate. Jesus! Sure! Sure! None of this is making any fucking sense! I don't want to hear any of this stuff. I don't want him to tell me anything ... explain anything. I'm afraid to know ... Don't be scared ... you'll be all right. I'm that consciousness which is within you ... Matthew 22: 43. After the defective tissue is dead, life goes on. Where? Heaven? Hell? Neither. Where then? Well ... that depends. That's why we need to talk, man. I need to explain. No! There's always a fucking catch. A price. A hidden agenda. Small print. Explain what? Why you should listen. Otherwise you'll die without having learned anything. Maybe I'd be better off. You'll only have to come back again ... *Eli Eli lama*

Sabachthani! I don't want to listen any more. He says there's a danger of getting stuck in a reincarnation rut if I don't. Go away! It might take me a million years to get out of it ...

Angeline stirred in the other bed. She didn't turn towards Francis, neither did she say anything. But he knew he was disturbing her. He didn't want her to wake because they'd only have an argument and he didn't want an argument because he was afraid to have an argument. He didn't want her to tell him again what he was ... like Alien was telling him. Like everyone was telling him. He didn't want to know. Ignorance was bliss. Who wanted to know anything? It was all a load of bollocks anyway. It definitely was! Divinely was! So he closed his eyes and allowed the shroud of sleep to be pulled down over his head — until the next day of dreams. When he'd once again face the growing threat of his own world.

chapter four

chapte r four

chapte r four

Francis Page was visited in Broadmoor by his defence team two weeks before trial. Not that there was much defence to be made. But mitigating circumstances could be taken into account and pleas entered for clemency and portfolios of other codifications put forward. Fiona came with them. Bastards at Broadmoor didn't want to admit her at first, but the solicitors insisted and she was eventually allowed to see her father. The legal beagles made themselves scarce for a while so the two of them could have a few private moments together. Francis had been solitarily confined for long periods and given large doses of drugs after the incident in the consultant's office. The psychiatrist who didn't run quick enough was lucky. Only concussion and nonlife-threatening lacerations to the head, face and neck. And it could have been a lot worse. The fact that Francis was still on the neuros, seds and tranqs at the time saved the sod. And prevented another murder. Or manslaughter due to diminished responsibility — and psychopathic personality disorder. Meant Francis wasn't allowed completely off the tablets during his trial. Although the drugs were being gradually reduced again so that he'd be seen as lucid — at least to some extent. But still groggy. And grotesque. And uncle John gone. Fiona sat opposite and was alarmed by his appearance. Hadn't seen him since that mad-dog day in the Pentonville visiting room and never before in this kind of state. Like Agnes D'Argensola, who was horrified when she saw him in prison and made the slags at the Ville bring him back to life. But Broadmoor was a different place altogether and these bastards were a law unto themselves and could do whatever they liked in the name of medical necessity. Francis didn't seem to recognise her at first. Looked through her. Like she wasn't there.

'Dad ...'

He didn't reply. His tongue protruded slightly from the side of his mouth and he twitched rhythmically from head to toe. Slumped over in the chair with muscles seemingly cemented in an abnormal attitude. Fiona a little afraid at first and looked around for re-assurance from the solicitors. But they'd left the room and were talking to one of the consultants outside the door.

'Dad ... it's me.'

'Who you?'

Francis had difficulty talking and slurred his words. As if he was drunk.

'Fiona.'

'Fiona?'

'Your daughter.'

'Drugs ...'

'What?'

'Heroin. You on heroin.'

She hesitated before answering.

'Who told you that?'

'I know! They told me ...'

'Dad ... I'm not on heroin ...'

'Show me the arms!'

'Dad ... I'm telling you I'm not ...'

'Let me see the arms!'

Francis tried to grab her but she pulled away from him.

'No!'

'You on the junk. You a junkie ... and it all my fault.'

'Oh, Dad! Dad ... Dad ...'

'Don't cry baby. I'll be out soon. I'll make sure everything is sorted. You don't cry baby. You don't cry. Out ... out ...'

Yet there's a spot. Where? Where? Out damned spot! out, I say! Let me see your arms. One: two: why, then 'tis time to do't. Don't do it baby ... you'll go to hell if you do it, didn't I always tell you that? Hell is murky. Fie, my lord, fie! A soldier, and afeared? Just for you baby, not for me ... What need we fear who knows it, when none can call our power to account? No! No! No power at all ... the junk will only kill you honey!

'Dad ... come back to me. Please!'

'It's your mother. Is she here?'

'She's not here Dad. Only me.'

The Thane of Fife had a wife; where is she now? I know it's you Angeline. What do you want? What, will these hands ne'er be clean? My hands are clean Angeline ... I'm sorry about Bertie. Sorry I lost my temper. But he asked for it. No more o' that, my lord, no more o' that: you mar all with this starting.

'Dad, I'm going to get someone ...'

'No. Wait! Wait! I've been down in the quicksand, Fiona. Something is breaking through ...'

'What are you talking about?'

'Let me listen. Let me listen for a minute ... before I sink again.'

Here's the smell of blood still: all the perfumes of Arabia will not sweeten this little hand. Blood? I'm no killer! Let me see it ... let me see your arms. Wash your hands; look not so pale: I tell you yet again, Banquo's buried; he cannot come out on's grave. Matthew is buried in Strangeways. I'm buried too Angeline. I'm buried in quicksand and I can't climb out. Help me! There's a knocking at the gate: come, come, come, come, give me your hand. Take my hand Angeline! Help me out! Help me! I just want a little bit of help. What's done cannot be undone.

'Oh, Dad ... listen, I do a little cocaine, not heroin. That's all. I'm not an addict. No big deal. Everyone's doing it.'

'I brought it in. How much?'

'Plenty of people are bringing it in ... not just you. Not that much. Don't worry about it. I can cope with it, Dad.'

'I'll sort it for you when I get out. Ok?'

'Oh I'm sorry. I'm so sorry. There's nothing to sort out, Dad. I'm so sorry.'

Fiona had already signalled for the others to come back in and the visit was ended. Francis led back to his room-cell and the legal team shook their heads in resignation while Fiona was eyed up and down and frowned at for upsetting her father. Again! Francis lay on the bed and held on to his head. Little shafts of light pierced through. Quick flashes like lightning. Bright for an instant and then black again. Trying to get through the invisible psychotropic straitjacket. The ortho-molecular docosahexaenoic eicosapentaenoic entity that he'd become tried to listen. And then waited. Waited. For the light.

Later that night he asked to be allowed to go to the prison chapel. Where he knelt and raised his head to the surrounding images of God. There was no one else to talk to now. Not Alien and not Animal and not Scientist nor nobody else. Only God now. Only God knew. What it was all about. Francis kept softly repeating the words — it won't be long. It won't be long. It won't be long. Over and over. Lips moving but barely making a sound. Justice will be done. Justice will be done.

Justice will be done. Over and over. I am the avenger of God. I am God's revenge. I am vengeance. I am vengeance. I am vengeance. I am Genghis. I am Gehenna. I am Geryon. I am Gayomart. God. Satan. God. Satan. God. I am God! Francis bowed his head and prayed. I am not yet born; O hear me. Let not the bloodsucking bat or the rat or the stoat or the club-footed ghoul come near me. I am not yet born, console me. I fear that the human race may with tall walls wall me, with strong drugs dope me, with wise lies lure me, on black racks rack me, in blood-baths roll me.

Francis stayed in the chapel until the whitecoats came for him. They stood in the doorway and watched him for a while. Sniggering to themselves. Then brought him back to his cellroom. They were pleased to think he might have found religion and would be less of a fucking problem for them from now on. With the help of God. All smiles and there now, Francis, things are never too bad to talk to the Lord about. Are they now? Never too bad. Talk to God. To God!

Trial day bright and sunny. Autumn beginning to show itself across the suburbs of West London as they drove east to the Old Bailey again in a white prison van. Screws either side and chains on his arms and ankles. Like he was some sort of fucking homicidal psychopath. Hannibalcannibal. Psychiatrists lightened the load of drugs even more in the last two weeks and especially as he was spending a lot of time in the chapel. Repentant? Remorseful? The prison chaplain even came to see him in his room-cell. But Francis wasn't interested. He wanted to talk *directly* to God. Not through any fucking intermediary.

Today he was feeling only half-fucked. Instead of completely comatosed as he'd been for an interminable time. And he was taking things in. Everything he could focus on. While the sense lasted. Sat in the dock and looked around at the fussing and flouncing of the learned friends and the clerks of court and newspaper hacks and public pricks and weirdo wankers who always went to these sorts of things. Fiona on her own. No one with her. No Angeline. No Glendora. No Sinéad. No Agnes D'Argensola. Francis saw Detective Sergeant Spencer down in the well of the court. Sitting. Smirking over at him. Come out of curiosity. Or maybe stitching up some other poor prick. And behind him Hatchet Harry Kane in a tracksuit. With one eye winking.

No jury this time round, as Francis' barrister had copped for a plea of manslaughter and the prosecution knew they'd get fuck-all else under the circumstances. Only a matter of going through the motions and the judgeprat putting his seal of approval on proceedings. And a life sentence of semi-consciousness. Francis sat through most of it with the words floating round the room and out through the windows. Off on the Autumn air. Some words were large and some small. Some nearby and others far away. Mostly red but some a different colour. Shades of intensity. They hummed and buzzed round his head and into his ears and out again. Flew up high to the ceiling and fell back down and crawled across the floor. Some were confident and strutted out of arrogant mouths. Others cowered inside on tight tongues and tried to sneak out unnoticed over reticent teeth. Some were spat out and some blown like kisses. All indecipherable. Incoherent. Intricate. Intolerant. Intimidating. Francis stood or sat as directed by the screws on either side of him. They took the chains off his arms but the ones round his ankles still clinked and rattled when he moved and he tapped his feet and made a little tune for a while until one of the screws stopped him.

Francis wasn't even sure what the outcome of it all was. Just the bad words. The black words. The slapinthefacewords. Like life and years and undetermined and the final fatalistic words of take him down. Francis spent some time in a holding cell after that — beneath the courthouse. While the screws had a cup of tea and cracked a couple of jokes with the barristers and another case came up before the judgebeak. Someone brought him a cup of black coffee and a cigarette and about twenty minutes later the slags came in and said it's time Francis. To go home. Handcuffed to one of them and on the way out of the building he asked to go to the lavatory. The screws frowned and wanted to know why he couldn't have went downstairs. Francis didn't have an answer. He remembered the word. Toilet. Above all the others in that day of words he remembered that one. Toilet. And where. Where was also important. *Where* he should ask them — to go to the toilet. He remembered that too. Francis didn't know how he remembered. Or why he remembered. But he remembered what and where. They took him up a flight of stairs to a remote lavatory and one of the screws checked first to make sure it was all secure. The man he was handcuffed to took Francis into the toilet while the other one stayed outside the door.

'Well?'

'Well what?'

'You said you needed to go, Francis.'

'I know what I said.'

'Well ... fucking go then. We haven't got all fucking day.'

'I want to have a crap and I can't wipe my arse if you're there stuck to me.'

'Oh, for fuck's sake ...'

The screw unlocked the handcuffs and Francis walked inside a cubicle. About to close the door, but the screw kicked it back open.

'You know the rules, Francis — visible at all times.'

Francis lowered his trousers and sat on the seat and waited. A moment later the other screw was flung through the lavatoryroom door by Hatchet Harry Kane. Holding his eyes and Harry holding a pepper spray and a small axe. Francis instinctively jumped up and struck his minder a doublefisted blow across the side of his square fucking head. The screw fell back across the floor but didn't go down.

Francis tried to kick the bastard but the chain round his ankles tripped him and he went over onto the piss-soaked floor. Hatchet Harry gave the screw a squirt of the pepper spray and clouted him across the head with the side of his axe. Slag fell unconscious onto the floor beside Francis. Blood running out of his head and ear. Harry helped Francis to his feet and then walloped the other screw straight in the face with the axe — to stop him screaming and staggering around the place. Went down like his friend with claret spraying from his left eye. Francis wasn't too sure what was going on but he didn't care. Old instincts started to surface which made him move and follow the flow.

'Quick Francis, we only got a few minutes ...'

'For what?'

'To get you out of course. Take that slag's uniform off before it gets covered in blood.'

Harry began to strip the man nearest to him and Francis copied with the other one. Kane took off his own tracksuit and dressed in the uniform — which had blood all down the front of the shirt. Francis couldn't get his trousers off because of the fucking shackles. Searched frantically in vain to find the keys and finally had to break the chain with the axe. Harry was panicking and urged Francis to fucking hurry while he propped the two screws up on seats in the cubicles and closed the doors. Francis still had the shackles round his ankles and wrapped the loose chain up along his leg and tucked it into his sock. His uniform fitted but Harry's was too small and a lot of blood on both of them. But no more time and someone could come into the jacks at any second. Had to chance it now or get caught and banged up for ever. Never see the light of fucking day again.

'Keep turned in towards each other, as if we're talking ... and don't look at anyone, Francis.'

They moved carefully downstairs and out into the courtyard and across towards the gate. Didn't hurry and pretended to be deep in conversation. Twos and threes of policemen and prison screws stood round smoking and talking to the white-wagon drivers. And small groups of solicitors and barristers and bench officials articulated in the September sun. Blathering legal crap at each other. Hatchet Harry steered Francis towards the exit and tried to be nonchalant and not get themselves noticed. Francis attempted to take everything in. Uncertain. Tremulous. Like waking slowly from a dream and not knowing where he was. Reality came in little eddies — until the dam broke and a great gush of relevance almost took his legs away. Harry steadied him and they proceeded. Gate getting further away with each step they took and every prick in the place staring at them. Or so it seemed. Ready to blow the whistle. Then they were outside! On the street! A metallic blue Audi pulled up beside them and Harry opened the door. Pushed Francis in onto the back seat and climbed after him. The car pulled gently away from the kerb so as not to arouse suspicion and headed uptown.

The men switched to a black Citroën at the Barbican.

'Well, Francis ... you're out.'

'Thanks, Harry. Thank you for ...'

'You're welcome, boy. I was hoping you'd remember my plan.'

'I forgot for a while, but then ...'

'Good man. Bastards wouldn't let me visit a second time.'

'I'm surprised you got in at all. How come?'

'I was owed a favour by one of the screws.'

Sense was slowly seeping into Francis. But even though he knew in a physical way what was happening — it was happening in an atmosphere of unreality.

'There's a thing I don't understand ...'

'What's that, Francis?'

'Why would you do this for me? Take such a risk and all? We hardly even know each other.'

'Don't pretend to be so fucking naïve, Francis.'

'Naïve?'

'Aye ... fucking naïve. You got twenty kilos of coke stashed. You and that paddy tosser ... Moore.'

'No. You're wrong, Harry. The rozzers got the charlie.'

'No they fucking didn't, Francis.'

Francis tried to remember. He thought he was right. But it was so long ago. Questions formed in his mind. And he was gripped with a real sense of fear. Not of Hatchet Harry — but because he couldn't remember.

'But ... that's how they convicted us. Possession ... bang to rights. The fucking judge even made a comment on the size of the load.'

'I'm telling you, Francis, the stuff's still out there.'

'I'm not trying to stiff anyone. Ask Matthew Moore ...'

'Can't do that, Francis.'

'Why the fuck not? Why not, Harry?'

'Because he's dead.'

'No he's not. How the fuck can Matthew be dead?'

Dead? Francis felt these people in the car were impostors. Lying to him. Telling him lies. Maybe not Harry Kane at all — but some robot double. Looking like a robot. Moving like a robot. And who the fuck was that driving?

Hatchet Harry Kane's robot double pulled a 9mm Browning automatic out from under the back seat of the car and pressed the muzzle into Francis' side. The Citroën sped on northeastwards through Shoreditch and Stratford and Snaresbrook and Francis noticed the face of the driver in the rear-view mirror. For the first time. It was a robot double. Of James fucking Greenwood.

chapter five

chapte r five

chapte r five

Birds lamented in a late Autumn tree outside the bedroom window of the house in Leytonstone Road. Francis Page stirred and opened his eyes. Light streamed into the room through a gap between the curtains. At first he wasn't sure if it was light at all. It seemed solid — a shaft of pure gold he felt he could touch. An omen. Some sort of portentous sign? Maybe today something would happen to solve all his problems and make the future bright and silver — like the beam of goldlight coming through the window. Francis looked at his watch. 2.00 p.m. He was alone in the bedroom and could hear noises coming up from downstairs. He didn't want to get up, even though he wanted to know who or what was making the noise.

He's asking if I think the *kaya* of Mary has to include that of Magdalene, Chela? It doesn't matter what I say. The cunt won't go away. Was that you downstairs? I'm everywhere. Shhh! Can you hear it? The noise ... from downstairs. He says it's probably part of the reality I can't live with and can't explain away. Why am I asking him? Am I going fucking mad? He's not here. I'm here, Chela. I'll always be here. No no no no no no no ... I got to get up and see who the fuck's downstairs. Might be them. Don't be scared, Chela ... even if it's death. He's saying once I subscribe to the hate thing, I gotta go on to the inevitable conclusion ... there's no way out. No escape, man. I just want to sort out who's downfuckingstairs! That's all! I ask what if it's a burglar? Should I show compassion and kiss the cunt? He says I ain't listening ... in spite of all the terror and bewilderment and confusion ... reality will remain itself. Real. It. Y. The inner light. Tells me I can be *yogin*, Chela. As he was to God. What terror? What bewilderment? What confusion? To come. To come. I ask him politely to go away. I'm asking politely because I don't want to get myself all angry. He keeps saying I'm not listening but I am, because he told me not to get angry and I'm doing my fucking best. But I've only so much patience. You know. I know. He's saying I can't do nothing to lose him, Chela, that ain't been already done. I wish I knew who he really is? You know! I told you ... I'm the Window in the Wall ... I'm who I've always been. I saw all the kingdoms of the earth and all the peoples as they lived and laboured for the flesh ... Luke, 4: 5. You saw nothing ... you see nothing ... you know nothing about me ... who I am. Leave me alone! I know you! I *am* you! You are me! I'm not a fucking alien ... In every man there's a Son like the Father ... John, 5: 44. You have the *phowa*, Chela ... the insight ... buried deep inside you. Some have it and some don't. Those who have it gotta practise *tonglen*, man ... otherwise it's a sin. You said there's no sin. No evil. That was death and evil and Matthew said it. Alcohol and drugs. Alcohol. Drugs. Cormorbidity. I don't understand. What does it mean? It's what affects you. It's what makes you human. It's against you. I'm not against you. I'm with you. It is. I am. It is I. I am I. I am. I am. I am. 1+1=1. 1+1+1=1. 1+1+1+1+1+1+1=1.

Footsteps on the stairs distracted Francis' attention. Who the hell should it be? He was worried. Pictures on the walls told him the bastards were out to get him. He didn't know who the bastards were — but they were out to fucking get him. Only a matter of time before he found out and then there'd be big trouble. In little London! His head suddenly jumped to one side and hung at an odd angle. Just as the door opened and Angeline came into the bedroom.

'What's the matter with you?'

Francis didn't answer. He continued to stare at his wife as if she was a complete stranger.

'Are you all right, Francis?'

Francis straightened his head and wiped a discharge of dribble from his chin. He pulled on his jeans and lit up a cigarette. Angeline crossed the room and opened a window, waving the cigarette smoke before her as she went. Francis stared at her.

'Why aren't you at work?'

'I've asked you not to smoke in the house ...'

Francis seemed not to hear her for a moment, then he flicked the cigarette through the open window making an arch of sparks. He took a fresh shirt from the wardrobe.

'Who were you talking to?'

'What?'

'I heard you talking to someone.'

'It was the radio. I switched it on for the news.'

'It's not on now.'

'I switched it off again ...'

Angeline looked behind the bedroom door. Then she opened the wardrobe and peered inside. She gave Francis a suspicious look before leaving the room and going back downstairs. He put on his socks and shoes and followed her. Angeline was in the kitchen, applying fresh make-up. Francis poured himself a cup of coffee.

'Why aren't you at work?'

'I've got to go up to Birmingham.'

'What for?'

'It's my job, Francis. I buy cosmetics, just like you punch people about.'

His hand tightened round the mug handle.

'Don't start, Angeline ...'

'At least you managed to find your way home last night.'

'I know my way home.'

'Maybe you shouldn't have bothered.'

'Why not? Why shouldn't I?'

Angeline pouted her mouth and applied lipstick before replying.

'You don't work till five in the morning, Francis. Then you were talking when you got into bed ... about Heaven or Hell or some other nonsense. You shouldn't be driving when you're so drunk.'

'I was fucking sober, Angeline!'

Even though he shouted — she didn't stop.

'And who were you with?'

'Nobody. I was with nobody ...'

'There was a smell of cheap perfume when you came in.'

'I thought you were asleep?'

'Who was she? Not that I really care. I honestly don't give a damn, Francis!'

'Then why ask? Anyway ... I just drove Agnes home from work.'

Angeline threw the make-up things into her bag.

'The Spanish tart. I see.'

'She's South American and you see nothing! I just dropped her off ...'

'Look, Francis, I don't really *care* what you did last night, or any other night either. I just came by to tell you I'll be late and could you please pick the girls up from school.'

Francis hated this. Hated her. Loved her. Sometimes. She was so fucking smart. Everyone thought they were so fucking clever these days. Lately. He looked at her and she smiled that smile of hers. As if she knew something he didn't. Was in on the joke — some secret and he wasn't. Left outside. Didn't know what was going on. Couldn't trust her any more — this woman whom he loved and hated. She let him down like they all did all the time until you couldn't trust them any more. Why didn't she love him? Keep loving him? What did he do? What the fuck did he do? Francis couldn't remember what it was he'd done to make her hate him so much. It was a long time ago. Her know-somethingyoudon't face made him angry. Heart. Beat. Stresstrigger! Heartbeat-panic-violence. He slammed his coffee cup down on the table. Angeline moved away from him.

'Oh yes, that's your answer to everything. If you can't win any other way, punch the living daylights out of it.'

'Why don't you leave me alone?'

'With pleasure! I've no desire to hang around here listening to your stories. Save them for your pals in the pub.'

'It's not a story, Angeline ...'

'Your whole world's a story, Francis. It's not real. It's just some little adolescent boy's game. If it wasn't for me you'd be in a cardboard box down on Millwall Docks ... or in some institution.'

'You fucking bitch! If it wasn't for you I'd be free!'

'There's the door, Francis.'

Francis turned away from her. Hated hated hated fucking hated this. Knew he'd hit her if she didn't fuck off. Didn't want to. He never hit her before but this was new. Lately. Edginess. He felt like it. Could only be pushed so far. She shouldn't push him like she did — with her words. And her cleverness and her fucking superiority and her holierthanthouness. Francis tried to calm himself but couldn't. Heartbeat. Heartbeat. Heartbeat. He poured more coffee and walked through to the living room. Switched on the television and sat down. Held onto the legs of the chair. A few minutes later the front door slammed and Angeline's car revved up angrily outside. Francis waited until she drove away, then threw the coffee across the room and jumped to his feet. He kicked over the chair and punched repeatedly at the wall. It took him a long time to get control back. Once the blood came down behind his eyes. He became a mad animal for a while. Insane animal. Heartbeat-panic-fear-violence. His brain closed down and refused to reason and he foamed slightly at the mouth. In this state he was capable of killing. Even though he wasn't a killer by nature. Naturally. Normally.

Gradually, the somatotrophin levels began to get back to a par. He sat heavily in the armchair and surveyed the damage. This was the third time he'd broken stuff in the house in the past couple of months and he knew he'd never hear the fucking end of it from the lovehate woman.

Francis could remember being violent as a boy. His South African father was called Konrad Fichte and he fucked off when he found out Annie was crazy. He was a merchant sailor and she was an assembly-line worker in a computer factory. He lived with them until Francis was five years old. The boy was called Francis Fichte then. The beforeboy. But Annie got worse and Konrad went back to sea. Never to be seen again. Annie changed his name back to hers — Page. It suited him better. The afterboy. Afterbirth. Madnesseepinginthewomb! Over the following few years Francis and his mother were in and out of institutions all the time. He was an only child and even though he was good at school in the early days, he was always in trouble. The teachers said he had potential. But the other kids wouldn't leave him alone about his mother being mad. So he beat the shit out of a few of them and was labelled difficult — aggressive and antisocial. Youth custody centres were the next stop and then prison. Once he was old enough.

Francis didn't like prison too much. Didn't like being locked inside for long and the place was full of smooth walls. And bright lights. And madness. That belonged somewhere else. For treatment. Not in there.

Needed doctors. Not witchdoctors. Not judges who didn't know who was crazy and who was callous. Didn't know the difference. Didn't fucking care. The cunts! It was a strange kind of reality on the inside. What was real and how did he know? Like a recurring nightmare that established itself on his waking thoughts. He was constantly being beaten up by the screws and thrown into solitary. Which he didn't mind all that much. The solitary — not the beatingsup. Preferred to be on his own — away from the rest of the shitehawks.

When he got out he made himself a promise never to go back in there again. Built up his body pumping iron and went into the bouncing business. Francis found his vocation! A legitimate way to channel anger and frustration — and get paid as well! His reputation grew and he was much sought after as a minder and bodyguard in the great heydays of his peak. He'd looked after the best — some of England's most famous singing stars, visiting actors, businessmen and other wealthy bastards. Along with gangsters and even politicians. His career was well on its way. Until something snapped in his head one day and he put a member of the paparazzi into intensive care. He lost it in front of the cameras and almost half-killed the bagofshit. Just for trying to take a photograph. Or for spying? Being a spy. A conspirator. A grass. A nark? Francis couldn't remember. Trying to take a picture for some perverted purpose. In any case. There was an outcry from the bleedingheart brigade and other freaky fuckers who relied on the likes of him to save them from the baretooths and burglars and batterers — when it suited them. They were the first to bawl and scream for help when they were being mugged and maimed. Couldn't fight for themselves but as soon as they saw a bit of blood they started pissing in their knickers and saying their fucking prayers.

The client paid for a good brief and Francis got away with a fine and a suspended sentence. But the damage was done. The newspapers hung onto the story and persecuted him for a while, jumping out from behind hedges and parked cars and ringing the telephone and the doorbell at all hours of the day and night until they found something else to get hysterical about. Nearly drove him to fucking distraction. Brought it all up again about his mother being in a mental institution until she died and how he'd led a life of crime and violence. And everybody knew schizophrenia was a genetically inherited disease. The bastards! The bad fucking bastards! The dirty fucking bastard bastards! After that the bigmoney jobs dried up and all he could get was doing the doors and the odd rockmusic concert here and there. And they all said he was mad too. Just like his mother.

Francis made money when he was at the top. He also spent it. Liked deepsilver time and reassuring things — expensive cars, expensive clothes and expensive gambling. The women didn't bother him that much. Although he seemed to bother them. That nervousness he felt towards females never went away — even at the height of his self-esteem. When the big cash dried up, Francis failed to cut back quick enough. As if he didn't believe it was over. He could see the before person — the ghost of Francis past. He failed to see the ghost of Francis future. Didn't want to see it. Was frightened by it! All he had now was his girls, the Jaguar and Glendora. Even the house was in hock with a couple of mortgages to pay off the gambling debts and Angeline was right — if it wasn't for her that would be gone too.

Francis watched an audience participation programme on the television. They were trying to tell him something. All standing up and screaming at him. He jumped to his feet and whirled round, half expecting to see Angeline with a knife raised — ready to stab him in the jugular. There was nothing. Nobody. Francis turned the set off and sat amongst the silences of the afternoon. Where were the bastards now when he needed them? They never talked to him when he was in this kind of mood. The fuckers ran away like everyone else. Shiteing on themselves. He didn't need them anyway. Well able to figure things out for himself. No. He wasn't. Wasn't able to figure anything out — especially why they talked to *him* — this Alienchrist and the others. Were they trying to warn him about something? Was the fucking world coming to an end? He knew about the conspiracy — maybe they were trying to tell him who it was — in some symbolic cryptic way. He just had to break the code and he'd have the answers. Thoughts began to run faster through Francis' head. He could keep up with them at first, but they kept going faster and faster until his mind was in complete confusion. Was it the craziness? Did he have it like his mother? Were they right? The bastards!

Francis stood up and put his hands to his head. Hurting now. He walked round the room in a circle. This was driving him up the fucking wall. Felt as if the world was nothing more than a savage shithole-animal. And he had to kick the fucker down before it did him in. Completely. That was the law of fucking survival wasn't it? The law of fucking nature! Naturalaw. Normalaw. The spider ate the fly and the bird ate the spider and the cow ate the bird. We ate the fucking cow and some deadly prehistoric micro-organism ate us. Full circle! It was all so fucking uncomplicated. You lived the best way you could. Then, when you died, your body rotted back into the earth and your soul went to Hell with all the rest of the fuckwits and television presenters and counterfeiters and conartists. Everything else was complete shit and confusing crap! No one he'd heard about was ever abducted by aliens — at least not in this part of London. There were a few fuckers up in Scotland looked a bit strange all right. But not the Mother of fucking Christ?

But in an obscure way it made some sense to him. Not in any way he could explain — but intuitively. As given. And Jesus Christ being from another planet and getting stuck in a reincarnation cycle and persecution and power and preoccupation and primary delusions and death and degeneration and genocide and. And. Guilt! What the fuck did he know about all that kind of stuff? What did he fucking care? A simple man. Only one fucking life. Only one wife! Only two chances — two children. One Internet. One world. One conspiracy. The ticking clock. The ticking clock. The ticking tock. The ticking clock attracted Francis' attention and he focused his mind on it. Gradually, the spinning in his head began to slow and eventually it stopped altogether.

Francis went back into the kitchen and poured himself another cup of coffee. He stuck two pieces of bread into the toaster and opened a tin of baked beans. Emptied the beans into a non-metallic bowl and put the bowl into the microwave for exactly one minute. Francis waited. The toast and beans were ready simultaneously and he considered *that* to be one of the wonders of his Universe. And most of the meaning of his life. He sat at the kitchen table and pondered the seemingly insurmountable problem of making some late money and getting out of the door game. Could Alien tell him how to do that? Could any of them?

Could they fuck, the pricks!

Francis spread honey on his toast. It looked so golden. So beautiful. He put some on his finger and looked at it up close to his face. Light from the window shone through it and it seemed to take on an alternative form — to become ethereal, spiritual, other-worldly. And he realised that humanity was only observable at arm's length. If you took a close or distant look, the humanity disappeared and the thing became disquietingly strange. Like a portrait — up close it was a mass of random patterns and abstracts and waves and from a distance it blended into the larger surroundings and was no longer divisible from them.

Francis studied the honey. This was God! This little piece of gold. This was the meaning of everything. This was the future. The golden future! The silver. Something?

chapter six

chapte r six

chapte r six

James fucking Greenwood talked incessantly up front in the driving seat but Francis Page didn't hear a word he said. Shite mostly. The black Citroën eventually turned up along a muddy track and stopped outside a remote country house in Essex. Greenwood got out and opened the door for Francis. If it was Greenwood. Hatchet Harry Kane followed them with his gun — across the coarse vegetation at the front of the house. Francis tried to get things straight in his head. What the fuck was going on? Matthew dead? Murdered? Was he? Who would do a thing like that? And Glendora as well? Same bastards? Maybe that put his daughter on the drugs. Maybe James Greenwood there. Or John Nightingale. Or the Yardies. As a way of getting back at him. Could even have been Angeline? No! Could! Or Konrad. Come back from Efrikaaner land. Francis needed to talk to God again.

'Is there a church round here?'

'A what?'

'A church ... a chapel or some other place of worship?'

'For fuck's sake, Francis ...'

'Did'ya hear that, Harry? Did'ya hear that? He musta got religion down in Broadmoor. Did'ya get religion in the nuthouse, Francis?'

James Greenwood laughed. Hatchet Harry didn't. If it was Hatchet Harry. Both looked at Francis and he looked back at them. Stared back at them. Burned holes in them with his eyes. Greenwood stopped laughing and looked away. Still talking shite. Mostly to himself.

The house was as derelict inside as it was outside. Harry raised the gun and pointed it at Francis' head.

'Don't get any fucking cute ideas, Francis.'

'You think I'm afraid of you, Harry? Or that boybastard there?'

'Maybe not. But I've got the fucking gun.'

'That won't stop me if I go ... Harry.'

Hatchet Harry Kane shot Francis through the left kneecap. He heard the bone splintering and smelled blood gushing out from his leg. A piercing pain ran the length of his entire body. A red-hot knife pain. Francis fell over onto the floor. The other two approached across the room.

'Not so fucking fierce now, are you Francis?'

'I'll kill both of you. I'm not a killer ... but they said I killed a screw, so if I did ...'

'You'll kill fuck-all. Now ... where's the cocaine?'

'There is no cocaine.'

'Listen, Francis ... we didn't want to deal with a mad bastard like you. We'd have preferred to deal with Moore. But the silly sod killed himself and that leaves us no option.'

Killed himself? Even though Hatchet Harry's double just told him — Francis didn't believe it. But he still knew Matthew was dead. It was just that something was telling him he did it. Francis did it. Didn't he? The robots were shouting the word cocaine at him. Over and over.

'There is no fucking cocaine!'

'Stubborn bastard ain't he, Harry. You're a stubborn bastard, Francis, I'll say that much for you. But we're in charge now, ain't we Harry?'

James Greenwood kicked Francis in the stomach. Then Harry bent down and put the muzzle of the gun to his other kneecap.

'This one next Francis, then you'll be a cripple for life. As well as being a fucking psychopath.'

Psychopath? Psycho! Spastic! Window-licker! Francis saw the mirror reflection looking back at him from the sneering faces. In the limitless space of the room. And the blinding electric light bulb overhead. He had to say something sensible.

'Fuck you, you stupid cunt!'

'Then your elbows ... or your bollocks. They say a bullet in the gut is a bastard altogether ...'

'God won't allow this. You try and see what happens ... go ahead, you piece of pigshit!'

Francis didn't know why he said that. Because he knew God would allow it. Greenwood's God and Kane's God. Robot Gods. Metal Gods. Machine Gods. He'd have to do something soon.

'I don't think the mad fucker cares, eh James?'

'Stubborn bastard ain't he, Harry? Stubborn fucking bastard!'

Greenwood kicked Francis again. The pair of pricks were now at a loss for ideas. Whispered to each other while Francis felt inside the uniform jacket for the small axe. Harry came back across and bent down close again.

'James here says that daughter of yours might know, Francis.'

'The junkie, Harry. I know her from the clubs ... I know a lot of people, Harry ... looking for the charlie most of the time but she takes the horse too for the paranoia and lying on her back for a fix. She knocks around with the low life, that one!'

'Maybe she's holding it for you, eh Francis?'

The robots strutted up and down the room. Jerkily. Unnaturally.

'And dipping into it at the same fucking time I betcha. She's bound to be dipping into it ... keep the crack and smack horrors out of her hair.'

'James says maybe we ought to go ask her.'

'Before it's all gone. Where does she live, Francis? Down by the polytechnic somewhere?'

'Maybe we'll bring her out here.'

Kane came back and pressed the gun against Francis' neck.

'And the two of you can have a little reunion. That'd be good ... mad dad and druggie daughter. Be easy enough to find her ... just go down the Charing Cross Road any night of the fucking week.'

Francis swung the axe and it chopped Hatchet Harry's hand clean off. Still holding the gun. James Greenwood stopped talking and backed off quickly. Kane's mouth choked and his tongue stuck out in surprise as he watched the blood pumping from his wrist. Francis grabbed him by the throat as Hatchet Harry gurgled at Greenwood and pointed towards the severed hand. Clasped round the Browning. The blabbermouth scared shitless now and paralysed with fear. Francis bit off one of Kane's ears and threw him to one side. He reached the hand first and prised the gun from its fingers. Harry came back at him with his face contorted and covered in blood. But Francis shot the bastard in the forehead and he fell over onto the floor convulsing in a macabre death dance. Francis pulled himself into a sitting position and pointed the gun at the boy. James Greenwood dropped to his knees and put his hands up to his head. Francis struggled with difficulty to his feet and limped across to where the mouthalmighty waited with panic screaming out from its hiding place behind his eyes. Grabbed Greenwood by the hair.

'Who's in charge, James? Who did you say was in charge? My God's in charge here! My God!'

Francis dragged the boy across the room and threw him down on top of Hatchet Harry's dead body. Then tore up a curtain to make a tourniquet. Tied tightly above his left knee to stop the stream of blood and used the rest of the material to bandage up the jagged wound. James Greenwood cowered on the floor — whining and whinging and begging Francis to let him go. Francis struck him with the axe. Greenwood screamed. Francis struck him again. Greenwood screamed again.

'Did I kill my friend Matthew Moore?'

'He killed himself, Francis ... he topped himself they said. Honest ...'

Francis struck him again with the axe. James Greenwood screamed.

'Who killed Glendora?'

'I don't know any Glendora ... who's Glendora, Francis? Jesus ... don't kill me ...'

Francis struck him again with the axe. James Greenwood turned over onto his back. Eyes streaming tears. Rolled down his face and mingled with the blood. The eyes pleaded with Francis — he could hear them. Prayed to him. He was their God. The Eyegod. Didn't want them looking at him. They knew he was a killer. Francis struck Greenwood in the face with the axe. The boy puked and looked with bloodfilled sockets at the bits of himself that were scattered around the floor.

'Who gave Fiona the drugs?'

James Greenwood couldn't answer because he was dead. Blood continued to gurgle up from his throat. Francis struck him again, almost severing the head from its trunk.

'Who grassed me to that pair of drugsquad slags ... Dunne and Spencer?'

Francis struck the body again with the axe. James Greenwood's head rolled away across the floor and his lifeless eyes stared at the ceiling. Francis struck the body again.

'Who's been reading my mind on the fucking Internet? Hey boy, you know!'

Greenwood's headless body twitched and spasmed in the pool of its own blood.

'Whose idea was it to get me out of that Broadmoor shithole? You two are not smart enough ...'

Francis noticed that the head had rolled away and limped across to it.

'Who's behind this whole conspiracy, boy? Is it Nightingale or Shillinger? Who is it? Who is it? Who is it?'

The eyes didn't answer. Glazed over. He didn't ask any more questions. Wasn't Francis Page any more. He was Genghis the Animalkhan. The Mahdi. He was a savage insect. Sardanapalus. Devouring its prey. And he beat James Greenwood's head with the axe until there was nothing left of it but a bloody pulp. Only when exhaustion overtook him did he stop. He took a packet of cigarettes from Hatchet Harry Kane's dead pocket and sat down on a chair. Francis struck a match and lit the cigarette and blew blue smoke into the blood-speckled air.

chapter seven

chapte r seven

chapte r seven

Once he'd rested for a while, Francis went back over to the bodies. Hatchet Harry was carrying a couple of hundred pounds and Francis took the money. Anything James Greenwood might have been carrying was too soaked in blood to be of use. He used the gun to blow the rest of the shackles off and nearly shot himself in the ankle while doing so. Francis' uniform was also covered in redblood and he searched through the house for something clean to wear. Big ramshackle place. With about a dozen rooms altogether. On two floors. Surrounded by a couple of acres of weed-filled garden and a high hedgerow that kept it secluded from the neighbouring farmland. No electricity — but running water and some tins of food in the kitchen. Francis found a room with a single bed upstairs — and a change of clothes for Hatchet Harry Kane. Otherwise the place was bare — except for a few chairs and a wooden table. Looked as if the robot bastards intended to keep him there for maybe a couple of days. Then kill him.

To Francis' best knowledge the house was somewhere between the village of Pilgrims Hatch and the border of Greater London. About twenty miles or so from the city. Flat farmland and thickashit swede-knawer country that might have suited Matthew Moore for rearing his alpacas. A shed at the back with garden tools and a wheelbarrow and other stuff.

The small wooden building was even more derelict than the house. Roof caving in and the smell of dung and decay everywhere. Francis dragged the two bodies out and threw them into the shed. Then he spread a sheet over the bloodstained floor.

Changed into the spare clothes for Hatchet Harry that were a bit too big for him but beggars couldn't be fucking choosers under the circumstances. Then made himself a cup of cold coffee in the kitchen and carried it upstairs. Francis lay on the bed and smoked another cigarette. The pain in his knee would have been unbearable for any other man. But still some sedative in his system. And lately he was insensitive to pain and had no awareness of heat or cold. To Francis the wound was a sign. From God. It was his cross. His augur's staff. His *tau*.

Outer reality was distinguishing itself from inner reality. Francis knew what was going on around him. What he believed was going on around him. Even though he was strangely detached from it. But the house was a friendly thing and it comforted him. Shielded him now from confusion.

The blood and unseasonable warmth of the Autumn weather attracted a swarm of bluebottles and greenbottles and every other colour fucking fly downstairs. Francis heard them buzzing and blowing — looking for a place to leave their larvae. Tired after the events of the day and the drugs still contaminating his blood made him drowsy. Out in the shed the dead bodies waited to be buried and the insects crawled all over them and the ghosts of their victims laughed and pointed with cold white fingers. Francis drifted in and out of consciousness for several days. Getting up only to drink cold coffee and smoke and piss. His affinity for the house grew — despite its remoteness. It seemed to cradle him in its arms and he felt safe. Secluded. Steel-clad. Shadows came and lay beside him. Lucrezia Borgia. Who thought he was her father. And *Le menu peuple*. And Dido. Who was looking for Aeneas with her hair and clothes on fire. And Xanthippe. Who knew he'd been drinking with Socrates and scolded him for it. And Oenone. Who told him the story of the rest of his life. *Soint bons, soint mauvais esperils, ilz me sont apparus*. And he knew somewhere in the back of his mind that now he was a killer. *La grande pitié*. A real killer. Despite how hard he'd tried not to be. Despite all his efforts to be harmless and human. Despite all Alien had told him about love and compassion. He had taken life. Deliberately. Not accidentally, like in Pentonville. He felt no compassion. He felt no remorse. And neither did God.

The weather got colder and Francis knew for some reason that winter was on its way. All the tins of food in the kitchen were empty and he ran out of cigarettes and coffee a long time ago. Had to go into town. Grown a bit of a beard by now and his hair was longer. So he hoped no Essex hick arsehole would recognise him. Tidied himself up and went out of the house for the first time in his new life. Citroën still parked where James Greenwood left it. Keys in the ignition. Francis looked at the money. A few red speckles of blood on the notes but unlikely anyone would know what they were by looking at them. Little flecks of life. Sparkling ruby atoms in the weak sunlight. Who would know. Anything.

Pilgrims Hatch was a small market village with the usual cross-section of commuters and clodtossers and farm labourers and layabouts and perty professional people and women with their noses in every other fucker's business. Except their own. Francis pulled up outside the supermarket and bought a few things without any problems. Then went next door to a tobacconist. Big stack of newspapers roared out at him from their headlines. 'Mental killer still on the loose'. And a mug shot of himself from Broadmoor looking like Hannibal the fucking Horrible. Francis paid for his cigarettes and the young assistant behind the counter gave him and his limp a suspicious look but said nothing. He drove straight back to the house and parked the Citroën round the rear. The sky closed in. Looked like early snow and Francis decided to make a fire. Have some hot fucking coffee for a change. Wasn't sure if he should risk it. If it was worth it. Didn't know who owned the house. Or if it was supposed to be occupied at all. Last thing he wanted was some candleater nosing around and maybe calling the fucking cops. On the other hand no bugger might notice and he wanted the hot coffee.

That night a comfortable little glow came out from the grate. Made by firewood Francis collected from the garden. And a cup of hot coffee in one hand and a cigarette in the other. And the silence of the country night. Maybe he'd stay there forever. Live like a hermit with his own thoughts for company. Nowadays he knew the pricks had satellites circling the earth and these things could pinpoint a fucking flea on a sheepdog's back. Better to stay in out of the way. Only problem was his knee. Beginning to smell like a dead goat and the fucking flies must have got at it because he could feel maggots crawling around inside the shattered bone. Next day, Francis shaped himself out a crutch from the branch of a tree and that took the weight off and helped him get around the house. He saw several large rats to-ing and fro-ing from the shed. Never got round to burying the bodies and it seemed to him probably a waste of time now. So he didn't bother.

There was a small church in the village. Francis noticed it when he went in for the provisions. Thought maybe he'd go back there after it got dark. Risk the satellites. And all the conspiracy cunts. Talk to God. Again. He needed to find out. Take revenge. Hatchet Harry and that talkofthetown James Greenwood were no fucking use to him.

Somebody had to know. God would tell him if they spoke together for a while. Fuck the rest of the bastards. Who did he need to find? Who had done all the bad things to him? That had brought him to where he was. Later that night he dug some of the maggots out of the knee before they started to feast on healthy tissue. Then he drove the Citroën back into the village and hid it in a remote section of the churchyard.

The side door was unlocked so he went down the darkened aisle and across the nave to the altar. Lit a couple of candles and spread his arms wide and looked up towards the high ceiling. God looked back down. And smiled. And Francis prayed. I am not yet born; forgive me. For the sins that in me the world shall commit, my words when they speak me, my thoughts when they think me, my treason engendered by traitors beyond me, my life when they murder by means of my hands, my death when they live me.

Francis took into consideration if he waited long enough someone was bound to show up at the house in Essex. Whoever was behind it all. Somebody to blame. For everything. A ghost to lay. But nobody did. A delusional conclusion. Kane and Greenwood must have been on their own in this thing. And every other fucker must've forgotten about him. Almost Christmas before the money ran out. Francis was going to go out to the shed to get whatever cash James Greenwood had on him. Wash the blood off. But decided the rats probably ate it by now. His knee was in a bad way. Full of little holes where he dug the rest of the maggots out. The wound looked clean and not red and angry like before. But Francis still believed gangrene would set in and the limb would have to come off. Sooner than later. Before it travelled up to his heart and killed him for being the murderer that he was. And sometimes he thought that might not be so bad. Death is the beginning!

Any lingering effects from the tranqs had long since gone and Francis now in a nervous hypedup state. All the Voices back. Bringing more with them. Jeering. Mocking him. Repeating what he said to himself. Fed up with the fuckers and only wanted to talk to God. But they wouldn't leave him alone and sometimes he wished he was back in the hospital. Even thought of going there. Giving himself up. Just walking casually up to the gate and saying 'I'm back. Take me in and send me down into the quicksand. Where I can be quiet.' But he didn't. Because no matter how bad things got he knew if he went back he could never come out again. And he couldn't be inside all the time. For evermore. He'd go fucking mad!

Francis visited the little church every morning in the safe early hours. Looking for love. Longing for love. And it was the only place he could get any peace. No real people around him. To comfort. Console. Someone. He'd lost the only person he knew completely intimately. Himself. And what took his place frightened him. Made him angry. A hostility that was self-protective. Against perceived hatred. Pain. Loneliness. Fear. Against the strangeness that inhabited his mind. Francis always brought the gun with him and a box of bullets he found in the car. The 9mm Browning had a fourteen-round magazine plus one up the chamber. As good as anything else. Better than some. He knew now where he had to start. Begin. At the beginning. The end for some. Of some. Things. And now that the money'd run out it was time to begin. Christmas was appropriate. Christmas. Christ. Mass. Massacre. Massmurder.

Cold winds blew down from the north and Francis could smell the snow on its way. From the north. North pole. Magnetic pole. Which he knew was not one stationary place. But moved around. As it liked. Here today. There tomorrow. Scientist told him there would be another polar reversal soon. Send the world into complete chaos. It was only right that it should. Poetic justice. Just. Ice. And he knew he couldn't bring an end to everything by solving all his problems at once. And maybe he got it wrong right from the beginning because the dream of normal — reason — rational — logic — was illogical. And there was a distinction between what could be said and what could only be shown and in the final analysis there was much less to be said than was originally thought. And there is no rhinoceros in the room. Prove it! I can't.

chapter eight

chapte r eight

chapte r eight

The Three Cripples was within walking distance of Leytonstone Road, in Maryland Square. Francis Page used the pub as his local. 3.40 p.m. and the public bar was quiet. A few thickshits inside bowed and scraped to Francis as he came through the door and the landlord threw him up a large JD on the house. Francis knocked the drink back and before he could open his mouth there was another one in front of him from his fan-club. One or two early boys were beginning to straggle in on their way home from work and drawn to Francis like moths round a dangerous candle. It wasn't long before he reluctantly had an audience. All buying him Jack Daniels and trying to be his best mate. Francis was always embarrassed by this kind of attention. He wondered why the fucks didn't go and live their own lives instead of latching onto his? Sometimes he felt as if his brain was dissolving when he talked to them — that they were sucking the life out of him. Muscles and bones and ligaments and lungs. Living off him and he was dying. Bit by bit. Yet he never reared up or done violence to any of them. After all, you had to talk to somebody. No man was an island.

'Tell us that story about the pit-bulls, Francis ...'

'I'm tired telling that one. Tired.'

'Benny here never heard it.'

Although Francis resented their intrusion, he increasingly needed contact with other people to be able to break through the unreality barrier that was growing around him. He searched for the right words.

'Well ... it was after a bit of a punch-up in the Cannibal up West in Golden Square. These pricks came back with a couple of dogs. Dogs ...

'Pit-bulls, Francis ...'

'That's right! And got them inside the club somehow.'

'For fuck's sake ...'

He felt a sense of anxiety as the crowd around him grew. The light was glaring down like a laser. Then he remembered the words of the story.

'Pandemonium. Punters screaming and the bulls savage and every-one trying to jump up on the stage or on tables or the bar ... anywhere. Anywhere ... get away from the fucking beasts.'

'You don't want to mess with those fucking dogs ...'

'I saw it on television where an American policeman put six bullets into one of those brutes and it still came at him.'

'Will you shut the fuck up and let Francis tell the story?'

'What did you do, Francis?'

The alcohol was loosening Francis up and he began to feel a little more at ease. Not so nervy now nor jumpy. Edgy. The situation at home wasn't good lately and he was sure it contributed to most of his problems. But at least he could forget in here. These tossers might get on his nerves sometimes but he was safe with them. A gut feeling. A gut in good shape along its whole length with healthy membranes and motility normal — was essential for the proper working of the brain. There was nothing in here that could harm him.

'I always keep a 9mm Glock 17 automatic in the glove compartment of the car but, as you know.'

'What?'

'Know what, Francis?'

'That would've been fuck-all good against those brutes.'

'What's a 9mm Glock 17?'

'A fucking gun you dickbrain!'

'For fuck's sake, Benny ...'

Francis lost the thread of what he was saying again. Just for a moment. Under the glare of the spotlight. He didn't recognise the people either — just for a few seconds. Then their faces came back to him.

'Anyway, Charlie ... the manager of the Cannibal, keeps this big tomcat for mice and rats. So I gets hold of it and ties a lamb-bone to its tail. Then lets it loose in the club.'

'Did the dogs kill it?'

'Not likely. This is a tough fucking cat. It took the right eye out of one of the brutes and split the other's nose. I opened the side door to the alley and the cat made a bolt out through it.'

'And did the dogs follow it?'

'No ... they stopped at the bar and had a fucking drink.'

'Sorry, Francis ...'

Roars of respectful laughter finished off the story and Francis clapped on the back and flattered beyond the worth of words. And broken leg can mend — broken mind can not. Other stories about the time some crackpot got into the Playboy in Piccadilly with a chainsaw and the headbanger who rode a horse into the Shakespeare on Shaftsbury Avenue and asked for a pint of lager and a bag of oats were inveigled with more drinks and Francis could hear his own thoughts inside his head before he spoke them. Thoughts that described the remembered events to him in the third person — as if they were telling him the tale before jumping out of his mouth to tell the others. Time seemed to be standing still. And the world wasn't moving on the outside of this public house. There was no tomorrow. No yesterday. Only today. Only now. This minute. Second. Chronon.

'So I said to this man, look ... you can either leave the way you came in, or with your arse in a carrier bag. It's all the same to me.'

'What did he do, Francis?'

'The man fancied himself. Big. A big man. A big bastard ... rugby player maybe. Or something. Put up his fists.'

'You're not serious?'

'On my children's lives! Like Maureen O'Sullivan's brother or some fucking thing.'

'Who?'

'Sullivan ... John L.'

'Oh ... sure ...'

'I said to myself, this poor fucker wants a fair fight.'

'The bloody idiot!'

'So I kicked him straight in the bollocks and then helped him to the door.'

The Three Cripples was filling up as the night nudged onwards. Francis felt his head go a little light, but he knew he couldn't allow these bastards to think he was getting strange. Fuzzy. Flooked. Comorbidity! For fuck's sake! Alcohol affects the brain. Drugs. But never show signs of weakness! First rule of fighting. Otherwise you're dead and fucking buried. He got up and walked steadily to the washroom where he splashed some cold water onto his face. Then he tidied himself up and came back to the crowing crowd.

'Who was the hardest you've seen, Francis?'

'I'd say Hatchet Harry Kane.'

'I'm asking Francis, not you.'

They all started arguing about who was the hardest. God was. Everybody knew that. Their tin voices screeched at him until he stopped them with his own words.

'Sure, I knew of Hatchet Harry ... about him ... never met ... met Lenny though.'

'Lenny who?'

'You know Lenny. He's dead now. A hard man. Toothpaste.'

'Jesus, you knew a lot of bad bastards, Francis. Did you get on all right with them?'

Francis was getting fucked up with all the questions. But they were holding him there — where it was real.

'I can't remember now ... which is more than I can say for most of the fuckers.'

'Was he the hardest, Francis ... apart from yourself, of course.'

'You listen to me, you shouldn't talk about hard this and hard that. Only those who are hard can talk about it ... and if they're really hard, they never do. Ok?'

'I didn't mean nothing by it, Francis ...'

'Those pikeys are the boys, if you must know. Most of 'em does the bareknuckle stuff. Barefaced bareknuckle ... heads like fucking breeze-blocks ... take a bullet to stop 'em. Maybe six bullets. There was a few one night. In the Saracen's Head, down Leicester Square way ...'

At that moment the pub door opened and Matthew Moore walked in with a young girl on each of his arms. Francis stopped telling his story. Matthew was another man he respected. Liked. Which was more than he could say for most of the pricks. Although he was only twenty-two, the Irish boy never passed remarks — unlike that American cunt John Nightingale. Insinuations. That he was — different. Different?

Matthew Moore kept himself to himself mostly and was efficient at his job. Preferred to talk people out of doing silly things in the first place, rather than let them do it and then beat their brains in. Learned that method from Francis. His mentor. And role-model in the dangerous world of the door. Real doormen didn't freak. Stay in control! And Francis liked him for his reliability and carefree manner. Came from a place called Carlow in the Irish Republic and had ambitions to move back over to that country some day and buy a bit of land to rear alpacas. A South American animal like a camel. Only smaller. And there was a fortune to be made from the fleeces and the meat was a delicacy that was sure to appeal to the Irish palate. Francis couldn't understand why he'd want to do such a thing. But that was the man. Maybe Agnes knew something about it all. Coming from the same continent. As the alpacas — not Matthew. Maybe give him a few tips. If Moore had a fault it was an over-fondness for the females. He was a goodenoughlooking boy and could attract the ladies at will.

'Francis, you bollix ... is that you slaggin' off my relations?'

'Matthew ... you're a male prostitute! And who are these young ladies?'

'This is Siobhán and that's Gráinne.'

'Good Irish names I'm glad to hear. How are you, girls?'

'We're lovely, thank you.'

'We're heading for a party, Francis. Down Wimbledon Way.'

The crowd of admirers dispersed about the bar as Francis lost interest in their obsequiousness and turned his attention towards this friend. Always necessary to have one friend. Just the one. Someone he could trust. The rest could go and have a crap for themselves. Francis looked sternly at a couple of likely lads who were giving the girls the eyeball. The men immediately gave up their seats for the women and sloped away. Francis called for drinks and a barman was sent running to his table.

'Guess who's coming to town?'

'Santa Claus ...?'

'For fuck's sake, Francis ...'

'How should I know?'

'The Antichrists!'

Alienchrist? How did he know? Did Matthew know? How much?

'Who the fuck is he?'

'Them, Francis ... them. American heavy metal band.'

'Band of gold. Golden Gate of America ... San Francisco.'

'Sure ... they're on the last leg of a European tour. Doing a one-nighter at The New-Rainbow. Percy Shillinger's running the show.'

Shillinger. That name. He knew *that* fucking name. Too well.

'As fucking usual. That prick's into everything.'

'He's looking for men for the night. Good payday, Francis.'

'How much?'

'Three hundred a man ... plus the perks. You know ...'

'That'll do me, Matthew!'

Tray of drinks came over and the barman refused to take any money. Siobhán and Gráinne giggled and exposed a little leg and looked enticingly out from under their eyebrows. Francis thought they were very young — even for Matthew Moore. Couldn't help realising that Fiona might look like them in a few years. Hoped she wouldn't be sitting in no pub taking drinks off some strange bastard like himself.

'Why don't you come with us, Francis?'

'No ... no girls ... I don't think so.'

Wasn't Francis' scene. But Matthew insisted and the girls kept saying ahh come on ou're that and he was a little disorientated by this time anyway. With the drink. They called a cab and piled inside to set off southwards across the city towards Wimbledon. Francis went in the back with Siobhán on one side of him and Gráinne on the other. While Matthew Moore sat up front giving directions to the taxi driver — who said he was born and reared in London and didn't need no directions from any fucking Irishman. But Matthew didn't trust none of the wankers who were all out to rip off the unwary foreigner.

Francis felt claustrophobic. The girls were leaning on him and he didn't like it. They looked grotesque. Images from a fairground hall of mirrors. All distorted and out of shape. Their voices sounded shrill and intense — grating on his nerves. He was glad when the cab finally turned into Queensmere Road, off Wimbledon Park Side. A well-heeled area with Georgian houses on either side of a tree-lined street. Francis wondered who Matthew Moore would know in a place like this. But Moore was a strange customer and full of surprises. Surprise! Surprise! IC10. DSMIV. Diagnostic systems! There was no sign of life at first, but when the taxi pulled up outside a house on the corner they could hear the sound of party music waving out at them on the night air. Matthew paid the driver and they climbed out and stood on the pavement.

'Listen, Matthew ... I'm not too sure about this ...'

'It'll do you good, Francis, you've been a bit wound up lately. Anyway, the cab's gone now.'

'I don't know ...'

'C'mon ou're that, man!'

The girls had already skipped ahead to the front door which was opened by a Liam Gallagher lookalike. Francis could see from the street that the place was full of all sorts. Kings and queens and teenies and meanies and chics and shites and a few old hippies giving it the big one in the hallway. Beyond that, the kitchen teemed with dope-heads and drunks and snow-noses and pseudo-intellectuals and poets and pimps. There were dames looking for dudes and toy boys looking for meal tickets and more mature magintys looking for a little lightnight deviation and a general collection of cunts and creepy-customers.

Matthew grabbed Francis' arm and led him through the front door after the girls. Nearly midnight and half the fuckers looked as if they'd been awake for weeks. Francis picked his way through to the kitchen and found a bottle of Bourbon. They were at it all over the place. Snorting charlie off the top of the washing machine and skinning up the ganja on the stairs. Somebody passed Francis a spliff and he took a drag just to be sociable. The weed reacted badly with the whiskey and he had to go and sit down.

A quiet dark corner which he thought was deserted but there was a strange woman dressed in black. Just across a low coffee-table staring straight at him and he had to look again to be sure it was a woman. Not some figment of his inebriated imagination. She had a little packet of whiz which she took up the nostril like snuff. The woman offered some to Francis without speaking and he decided why not? Keep him on his feet for another couple of hours if nothing else. Matthew and the girls disappeared into the drug-haze and Francis sat back with the bottle on his lap. The music was too loud — which disturbed him. Seemed to be acutely sensitive to noise lately. All coming at him and sometimes he couldn't select the relevant sounds. Everything with the same intensity with no emphasis nor focus. Didn't seem to be any smack around and Francis was glad about that. He didn't like the junk and he didn't like junkies. Unpredictable — and an unpredictable man was a dangerous man. Or woman!

The dark woman looks straight at me and says Jalal al-Din! I will cleave your body in two! For fuck's sake ... Who? She says you ... Jalal al-Din. I tell her she's got the wrong man missus, not me this Jalal joker. I ask her where might we have met before and she says she knows who I am. And who the fuck are *you*? Says she's Animal ... the great Genghiskhan. But you're a woman! She spits at me and says she would have killed me for calling her that ... tells me she's the greatest of the Khans. And I'm the king of fucking Croydon! You are Animal too, Jalal al-Din ... like me. Forget all these people about you. They are not like us. They are full of fear. And I think maybe it's not a bad thing to be a little bit cagey sometimes. No! Forget about fear she shouts! And words are the worst of all enemies. I go along with that! She says I am inside you, Jalal al-Din. I am part of you. We are indivisible from each other. You say you're ... Genghiskhan, the greatest warrior this world has seen. But I don't believe that. Because Agnes D'Argensola would make shit of her. She wants to know if Agnes is a great general? And I say she's a woman, like you. She spits at me again and shouts do not call me that! I am a man! For fuck's sake ... And a man was made to fight. If he does not ... then he is a woman. I tell her I'm not afraid to fight. If I have to ... and I'm no killer if that's what she thinks. Just tired a bit. A little bit tired. A bit sick of the sight, if she knows what I mean. Tired and sick. No sense! No sense! Never! She says she was never tired, Jalal al-Din. Never sick. And still conquering the world when she died. You? I struggled against and overcame all adversaries. And I tell her I've got a few adversaries of my own. She asks me if I'm a warrior? War. I. Or. And I suppose you could say I am in a way ... was ... I think. Then it is your heart that will count, Jalal al-Din. Heart! If I have heart I'll win. Heart is everything! And I kinda like this Animal, she has a bit of balls. She spits at me when I say ... for a woman. I say sorry ... sorry. Her name is Universal Ruler and she ruled the Universe. There aren't many women this fucking interesting. Sorry ... Sorry ... I only came over here for a sit-down. Where is your empire, Jalal al-Din? Where's yours? I subdued the Naiman the Irtysh and the Tangut. I could have done that. I know I could have done that. Could you, Jalal al-Din? I conquered China, Russia, the whole of Islam and as far west as Hungary. Me too! Me too! I did the fucking same. Are you such a man? A king amongst common fools? And you say violence is a good thing Khananimal? A necessary thing. She's telling me the dream of the *arhat* is absurd. It will fail. Her word is Hate! Hate will always triumph. And everything's changing. But everything's changing ... minute by minute. Her word is violence! Everything inevitably resorts to violence,

Jalal al-Din. It is implicit in nature ... implicit in all tribes and religions and moral principles. And death is the beginning! I shouldn't be listening. I know I should not be listening. But I thought for a while back there that I was going mad.

And now I know it for sure.

The woman in black listened to Francis with great interest. He was talking to her but she couldn't understand what he was saying — no matter how hard she tried. She was smoking marijuana, so it was really all the same. To her. One way or the other. Francis smiled at her and she smiled back and offered him more billy. The bottle at his feet was half-empty and he decided he'd taken enough intoxicating substances into his body for one night. He moved out of the corner, looking for a toilet. 2.00 a.m.

Francis came to slowly. Lying face down on the bathroom floor. He could hear people banging on the door to get in. Gradually pulled himself into a kneeling position over the lavatory bowl. Spat down into the urine and then stood up. He ignored the banging on the door while he washed his face and hands in the basin. Combed his hair and brushed down his clothes. Then he opened the door. Several irate women accused him of interfering with himself, but he said nothing — just slipped back downstairs. Looked at his watch. 3.30 a.m.

The tempo of the music had slowed down considerably. A tenor saxophone blew late night blues from the compact disc player and the few people who remained standing clung to each other for support as they dragged their feet around the floor. The rest mingled in a tangled mass all over the room. Some slumped on tables and chairs and others lay along the hall. The smell of dope could have choked a carthorse and glass straws and razorblades littered the high tableau. Francis looked around for Matthew Moore and finally found him asleep in the kitchen. No sign of Siobhán or Gráinne. Time to fuck off.

Outside, the early morning air blew some of the shit from Francis' brain. He looked up and down the street. This was unfamiliar territory. Didn't know whether to go right or left to find civilisation. He chose left because he could hear the sound of trafficnoise down that direction. Street dark and deserted as Francis stumbled along. Falling over dustbins and frightening the cats. A couple of sanctimonious lights went on and net curtains peered through at this shitehawk who was disturbing the peace of their pleasant little suburb. Francis ignored them and drifted on till he came out at last into Wimbledon Park Side. Hailed a taxi and sat back to see the waking city flash past his window.

Francis was tired. Fell into a fretful sleep and dreamed about Glendora. He wanted to see her right now, but he knew it was better if he didn't. She was already too dependent on him. Or independent of him. Which was it? Little delicate sophisticated girlwoman who'd had it rough. Even rougher than him. Father and fucking uncles abused her and sold her off for favours to their fucking friends when she was no more than twelve years old. Ran away from her home in Liverpool when she was sixteen and ended up in London on the game. Francis found her in an alley one earlymorning when he was leaving the Barracuda Club down near Soho Square. She was dehydrated, hypothermiated, fucked, freaked-out and nearly dead from a drug overdose. He took her to the hospital and she survived.

Later on, when she recovered, he visited her and the relationship grew. They were an odd couple. A middle-aged scarface bouncerbastard and a young beautiful black woman. Everybody thought she was some famous film star and he was her minder. She didn't want much from Francis — just to be protected from the whole wide fucking world. He liked her because she accepted him at face value and didn't look for the man underneath. The man she saw in front of her was good enough. And she told him so. Everybody needs somebody! Francis helped Glendora get a new flat up in Hackney and a new job as a croupier at the Cosa Nostra Casino in Gloucester Place. They shared a bed together every so often but took precautions because she was HIV positive. She didn't have AIDS — just the virus. Doctors told her she might never develop the disease. Then again she might. And even if she did, it was a thing you lived with these days — not died from. If she survived for five years she had a good chance. Maybe they'd even find a cure before anything bad happened. Neither of them spoke about it. They both knew about it but didn't speak about it. Sometimes it was like the spectre at the feast when they were making love. But they still didn't speak about it. Better like that. No sentimentality and no shit! Glendora was happy — as long as Francis was there when the world tried to take a bite out of her. And he was always there.

Taxi pulled up outside the house in Leytonstone Road. Francis paid the driver and stepped out into the street. After 4.00 a.m. and no lights on. Again he thought of not going in at all — of just fucking off. Just walking away down the road and never coming back. He took a deep breath and headed up the driveway towards the front door.

chapter nine

chapte r nine

chapte r nine

Francis Page sensed something as soon as he came into the house. Same feeling he got when a punch-up was about to kick off in one of the clubs. He moved cautiously, leaving the lights and making no sound. He waited at the entrance to the living room. Listening for any noise. There was nothing. Francis moved into the room, keeping his back against the wall and trying to acclimatise his eyes to the gloom. Nobody. He was just jagjumped. It was those fucking Voices — they were jangling his nerves. He relaxed, taking off his jacket and throwing it over a chair. Francis made his way to the kitchen and turned on the light. Angeline sitting at the table, face black and bitched. Stopped in his tracks. Heart. Beat. Hate. Love. Looked at her without speaking.

Angeline was still an attractive woman, in an affected sort of way, despite the years of controversy and confrontation. But she'd grown hard since he first met her. Tough and independent and the years with him made her cynical and difficult. It showed in her face. Even her expensive make-up couldn't hide it. Why the fuck was she sitting there? She never waited up for him this late. It always took Francis some time to realise when things were changing and to figure out what the cause was. Why should they have to? Why should he have to? What made it so?

Some of Angeline's friends may have viewed her as a victim, but she didn't see herself the same way. At least not in the sense of some women who are physically abused by their men. Or psychologically. He didn't do that kind of thing. At least not yet. She blamed herself and her youthful naïvety for the situation, as well as Francis' ongoing immaturity and ineffectiveness. She blamed the infatuation she had for him fourteen years ago. Infatuation. Because love was a word she didn't believe ever applied to their relationship. She blamed her parents' religious beliefs for keeping them together. She blamed the vodka she drank that night they first made love. And her stupidity in allowing him into her without protection. That was all. Circumstance. Not victimisation. It was a circumstantial problem that had endured for fourteen years. There had been no solution. Until now.

Francis didn't see her as a victim either. In a way, he was more afraid of her than she was of him. He saw her as increasingly aggressive. Increasingly selfish. Increasingly threatening. As the frustration of the relationship grew, so did his fear. There was a physical base to personality and he was the product of his biochemical make-up. So was she. And maybe he was the victim. Because he always expected life to stay as it was. Expected the people around him to remain in suspended animation. But life didn't work that way and, no matter how frantically it tried, his brain couldn't sort out all the strange changing messages it received. And produced equally strange explanations to allow him to cope. To continue. To survive. Always with a sense of uncertainty, self-consciousness and guilt. Francis had grown up slow and was only finding out that life changes all the time. But it still took him a little while to understand what was going on.

'Tell me it isn't true.'

'Tell you what isn't true?'

'That you're sleeping with a woman who has AIDS.'

'It isn't true.'

She wasn't going to stop. He knew it.

'Where have you been until now?'

'Who told you I was sleeping with a woman who has AIDS?'

'Does it matter, Francis? I had a phone call.'

'From who?'

'I don't know.'

'Male or female?'

Angeline threw her arms in the air.

'For God's sake! Where have you been, Francis?'

'With Matthew Moore.'

'Liar!'

He wasn't a liar. Why wouldn't she stop?

'Fuck off to bed, Angeline.'

'No I won't! Not until I say what I have to say. Why didn't you pick the girls up from school?'

'Oh shit ...'

'Precisely!'

'I forgot. I forgot. Fuck! Did they get home all right? Fuck! Fuck! Fuck!'

Heartbeat.

'They shouldn't have had to get home all right ... on their own. There are too many bloody maniacs like you out there, Francis.'

'I'm not a maniac. Don't say that to me, Angeline ...'

'You obviously have as much respect for your daughters as you have for me.'

'I wouldn't let anything happen to those girls ...'

'How would you know if anything happened to them? You're a retard, Francis ... a bloody retard with as much sense of responsibility as a ten-year-old child.'

Heartbeat. Heartbeat.

'No ... I'm not that! Don't be like them in the schoolyard ... go fuck yourself, Angeline!'

'Oh I do, Francis, I do. It's certainly safer than letting you fuck me.'

Francis picked up a glass and smashed it against the wall. Stresstrigger! Heartbeat-panic-violence. The neurotransmitters in his brain were overheating. The histamine was high and the dopamine was drunk. Homocysteineheartbeat. Heartbeat. Heart! Beat! Control ebbing away. The side of his face began to twitch and his mouth opened and closed as if saying some silent prayer. Splinters of glass rained down on the table but Angeline didn't move. The watershed had finally come. The point of no return. Francis was agitated by her intransigence and surly stare. He hated impersolence. Especially in women. They weren't supposed to be like that. His mother was vulnerable and persecuted. Women were supposed to be looked after — protected from the world. He couldn't protect his mother — too young. Couldn't protect Angeline either. How could a man protect a woman who did it for herself? It wasn't right. Against the natural order of things. Francis didn't know how to cope with women who lived outside that pattern which God and man had imposed since time began. He tried to come to terms with it all — change, time, change, life, change, madness, change, women, change, money, change, violence, change, change. Change!

What the fuck was going on?

Francis kicked one of the cupboard doors off its hinges. Angeline flinched but held her ground. She was getting on his fucking nerves and he would normally have fucked off to bed by now and not have allowed the situation to develop to the next stage. But an edginess was inside him. New. He swept all the saucepans off the cooker with his arm. They crashed to the floor and the lids rolled round in circles. Francis kicked them out of his way. Why was she staring at him like that? Something was going on. He knew they were cooking something up. Maybe she was in on it now and who else? Couldn't trust any fucker — even his own wife. Francis raised his fist and held it in mid-air. Threatening. Tears in his eyes. What now? What now? What now? Listened. Footsteps coming slowly downstairs. Fiona entered the kitchen cautiously — followed by Sinéad carrying a well-worn doll. The girls stayed near the doorway, not wanting to come any closer yet worried for their mother. Francis calmed down when he saw them. Heart. Beat. Sinéad was crying, but Fiona just looked straight at her father. Angeline immediately left the chair to console her daughters.

'Now look what you've done, you bastard!'

'I'm sorry, girls. Sorry, sorry ...'

The just-turned-thirteen-year-old was about to go to Francis.

'Mind your feet on that glass, Fiona.'

Angeline pulled her back to the doorway.

'Go on back to bed. Me and your mother are just having a little talk.'

'Leave them where they are, Francis.'

'Go on, girls ... go, go ...'

'Let them see what a big ignorant bully they have for a father.'

Francis moved towards the girls, crunching the glass under his boots. Sinéad began to sob even louder and huddled close to her mother. Fiona didn't move. Angeline had an arm round the older girl, but she wasn't frightened. She was fascinated by her father and stood facing him, not saying a word. While her sister held onto their mother for some sort of stabilisation. Francis moved closer, finger up to his mouth and lips saying shhhhh. He bent down and smiled at Fiona. The girl smiled back. As he reached over to touch Sinéad, Angeline picked up a heavy saucepan from the floor and struck him a solid blow across the side of the skull. Francis was motionless for a moment, the smile still painted across his drunkdrugged face. Then he sank slowly to his knees and remained in that position. Angeline dropped the pot and quickly moved the girls away from him.

He's telling me now I gotta learn to be more careful, Chela. She sideswiped me! The bitch! He says I'm not to be mad ... because the woman's only my alter ego, man. Remember my word. Hate? Love. Remember Magdalene and the guy who cast the first stone. Who did? Nobody. My earth-mother loved me. So did mine! Tried to love me. I tried to love her. We were dealt a dud hand. He's saying that woman and man together is *lü* ... for him who understands my teaching there'll be no meaning in father or mother or wife or child ... Luke, 14: 26. My word is Love, Chela. Love ... Love. All you need is. Love is all you need. Sometimes love isn't fucking enough! Dismas loved me when I was dying on the Roman cross. And he was enlightened and lived. Gestas wanted me to save his earthly body and he died. But Animal tells me to hate. Who? Animalkhan. He's the *dakdzin* ... the *tsatsa*. Why're you listening to that guy? Her! I'm not a killer. Then don't listen to one! Did you see Riazan when he was finished with it? Or Kozelski ... or Pest? If you had you'd know him ... the meaning of him. I say she has heart! He says but no soul. Heart will leave you, soul won't. Soul won't save you when they're trying to break your bloody neck. But it'll save you from yourself ... my Father ain't flesh but spirit and I live by Him and Him alone I honour ... Matthew, 4: 8. I don't need saving from myself. He's asking if I even know who I am, Chela? Yes. No. Sometimes. Says the sum total of myself is greater than the inconspicuous few moments of a lifetime. Leave me alone! Says my anger is never justified ... and the anger of others is never causeless. Fuck that! Mother ... Annie ... they said you did it to me. Windowlicker! And consciousness can easily be overwhelmed by irrelevancy, Chela. Psycho! Asking if I'd go back to my youth and give up the bit in between?

Maybe. But to do that I'd have to hate what I am and if I hate what I am why would I want to become it again? Nutter! When I was young I believed everything would always stay the same. All kids do ... do they? Don't they? Animal! Yet you see now that you were wrong. Because he left us. Konrad left us! Spazo! Things have changed for the better for me. They have! The future! I live for the future, Alien. Or have you just learned the imposed constraints of the past? I've learned that when you trust some fucker he leaves you. She leaves you. Now I trust no bastard ... including you! He's saying I'm really back where I started, man. At the beginning. Maybe I want to go back to the beginning. Have a go at it all over again. He's calling me a child. Saying I'm a child again. I'm not a child no more. No longer a child! Don't say that to me, Alien. *She* said that to me. I know well there's more to life. I have it under control. There's going to be more to my life ... To existence, Chela. He says I should live in the present ... don't try to go back and when the future comes its trouble will come too ... Matthew, 6: 32. Contradictions! Contradictions! What does it all mean? I can't understand what they're telling me ... what's the code? What's the secret? Don't you know? You're the alien ... the fucking philosopher ... you tell me! I can't tell you, that's the point. I can only show you. Show me then! Show me the silver! First you have to be able to see. I can see! Look then. Not with your eye, man ... with your *samadhi*.

Cold water struck Francis straight in the face. He spluttered and shook his head. Still in a kneeling position. Heart. Angeline stood over him. Beat. Wearing her overcoat and holding an empty water jug in her hand. Francis made an attempt to get up and she stepped back, ready to run. But dizziness overcame him and he slipped back down again. He felt the side of his head. There was no blood, just a large lump still growing. He felt a pain in his knee and looked down to see blood oozing from a cut in his trousers where a shard of glass had penetrated. Angeline was half-way down the hall.

'I wanted to make sure you were all right before we left.'

'Left what?'

'We're going, Francis. We've had enough.'

He heard the words but they were meaningless. Apart from the threat of them. The meaningless threat. Francis tried to focus.

'Where are the girls ...?'

'They're in the car.'

'You can't, don't Angeline ... do that!'

He knew she couldn't do it. But she was doing it.

'We'll come back when you've gone.'

'I'm not going anywhere. Where? Gone where?'

'This is my house, Francis. I want you out of it.'

Lucidity was like a light. She was leaving. He wasn't leaving. She was.

'It's my house too. I'm not leaving ... the girls.'

'Who pays the bloody mortgage?'

'My money pays for things ... you know I pay for things.'

'Sure you do, drugs, drink and whores.'

Heart. Beat.

'I'll get you back if you do this, Angeline.'

'I'm not afraid of you, Francis.'

'I'll kill you!'

Heartfuckingbeat!

Francis lunged at her from his kneeling position. Heartbeat. She easily evaded him and ran to the front door. He struggled to get to his feet, but could already hear the car engine revving up as he followed her down the hall. By the time he got outside, they were reversing down the driveway into the road. Francis ran after the car. Could see Fiona's face pressed against the back window. Smiling and waving him good-bye. His mother's face was beside his daughter's — mouth open in a silent scream. Heartbeat. Heartbeat. Heartbeat. Francis hurled himself down the street, but the car had already turned the corner and was out of sight.

A few early birds on their way to work. 5.30 a.m. The milkman gave him a dirty look as he passed but Francis didn't even see him. He stood there for a long time, looking down the street in the wake of the car. Time standing still again. Yet externally it was rushing past his motionless body like an express train. Something had changed. Francis tried to understand — to work out in his head why this should be. He stood there in the street, trying to see through the mist. Why should it be like this? Why should this be like this? Why should this be what it is? What it is? Faint fingers of light beginning to appear in the eastern sky across the marshlands and out where the sea lapped up against the land at Southend and the Isle of Sheppey. Francis felt as if he had turned to stone, with more and more people passing by on their way to whatever their business was. They were all glaring at him through their car windows and beeping horns at him to get out of the way — but he didn't notice any of them. Just continued to stare down the road. Felt sick. Vomit erupted from the pit of his stomach and spewed out of his throat. He watched it hit the ground in slow motion and splash back onto his boots and trousers. Francis wiped his mouth with his sleeve, then turned and walked back up the road. What was he going to do now? Didn't give a shit whether Angeline left him or not. Even though he loved her. Hated her. She shouldn't have taken the girls! She could not do that! And she wasn't getting the fucking house either. Fuck her! The fucking fucking heartbeat whore! He traipsed into the kitchen and poured himself a glass of water.

Francis walked through the house. What the fuck was it? What was it? A house! Not a life. Nor an existence. Not a heart. Not a soul. What was it? He didn't give a shit about the house. Fuck the fucking house! But he wasn't going to let her do this to him. His worst fears were realised. She was gone. And taken his girls. Everybody was gone. Fuck the house. Burn the bastard down to the ground if it tried to leave him! Francis held his head. The woman fucking hit him. He always knew she was going to. Took her fourteen years but she done it finally. Like he knew she would. The witchbitch! The lovehate woman. If he let that go — if it got out, every fucking toerag in London would be trying to do the same. He wondered where she'd gone with the girls. Could be any place. One of her noseintheair friends or her fucking family. Some of the bastards lived down country in Kent and she had a brother over in Hampstead. Maybe the woman had another man somewhere. Some fucking prick with a bow-tie on his bollocks. Francis didn't give a shit about that either. Even though he lovehated her. But no bastard was having his children! No fucking ratbag slag fucking paedophile wanker! He'd halfcripple the cunt! Heartfuckingbeat! Fear-panic-anger-aggression-violence-symptomology. Burn the bitch! Burn the witch! Hunt the witch. Doctor!

Francis kicked tables and chairs around the kitchen. Picked them up and smashed them to smithereens. Only when there was nothing left to break did he calm down. Slowly climbed the stairs. Angeline had taken most of her stuff but Francis could still smell her in the bedroom. The smell of her was in the curtains and carpet and wallpaper and bed-clothes. All around him. Spying. Telling. Going through his fucking pockets. He caught his own reflection in the dressing-table mirror and turned quickly away. Didn't want to see. His own face. Hated himself. Hated the dressing-table for reminding him and kicked it across the room, shattering the mirror into a million slivers of glass. The girls' wardrobes also empty. Francis sat on the side of Fiona's bed. He knew the girls loved him if no other bastard did. Saw it in Fiona's smile. Sinéad was too young to know what was going on. But Angeline wouldn't have it all her own way with Fiona. She was her daddy's goodnight girl.

Fatigue finally overcame Francis and he lay back on the bed. He stared up at the ceiling for years. Day into night into day into night into day into. Into. Maybe it was all his fault. Maybe he was a worthless evil psycho bastard. Like they said. Maybe he was fucking mad. Maybe they were all right? Showing weakness now and he had to be careful because the wankers could read his thoughts as well as everything else. Fatigue became an entity in the room with him. It lay beside him on the bed and forced his eyes to close so that the sleep could come and bring with it the familiar dream that never ended.

chapter ten

chapte r ten

chapte r ten

Francis Page waited for darkness to fall and then waited a while longer for everything to settle down and every arsehole to get home out of the Winter night. Where they should be. And not out minding other fucking people's business. Sit by the glowing fire in their smug armchairs and dream little complacent dreams of wellbeing and wish-fulthinking.

He closed the front door of the house in Essex and drove off towards London in the black Citroën. Francis cruised down the M11 into Woodford. Then on through Wanstead and Stratford. Stopped the car in Leytonstone Road across from his ex-house and sat there watching for a while. No one came in or out. Whole street silent. Holding its breath. Smoked a couple of cigarettes and saw the dogs again and drove on. West past Pentonville Prison where he thought about screaming out at the shining smoothwalls. But he didn't. Because he was afraid they would reach over and pull him back again. To the false shadows and the symbols and the searing rage. He stuck his fingers up at the looming monster and drove on south by King's Cross and Farringdon to Holborn. Parked the car near Hatton Garden and walked along Greville Street to Brooks Court. Where Fiona had a small flat. He remembered because she told him he could come there to live when he got out and it stuck in his mind. Lodged there. Because he was in prison at the time. Prison. Crooks. Court. Crooks Court. Brooks Court. He passed the small medieval Church of St Eduard the Martyr and wanted to go inside. To pray. Decided against it for the present at any rate. A soft crimson light in the flat window and already 2.20 a.m. by Hatchet Harry Kane's watch. He was jumpy. Nervous. Edgy. Didn't know who could be inside. Even if Fiona still lived there. So long since he saw her. And he was well tranq'd out of it then. Someone might even be watching the place. Some police slag. This was taking a chance — but chances had to be taken. Had to make his move now. This move. Now!

A man emerged from the flat just as he approached. Francis drew back into the shadows and waited while the man looked around, then pulled his collar up and made his way quickly to a parked car. Francis didn't move until the car was out of sight and then came carefully back to the door. He knocked lightly. No reply. Listened for the slightest sound. Ears acutely sensitive to any audible danger. Knocked harder and a light came out from under the door. A small voice after it.

'Who's there?'

'Fiona?'

'Who's there?'

'Is that you, Fiona?'

'Yes ...'

'It's Francis. Dad. It's Dad.'

The door opened just a crack and a frightened eye peered out into the blackness of the hall.

'Dad?'

'It's me. Let me in.'

Hesitation behind the door. Francis could feel the fear. Touch it. The small voice talked to itself for a moment. Sobbed a little. Then opened the door. Francis stepped into the flat. He looked like Bunyip on a bad night and Fiona looked like she hadn't eaten for a year and a half. Black circles around her eyes and teeth discoloured. Hair like a boy's, short and cutscabs on her head. The flat was dirty and smelled nearly as bad as Francis' knee. But they were glad to see each other and hugged and held on for a long time. Needed someone to love. Love them. Anyone. Someone. Tears fell down both faces until Francis picked her up in his arms and carried her through to where he could lay her down on a sofa. He was back. To take care of her again. His vulnerable little baby. And she was. Glad. He'd allow no further fucking about. From no bastard!

'I'll look after you now, honey.'

'Will you, Dad? At last? After all this time?'

'I promise. Was that your boyfriend?'

'I have no boyfriend. Who?'

'That man I saw leaving.'

'There was no man leaving, Dad. He didn't come from this flat? Maybe next door.'

Francis agreed. That it was probably the flat next door. Or his imagination. Covered her with his coat and watched her until her eyes closed. Then lay on the floor beside her and they said nothing more. She slept unsoundly through the rest of the night and he smoked cigarettes and now and then got up to make coffee. And watched over her.

A weak sun from the east struck the window pane a glancing blow late next morning. Shining from somewhere out in the North Sea. Fiona stirred and opened her eyes. Startled to see Francis standing over her with a cup of coffee. He looked like a complete stranger. A tramp off the street. With his long hair and beard and dirty clothes and cyanosis of the hands and feet and oedema of the nose and ears and a smell that she couldn't put a name to. Like death. He smiled and she remembered the night before. Took the coffee and sipped at it while he sat on a chair nearby.

'Sorry about the state of this place, Dad.'

'Don't worry, you should be where I've come from. Have been.'

'Where?'

'What?'

'Where have you come from?'

Where had he come from? The house. His friendhouse. He missed the place and was feeling anxious to be so far away from it.

'The country.'

'It was in all the papers ... how you escaped with that other man.'

'Hatchet Harry.'

If it was Hatchet Harry. Francis still wasn't sure.

'That's him. They said you nearly killed two guards. One lost an eye and the other had a broken skull and suspected brain damage.'

'And Matthew? Did they say I killed Matthew?'

'No ... no killing. What happened, Dad? You look terrible.'

'So do you. You back on the skag? Junk? Shit?'

'Dad ...'

'Are you?'

She wasn't afraid of him — had never been. Even though she thought she ought to be.

'I told you ... I just take a little cocaine. Everybody does. It's nothing to worry about. Where are you living, Dad?'

'Nowhere now. I was in the country. Can I stay here?'

'Sure. I'll clean the place up today. We can stay here together. That would be great.'

'Not forever. I have some business here in the city, then I'll be going back to the country.'

Back to the comforthouse. Where no one could touch him.

'I could come with you.'

'What about your college?'

'Don't worry about that. I can pick it back up later.'

He kissed her on the forehead. Then fell asleep in the chair. She shook him awake and took him through to the single bed where he slept all day. While she cleaned up the flat as best she could and hid the rock pipes for the crack and syringes for a little smack to get her down easy off the high. She opened the window and let in some air and took a shower and did her hair. The only one who ever loved her was here. And she was happy for the first time in a long time. If ever. Apart from a few Sundays a long time ago when she used to go for drives with a big man in a bottle-green Jaguar and he bought her things and they laughed together and hugged each other and he kissed her and she knew he was on her side. If nobody else was. And it ended then but now it was back again.

Darkness down by the time Francis woke. Fiona cooked beans on toast and they ate together and afterwards he had a wash and she had a look at his leg which was in a bad state and she couldn't understand how he was able to walk around at all. Even with his crutch. He refused to go near a hospital so Fiona cleaned the wound up and disinfected it and dressed it. She gave Francis a couple of strong painkillers and he seemed to settle down a bit. Not so edgy. Explosive. Eat you with a grain of fucking saltive. And he felt he was home. After being away so long. She trimmed up his hair and his beard just a little bit. Because he wanted them both left longish. For camouflage. That night Fiona slept back in her bed and Francis went up to the Church of St Eduard the Martyr. He entered through the medieval arch and made his way cautiously in the dim ghoulshine across to the nave. No one about. He stood upright in front of the altar in the eerie flickerlight from the candles. A scene from a different age. An earlier time. Dark age full of ghosts and grotesque gothics. Spectres and wraiths played hide-andseek amongst the shadows and the silence screamed with bloodfreezing cries of Hell. And damnation. And down down down down into the depths. The jaws. The bowels. Of misguided belief.

I am not yet born; Oh hear me. Let not the man who is beast or who thinks he is God come near me.

'You're here late.'

'Is it late, Father?'

'Early then.'

'God talks at all times.'

The priest looked Francis up and down.

'Quite true. Are you a local?'

'Just moved into the area, Father. From the country.'

'I see. Is everything all right?'

All right? Did he know something? What did he know?

'Yes. I mean ... how do you mean?'

'Well ... I'm sorry, I don't mean to be discourteous ...'

'Speak your mind, Father. You're in God's house.'

'It's just ... you look a little ...'

Francis realised what he must look like.

'Down. Down and out. Down?'

'Yes ... I mean, yes ... sort of ...'

'I've just come out of hospital, Father.'

'Oh, I'm sorry. I mean, I'm glad ... that you're out, of course. Anything serious?'

Serious? Only if losing reality and living in the land of turmoil was serious.

'You could say that.'

'Well, I certainly hope you're on the road to recovery.'

'Oh I am, Father. I am indeed. Now that I'm here.'

The priest genuflected and crossed himself.

'Faith is a great healer. Do you have a place to live and job to go to?'

'A place to live I have, but a job ... not yet. I'm looking around for something though ... just to tide me over for a while.'

'What sort of work do you do?'

'You could say, Father, I'm kind of a handyman. A bit of hammering here ... a bit of banging there.'

'Well now, isn't it just the most extraordinary thing ...?'

Francis didn't know what he meant. Maybe it was time to go. He made to move away, but the priest caught his arm.

'What is it? What can it be? Father ...?'

'We've just lost our man here ... at St Eduard's. We're looking for somebody. A caretaker-type person. The pay isn't a fortune, of course but ...'

'I'll take it. Does God move in mysterious ways?'

'Quite. He does.'

Francis asked if he could work at night instead of during the day because he had a clinic to go to and the priest said it was all right as long as everything was done and Francis promised him it would. Get done. Everything.

Francis worked as general caretaker at the Church of St Eduard the Martyr over the next few weeks and through the Christmas holiday and on into the new year. He lived with Fiona in her little Brooks Court flat and almost completely forgot about the house out in Essex. Even tried to get her off the crack and found a rehab clinic for his daughter. With the help of the priest and made her promise she'd go there on a regular basis. Carbon copy of that other time. When he picked another girl up out of the junkie gutter and brought her back to life. Second chance for him. Life repeating itself. Going back on itself. Déjà vu. Only simpler now. Not so complicated — in the actual physicality of it. Just the turmoil in his head. Constant. Except for brief windows of reality which could come at any time. In the middle of the Voices or when he felt suicidal. Bringing him back to life. He didn't go far. Just from the flat to the church and back again and sometimes to the shops. Occasionally when he felt up to it he drove Fiona across to the rehab clinic in Cheapside. To make sure she was still going and not pulling the wool and meeting pusherpricks and pimps who would only destroy her precious little life. Fiona was on benefit and between them they just about managed. The bones in Francis' knee knitted back together in a disfigured mass and scar tissue grew over it all. Leg twisted into a crazy shape as a result and he walked with a pronounced limp. Even when using the crutch. But as long as it was hidden underneath his trouser leg. It was invisible. The newspapers forgot about him. Always some new scandal to shout about. But Francis still didn't trust the bastards and kept watching all around him. All the time. Every move. In case the fuckers crept up on him. Again.

Fiona didn't like the gun in the flat. Francis told her the weapon was only for their own protection. He took it out and cleaned it every night before going over to the church and counted the bullets and clipped them into the magazine and out again. Several times over. She said nothing. Francis also kept a kind of journal — a diary. She looked at it once when he was out of the room but each page consisted of one word only — repeated again and again and again. Like killer killer killer killer killer killer continued on down to the end of one page. And love love love love love love down to the end of another page. And hate hate hate hate hate hate to the bottom of another. And God God God God God God all down along the next. Then mad. Then normal. Then other pages full of names. Like Glenny and Annie and even her own — Fiona. Also other names she didn't know — and one she did. Some pages had no words but only sketches. Small little pictures cramped into a tight corner and the rest of the page blank. And some just a mass of scribbles all over the place and completely indecipherable. Other drawings were dark and had faces of fear and things that she'd only seen before in her nightmares. The journalbook was almost full up and only a few blank pages left. She wondered how it would end.

Fiona thought of talking to Francis about his diary but she decided it was best to leave well enough alone. So she said nothing. Had her own problems. Said nothing. Francis locked the gun and the journal away every night. Before he went to work. And pray.

Killing is killing. And a killer is a killer is a killer. It's all the same. What's the difference between a bomb falling out of an aeroplane or in the boot of a car? Nothing! No difference. Killing is killing! Killer is killer! Who would I give my life for? What? Only for myself. Because I know now there is no death. There is only *me* ... *me* who is going to die! I alone in the Universe know I cannot escape death. But I will not die. I will be killed. And I will not know the moment of my death. It will be determined by the choices I make. Just as I am now the result of the choices already made. A self-created reality. But to know the end I need to know the beginning. Death is the beginning! Know death. Know birth. Understand. No act and no consequence of that act can be judged in isolation. I have died before. Many times. It is not a unique experience. I have seen the words. Even the unseen words. And when the agonal moment comes I will be calm. Infinity in the palm of my hand. I *will* know again what the child knew. Always knew. Knows. Now.

He told everything to God and God understood and nodded his approval but said nothing in reply.

Francis saw Glendora asleep in the bed when he got back to the flat next morning. The black girl looked so vulnerable. So slight and breakable. He moved towards her as if being pulled by some old magnetic force. Almost forgotten. Took off his clothes and slipped in beside her. Into the bed. She was warm and brittle and he touched her sad small body and it shivered. She opened her eyes and looked at him in quiet surprise. At first she didn't recognise him. But she looked deep into his soul and knew he loved her and it would be all right again. Like it was. Just the two of them. If nobody shared what they had but the two of them. Because nobody else understood what was between them. They were alike. The same. Two of a kind. And it was appropriate now that they should become one of a kind.

He began to shake. With emotion. Uncontrollably. But her small hands steadied his shoulders like they used to in the old days and it stopped. Went away. She smiled and her lips came up to meet him. They touched. Brushed by each other. A gentle glow enveloped the room. Brought in by the pale Winter sun. Melting over the walls and velvetsilk across the floor. Her breath enveloped him. Held him in a sweet chrysalis. His body was clumsy with misuse. But hers was serpentine. Moulding itself around him. Into him. They spoke to each other in a language that neither understood and their fingers played across the membrane of pleasure that enveloped the bed. He looked for protection when the appropriate time came but she said softly there was no need because she hadn't had a period for a long time and he was happy that she was cured at last. From the disease. They laughed and kissed and he entered her. And they absorbed each other's essence. The essence of each other. And became one flesh. One world. One deion.

chapter eleven

chapte r eleven

chapte r eleven

Francis Page and his associates had free access to the Hardcore gymnasium on Oxford Street because it was owned by a friend of Percy Shillinger. Some said it was part of a protection package but nobody gave a shit once they got in gratis. Fitness centres were expensive if you worked out three times a week and bouncers and bodyguards had to keep themselves in shape — otherwise every wiseguy wanker in the city would be knocking lumps off them.

Francis pulled himself out of bed in the late afternoon. Didn't want to get up. Becoming more difficult every day. Sometimes he just wanted to lie there and never move again. He put it down to age. Or maybe he was turning into a vampire. Awake all night and asleep all day. With the metaphysics of the Voices and the disillusionment of answers for everything but explanations for nothing. At first the events of the night before didn't come back to him. Knew something bad had happened. What? Wandered from room to room trying to get things straight in his head, slowly piecing together the reality of the situation.

The witchbitch had left him at last and he cursed her for the lovehate tramp she was and always would be. Francis stuck his head under the cold tap in the bathroom. Normally quite meticulous about his appearance, but today he couldn't be fucking bothered. Just dressed quickly in a tracksuit and drank black coffee. Matthew Moore called to the door and they drove uptown in his car. Francis remained silent on the way and Matthew knew better than to bother him with small-talk. They climbed the stairs to the gymnasium changing rooms. Matthew was ready quickly. While Francis just sat staring at the wall. He was sorry now he'd come. Didn't want to talk to any of these tossers and only wanted to stay indoors — away from the staring eyes and pointing fingers. He thought about getting hold of a machine-gun, just in case some of the fuckers tried to get into the house. To kill him. Blow them all away. Like thistledown. Hither. And thither. Matthew left him to the woolgathering and went out to start his session.

Something in my head or maybe not, saying that contemplation is the first step of science. Calling me Shegetz. Und science is ze first step of understandink. An evolvink classroom! Ask if it's talking to me? It replies I am reason, Shegetz. I am logic. Und zere is no other *mensch* here, so I must be talking to you. I say there's no logic any more. It says of course there is. Tells me it belongs to a mathematical physicist, so it should know. I just wish ... I just wish ... I just wish. A mazematical physicist is a *wissenschaftler* who does not believe zat science is ze be-all und end-all of everyzink. But I can teach you to think. I say I don't want to think. For myself. I don't want it! It tells me of course I do. Says it's very easy to understand Shegetz, ze fundamental laws of physics are all around. Where? Everyvere! I ask what's a fundamental law? What's logic? What's reason? What's any fucking thing? A fundamental law is a fundamental law it says! Asks me if I'm a complete *naar*? I shout be careful what you call me, Scientistvoice! Especially at this moment of now ... because I'm ... I'm. I'm I'm. I just wish ... are you another alien? It says its word is normal, Shegetz. Everyzink is normal. Ze Universe is normal. I ask if a fundamental law is normal? And if it's a fundamental law, does that mean it can't ever change? Never change? Of course it can! Everyzink changes. Don't you know zat? Ze vorld vas once flat, vas it not? No it wasn't. Every *meshugina* believed it vas ... it vas a fundamental law. Ze atom could not be split ... I ask can one and one be equal to one? Tell me that, Scientistvoice! Is that normal? Is that reason? Logic? If you believe it is ... it is! I tell it I know it's only a cartoon character and not real like blood is real. Or braincells. It agrees — says that's true ... I am a cartoon character in a theoretical position vich turns out to be a joke. But isn't zat vat everyzink is? What is what everything is? Atomic. A. Tom. Ic. I ask more questions even though I don't really want to know the answers. Like ... about these atoms? Ze smallest unit of matter zat can take part in a chemical reaction. How small is that? Small! It says that atoms are largely nothing, Shegetz ... chust protons und neutrons surrounded by electrons. Five millionths of a millimetre in diameter ... und ze nucleus is much smaller. I say like tiny little worlds then ... Precisely! Und zey rotate. So ... everything is really a big spinning fuck-all? Somezink like zat. And is that your word? Is that normal? It is. I ask how it knows it's right? How can you be so sure of everything? Scientistvoice? If you can't see it? It says you don't need to see something to know it exists and asks me if I've seen Africa? I've seen God. Und does He play dice? My little girls ... my girls. I left Lieserl. I left her, Shegetz. Don't be like me und break your own heart. It's already broke. Telling me now the tragedy of physics is zat it explains ze objective Universe at ze cost of subjective intuition. Why am I who I am? Like I am? It is all relative, Shegetz. Warning me not to rationalise too much or I'll go mad. Vonce you go through zat door you vill neffer be ze same again ... you vill be foreffer tryink to understand ze relationship of systematic reasonink to ze truth it can neffer explain. I ask if death is the beginning? Scientistvoice? Is it the meaning? It says that neither death nor science exist in themselves ... both are merely reactions to experience. Is it an end? It is an end und a beginning. Is it good? It says good is a value judgement zat science does not recognise, Shegetz. And I ask who's to say there ain't tiny little people living on these tiny little atomworlds? Little vorlds of protons, neutrons und leptons ... vhy not? Maybe the lights we see in the sky, Scientistvoice, are really big electrons whizzing round our own little atomplanet. Is death ... is death ... is death ...? Is our sun und solar system part of some gigantic molecule? Maybe a little part of some gigantic horse-shit! Is ze Universe itself nozing more zan a super fundamental particle? Do you know ... Einstein?

Do you know? Of course I do!

A bunch of squashrackety nancyboys burst into the changing-room. Looked across at Francis in suspicious manner. Surly. Skulking. He knew who they really were, but didn't let on he knew. Stood up quickly and growled, then left them to their fucking plots and plans. The weightroom was spacious, with a wide variety of benches, barbells, pec-decs, hack-squats, dipping frames, chinning bars, leg extensions and all the other paraphernalia required to get the well-paying punters all isotoned and adrenalined. Matthew Moore was pressing out a hundred-kilo set on the multigym. John Nightingale and some of his fairy friends from the Backside Bar were using the squat-rack. All feeling up each other's arses. Francis joined Matthew on the bench-press.

'Let me slot in there ...'

Matthew got up and let Francis onto the press.

'Jesus, Francis, I didn't like to tell you but you look fucking rough.'

'Then why are you telling me?'

'What?'

'If you didn't like to tell me before, why are you telling me now?'

'No reason ... I just thought I'd say it, that's all.'

'Well, mind your own fucking business in future!'

Francis pumped out a set of ten. Then he got up and let Matthew back on.

'What the fuck's up with you?'

'Nothing!'

'Was it the party?'

'What party?'

'Yesterday ... last night. Don't tell me you can't remember?'

'I can ... and I'm all fucking right!'

Matthew knocked out his set. He stood up and looked at Francis.

'The side of your head don't look all right. Did you get some grief somewhere?'

'I'll give you some fucking grief in a minute. I told you to mind your own fucking business!'

Matthew Moore decided to say nothing more. Francis was in a bad mood and it was getting worse by the minute. He knocked out another set of ten reps. Counted each one loudly, then sat up on the bench to catch his breath.

Heart. Francis saw John Nightingale looking his way. He hoped the bastard wouldn't start. Nightingale locked eyes with him and grinned. Then he broke away from his company and sauntered across the gym. Beat.

'Boy ... you look like crap, Francis Page. *Cotidie morior ... coditie fleo.*'

Francis didn't want to reply. But he knew he had to. Again he searched for the right words.

'Just fuck off, Nightingale ... and leave me alone. I'm not bothering you.'

'Maybe you should try to get in the aerobics class with the rest of the old broads?'

Matthew Moore pushed his way between the two men.

'Leave him alone, Nightingale.'

'Mister Moore ... my man. You his pimp or something now? Can't he talk for himself?'

Francis wanted to talk for himself. But the turmoil in his head made it difficult to know how. So he said stupid things. Or things he thought were stupid. Because he himself was stupid.

'I'm getting pissed off ... all this Latin shit. Let's sort it out ... you and me. Once and for all!'

'Wow! Don't get sore, Francis Page. Sounds like the lady doth protest too much. I just came across to wish you luck with your big deal.'

'What big deal? What deal?'

Nightingale put his hands on his hips and looked at Francis as if he was a kid.

'Your joint, Francis Page. The joint you're gonna open. The Furry Fanny, ain't it? Some shit like that.'

Matthew Moore was still trying to stay between them.

'Leave it out, Nightingale! Take no notice of this cunt, Francis.'

'When's opening night? When Agnes D'Argensola wins Miss Personality of the Year? You want a good guy for the door?'

Francis was confused. Nobody knew about his plans. Some people knew, but not this Yank bastard. How did he know? Who was talking to him?

'Who told you? Who? Who the fuck told *you*?'

Nightingale touched his lips with his forefinger. He blew a kiss at Francis, then turned to walk away. Stresstrigger! Heartbeat. Francis was up and onto him before he took five paces. Bars and bells sent sprawling across the floor as the two men wrestled and punched. Matthew Moore tried to get in between the blows and bites assisted by a couple of bodybuilders. The rest of the clientele scattered quickly, before they got a clout of a five-kilo disc or a swipe of a tricep-bar. Gym instructors came flying from all over the centre and after a sweatpumping struggle, the protagonists were pulled apart. Nightingale took the worst of it and was led away bleeding to the changing-rooms by his pansy pals blowing back another kiss at Francis and muttering — *vulneratus non victus*. Francis had a split eyebrow and he stood against a wall holding a towel to the cut. Heartbeat. Instructors patrolled the gym area to make sure there were no further outbreaks. Of that kind of carry on. Give the fucking place a bad name. And the management trying to pull in a cuter class of client in these upmarket days. Francis lit a cigarette to calm his nerves. Heartbeat. The nearest gym guy knew this was against the rules of fitness and fair play to the rest of the equipment users — who had all fucked off by now anyway.

'Put that out!'

'Go piss up a rope you fucking tosser!'

The instructor snatched the fag from Francis' mouth and stamped it into the floor. Francis jumped on the prat and the swinging and swiping began over again. All into it once more, temporarily forgetting about the good name of the establishment. Reinforcements called on radio phones and although Matthew Moore weighed in on Francis' side, the two of them were seriously outnumbered and eventually surrounded and persuaded after a good deal of loudlanguage to leave the premises peacefully.

Outside on the street. Examining a few minor cuts and bruises and picked kit-bags from the upturned pavement. Wankers! Arsefucking-wipes! Bagsofshite! Heartbeat. Beat. Beat. Francis lit another cigarette and blew smoke up into the London sky.

'Don't worry Francis ... the fuckers won't bar us, Percy will see to that.'

'I'm not fucking worried at all!'

But he was. Worried all the time. About everything. Some things having precedence at some times and other things at other times. Right now he was worried because this thing between himself and John

Nightingale was getting out of hand and he didn't know what started it or how to stop the rollercoaster. Someone was going to get seriously hurt.

'How did that bastard Nightingale know about my club, Matthew?'

'How should I fucking know?'

'Well, Glendora didn't fucking tell him, Matthew ...'

'I might have let it slip ... it's not a fucking secret is it?'

'I don't want that shitslime slithering at me all the fucking time.'

'Come on, let's get a drink.'

'I don't want a drink.'

They'd got to Matthew's car. Francis wouldn't get in.

'Suit yourself!'

'I will!'

'Go home, Francis. Chill out for a bit.'

Matthew got into the car and drove away. Francis watched him go.

'Fuck the lot of you!'

Francis walked away up Oxford Street. Fuck the bastards! He could do without them. Fuck Angeline too — and her whole fucking family. The girls would come back to him. They would want to be with him. He was their father for fuck sake! Find out where they were. Go round there and kick the livingcrap out of anyone who got in his way. Francis turned slowly into New Bond Street. The people around him looked odd. Suspicious. How many fucking aliens were walking the streets of London? Maybe they were all aliens and he was the only true fucking human. Being. Francis went up close to one or two of them. Put his face right up to theirs and stared into their alien eyes. Fuckers so frightened they nearly fainted. Pulled away. Faces shocked. Horri-fuckingfied! But hate hurts the hater as well as the hated.

Francis passed aimlessly along by the fashionable megastores. Maybe he'd get away from London altogether. Go to America. New York. People were more perpendicular over there and a man could make a lot of money if he had the balls and blood for it. And the heart! Should have fucked off long ago — when he was younger. Might be a millionaire by now — or a management executive of some fucking sort. Instead of marrying Angeline and fucking up his whole life. Body and soul. Body. Fortysix chromosomes. Fortyfour autosomes and two sexomes. Three billion base pairs of DNA. Adenine base with thymine and cytosine with guanine. Genome of eighty thousand genes — sequenced pairs along the chromosomes. And soul? Maybe it wasn't too late? Maybe it wasn't. Was it?

Francis saw the strange woman from the nightbefore party weaving through the West End crowds.

I can hear her even though she's a distance away. Saying she sees I'm a man who is not afraid to fight, Jalal al-Din. Animalkhan! And not afraid to die? I think I might be afraid to die all right. Never! She says the man who has not learned how to die has not learned how to live. Death is the beginning of life? Without death, the world could not continue to live. Listen Khananimal, we're in the middle of the West End ... Death is progress. Death is growth. Asking me who are all these people of fear, Jalal al-Din? And I'm not sure ... some of them might be aliens. All of them are afraid to die! Afraid to face the great challenge. Maybe the fuckers are just afraid of what they don't know. Everyone knows they must die she shouts! It is only a matter of when and how. I say those are fairly fundamental matters to most people ... But she sneers at me and says it is the quintessential dilemma of an immortal ego trapped within a perishable body. Telling me not to be afraid, Jalal al-Din ... I will never know death. Never, Genghiskhan? Death is not an event in life. It is not lived through. It is just the end result of dying. She's saying I'll always be alive and I'll always be dying. Until I die! And you will not know you have died. It is only the anticipation which causes the fear, not the event itself. If I don't worry about it I won't worry about it? Yes! Easier said than fucking done. She says she'll teach me. Will you? Of course! Her voice grows soft and shivers when she says what a terrible fate it would be to live forever. To see your comrades grow old and die, your children grow old and die, your grandchildren and their children ... everyone going the natural way of all things and you ... left behind amongst strangers. Alone. Forlorn. Sad and desperate, unable even to take your own life ... to end the horror of it once and for all. How terrible! Jalal al-Din.

Francis lost sight of her as he reached Piccadilly — and the aliens were staring at him. Two of the fuckers were wearing blue uniforms and walking behind him. Waiting to see if he became abusive to the general public. Or was going to fall down in an epileptic fit and foam at the mouth. Francis looked back at them and realised they had him under surveillance. Bastards ready to pounce at any minute and drag him into the nearest station where a dozen others could kick the coloured crap out of him. He knew they knew he was on to them. Knew they knew he had sussed out their little fucking strategy. Francis quickened his step. They didn't try to keep up. Soon left them behind and turned along Shaftsbury Avenue. He remembered he was working at the Pink Peacock later that night so it was better if he didn't go for a drink. Could have done with one though — at this very minute. Remembered Nightingale the tonguetwister. The smartalker. Tantaliser. Get what was fucking coming to him all right. One of thesefinedays! Francis didn't give a fuck what connections he had with Percy Shillinger or the Army or any other bastard for that matter. He could feel the tempersap rising again. Beat. Beat. The heat in his head and the blood behind his eyes. Madness was merely a raised temperature. If one of these wankers on the street so much as brushed against him he'd choke them to fucking death!

Francis stopped walking and leaned up against the railings by the Globe Theatre. No killing! He felt like one of the forgotten people. Needed to get himself under control. Thought about Glendora. Maybe this would be a good time to go round and see her. No. She'd be asleep and anyway he'd only end up snorting fucking snow and getting paranoid on the door tonight. Hailed a cab instead which took him away from the threatening West End and out to the quieter streets of Stratford. Thoughts in his head running mad all over the place. Things he'd always dreamt of but which now seemed more urgent. Critical! Things like life and death and love and hate and heaven and hell and the fact that his skin was creeping and something was interfering with his intestines. All melding his mind. And the hot brain only an organ Part of a body.

Francis could smell the taxi driver, like an animal smells things. Like a dog. Was he going off his fucking head altogether? Brain? Ventricles. Frontal cortex. Striatum. Substantia nigra. Mesolimbic pathway. Hypothalamus. Synapses. Neurotransmitters. Cerebrospinal fluid. Receptors. Tracts. Nerves. Him. Him. Where was Him? He'd heard about the male menopause and hormone deficiencies and men leaving their wives and children for young girls. Maybe they heard voices as well — telling them to grow goatee beards and get their nipples pierced and sing in kareoke clubs. Was he different? Was this different? What the fuck was happening?

chapter twelve

chapte r twelve

chapte r twelve

Francis Page stood the door of the Pink Peacock nightclub with Agnes D'Argensola. She was keeping her distance since the other night and Francis hoped she'd given up on him at last. Maybe leave him alone from now on. One less thing to worry about. But they'd worked together long enough for him to know Agnes was a determined woman. Strongwilled South American who always went after what she wanted — or thought she wanted. An ex-conventgirl who went to college and had a bit of a brain on her and was never happy about settling for statusquo. Whether in life or love. Agnes had connections at the Bolivian Embassy on Eaton Square and was able to hang on to her work-permit longer than she should. Had her own place just south of the River and she liked her job. It paid well and was safer than prostitution. Anyone looking would say Agnes was independent enough. But deep inside she knew time was running out. Becoming increasingly difficult to get extensions to her visa and sooner or later she'd have to go back to the yungas and the ruins of Tiahuanaco and the turquoise waters of Lake Titicaca.

Agnes believed a child could save her. An English citizen. Her own little *chavalito inglés*. Knew she had it in her to be a good mother and wanted the one *bebé* — just one. As soon as possible. Agnes was also particular who she had the child for. Didn't want any of the *cabrones* who were just waiting to jump into her *bragas*. And there were plenty of them. Every *idiota molestia* she ever met. If Agnes wasn't classically beautiful she was certainly what was called sexy and her body more than made up for any shortcomings of the features. She selected Francis Page because he was different and because he was difficult. It started out with her making a bet with herself that she could do it — for the singular reason of satisfying her own ego. But since then it had become serious. She saw something deeper in him than the average bonehead bouncer. A man behind the man. Became intrigued by the enigma and was determined her son would be part him. This man. This *hombre entre todos los hombres*.

Agnes knew about Glendora. Although she didn't know the full extent of the relationship between the blackgirl and Francis. There were rumours about AIDS. But Agnes took them with a pinch of salt and reckoned Francis wasn't stupid enough to jeopardise his life for *un poco de basura negra*! Anyway — she figured they could use *condón* protection until a blood test and even if necessary an in vitro egg fertilisation could be arranged by her connection at the Embassy. No matter what — you couldn't be too careful these days. And she didn't really want a husband. Or even a full-time lover. Just a stud for a stipulated period of time. Until *concepción*. After that it would be ok. Plain sailing to the little baba *bebé* of her dreams. One quick spermsample. Maybe two. Or three. Agnes wasn't worried that Francis was almost twice her age. No problem about him growing old before her. No problem about him dying before her — as long as she had the child. That was the main thing. There was really nothing else to worry about. Just the baby. As for his wife, Agnes knew Francis hated the *blanca* bitch and she wouldn't pose any problem. The two daughters made no difference to her. They were his business and nothing to do with her plan. There was nothing else to stop them. There were no other *problemas* on the scene. Just the *mujer negra*!

Now and then Francis caught Agnes looking at him. He pretended he didn't notice. Went through the routine of patrolling and frisking and talking sense into the odd young tearaway. His head had calmed down since the earlier gymincident. Though he was aware that John Nightingale was inside the club with Matthew Moore. Madness was only a change in personality due to alterations in brain chemistry caused by something physical. A sore toe? Francis felt unusually peaceful in himself and he kept seeing words like Nazka and pampas of Peru and Shaman and cactus and straight lines in the desert. Didn't know what the words meant and didn't care. They were somewhere inside his head. Made him feel well. Like glowing landscapes of inactivity. Fields of peace. Psychiatric came *after* physical. Physical came *before* psychiatric.

A black limousine pulled up to the kerbside at the entrance to the club. Couple of minders emerged first, followed by Percy Shillinger. Francis and Agnes held the punters back while the men made their way inside. Shillinger nodded briefly to Francis on his way past and the hint of a grin broke across his mouth. The two men knew each other well. Francis would have been out of Shillinger's pricerange back in the good days. Now it was different and Shillinger took a perverted delight in having a man of Francis' calibre doing his doors and nodding condescendingly to him on the way through. Like some twopennyhalfpenny hacker. Francis saw Glendora coming up the street and brought her straight to the front of the queue.

'Not working?'

'Night off. Thought I'd come down and see you.'

'That's nice.'

'She has to be searched if she is going inside.'

'No she doesn't, Agnes.'

'You know the rules, Francis.'

'It's all right, Frankie ... I don't mind.'

Francis fumed while Agnes searched the black girl. Roughing her up a little when he looked away. The doorwoman deliberately inspected each item in her bag and the *mestizos* eyes burned like embers into Glendora's. Francis lost patience and pushed Agnes away. His good mood was going.

'No need for that!'

'*Excusa* ...'

'Go inside, Glenny. I'll be changing over in a minute.'

'*Go inside, Glenny* ... Glenny, Glenny!'

'Shut up, Agnes!'

'I heard she has got the AIDS.'

'Well you heard fucking wrong. And it's fuck-all to do with you anyway.'

Agnes laughed out loud and walked away down the queue, roughly pushing some of the young girls to one side. Francis waited outside for John Nightingale to relieve him. Glendora didn't have AIDS. She was HIV positive from the needles and that was a different fucking thing altogether. People were ignorant and didn't understand. It wasn't her fault she got the fucking virus. Some dirty bastard she shared a needle with in the bad old bygones — if Francis ever found the fucker he'd kill him stone dead. No killing! Hurt him bad. HIV was still a dirty word despite all the investigations and research and analysis and conclusions. People backed off. Ignorant. If you tested positive they thought you were some sort of sewerstinking pervert with dirty filthy habits. But he knew that many innocent people had it too — haemophiliacs and silly types who'd been taken in and children who done nothing to deserve it. All a complete fucking shame. He could have sex with Glendora. As long as they used protection. They could kiss and hold each other and lie together in bed and make love without him catching it. What did the wankers know? Ignorant fucking shit-heads!

John Nightingale sashayed out of the club. He held the doors open for a moment, then let them swing back behind him in flamboyant fashion. For Francis' benefit. Left eye swollen and he had cuts to the face and forehead. Nightingale didn't speak. Just mincemeated up to his place outside the door — but inside he was saying *hodie mihi cras tibi*. Francis gave him a long look as he passed by. On his way inside.

The Pink Peacock was hot and noisy. Glendora sat at a remote table which Francis liked because it was away from the lights and the distorted crowd. Made his way to her and they kissed. He sat down and she smiled and touched his hand. They didn't speak. Didn't need to much. She was beautiful — despite the hardships she'd been through. Hair plaited with beads and she wore a short black dress which highlighted her slim body. Difficult to believe she was twenty-five. Looked so much younger. And hard to believe she was only twenty-five. Seemed so much older.

'I thought you might have come round, Frankie.'

'I wanted to ... but things have been happening.'

Things were always happening where Francis was concerned. She wanted to ask him what things. What kind of things? But she didn't.

'It's ok.'

'How have you been?'

'Missing you.'

'Any problems?'

Of course there were problems. But she believed Francis didn't want to hear about them. He had enough of his own.

'No. I just get anxious when I don't see you, that's all.'

'I mean any ... bad symptoms, stuff like that?'

'No. Still stable.'

'Good. Listen, I've got to go on duty inside with Matthew. I'll come back over when I can. Wait for me 'til I finish. If you want anything at all, just tell one of the bar staff.'

'Ok ...'

Francis walked away from her. Looking back every now and then to make sure she was still there. Still ok. Still safe. Still stable. Most of the regulars to the Peacock knew she was his girl and didn't bother her. Those who weren't aware of it found out the hard way. And everybody had the right to be cared for. The right not to be unwanted, neglected, abused, ridiculed, despised, criminalised.

The night dragged slowly for Francis and he was back and forth to the table. A little word and a laugh and a touch and a tenuous thread of something delicate. Something worth something. Cleared the crowd quickly at closing time and gave the slackers no time to finish their drinks. Percy Shillinger remained behind when the doors closed and so did Glendora. Shillinger held court at the bar while the coloured girl sat quietly in her corner. Waiting for Francis. He made little signs to her that there was a bit of business but it wouldn't take long.

'I want six men front-of-stage for the flyers.'

Francis saw John Nightingale smile across at Glendora and give her a little wave. Heart. Had to concentrate.

'I thought this was a minding job.'

'Listen, Francis, these people have their own minders.'

'Yanks eh ... won't be worth much without their fucking guns.'

'Who says they'll be without their fucking guns?'

Nightingale looked away from the black girl and turned his sinister smile on Francis. It said try me. Sometime.

'Out front is fine with me, Percy.'

'Good man, John, what about you, Matthew?'

'Count me in.'

'Agnes ... could do with you on the door. For the girls.'

Agnes paused before answering. Everybody looked at her, but she only looked at Francis. A smouldering look. Straight out of the Diablada. That she knew Glendora would notice — even from her table in the corner.

'Ok.'

'What about the mazuma?'

'You know my motto, Francis, you pay peanuts you get monkeys. Three hundred a man ... and woman. Be a bit of a bash afterwards of course. And, if all goes well, I might have more of the same coming up.'

Matthew Moore sensed the tension in the atmosphere . He wanted to get Francis out of there and wished his friend wouldn't keep prevaricating.

'C'mon, Francis ...'

'Ok, I'm in it. I'm in it.'

'Just so long as you all know I don't want any silly stuff. Real doormen don't get silly!'

'Everything's cool enough, Percy.'

'Good. Keep it that way. George ... set 'em up again here for the boys and girls.'

'I'm away. I've got someone waiting.'

'Fair enough, Francis.'

Francis walked across the club to Glendora. Knew the bastards were talking about him behind his back. How he had head problems and his girlfriend was a junkie and his wife left him and his mother was mad and flies die like flies and there'll be a ball of maggots as big as the fucking earth.

The Jaguar moved easily along the dead roads. Turning up past Euston and heading north-east across the city into Hackney. Dalston Lane was that part of the A104 which ran from Kingsland to Pembury and Glendora's flat was on the corner of Spurstowe Terrace — across from an empty shop that still had the sign 'Vic's Velodrome' above the door. She held onto his arm as they climbed the stairs and unlocked the heavy wooden door on the first floor. The flat was spacious inside — large bright reception with parquet flooring and a high ceiling. Well-equipped modern kitchen and the bedroom warm and sensuous with deep colours and framed prints of pictures by Pablo Picasso on the walls. Both of them felt at home in the flat. It didn't bother either of them that this area of London had a bad name for drugs and guns — it was a little oasis in a crazy world. Nothing could get in once the door was locked. They could be themselves. Forget whatever it was that had hurt them — whatever it was that had disfigured them and made them ugly. In here she felt safe and he felt secure. Francis could hold himself together and Glendora could find sanctuary behind the heavy door when she was alone. Didn't want to be alone. Wanted Francis to live here with her all the time.

Glendora didn't want children either. Knew she could never have any and didn't want to bring a baby into such a savage world. But she needed the security of Francis all the time — not just when he decided to come over. It was all right when he was here. But when he wasn't the anxiety came back. And the addiction. Always there. Always calling to her. Calling her back. And she held onto Francis while it tried to suck the life out of her.

Glendora turned on the imitation coal fire and they lay on the floor in front of it, leaning their backs against the sofa. Watching the dancing gas flames. Francis seemed mesmerised by the movement and they were still and silent for a long time. Glendora eventually pulled a cellophane packet from her pocket and set out two lines of cocaine on the polished wood of the floor. She rolled up a crisp new twenty-pound note and took one of the lines up her left nostril, then passed the moneystraw to Francis. He looked close into her darkeyes.

'No junk?'

'Of course not ...'

'Promise?'

'I promise, Frankie. You know I've been clean ...'

'I know.'

'Then why do you keep asking me?'

'I'm afraid you'll go back to it.'

'I won't! I won't, Frankie, I won't!'

She took his head in her hands and kissed his eyes. He wished he could trust her. Knew he couldn't trust anyone else. Even Matthew Moore had let him down now. So had Angeline — but he had to trust somebody. Everybody needs somebody? Francis took the line of cocaine up through the twenty. It hit him immediately, sending his worries away and making him feel confident again. A new man. A man again. A man.

'I'm glad you're here, Frankie.'

'Glad to be here, Glenny ...'

'I love you so much.'

'Do you? Do you know how sure you are about that?'

'Course I'm sure!'

'Why?'

'Cause you're my man. No one can hurt me with you here.'

Francis turned to look at her.

'Who would want to hurt you, Glenny?'

'Nobody ... now. They're afraid. But you know people have ... in the past.'

'I know, I know. Shhh, forget all about those bastards.'

He didn't want to talk about it and it made him angry to think about it.

'I was a baby ...'

'You're my baby now.'

'You keep me warm, Frankie, keep me warm and safe.'

The fire was warm. The light was warm. The woman was warm.

'I'll mind you, baby.'

A sudden streetnoise brought the world back in. Francis sat up. The realworld tried to creep back.

'Mind me forever, Frankie.'

'I'm not going to live forever, Glenny.'

'How do you know?'

'A man told me.'

'What man?'

'Genghis Khan.'

She didn't query the unlikelihood of this. Like she didn't query much that he said. Or did.

'And you believe him?'

'Yes.'

'Then I'll die with you.'

'Don't talk, Glenny. People talk too much. Too much talking isn't any good for you.'

Felt her breath on his face and neck. A scent of jasmine in the room that filled his head. He could touch the fragrance of her. The woman. Smell her woman's smell and taste her woman's taste. Taking the fear away. He kissed her breasts and her stomach, opening the black dress as he went. She undid the buttons of his shirt and jeans and licked at his ear with her cyclamen tongue. Francis stopped suddenly as the room grew starbright for a moment — then darkened to deathness. His face contorted into a clurichaun's. Body rigid and began to convulse in short spasms. But Glendora knew this thing and she held his shoulders until it stopped. The thing that came over him every now and then. Hold on. Hold on. It stopped as it always did and they relaxed again and made their own kind of music until the critical moment. Then she produced a condom and fitted it over him and they came together. Into one thing. Rolling over and over across the floor until the wall stopped the progress of their passion. Two bodies like one strange animal, black and white, frail and strong, positive and negative. Wordless voices reverberated round the room of desire. Faces pressed together in an overflowing of little bites and Glendora's legs locked round the small of Francis' back. He heard the Shamen singing somewhere in the desert as his muscles tensed up tight and a symphony of excitement exploded all around his ears. They lay still and breathing heavily for a long time. For all time. She continued to hold him with her legs and the sweat from their bodies made a wet trail across the wooden floor.

Francis carefully discarded the Durex — then crawled back naked to the fire and they smoked a couples of spliffs. Lay in the artificial firelight and Francis felt good. Forgot about Angeline and every other bastard. All the steady people. Sure people. Sane people. Wasn't long before the warmth and the weed lowered Glendora's eyelids and she slept beside him on the miniver rug. He covered her with a blanket from the couch and lay there beside her with a cushion under his head.

When he looked again he was lying beside another woman.

She's saying instincts, Jalal al-Din ... feeding, fighting, fornicating. That is all there is. Sin and evil exist only in men's minds. Women's too! Says it's my strength that will save me. I'm Animal like her. Am I mad Genghiskhan? Telling me they said *she* was mad, Jalal al-Din. Did they? Called her the madman of the Steppe ... the scourge of Asia ... and many other things. And were you? What? A madwoman? She spits and shouts I was strong! Says it was her strength that saved her. Tells me I must be ruthless in this world. Take what I want. Kill those who would hurt me. I say sure ... she's right. I understand, Animalkhan. I'm stronger than any woman. I don't need to worry about any of those conspiracy cunts. I'm strong enough to win, aren't I? If you are ruthless.

If you kill them all. I can't kill. You can! I can't. You must! I'm not sure. Never sure. Do not look for explanations. Excuses. Tell me the truth then. She says to find the truth I must destroy everything ... including yourself, Jalal al-Din. The meaning of my life lies outside my life. In the woman who made me? Tells me not to be that kind of man. What kind of man? The man who looks for explanations. The blaming man. The normal man? God? Jesus ... no! Jesus? Why am I knowing all this now? Because you want to know. I say you asked me, Animalkhan. Didn't you ask me? What would I ask you, Jalal al-din ... what could you tell me? She says I take the drug and she took the drug. The drug? Every man has his own drug. And woman too. The urge to escape is in all of us. Saying her drug was power and she killed and killed and killed and killed. Saw in her killing what Adam saw on the first day of creation ... the savage miracle of naked existence. Says she was in the unexplored place, Jalal al-Din. The back of the mind ... where the music of murder washes over your soul with a frenzy of paranoia. Where the more you kill the more you have to kill. Will smoking hash do that for me, Animalkhan? Of course not! But there is an inside to experience as well as an outside. Maybe that explains why it makes me feel good when I feel bad sometimes ... She tells me every man must get away from his own reality. And you only go mad when you refuse to come back again. Nobody can stay out there for ever. She says she tried, Jalal al-Din. To go as far as could be gone. Where only Gods had gone before. She fell from her high horse in the end. Like any other man. Or woman? Even though she was a God. And that's the problem with Glenny. That's what was wrong with her. Reality was too cruel for her. She needed her drug to make it bearable. But not any more ... not now I'm here. She's asking now what man is ever to know, Jalal al-Din. I know! I'm happy here at this small nowmoment Genghiskhan, so please don't go telling me wrong things. I really just want to be left alone. She's angry and asks if I don't trust her, Jalal al-Din. Says she's my friend ... my only friend. Women get me confused ... and the others. Do not listen to the others. Only to me. You know my word, Jalal al-Din. I want to be left alone. You have heard my word. Remember Jalal al-Din, my word when things come. There are things to come. Worse things ... many worse things ... much worse things ... you know it. Jalal. al. Din. Animal does not care what is said ... only what is.

And death is the beginning.

Francis opened his eyes. Glendora still sleeping by his side. The artificial fire still flickered and the first rays of dawn assaulted the curtains of the flat in Dalston Lane. Seemed as if he'd slept for a week. Still inhumanly tired. Lethargic to the point where he would never be able to stand up and walk again. Francis shivered and pulled the blanket over his shoulders. While outside on the streets the strangeness — the sinister and chronic otherness that hides in familiar things was waiting for the new day.

chapter thirteen

chapte r thirteen

chapte r thirteen

The New-Rainbow Arena in North London was completely full to capacity. Inside and outside and girls screaming when the Antichrists arrived and doorpeople barely able to hold the heavymetal fans back. Chaos filled the auditorium. Bikers and bullshitters and longhaired hijackers and tattooed women with spiky hair and hard faces and the high sweet smell of marijuana and the stink of beersweat. Agnes D'Argensola worked outside on the street with a couple of big back-ups while Francis Page, Matthew Moore, Jack Black, Jim 'The Neck' Jones, Muhammed Sharif and John Nightingale faced out to the frontofstage fuckology.

Francis knew Nightingale was keeping one eye on him as well as one on the rockers. The smartman might have been a pisstaker and a shirtlifter, but he was clever as well and didn't want a smack of a blunt instrument across the back of his head in the heat of battle. *Vis consili expers mole ruit sua*! Not that Francis was an ambusher or anything. Always facetoface. At least onetime it was like that. Now anything was possible. With the new thing. Edgything. Inside him. Nightingale knew Francis was a bit crazy and that was half his fascination with the man. How far could he be pushed? Before going over the edge. How far could any man be pushed before he broke? It was a kind of psychology game that would stand him in good stead. For the future. On the door. The other half of the fascination was fancy. Agnes was right. And he was afraid of this. Dangerous. But being gay and from a military family at the same time taught him how to survive the conservative prejudices of Hartford, Connecticut and the false approbation of his university peers and army siblings and the persecutions of West Point and the sneers of these dumblimey fucks in the door game. Even though they were all at it and each any every one had it inside themselves — if they had the courage to look. No different. To the Alma Maters and majors. The coarse, the ignorant and the hormonally correct. Opinions on everything and information on absolutely *nihil*. Typical thick tabloidreading gorillas. But Francis Page was different. More dangerous. In the long run. Nightingale wound him up because he could do it and Francis had no weapon against it. And that was dangerous. On the edge. Like a rush. A highball buzz. But the smartman was cautious not to push the psycho too far. The episode in the gym was close enough. *Ipso facto*!

Jack Black was the best man to eat in the south of England and he frequented a few posh restaurants and had a little bit of background on John Nightingale. Born a New England silverspooner with an education that was common knowledge. Constantly yapped on about the classics he studied and made those little comments in Latin to show how clever he was. Didn't like London or the commonherd and only waited for the day when he could return to the bosom of those he considered to be his intellectual equals. *A fronte praecipitium a tergo lupi*. Even if his conduct at West Point was a nevertobeforgotten embarrassment to some of them. He wanted to spilt from here. Away from the prejudice and the crass nazi company of 'the door'. And yet he wanted to stay. Nightingale lovehated doing what he did. It had its own fascination. Its infatuation. It wasn't a love affair and he hoped it wouldn't last for ever, but he was with it now and he couldn't be sure if it would ever let him go. Back to the society he belonged to. Or believed he belonged to. Before he became a Francis Page. In his own way, he was as bigoted as any black or bengurion or bumboy basher and was seduced by the sense of control.

Fucked the young cadet son of a four-star General in his initiate year at the military academy — reportedly against the boy's will. Family connections managed to stave off an assault charge to avoid mutual bad press and got him away to the anonymity of New York before he was exposed and some of the hypocrisy of his class laid bare along with him. Spent some time idling around Greenwich Village with his head down and his ass up but he couldn't and wouldn't compete with the younger kids in a lifestyle which he considered worse than being in the fucking Marines.

He got to know the owner of the Pink Peacock through an Internet Latin club. As a child, Percy Shillinger had studied the old language in a Jesuit orphanage. Shillinger was bisexual and had invited John Nightingale over to London as a procurer of young men of homoliberal leanings — and a bit of style. The thing that couldn't be bought with dirty money and a few words in a dead language. Life was just lying low at the moment. But Nightingale was young and had the time. Enough dough coming in and this was as good a place as any to wait out the winteryears. Very few classics scholars doing the door and he didn't exactly miss the aesthetic debate within the halls of academe. It was just as the old professor said — some queers are tough and some toughs are queer. *Bona fide*!

The Antichrists hardrocked the crowd into fever pitch. Bouncers behind crash barriers located between themselves and the crowd.

On-stage, indecipherable lyrics and relentless electric guitars went through Francis Page's head. He looked out over the sea of hair and waving arms and smelled the sweat and leather and even the blood of menstrual women. Every now and then the crowd surged forward. Barriers swayed and the men behind them had to work hard to avoid being crushed against the stage. Flyers came over the heads of fans. Running on top of a sea of bodies and launching themselves towards the band. The bouncers grabbed them and flung them back into the seething mass. Stewards along the perimeters helped those overcome by it all to get outside into the air — where ambulances waited in case of casualties. Some of the women stripped naked and hurled their underwear at the Antichrists. Most of the clothing items fell short of the mark and into the nomansland between crowd and stage — inhabited only by the bouncers. Knickers, boots, brassieres and an assortment of sanitary protection pads flew towards the band. Francis and the others had to duck and dive to avoid the missiles. At any opportunity naked girls scrambled onto the proscenium and had to be dragged away screaming and swearing and scratching.

The bass guitar player was called Pigg. He taunted the crowd continuously and encouraged them to come and get to him. Making the bouncers' work even more difficult than it already was. Francis could hear the fucker screaming in a thick Appalachian accent that grated on his nerves and he wanted to climb on-stage and break all the bastard's teeth. Heartbeat. Bollocks deliberately agitating the greaseheads so they'd get hysterical and Francis was beginning to wonder if the fucker wasn't some sort of Internet agent provocateur. This whole thing was getting out of hand and Francis was beginning to see blood. Normal modes of control were failing. Failsafes fusing. Bloodbeat. He started to laugh even though he felt fucking wild. Wasn't that he *wanted* to laugh. Couldn't control it. Laughter raged out of him in the direction of the crowd. Those at the front were bemused and began to laugh with him.

Pigg thought they were laughing at him. The bass guitarist unzipped his leather trousers and pissed in the direction of the distorted faces. Francis felt something wet and warm on his shoulders and turned to see Pigg spraying an arc of urine in his direction. Francis stopped laughing. Heartfuckingbeat! About to climb on-stage and pull the cunt's cock off when the crowd surged forward again. This time the barriers gave way and the rockers at the front were pushed into the no-go area.

Kill them! Kill them! Kill the sons and daughters of Samarkand! Temujin says spill their blood and feed their entrails to the wolves. Flay them alive! They are your enemies and will send your kindred to the grave if you allow it. Killbeat. Killbeat. Killbeat. Francis began to punch, kick, gouge and bite with the ferocity of a wildanimal. Animal. A. Nimal. Anyone close enough got clouted. Crowd tried to get back away from the madman but those behind pushed them forward again. Bodies fell to the floor and were stepped on by others. Blood splattered on the screaming faces of girls and the area surrounding Francis became a scene of crimson carnage. Split their skulls and send a river of blood back to warn all others that the hand of the Great One is a cruel unmerciful hand. Then they will be afraid! A. Fraidbeat! Francis began to advance further into the mass. Lashing out at everyone and anyone as he went. Some tried to fight back but were immediately poleaxed by a swipe from either fist. Francis himself was covered in blood and the panic-stricken crowd tried to part to allow him through — then closed behind him until he was swallowed up and no longer visible to the other bouncers. Kill them! Strike them from in front of you! No man or woman can stand against you. Kill them all! Crash barriers were re-set and the other bouncers gradually restored order at the frontofstage. The Antichrists kept playing and most of the crowd unaware of the slaughter going on in their midst. Screams and cries drowned out by the music and the pile of bodies and pools of blood on the floor overrun by baying bollockbrains.

Matthew Moore and Jack Black grabbed Francis from behind and pulled him back through the crowd to the security of the barriers. Francis tried to swipe them and the others had to join in to subdue him. Matthew's face swam around the room. Beat. The man's mouth was moving but no words emerged. Blood on his face and hands and Francis wondered where it came from. He looked into the crowd and saw more blood. All over the place. Stewards and ambulance men trying to carry bodies out from the mêlée of metalmusic and madness.

'Francis ... for fuck's sake!'

He heard Matthew Moore's words this time and his head focused on where he was and what he was here for. Heart. The noise of the band faded into the background and the crowd were far away. Beat. Voices a distant hum and faces deathly white under streaks of crimson. Who got killed? Matthew wiped the blood from Francis' face and told him no one was dead. As far as he knew. Francis took a short break to clean himself up. Then went back to work.

The rest of the night moved along in a dream until Francis found himself back at the Hilton Hotel on Park Lane with the others. He could only barely remember the concert. It might have been five hours or five weeks ago. Deep voices spoke in slowmotion around him as they ascended in an elevator and then walked stepsilently down a deepcarpeted corridor. Floor made of marshmallow and walls on either side converged at the top when their feet sank into the softness. Francis thought he was someone else. Not himself. Lost identity. Didn't know who he was or who he was supposed to be. The Antichrists had the best suite in the hotel and one of their American minders opened the door to the bouncers. Big man. Seven feet tall and three-hundred pounds at the very least. Two others equally big and dressed in dark suits stood inside the room. Looking towards the door. Jack Black pushed past and immediately attacked the food. Percy Shillinger and halfadozen groupies in miniskirts and laddered stockings beckoned from inside with the band members. A low table in the middle laden to the legs with bottles of spirit and everybody in a raucous mood. Except the minders — looking as if they expected an assassination attempt at any minute.

'Come on in boys ... and girls. Help yourselves to drinks, or *food* if you want, Jack! You all right, Francis?'

'Why wouldn't I be?'

Shillinger watched amused as Jack Black went straight for the grub, then turned his eyes back to Francis.

'Bit of bother there for a while.'

'That bastard started it.'

'What bastard?'

'That bastard there!'

Francis pointed. Shillinger followed his finger.

'Jesus Christ, Francis ... that's Pigg.'

'He *is* a fucking pig.'

'He's the band leader.'

'He pissed on me.'

'High spirits ... look, have a fucking drink and calm down.'

Percy Shillinger clapped Francis on the back and went to introduce John Nightingale to his fellowcountrymen. Party getting into full swing and cocaine floated on the heavy air like morning mist. Pigg and his pals tried to fuck the women on the floor but were too far gone to perform properly. Just rolled around laughing like little kids. Francis poured himself a Jack Daniels and stood to one side. His hand trembled. There was an entity inside him. That had no particular symptoms. Followed no particular course. Responded to no particular panacea. And had no particular origin. He felt he had to get out of London. Move on! Make tracks. Soon! Shillinger later called his men around him and doled out pay for the night's work.

'Listen men, the band were impressed with your tastiness tonight and want to take some of you on tour with them.'

'Where to?'

Francis wasn't listening. He was looking at the boy they called Pigg. Who was sticking something up his nose. And the noise in the room began to pierce his brain.

'America.'

'When?'

'They're going to rest up for a bit now and they'll let me know when they get it organised.'

'Great!'

'What's the deal?'

'All expenses of course ... and you'll be earning five hundred a day for six weeks!'

'Pounds?'

Shillinger's words registered with Francis. He heard — and the room noise began to fade away somewhere. Not altogether, but far enough for him to concentrate. He could also hear the other men now.

'Dollars.'

'That's fucking wedge enough.'

'And a bit of a bonus at the end if everything goes nice and smooth. Be sensible with your money and you could come back with a nice little nest-egg. Who's interested?'

'Me!'

'Me too!'

'I'll go!'

'Francis?'

Percy Shillinger was watching Francis. Nervous. The room was nervous. Francis focused.

'Sure ... why not ...?'

'Right! Get your passports sorted out then boys.'

That was it! What Francis was waiting for. The big banana! Buy him into his own club and the future would be happy ever after. Hisownclub. His. Own. Club. Francis knew the place well. The place he wanted to be his sanctuary. His haven. His asylum in an arsehole world of wankers. Been up there to see it — in the Charing Cross area. St Giles. Stood outside it. Felt the texture of its walls. Smelled the security of its lowlight smothering. Francis knew the owners and they'd promised to give him first refusal. But he needed the deposit. The downpayment. The dooropener. And this American tour was it! Knew if he waited long enough the opportunity would come along. Said it all along. Silver angel on his shoulder. Glendora would have mixed feelings. She'd be glad for him but afraid for the six weeks he'd be away. Couldn't be helped. Everybody had to compromise to some degree in life. This was his dreamtime fairytaletime. Coming true. His own place! A piece of. Live on the premises and Angeline could have her fucking house back. The girls could come and stay with him on a regular basis. Glendora could give up the casino and help him manage the club. This would sort out all the shit. All his problems. In one go. Thank you God! Now every prick would see. What was he made of. How far he could go. He'd go far. He'd come a long way. Many memorymiles.

He says to be careful what I ask for, Chela ... it might come to me. Tells me to be satisfied and sufficient in my *bindu*, man. Asking if I've really come a long way? Since my first steps in the young Universe? I tell him this is a fucking party and nobody's fucking interested! But he won't let go ... says there's beauty in quiescence and mystery in melancholy, Chela. Look for it! You look for it! Won't stop. Saying higher order prevails even in disintegration ... the totality's present even in the broken pieces. Listen to my word, Chela. Not now! Go away! It ain't survival of the *sem* that counts. Who cares? It's discovery of the *dharmata*, Chela. I'm shit on so! I'm the knowledge you're looking for. I'm the mystery. I'm the future. I'm the meaning. I'm everything you need,

Chela. The true light always existed in the world but the world didn't retain it ... John, 20:9. Asks me if I feel it? No. Sure you do! I know what I know! All this love shit. I know it ain't mine. Ain't for me. Annie never taught me. Konrad never taught me. Angeline never gave it to me. How would I know? Anything about that kind of thing? He says I have it for others. Have I? Have I? Who am I? You're you, Chela. You're me. Tells me I'm trying to take refuge from real reality in my little familiar meanings of commonsense and shared symbols. Real. It. Y. There are higher things. Higher. Higher. Into the nonexistence of the *sipabardo*, man. Into the *amitabha* where everything is possible and only what's observed exists. Asking me what I want to be, Chela? I don't know ... more than what I am. What I ought to be. Like him. I'm Christ. Like Animalkhan? She told me to kill every cunt. Tells me to look at the *dharmakaya* ... it'll keep the *maya* away. Don't live in darkness ... in the shadow of death ... Matthew, 4:14. I must see the *amitabha*. There still exists what was before and there already exists what'll come after the end. Asks me if I understand, Chela? No I don't! I don't! I won't! Saying I must walk a tightrope between two states ... *tögal* and *kaya*. Leave me alone! I just want to live ... nothing else ... just want to ... to ... You've always been where you're going. And it's never as it seems, Chela. One plus one plus one plus one plus one plus one plus one plus one equals one. Where's the savage? Where's real mansavage? I want to see him! I know he's there!

'Who are you talking to, man?'

'No one.'

'Why don't you git me a drink then?'

'You want a drink?'

'Yeah ... that's your job, git me what I want.'

Francis smiled a smirk at Pigg as he picked up a glass from the table. He slowly unzipped his trousers and pissed into the glass. Held it over to the band leader. And madness was just a value judgement on people's behaviour. In a classist society. It was a weapon to devalue and reduce people to objects. To feel safe and superior. That's what it was!

'You're a fucking crazy mother ...'

'Don't call my mother crazy, you cunt!'

'You're fucking spaced man.'

'Don't you want your drink?'

Francis was attracting the attention of the big minders. Heart. Beat. He grabbed Pigg's head and held it back, forcing hot piss down his gurgling throat. Then smacked the bass guitarist in the eye. Pigg fell to the ground screaming and spitting. Minders across the room. Stresstrigger!

'Come on then you yank fucks ...'

'Francis ... for Christ's sake ...'

Percy Shillinger nearly had a fucking heart attack and signalled to his men who swiftly shot between Francis and the Americans. Shillinger knelt down and wiped Pigg's face with his handkerchief.

'What the fuck did you do that for, Francis?'

'The bastard pissed on me.'

'These are wild boys ... they do what they like.'

'Not with me ...'

'Look, Francis ... everyone's had a good skinful. Why don't you go on home. Matthew ... take Francis home like a good boy. We'll talk tomorrow.'

'I don't need anyone to fucking take me home.'

'Of course you don't. What am I thinking of?'

Francis stared hard at Percy Shillinger for a moment. Heartbeat. Heartbeat. It was all that shit's fault. Shillinger brought him down. Didn't he? Keeping him down now. Enjoyed it. The prick! Francis fixed a savage eye on the minders. Then turned and left the room. Slammed the door behind him. Outside the suite, the corridor had returned to normal. Carpet stayed put under his feet as he walked to the elevator.

He felt a bit claustrophobic in the lift and was glad to get out on the ground floor. A cab called by the hotel commissionaire in Park Lane and a sigh as the driver took him away from the shit and shouting and fucking savages. And he wondered if there was really a spiritual part of him. That was nothing to do with genes and the workings of brain cells. Who was? His God.

chapter fourteen

chapte r fourteen

chapte r fourteen

Shitelogic! Normal? Why then? I don't want it ... these people talking to me all the time. It was better before ... like. I don't want this either. But it won't leave me alone. I mean ... it's not normal, is it? Is it normal? Reasonable? Reason. Able. How to make money ... that's rational. Logical. All this shit about ... about ... I don't know. What's it about? Where's it all going to stop? Is there going to be an end to it? It says maybe, Shegetz ... if sequencing ze genome engenders ze sixth extinction. Thinkink involves ze consideration of alternative responses ... zat is all, Shegetz. Don't think. Don't think. I say it's not real ... and ask where the fuck is it going to end? I've chust told you ... zat depends. It says I'm like a lost child ... looking for a place I once knew. In the remote future. That's crazy! I'm not crazy! It says it's Scientistvoice. Then it should know, shouldn't it? Physics und mazematics are not quite psychiatry. I'm not fucking mad! Mad, schmad ... mad is relative. Something inside my head or maybe not says insanity is a cruel hoax, perpetrated against those who can't think clearly by those who won't think clearly. It runs in families! Everyzink runs in families! It's telling me that society takes it upon itself to decide who's mad, Shegetz. Und vat qualifies zem to draw such conclusions? How do zey know zey are not mad zemselves? They're all talking about me behind their fucking hands. Three hundred years ago nobody vould haf understood ze laws of aerodynamics or digital technology ... zese thinks vould haf been viewed as vitchcraft. Asking me if we've come any further in our perception of things, Shegetz? But I don't know. Have we? It won't tell me ... I keep asking all these fucking questions that never get answered ... that are in my head ... put into my head. The truth! I shout at it to tell me. Tell me! I know it knows, so why won't it fucking tell me? It replies that when it comes to explanations, Shegetz, zere is somezink infinitely futile und presumptuous about speech. It is ze ladder which must be destroyed vonce it is climbed. You're not helping me ... I vould if I could. It says there's infinitely more to everything than is obvious to us poor *schlamazels*. I must look at it directly, not through half-opaque symbol systems und concepts und generic labels und explanatory abstractions. I can't! My brain ... brain ... brain ... brain ... won't take me there.... It says that brain is only a filter, Shegetz. Everyzink is out zere but ze brain only lets through vat is biologically relevant. When will I understand, then? When will I know? Telling me the brain dies at death und mind-consciousness is exposed to everyzink. So ... death is the beginning? Ze vords zemselves are inadequate to describe vat zey attempt to describe. I don't want to die ... or be killed ... or kill ... or listen any more. It's sorry there are no clearer explanations, Shegetz ... but science gives no human dimension to ze facts it presents. Fiona! Lieserl! Zen of course, zere is alvays ze quantum und ze quark.

'Francis ...'

'Matthew?'

'You were talking to yourself again.'

'I was not!'

'You were.'

'I was fucking not!'

'Ok, ok. Only I'd go see a doctor about it if I was you.'

'Well you're not fucking me!'

'That's true too ...'

Francis Page and Matthew Moore emerged from the showers of the Hardcore gymnasium. Fixed for them to get back in again by Percy Shillinger — on the strict understanding that Francis and John Nightingale trained on alternative days. And that was ok. Fine. Everythingfine.

Or was it? Francis was beginning lately to feel painfully self-conscious. About every move he made. People watching. Every move he made. Accusing looks about every thing he did. Every comment a fucking criticism. Jumpy. Agitated. Edgy. A general evasiveness in the air since the episode at the Hilton. Francis wanted to find out more details about the American tour, but Shillinger was always too busy to talk about it.

'You heard any more about this tour, Matthew?'

'Not much. Supposed to be sometime in the New Year.'

'Be nice to get away somewhere warm for the winter.'

'They'll be playing all over, Francis, ending up in New York.'

'Who told you that?'

Francis stopped packing up his sports bag. He looked at Matthew. Matthew's Goatgod wouldn't look back.

'The lads.'

'What lads?'

'The lads ... you know ...'

Francis didn't know anything. Anything. Anything. Any fucking thing.

'How come no one told me?'

'I don't know.'

'Bastards!'

Midautumn leaves blowing onto the city streets from the parks. Days pulling in and Winter on its way. The two men emerged through a side door onto the corner of Holles Street and Cavendish Square. Francis turned the collar of his coat up against the north wind that was cutting down Regent Street from the Park. People passed by in a hurry to get wherever it was they were going. Some things just wouldn't wait. Mental. Everyone was mental. Good mental or bad mental? Depended. On a gene on the short arm of the x chromosome coding for synaptophysin and maybe as well on the number 6, 8, 10, 13 and 22 autosomnal chromosomes. Who knew? Quick! It was a quick thing. You had to be quick or be dead these days. Push the pricks out of the way before they trampled you down into the dirt. Grab the prize and hold it up over your head before they could get their dirty fucking maulers on it.

'You sure you haven't heard anything from Shillinger?'

'Honest, Francis!'

Matthew was looking away again. Francis didn't like it. He didn't like people looking at him but he didn't like Matthew looking away either.

'This trip means to me, Matthew. A lot!'

'So it does to us all.'

'Set me up.'

'Me too. I can go back home to Ireland and get the alpaca farm going.'

Francis grabbed Matthew by the arm. Everything stopped in the street.

'Fuck the alpaca farm. Agnes told me it'll never get off the fucking ground.'

'Fuck Agnes! What does she fucking know?'

'She's South American.'

'Bolivian! The beasts come from Peru, Francis .... Up in the mountains.'

'No they don't! They got them in Bolivia as well. Agnes said. Mountains and beasts. Any mountains where you come from, Matthew?'

'No ... but that doesn't matter. I've done my research. The climate will suit them.'

They started walking again and the street came to life again.

'It's too dodgy, mate. Come in with me and we'll run the club together. I've seen a place we can get ... down near Charing Cross. Twenty grand. I've talked to the men ... twenty fucking grand and we're in the fucking door.'

'No way! What about the rest?'

'That's what I'm saying ... I know a couple of backers from the old days. Big backs. Big bucks ... who'll come in with me, Matthew. Silent partners.'

Matthew Moore didn't like the way Francis was talking. It wasn't the first time. Saying words that didn't make sense. Like he was on something. Maybe he was.

'Jesus, Francis ... you're beginning to sound weird. Who'd have control?'

'Us, of course. These pricks don't want to get their hands dirty. I'll do the dirty. All they want is a good return on their money. Dirty fucking money.'

'No way, Francis. Thanks all the same, but I'm getting out of this game.'

Matthew walked a bit quicker. As if he was trying to get away. Francis matched his pace.

'Buying into your own club is a bit different from doing the door!'

'Not for me. But I wish you the very best, Francis. I mean it. I hope you get everything you want.'

'I will, Matthew. Good as gold, boy. Solid as silver! Once the thing gets moving and making, I can get the fucking banks involved and expand. Simple!'

'Sounds ok on paper ...'

'It *is* fucking sound, Matthew. It's a gilt-edged goer. I've talked to all the people ... they're all in. Just needs the money now, that's all. Better than a fucking alpaca farm out in the backhole of the arse of beyond.'

Matthew Moore fell silent, like he didn't want to discuss the thing any more. Francis was still enthusiastic and waffled on for a while about interior designs and how he'd made initial approaches to a couple of banks and backers and how they were all up for it and great golden opportunities and preconditions and profits — but the other bouncer didn't reply. Francis noticed his reticence. Something was up.

'What's up?'

'Nothing.'

'I said what's up, Matthew?'

'Nothing ... I just don't like counting the ould chickens, Francis. You know ... something always happens ...'

They reached Moore's car and Matthew jumped in and slammed the door. Francis ran round and climbed in beside him.

'Like what? What can I do wrong? Commit some fucking crime? What happens?'

'Nothing ...'

'What the fuck can go wrong?'

'Nothing ... I suppose ...'

Glendora was waiting for him at the Cajun Chicken on Argyle Street. Francis decided not to take the matter any further. For now. Matthew Moore drove away with an ambivalent face and Francis wondered about him for a few seconds. What crime? No one wanted to talk about it. Must've been some fucking thing altogether. Some fucking thing. Then maybe the boy was just annoyed because he tried to make him have second thoughts about the alpacas. Alfuckingpacas. Agnes told him they were related to the fucking camel — and they wouldn't be suited to the topography of south-east Ireland. And Francis was sure the indigenous farmers wouldn't tolerate an alien species rubbing flanks with their sheep and cattle.

'Hiya, honey!'

'Hi.'

'Ordered anything yet?'

'No. I was waiting for you.'

'Getting cold out there.'

'Have some coffee.'

Glendora poured some from the glass pot on the table. He sipped it slowly and warmed his hands on the cup. Tasted coppery. Like copper. Camouflaged. Contagious? She looked at him quizzically and he decided it was his imagination. Of course.

'What d'you want? Waitress!'

'I'll just have a salad.'

'Too cold for that crap, Glenny. Have something substantial.'

'I'm really not all that hungry, Frankie.'

'I insist! You eat something. Eat something!'

Glendora was startled by the tone of his voice. She took a long pull from her cigarette.

'All right. I'll have the chicken Creole.'

'Is that all?'

'It's enough for me.'

'Anything to start, sir?'

'Glenny?'

'No. I'm ok with the coffee.'

'We're ok with the coffee, thanks.'

Francis ordered jambalaya pork with fries and black-eyed peas and poured another cup of coffee. Smiled across the table at Glendora. She seemed distant today and her eyes looked through him. And he worried all the time in case she went back on the shit. Francis reckoned he'd know if that happened but you never could tell with a woman. Maybe she already had. Maybe it was all just a front. No. He'd know about it if she had. The restaurant was warm and the Cajun and Creole smells seemed to reassure Francis. He looked around. A few other diners — all engrossed in themselves and what they were doing. All looking at their food or chatting to acquaintances or calling the waitress or just sipping coffee or reading a newspaper. Safe. Nothing suspicious. A relaxed easy scene. The coffee warmed him and he felt guilty about doubting the black girl. She was a good kid and she knew what was at stake.

Francis ultimately ended up feeling guilty about all the females in his life. Felt guilty about his mother, about Angeline, about Sinéad and Fiona — even about Agnes D'Argensola. Now he was feeling guilty about Glendora. Fucking ridiculous! He put it down to the financial pressure he was under. Once things worked out he wouldn't feel guilty about anything any more. It was just the fucking money. He missed it. Wanted it back. It was security and it made him feel good. Not just walking around money. Real cash! He caught Glendora's eye and she smiled and looked away. Definitely distant today. But she was often distant — as if she was thinking back across time to Liverpool. The black girl rose from her seat and told Francis she needed to go to the toilet.

J'ai parlé à Dieu, Dauphin. What? *J'ai parlé à Dieu*. When? When have you spoken to God? Who? Who's spoken to God? *Moi, Jeanne d'Arc ... la pucelle d'Orléans*. We have both spoken to God ... you and I. No ... I haven't. I want to ... but I haven't yet. *Il n'y a pas de quoi avoir honte*. It will come. When? I have spoken also to St Michael, St Catherine and St Margaret. I've also spoken to Alienchrist, Scientistein, Animalkhan and others as well. Listen to no one but God! My word is God, Dauphin. Only God! I was His handmaiden ... *sa vierge*. I was pure ... as you must be. I'm not pure. *Vous sans péché ou mal*. Why would He want to talk to me? Because you are an innocent, Dauphin.

No! He chooses you ... just as He chose me to be His voice on earth. And did you speak for Him? Of course! What did you say? I said liberation and they burned me in the market-place at Rouen. Jesus fucking Christ! *Il n'était pas là*. What sort of bastards would do such a thing? You did, Dauphin ... the bishops ... the English ... everyone. Not me ... I'm no killer! You said I was a witch. Not me! Why didn't God save you? *Telle était sa volonté*. How d'you know it was God you were talking to? I knew! But how? *Je l'ai ressenti dans mon cœur*. For God's sake! For your sake, Dauphin. It *was* God! Maybe it was only a dream ... maybe you were dreaming? *Non*! Do you not think I would know the difference? Sometimes I can't tell whether I'm awake or dreaming. Don't ask for the dreams ... they just come ... dreamworlds ... symbols ... real. *Nos rêves nous font comprendre nos désirs secrets et nos craintes*. My dreams are real, Jeanne. You can dream in the womb without knowing about time ... change ... while the madness seeps through. My father and mother come to me in my dreams and tell me that I'm the useless product of them both ... why would they do that if it wasn't real? Real. I feel real when I dream ... not the fake phoney person I feel like when I'm awake. *Votre rêve vous indique* what you must do when you are awake. What must I do? What is it telling me? Listen! You are not listening. You are hiding behind *le masque des convention*? Imposed by the society *dans laquelle l'on vit*? Conforming to avoid being different and censoring to suit *les normes établies*? Who am I, Jeanne? Who was I and who am I becoming? Who am I really? Who am I? Am I the awake person or the dreaming person? I feel strong when I dream and weak when I wake ... and sometimes the other way round. *Pour moi*, dreaming *et* waking were one. But that's so fucking dangerous. Of course! I told you, Dauphin ... they burned me. *Peut-être vous brûleront-ils également*!

'I didn't know you spoke French?'

'I don't!'

The waitress hovered at the next table — clearing plates.

'What was it then?'

'I wasn't speaking ...'

'Frankie, I heard you when I was coming back to the table.'

'Not me!'

'There's nobody else ...'

Nobody else? Was there nobody else? There had to be somebody else. He didn't even speak French — or Latin — or German — or Alien — or Mongolian — or English. Even if he could understand it all.

'What about the waitress?'

'It was a man's voice ...'

'No it wasn't!'

'Then you heard it too?'

'Course I did ... it was the waitress. It's a Cajun restaurant isn't it? Cajun ... she's bound to be able to speak French.'

Glendora looked at him suspiciously, but decided not to argue the point. She didn't like to argue with Francis. If she argued with him he might pull away from her and never come back. Leave her to the wolves of the world. What would she do then?

'Why don't you move in with me, Frankie?'

'I told you ...'

'But Angeline's not coming back.'

'I don't want the witchbitch back ...'

'Then why?'

'Because I need the house for another while.'

'What for?'

'The girls, Glendora! Until I get the club.'

'You won't get the girls, Francis.'

Stresstrigger! Francis struck the table with his fist. Heartbeat! The force threw cups and plates and cutlery into the air and turned heads in their direction. He didn't know why he reacted like that. It was spontaneous. This new thing. Edgything. His face flushed and the muscles tightened on the back of his neck. Neckbeat! There was fear in the room. Francis could smell it. Didn't know if it was his own fear or somebody else's. An eerie silence descended and everybody seemed to be looking at him. Including Glendora. Francis hated that. Hated people looking at him. Hated being the centre of things — the centre of the fucking Universe. Fuck off! Fuck off the fucking lot of you! New feeling. Frustration. Not new. More intense. Dangerous. Silence continued. Even the traffic out in the street made no sound. He opened his mouth to speak but no words came out. They all stared. As if he had two fucking heads. As if all the customers were frozen in that position. Maybe he ought to kick a couple of them. Kickbeat! Killbeat! Glendora touched his arm.

'I'm sorry, Frankie.'

'No, no ... it's me. I'm not in the best of manners ...'

'Let's forget about it?'

'Listen, once this American tour is over things will be different ...'

'It's ok, Frankie ...'

She reached out to stroke his face with her hand but he pulled away. Her hand followed and he winced when it touched him.

'... I'll bring back enough money to do what we talked about ...'

'I know you will.'

'We can both be together then, with the girls. Angeline can have the fucking house back, but only when I'm fucking ready ...'

'That'll be fine.'

Francis leaned across the table and kissed her on the forehead. He paid for the half-eaten food and they stood up and put on their coats. And as they went out through the door, he thought he heard the waitress saying — *mais pouvez-vous transformer vos rêves en réalité*?

chapter fifteen

chapte r fifteen

chapte r fifteen

Late when Francis Page arrived back at the house in Leytonstone Road. Glendora keeping on at him to come home with her and he had to get a bit cross in the end. Didn't want to. Never done it before. She cried. He said sorry. Sorry. Sorry. Arms around each other. Tearwipes. Away. He sat outside the house in the Jaguar for a while half expecting that Angeline might have returned by now and brought the girls back with her. Surely she realised she couldn't keep them to herself? Sooner or later they'd want to see their father and how could she stop them? They'd run back to him. Race back to him! Away from her, the witch-bitch. The lovehate woman. Francis lit a cigarette and climbed out of the car. He thought he saw a light inside the house. Was it a light? Or just the reflection of a streetlamp? If somebody was inside — was it Angeline? Or some other sorts? Them? The Sons of Samarkand? The conspiracy cunts? Francis advanced slowly up the drive and stopped at the front door. Listened. No sound. Nothing. Or was the silence just an illusion? Was there an unbearable roar of noise all around him and he just couldn't hear it? Had his brain closed it all out — shut it all out? Maybe the whole fucking city was collapsing under the weight of its own crap and he just couldn't hear it. Francis tried to understand why these crazy thoughts should keep coming into his head. All the stress he'd been under lately. Stress and shit. Stress and shit! Illness and injury. Ill mind — ill self — ill soul. Shit and more shit. Be out from under it all soon. Into the world he wanted. Not what any other bastard wanted for him. What *he* wanted! Just him. What did he want? What was it he wanted? What he wanted — not any other bastard! Francis unlocked the front door and stepped slowly into the dark hall. Listened again. Nothing. Moved into the lounge and switched on the light. Nothing and nobody. Maybe they were in bed. It was late. Francis climbed the silent stairs and looked into each of the bedrooms. Nobody. The lovewitchhatebitch! He thought he heard a noise from the kitchen.

'Angeline?'

Francis rushed back downstairs. Ran down the hall to the kitchen and switched on the light.

'Fiona?'

Nobody and nothing. The fucking fucking fucking witchlove-hatebitch!

The kitchen was a mess. Pots and pans and cups and plates piled in the sink. Ashtrays full of dogends and the smell of food gone off. Francis stopped cooking for himself some time ago. Ate out or called up a pizza or a Chinese or an Indian. Boxes of congealed beansprouts and cartons of half-eaten curry strewn around on the table and work-tops. Couldn't be bothered to clear it up. Or eat properly any more and seemed to have acquired a fancy for junk food of all descriptions. Also drinking endless cups of coffee that kept him awake all night when he wasn't working and chainsmoking cigarettes that made him cough and wheeze and cut the fucking chest and lungs out of him.

Francis made a cup of coffee and went back to the lounge. Lit a cigarette and turned the television on and immediately turned it off again. Some prick he couldn't stand shiteing on about security cameras in highcrime areas and political prying and the spy satellites in space. Focused directly on his house! He quickly closed the curtains and switched on the CD player to confuse the eavesdroppers. The room immediately filled with the music of Gustav Mahler. Francis was startled and didn't know for an instant where it came from. Never heard this sound before. And it seemed so significant. Saying something to him. Francis turned the volume up and sat in an armchair. Notes and phrases and melodies and themes and structures played with mottos and expressions and syncopated accents as *allegro con brio* became *adagio assai* and then *scherzo* and back to *allegro* again. Francis found himself flowing with the music. Like being high. Above all earthly things — all mundane matters and stuff like money and mortgages. Why hadn't he heard this before? Whose music was it? Angeline's? Maybe. Because she was a stuckup mare and liked to pretend she was sophisticated. But she could never understand that sound as he understood it right then. All she really knew about was powder and perfume and frogspawn foundation and moneycosting makeup. But she thought she knew more. Like a load of other fuckers as well.

The CD ended and Francis played it again — from the beginning this time. It seemed to start quietly. Like someone tiptoeing unseen through a forest or a wood or something. That picture came into his mind. A glowing landscape which did nothing more than present the facts. Then louder. Darker. Louder. Darker. Louder. Darker. So loud it nearly blew his brains out onto the carpet. Brains that died at death. Then it quietened again. Became slow and sad. Slow and? Slow and? Francis lit another cigarette and listened. He topped the fag onto the carpet because there was no ashtray nearby and he didn't want to move. His attention was attracted to a minute area of discoloration on the ceiling. Couldn't have been more than a couple of inches square but it occupied his complete concentration, along with the music which filled the room like an entity. Huge. Overpowering and intimidating.

I could lie down like a tired child and weep away the life of care which I have borne and yet must bear till death, like sleep, might steal on me. Softwhisper. Softwhisper.

I hear him whispering that music has the beat to soothe a savage breast, Chela. And I cry into my hands ... no ... no! Can't I have any fucking peace? He's asking if I think I might hear this music after I die? No! Saying its light and colour and significance don't exist in isolation, Chela ... they're essences of you. If I live on, it will live on ...? I see I see I see I see. He tells me the *lü* and the *chö nyi* are separate entities. Or do I think mind is inseparable from brain ... only a perplexing part of a sophisticated machine? Brain dies at death. Brain dies at death. Can't you just leave me alone for five fucking minutes? Asks if I believe the *sem* is a temporary vehicle for the *skandhas*, which are immortal? I don't know! D'you have a soul, man? I don't know! I don't know! I don't know! I don't fucking know! Who the fuck I am? Who was I and who will I become? This is getting away from me now. Too far away from me. So far away from me. Matthew was right ... doctor!

I am Alien. The Enlightened. I am the Buddha and I am Guatama Siddhartha and I am Muhammad and I am Abraham and I am Krishna and I am Amarerasu and I am You, Chela. I acknowledge the spirit of the father, the source of everything in heaven and earth, who has revealed what was hidden ... Matthew, 11:25. He's telling me existence is necessarily miserable, Chela ... and non-existence is bliss. In other words ... shoot yourself in the fucking head, Francis! Death is the meaning? Is it? You must believe it, man. I don't know what to believe any more. So many of you fuckers telling me different things ... I don't know what to fucking think. I just want to listen to the music. Listen to the *prana*, man. Listen and understand. Understand understand

understand understand what? Not what, Chela ... who. Who what? Who you are. I know who I am. Do you? I'm *I'm*. I'm just *I'm*! In a Universe of logic or chaos? Which Universe? Scientistein said structure ... order. Normal. Reason. Logic. Apart from quantum. He laughs and says human life sure is an unfair thing. I know that! But I don't want to disagree and I don't want to agree either ... what if I agree ... what if I disagree ... what if it seems reasonable? Normal? I want to be normal! He's asking why is he Alien? Why am I, Chela? How do I know? Why are some guys rich and some poor ... some healthy and some diseased? Some sane and some mad? I'm not mad ... it's relative. He keeps asking me where's the logic, Chela? Why do some dudes sail through with beauty and intellect and an unshakeable belief that they'll pass unimpeded into some abstract heaven thing having had such a soft little vacation on this planet? While other softintheheads suffer poverty and doubt and rob and kill and take their chances with the hell thing? I tell him life's a fucking unfair thing, everybody knows that. Ask anybody! Then it ain't logical! Ain't there no *nadi*? No *dzogchen*? Why should some guys have such a head-start? Where's the fairness? Where's the *chakras*? Where's the order? He's asking me to tell him how it could all be made fair, Chela? But I don't know the answer. Someone told me not to think ... or I'd get stuck in a rut. Reincarnation he shouts ... sure, a series of *tulkus* where the *dak-dzins* experience and grow, until they got enough *terma*? The road to perfection of the spirit through experience and eventual escape from the *samsara*, man? That's what I was told. Is it right? Is it wrong? Unfair! Not normal? Not Rational? Reasonable? Inconsistent. Unbalanced. He laughs at me and says some people still got advantage over others. Still no true order. No normal ... no normal. I ask him where the normal is then? And he says it would have to be identical for everyone. Identical? Identical! I don't know how that could be. How the fuck can that be? But he says it's easy. All. Just all. I say that can't be ... Everyone? I want him to stop messing with my mind. Because I know there just wouldn't be enough time ... He says if Time's just an illusion? If it's all kinda ... parallel? Then ... Yeah? Then ... Yeah? Then ... I'm everybody? Everything! Everybody is everything. All should be One ... John, 17:23. It's One-Ness, man. Lift the clouds from your horizon, Chela. Stop thinking in symbols ... symbols destroy reality. You can't play the cosmic game by human rules. Love. Love is my word. If you show some compassion, it's for yourself. If you got the hatred ...

All she fucking knew about was perfume and powder — fucking mascara and masturbation. Something suddenly dawned on Francis. He jumped from his armchair and raced back upstairs. No cosmetics on the dressing table. Everything gone. She *had* been back! Francis pulled the door off the wardrobe. Everything gone. The rest of her clothes. He ran to the girls' room. Everything gone! All their stuff — clothes, books, computers, compact discs, little toy things. Every every every fucking thing. The fucking hatebitch!

'Fiona! Sinéad!'

Gone! The fucking fucking lovewitch! Heartbeat! She must have been watching him — came back when he wasn't there and took all the stuff. Twice that fucking game could be played! Francis began to punch the walls. Wallbeat! Punched holes in the doors until there was no skin left on his knuckles. Blood from his fists streaked the curtains. Bloodbeat! He kicked at the furniture, smashing everything that would break and screamed like some demon. The music downstairs stopped and there was a quietness — except for the animal noises that came up from inside him and out like vomit from his mouth. The rage stayed with him forever — until most of the house was broken up in bits. Then exhaustion set in and the fury ebbed away. Francis sat back down in the armchair. Sipped some of the coffee that had gone cold in the dirty cup and lit another cigarette. The night was silent now and he left it that way.

Francis must have slept. Didn't remember sleeping but he must have. For a while at least. Sleeping worried him sometimes. Felt like he was choking when he closed his eyes. Sometimes. Die. Murdered. Sleep. Brain. Silver streaks of light poked through the window and early morning sounds from the street outside. He was tired. Wringing with sweat and emotionally drained. More than tired. Fatigued. Exhausted. Weak. Defenceless. The light again seemed tangible and he reached out his hand to touch it. It felt cold. Like death. Brain. Francis went to the kitchen, made another cup of coffee and returned to his armchair. He looked up at the small discoloration on the ceiling. It didn't have the same significance as earlier and he quickly lost interest. Something else attracted his attention. A small pink envelope propped up on a shelf just inside the door. He hadn't noticed it before but now the light struck it and the pink colour seemed to diffuse into the room. He could smell Angeline. Francis wanted to see what was inside but was too tired to get up from the chair. He just stared at it, trying to see through the envelope at the bad news inside. Could hear Angeline's voice. Her words came from the envelope and sounded superior. Condescending. Sarcastic. Lovehate. Francis threw his cup at the shelf. The envelope fell to the floor and a wet stain of coffee spread out over it, turning it from pink to dirty brown. Angeline's voice stopped.

Francis tried to concentrate on what Alienchrist told him. But it was too difficult to get on top of. Made a kind of sense but was too big. Too elusive a thing for his tired brain. Death. Maybe think more about it later. Strange to be even interested. Tried to remember what Scientistein told him was normal. Couldn't remember. Thought about Animalkhan and killing. Wasn't ready. Was he slipping deeper into whatever was wrong with him? A nightmare that waxed and waned — came and went. What was wrong with him? Was there something wrong with him? There was fuckall wrong with him! Heard the Frenchwords of *d'Orléans* in his head and felt at home again.

Time for bed. Getting up from the chair was an effort, but he managed it. Francis walked slowly from the room, stepping on the wet envelope as he went. Seemed to take forever to climb the stairs. The steps went on and on when he looked up. Couldn't see the top. But he kept climbing. For hours and hours. Eventually Francis sat down, unable to climb any more. Then realised he was on the landing. Crawled on hands and knees to the bedroom and pulled himself up onto the bed. Not bothering to take off any clothes or cover himself with the quilt. Francis lay face down and breath came in long sighs. Unable to tell whether his eyes were open or closed. Aware of a profound significance. What it was he didn't know nor did he understand the feeling fully. A kind of sense. Like a sixth sense. It was there. The significance — so close he could almost touch it. Yet still just out of reach. Maybe he was ill. Schizoid! Coming down with some fucking virus that was making him imagine things. Psycho! He never got sick. Windowlicker! Not like other people. Maybe it was because he was getting older.

Francis wasn't a lazy man by nature, but lately everything was too much fucking trouble. Couldn't be bothered with this or that or the other. The music started up again downstairs in the lounge. Quieter now — in the background. Francis tried to think what day it was — if he had to work. Was it the weekend? Wasn't all that important and he soon grew tired of racking his brains. Just wanted to rest and not worry about anything. Any. Thing. Bedroom cold and he could feel a zephyr blow across the back of his neck. The door creaked open and out on the landing something came and peered in at him. Then went and came again and went. He didn't move. Sleep would soon take him away. And then he'd dream and become the dreaming man. He would become the real man like *Jeanne d'Arc* and he'd know his true self and become strong again. Couldn't afford to get sick now. Everything was about to happen. Had to get his energy back. It would come back once he slept and dreamed of the things that were real and the things that were right and the things that should have been but weren't and soon would be. The bedroom had a sinister feel to it which he didn't like and he wanted to get out of it as soon as possible. His dream would be warm. The sun was rising on the day — or was it setting? It might have risen while he lay there and was now going down again. Too difficult to tell. Francis wished his mother would come and talk to him. Sing to him. Tell him a story with a happy ending. But he could hear her crying in the next room and he knew she wouldn't. Couldn't.

chapter sixteen

chapte r sixteen

chapte r sixteen

Late autumn colours highlighted the leafbordered street where Francis Page waited in the Jaguar. Hampstead had a softness that was nice at this time of year. Neat! All golden and waiting for the Winter. With the city silhouetted on the skyline to the south and an affluent airflow blowing down from the shires to the north. Francis smoked a cigarette and tapped the ash out through the half-open window of his car. Mid-afternoon and kids coming home from school. Nice over here all right. Nice houses and nice cars and nice kids. Couldn't be legal, Francis conceded. Must be some fucking fiddles going on somewhere. The genetic picture wasn't clear. At least not yet. Metabolic errors. Polypharmaceutical. Psychopharmacological. Bertie the bollocks lived up the street with his two shithead sons. Francis had met him only twice — once when he married Angeline and again when Sinéad was born. Other than those times the prick kept himself away.

Bertie was a bit like Angeline. Two years older but nonthefucking-wiser. Bastard thought he was fucking royalty or something. Until his wife ran away with another woman and left him and the twins to fend for their fucking selves. Francis never met the boys at all. Before. But he knew they must be full-grown by now — going on twenty. No sign of life from the house and no sign of Angeline's car either. Francis wondered if he was on some chickenchase here but he had to start looking somewhere. Now that his wife meant business and it was no good sitting back any more and waiting for her to come to her fucking senses. Break down of her senses. If something was going to happen he had to be the one to make it happen.

Francis was parked out of the way and the Jaguar couldn't be seen from Bertie's house. He scanned the children on the street for any sign of Fiona or Sinéad. The road ran down behind him in the side mirror and his eyes darted to and fro in anticipation. The girls would be glad to see him. He didn't want to take them away or anything — just talk for a few minutes and say he loved them. He felt like some kind of villain, hiding there in the car as if he'd done somefuckingthing wrong. When all he wanted was to see his own children. It was a mad fucking world when a man had to hide like a hunkerdown to see his own kids. It was a bastard of a thing altogether! Heartbeat. But anger was no good here. That wouldn't do. Had to be calm and collected. No fucking fighting! No killing. That wouldn't do any good at all.

He saw a familar figure in amongst the school mothers.

Her lips don't move but I can still hear her voice saying that violence cannot be avoided, Jalal al-Din! Devour or be devoured, that is the great irony. We must eat life to live ourselves. She says there's no other way. And we must continue to devour until there is nothing left. Genghiskhan? I tell her I'm waiting for my girls. She says the world is an insatiable animal, constantly devouring itself. Devouring? Consuming. Consumer? Carnivorous fucking coward cunts! She says I'm a man like her and not one of those women. But you're a woman ... Spits and screams I am not! I am Genghiskhan! You are ... I saw you. Screams if I called her a women when she was alive, I would be dead now. Don't scream! Don't shout! Asking me what I'm doing here, Jalal al-Din? I say I already told her but she wasn't listening ... waiting to see my children. She can't understand why my children aren't with me? So I tell her my wife took them away. Kill her! I can't do that. You *must* do that! I think she might be living out here with them ... in her brother's house. Kill him also! You don't understand ... I understand this, you must kill them all. Not my daughters. If they reject you. No! Then kill your wife and her brother. No! She says maybe I'm not the man she thought I was. I'm not a killer. Every man is a killer. And woman too? We must kill ... telling me now it's our nature to do so. If we do not kill we die. Says none of us can live without death, Jalal al-Din. Consumers can. Can can. Candy colours can. Cunning manipulators can. Whispering to me if my wife takes my children it's like striking me with a sword. I might die from the wound. To prevent this I must take the children back. To achieve this my wife must die. Not necessarily ... What else can you do? Alien told me to talk. Love. For you and me and everybody. Weakness. My word is ... No! You will be at her mercy. No! Telling me how, when they resisted her at Bukhara and at Herab, she slaughtered them all ... men, women and children. I destroyed Liegnitz and Kiev and Volhynia and Lvov to show others that it was futile to oppose me. Why am I fucking shaking? She says it's because I know her word, Jalal al-Din. If I'm shaking does it mean frightened ... or does it mean freaking out? Coward or killer? She says I must show my strength, then I'll be feared. I don't want to be feared. I can say what she wants me to hear. Just respected. It is the same. It is? Yes. Is it Khananimal? It is. I'm like you, aren't I? Apart from ... you know. You are a man, Jalal al-Din. That's what I mean ... I'm a man, not a mug. Take what is yours! I will! Take it! I will! And kill all those who oppose you. I will! No ... Yes!

I can't kill ... You *must* kill!

Francis saw Angeline's car approaching in the mirror. He waited until it pulled up outside Bertie's house. Then swung his legs out of the Jaguar. Angeline emerged first, then opened the rear door for Fiona and Sinéad. The girls climbed out in school uniforms, carrying their cases. Francis ran up the road. Leaving the door of the Jaguar swinging open in his wake.

'Fiona! Sinéad!'

Angeline watched in disbelief. He was back. The man was back. Running up the road. She thought she'd put a full-stop to that part of her life. Her infatuation-turned-failure-turned-fourteenyears-turned-yesterdaysregret-turned-goodriddance-turned-runninguptheroad. Threatening to turn into her nightmare. If she wasn't careful. If she allowed it. Couldn't allow it. Had to stop here. And now. Tried to gather up the girls and get them inside the house but Francis was already on top of them. He lifted his daughters up in his arms and kissed them. Fiona hugged and kissed him back but Sinéad started to scream for her mother. Before he knew what was happening Angeline was hitting him and trying to drag the girls out of his arms. Francis resisted her at first, then put the girls down. Sinéad ran for her mother but Fiona stood still — smiling up at her father. Angeline's brother Bertie and his twin sons appeared at the door. Francis wondered if any fucker worked up this way or were they all either pulling fucking scams or spying for the fucking Government. Halfway houses. Luminous faces. Transparent skin. Francis reached out to touch them. Tentatively. Pulled away. Aliens? Angeline ushered the girls towards the door and one of the twins took them inside.

'Why did you do it, Angeline?'

'You know why.'

'Why did you take my girls?'

'They're not your bloody girls, Francis.'

'I'm their father, Angeline.'

'Who says?'

'Fucking hatebitch! Witchbitch!'

'Well ... that's beautiful, Francis ...'

Kill her! Francis raised his fist and moved threateningly towards Angeline. Heartbeat! She didn't believe he would strike her. Never did before, despite his hardman image. But he seemed different today and she backed up against the car. Just in case. Something in his eyes that she hadn't seen there before. Strange. Edgy. Madlook. Bertie and his boys watched from the doorway but Angeline made hand signals for them to stay where they were for the moment. She was afraid of this man for the first time. As if she had never seen him before. This side of him. But inside her she believed she could handle the situation. Like she handled all previous situations. With sarcasm.

'You should know all about bitches, Francis.'

'Know about you. You! You!'

'What about the black one ... ?'

Angeline became part of the car. Metallic. Robotic. Not human. Not flesh and blood and her words were made of tin.

'Don't do this now, Angeline ...'

'It doesn't really matter, Francis. It would have happened with or without her.'

'Why did you come to the house?'

'We needed our stuff.'

'You didn't have to go behind my back ...'

'Is that so? You'd have just let me walk in and take it?'

'I might have ... we could have talked. Talk to Alien!'

'Who? Like this rubbish you're talking now?'

Francis slowly lowered his fist. Heart. Angeline was defiant. Arrogant. He wouldn't do anything. Because he never did anything. Only dream some littleboy dream about owning some sleazejoint in the West End. He'd back away from her and go home because he couldn't face her argument. Her logic. Reason. Normalness. Brother and nephews waited in the wings. Francis hesitated — then began to move away from the lovehate woman and towards the door. Beat. Angeline moved with him — sliding herself along the side of the car.

'There's nothing left to say, Francis.'

'Please ... there must be!'

'No ... there isn't.'

Francis wasn't sure whether he was talking to Angeline or the car.

'I want to see the girls, Angeline ... that's all.'

'They don't want to see you.'

'Fiona does. And you've brainwashed Sinéad.'

'I don't believe I'm hearing this ...'

'You're not wanted here, Francis!'

Bertie's words distracted him.

'What did that bollocks say? That fucking brainwasher ...'

'He said you're not wanted here.'

'Stay out of my fucking way, Bertie. My girls, Bertie.'

'Just go away, Francis.'

'Let me see my girls! Just let me see my lovely girls ...'

Francis had come close to the door. Bertie and his boys blocked the way into the house. Heart. Beat. Francis faced them and called out to his daughters.

'Fiona! Sinéad!'

One of the twins pushed him in the chest. Heartbeat! Heartbeat! Heartbeat! Kill them! Killbeat! Francis lost control and rushed the door. Bertie grabbed his coat and Francis punched him in the face. Bertiebeat! The brother flew back into the hall with blood spurting from a broken nose. Angeline jumped onto Francis' back while the twins attacked from the front. Brainbeat! Deathbeat! Francis grabbed one of them by the throat and sank his fingers into the boy's windpipe. Kicked the other cunt between the legs and the twin screamed and doubled up in two. Angeline was digging her nails into his face and he could feel the warm blood running down onto his shirt collar. Kill her! Threw her over his shoulder and she landed halfway up the hall. Bertie regained his balance and came back at Francis — screaming out at the same time for someone to call the police. Francis hit him in the face again and blood splattered over the walls and up onto the ceiling. Still had a hold of the other twin's throat with his left hand and the boy's face turning blue. Kill the cunt! Angeline screamed at Francis to let go and threw a chair at him when he wouldn't. Francis ducked and the chair flew out and smashed in the driveway.

Crowd of nosy fucking neighbours peeping through their curtains and out from behind half-open doors as Francis growled like an animal and Angeline screamed and the twins cried and Bertie tried to wipe away the blood from his pulped-up face. Not used to trouble like this up here in Hampstead. Angeline up again and sank her teeth into Francis' fingers to make him let go of her nephew's throat. Not before the boy lost consciousness and collapsed onto the floor like a rag doll. Francis advanced punching and kicking into the house. Punchbeat! Kickbeat! Bertie lay in bits on the floor and Angeline bled from where the side of her head had banged itself against the wall. The other boy barred his way by pushing something heavy up against the inside of the hall door. Francis could hear the girls crying behind it and tried to break the whole wall down. Kill the fucking coward! In a frenzy now and almost through the door when the highpitch sound of sirens wailed outside the house.

Policemen down the hall and grabbing him from behind. Dragged Francis backwards out onto the driveway. Three patrol cars with flashing lights parked in the street — and a police van approaching at speed along Haverstock Hill. Four of the fuckers holding onto him while a policewomen examined the carnage in the hall. Crowd gathered at a safe distance as Francis threw two of the young police officers into next door's garden. The WPC came to help and Francis headbutted her in the face. Batons drawn! Painbeat! Fearbeat! Forlornbeat! They hit Francis on the legs and in the kidneys and across the back. But he felt nothing. Saw the hordes outside the gates of Premysl and the rivers of gore and tasted the bitter blood inside his mouth. Francis ripped the baton from one of the officers and smashed the man in the face with his own weapon. The policewoman was back on her feet but reluctant to come near the madman again. Francis beginning to get the upper hand when more lightflashings appeared. This time he was over-powered by an army of uniforms and beaten to the ground. Hands forced behind his back and handcuffed. Then dragged towards the van and flung into the back. Several officers climbed in after him and kicked him into a state of semi-consciousness. Kill the cunt!

He's laughing at me again. I wish he wouldn't do that. I don't fucking like it. And saying it's a pointless exercise, Chela. What? The violence. The hatred. There's just ain't no meaning. Tells me to forget the fear. I ain't scared of anything because I live in the light of understanding ... John, 11:19. I'm not afraid. Sure you are, Chela ... because you're halfway between ape and angel. Says I should fastforward the history of the earth in my mind ... since the creation until today. Let the lightyears be nothing more than minutes. How can I? Do it! I'm trying ... Do it! Yes ... See what's emerging? Yes. D'you see it now? Yes! Like an insect that lives just for the moment. See the simplicity, Chela. Alcohol and drugs shorten your stay. And boredom is fucking butchery. Humans. Some babies die. Very young. Don't you see the point now? I see the glare ... without shadow or relief ... ubiquitous and implacable! To some dudes the inner light of all things is menacing. To some it's hell, man .... He says they make their own hell. It's of their own doing, Chela. Some? Like me? Maybe. So also at life's end all that was temporary illusion will die and the true life of the spirit will alone be left ... Matthew, 13:30. Death is the meaning? No sin and no evil? I didn't say that. Life itself is such a transient damn thing. So short, man ... against the longer time of all. I may have to kill. He asks who told me that? You know who told me ... you're everybody ... you told me! You ain't no killer. I may have to become one. I went from God to God until they cried from me in me ... O thou I! *Tat tvam asi*! For what reason? My own. Reason. Logic. Normal. Love, Chela. He says advantage can only be gained at some other guy's disadvantage. Cause and effect. The bread you eat is only yours when no one else wants it. Life ain't given for yourself personally but only for the fulfilment of the Father's will, which alone saves from death and gives life ... Luke, 19:11. Look at it! I can't! Look at it! I won't! On and on and on and on ... the little life of the insect ... the chain ... up and up and up ... to what? And so on. And on. And on. You've seen it. When? Just now. No ... no ... no ... no! If there's no sin and no evil then killing can't be bad ... Khananimal might be right. I was blind but now can see. Now can kill. The dying of body is inevitable, Chela. He who don't give his body for the life of the spirit ain't got no real life ... John, 6:53. Maybe at some earlier point you understood more. Before the waters got clouded. Human is the real savage beast, Chela! The pathpoisoner. The power-player. And fucking fingerpointer! Say which tools, Chela ... not why build. Me first! Me first! I can't love. I can't love. There's no love left in me. Sure there is! You're fifteen thousand million years old! Alien? Aliens! We have to kill all the bastards. Just like Animalkhan said. His word is hate, Chela. Her! My word is love. Then you're a fucking woman like the others. You know it, Chela. You can't deny it no more. I do not! My love is like a rainbow. And sex is a straitjacket. Life is lousy. And lovely. And lousy. And love is like. I'm tired listening to you, Alienchrist! Then you'll die, Chela. Just leave me alone! Let me go!

'Let you go? Can't do that, mate. Mister tough guy, eh?'

'You fucking featherheaders ... slags!'

The officers gave Francis another few kicks as the wagon pulled up outside Maida Vale police station. Hauled to his feet and dragged inside. Heeeaaarrrttt. Beeeaaattt. Where the desk sergeant smirked at the bloody state of him and asked if he wanted a doctor.

'Just so you don't scream police brutality.'

'I want to make a phone call.'

'Later. Do you want a doctor?'

'I want my phone call.'

'Right!'

Took his belt and shoes and threw him into a cell. Francis called them a shower of alien bastards and then sat back on the bunk. Adrenaline receded from his blood and sharp stabs of pain began to break through. Heeaarrttbbeeaatt. He watched the door in case the slags decided to come back and give him another going over. The toerags didn't like you clouting one of their own. Always tried to make an example of anyone who stood up to them. On street corners. In cardboard boxes. Scraping out dustbins. Normalised. Deinstitutionalised. Down. Down. With the skinheads and shitbags and scavenging scarecrows. In singleroom occupancies and slumhotels with the callous and uncaring and being robbed and assaulted and raped. Francis knew this situation would be difficult to get out of — especially with his record. The cowards didn't come back and after a while he relaxed against the wall and wondered if there was really such a thing as sanity. Or just different degrees of madness.

chapter seventeen

chapte r seventeen

chapte r seventeen

Vous rêvez, Dauphin ... or is this reality? Jeanne? *Oui*. My reality maybe ... but I don't know what's real any more, do you? *Oui, je l'ai toujours su*. You're lucky. They said I did not know. Some said I lived a dream ... *que je rêvais*. They said I was insane and to make sure *que j'étais une femme* they stripped me. To establish *que j'étais vierge* they examined me intimately. And were you? Of course! So am I. It was they who were living the lie, *pas moi*. Like these slags here ... even though you wore men's clothes? Did that make me mad ... *le fait de porter des vêtements d'homme*? Should I have burned for it? They killed me not because I denied my sexuality ... not because I was touched ... or androgynous. But because I said the word. What word? *Dieu*! And I am now a saint, Dauphin, *parce que ça sied* the madness of the day ... the madness of the cause. I am a neuropolitical saint. A saint for all seasons. All men use my image, *pour vendre leurs propres psychoses*. At least you're out of all the shit now. *Le suis-je*? Aren't you? I am if you are with me, Dauphin. I was in a hopeless cell, *exactement telle que vous me connaissez*, but strength was given to me by God. He liberated me. With fire I was freed. No thanks! You must your own salvation choose. What does that mean? *Vous savez*! No I don't ... *Vous savez*! *Vous savez*! Are you telling me to kill myself? I am telling you to free yourself from your chains. A solicitor can do that for me. But still you will be a prisoner of your time and condition, *tout comme moi*. I am not! You will be. I have to learn, Jeanne ... I want to live until I learn how to die. You tell me if death is the beginning. You tell me!

La mort est la fin de tout, Dauphin!

Francis sat up and readied himself when he heard the metal door being unlocked. Two officers stood in the open doorway.

'You wanted to make a phone call, Page?'

'About fucking time!'

'Watch the language, now.'

'Any chance of a cup of tea?'

'He's serious ... will you just *fuck* off!'

Francis pushed through the door and followed one of the officers down the corridor. The other marched behind. In case the prisoner made a sudden break for it. Both the bastards smirking and taking the piss and talking in a sign language Francis couldn't understand. He realised Percy Shillinger was his only chance of getting out of this fucking situation — so he called Matthew Moore and told him the story. About everything. Life and death and space and time and trouble and terror and realitytesting. Matthew was a friend and wouldn't let him down. Even if he already had. Down. Down.

Escorted back to the cell and the door slammed behind him. Francis felt safe in the locked room and slept fitfully for a while and the policemen could hear him raving to himself and laughed at the crazy mad cunt. Except for the ones he'd hit — who weren't laughing at all. Couple of hours later the cell door opened again. Francis' face had swollen up and it was difficult to talk because of the congealed blood inside his mouth. Led to an interview room occupied by Matthew Moore and a man in a dark blue suit.

'You stupid fucking bollix, Francis!'

'Thank you, Matthew.'

'What the fuck were you thinking about?'

'I don't want a lecture.'

'You definitely deserve one then.'

The other man sitting opposite was young. Arrogant. With an arrogant mouth. Like he knew something nobody else knew. In his fucking blue suit.

'Who the fuck are you?'

'Your solicitor.'

'Compliments of Percy Shillinger, Francis.'

'Just do whatever has to be done to get me out of here.'

'You think that's easy, do you?'

'You said you're a fucking solicitor, didn't you?'

'Listen to the man, Francis.'

Matthew looked tired. Like a statue looked tired. Matthew's statue. Statue Matthew. 'S that you, Matthew? And his voice came out slow. Like it was tired too.

'Your wife and her family are pressing charges.'

'Fuck her ... them!'

'So is the WPC you headbutted.'

'Headbutted? Who? Self defence!'

'Is that so? She sees it a different way.'

'Whose fucking side are you on?'

'These are serious charges ...'

Everything was fucking serious. The fact that reality was slipping away was serious. How serious could it get?

'Everything's fucking serious ... sir!'

'Jesus, Francis, the man's trying to help you.'

'Can he get me out of here?'

'It's already been arranged.'

'Then, why are we still sitting here ... in this dirty dump?'

'Just fucking listen, Francis! Shillinger had to pull strings to get you out. High up strings, if you know what I mean.'

'I'm in his debt forever! He owes me ... the fucking impostor!'

Despite the nightmare terror that came and went inside him Francis tried to keep an outward air of normality. Of his old self. Whatever his old self was. Used to be. So people blamed him for what was outside his control. Like Matthew. Who shrugged his shoulders as if he was dealing with some small bad child. When all the time Francis was just trying to hold himself together.

'Just take the fucking thing seriously.'

'I will, I will.'

'Keep your nose clean until the case comes to court, otherwise you'll find yourself on remand.'

'Rem. And. Let's get the fuck out of this place.'

Francis poured himself a Jack Daniels when he got back to the house in Leytonstone Road. Needed something to take the pain away. The spirit stung his mouth but he forced it down. Wanted to ring Glendora. Needed her right at that moment. But he didn't make the call because he didn't want her to know he needed her. Need made him vulnerable. Need was dangerous. When people found out you needed something the price went up. Francis moved aimlessly around the house and tried to remember when he was working next. Tomorrow? Or the day after? An overwhelming urge inside him. To move on. Go away. Somewhere. Get out. That very minute. But he didn't. Francis looked at the laughing man in the mirror. Have to cover up the marks on his face. Otherwise he'd look a proper fucking sight outside the clubs. Be a target for every wiseguy in the city.

He shouts don't do it, Chela. And I know there'll never be no fucking peace! Ever. Again. To meet evil and not be infected by it conquers evil. I don't want to hear about it. I told you I don't want to hear about it! Tells me to turn away from the *maya*, man ... otherwise everything becomes self-validating. Proof of the conspiracy. Everywhere. I've had a bad fucking day. He knows I have, Chela ... but I need to recognise what it is I'm seeing. What is it, then? Just tell me what it is and leave me alone. Saying don't get distracted by the *skandhas* of your life. Concentrate! Try to remember. I can't remember who I was in *this* life ... never mind any other. The man now is not the boy then ... Everybody carries the genes of Adam and Eve. It's now! Now! Now! Now! That's the thing ... that's the bad thing. Now is nothing, Chela. No. Thing. The rock. The rock. One mile high and one mile wide and one mile deep and the small bird comes — every hundred years to sharpen its beak. When the rock's gone — that who you are. Now ... Tells me to think of the insect, Chela ... Fuck the insect! Again! Its own size is all there is. Optimal. Everything else is either bigger or smaller than the ideal. It don't want to be anything else, man. Don't covet its neighbour's wife. Or its neighbour's car. But it kills, Christalien! He says to kill and be unaware of the implications ain't to kill for the sake of killing, Chela. Now? Never? That's all right then, ain't it? Sometimes my body feels as if it's closing in on itself ... growing more dense ... more tightly packed ... like a lump of condensed shit ... like something that can be held in the hand. And squeezed. Packed tighter and tighter. Crushed. Ground down smaller and smaller. Even the people around me are becoming alien ... but not like him. Not human. Inhuman. I'm solitary in a crowded street. There is no reason. No logic. No normal. No hope and no fear and no pain. No love. No hate even. Nothing. Nothing. Don't isolate! To isolate is to give absoluteness, Chela. Forget the Pharisees of verbal orthodoxy. Find the stillness of unsystematic direct perception. Can I do that?

Trekchö. Trekchö? Tsul trim trekchö!

The telephone rang loudly. Startled Francis. He picked up the receiver.

'Hello?'

'Frankie ...'

'Glenny?'

'I was thinking about you.'

'Were you?'

'Yes. Were you thinking about me?'

'No.'

'Bastard! Can you come over?'

'You come over here.'

'Now?'

'Sure.'

Francis made a feeble attempt to tidy up the house while he waited for Glendora. But soon got fed up with the effort and sat down on the sofa with his drink. His mood swung before his face. Across the room — from wall to wall. Back and forth. Black to white and all shades in between. Glendora arrived quickly. He heard the heavy engine of her white convertible sportscar, which she paid for with the money she made at the casino. And didn't spend on heroin. Any more. Francis thought the car was too flash but she said the same about the Jaguar so he didn't push the point. The key turned in the door and he didn't get up when she came in. She took the empty glass from his hand.

'Another drink?'

Francis didn't answer. He stared at the opposite wall while she looked in amazement around the scene of destruction inside the house. Something was happening to him and she didn't know what it was. It frightened her. He was disintegrating. He couldn't do that. If he did that — who'd mind her? Glendora knew she had to help Francis but wasn't sure how to go about it. Maybe if he left the house and came to live with her. But he wouldn't. She asked and he refused. Like he wanted to self-destruct. She knew that if anything happened to him her old boyfriend would come back. The one who never stopped calling her. The one she was addicted to and would never be able to do without as long as she lived. But could keep at bay as long as Francis stood between him and her. She wanted to go back. How she wanted to go back. And Francis held onto her and she remembered how it was and she turned away and he held on and held on and held on to her. Until it passed and she loved him again. And then the next time would come. Glendora poured two bourbons and sat beside him on the sofa. Gently touched his bruised cheek and began to sob very softly.

'Don't cry ... it's ok.'

'What happened to you?'

'Nothing. Don't worry.'

'I have to worry about you, Frankie.'

'It's ok, just superficial.'

Not true. Glendora knew there was something deeper. Wrong. Deeper than the superficial.

'And look at this place ...'

'What's wrong with this place?'

'Looks like it's been turned over.'

'It hasn't.'

She didn't believe him. Something evil had been here. Maybe it was time for her to ask some questions. Before it went to far.

'Who's been round here, Frankie? Has someone come for you?'

'No one's come for me. I did the damage in here myself.'

'Why?'

'It doesn't concern you, Glenny.'

'Of course it concerns me ...'

'Just leave it alone!'

Heart! Francis shouted at her. Not again. Beat! Getting annoyed. Leave her alone. Hated questions. Just wanted to get on with things without every fucker knowing all about it. She was silent and he was sorry for shouting. Put his arm round her and kissed her forehead. She kissed him back. Lips on his marked face. Making the pain better. She moved away for a moment and the dress fell from her shoulders. Nothing underneath. Francis watched the shape of her slim body. She was slightly muscular, like a boy. With small breasts and a waist so narrow he could have broken her in half. If he wanted to. Black pubic hair trimmed to a neat triangle and her legs carried old scars along them. She moved back and pressed his face into her chest and ran her hands through his hair. Francis could smell the scent of coconut oil from her silk body and taste the spices on her skin. Soon naked too and they lay together on the big settee. Kissed her breasts and stomach and back and thighs and she moved her body across him so lightly it was like making love to a shadow. And when the time came she discreetly produced protection and fitted it almost without him knowing. He turned her on her back and entered her while supporting his own weight with his arms. She held him with her legs and her fingers touched his stomach and chest while the long strokes of intercourse gradually increased in speed until climax came bursting in upon his brain. Dead. Francis shouted and Glendora sighed with satisfaction as his teeth came down to bite at her neck and the breath pistoned from his nose and mouth. Then it was over. Francis waited a moment before withdrawing. Quickly got rid of the condom and returned to the black girl with a blanket. They lay together smoking and sipping bourbon until the room grew friendly. Francis didn't turn on the light and Glendora didn't want him to. There was a velvet texture to the night — to the woman. And when she fell asleep he slipped out from underneath the blanket and stood naked at the window.

Outside, the sky was full of fire. Electromagnetism in the air. Particles flying everywhere. He could feel the fundamental forces of nature all around in the darkness. Waves of photons went through him. Filled him. Became him. He was part of all things. Just like Alien said. Francis could feel it now. Could understand it all — what it all meant. Knew now the reality he observed was being altered by the act of observation and he had to choose his own path through the many parallel dimensions of the quantum. There was a sense of deeptime. He could comprehend the billions of galaxies in the Cosmos and the duality of linked opposites. He alone in the Universe could stand there naked and shout ...

'I know that I know!'

Glendora stirred on the sofa behind him. Francis turned into the dark room and forgot what he was thinking about. Something fucking weird. Those bloody Voices had him all fucked up.

Something inside my head or maybe not asks me if it's difficult to grasp, Shegetz? I say, see ... that's exactly what I fucking mean. I don't know whether I'm coming or fucking going. Is it surprising? *Oy vey*, zere has been change. Change change change. Und ze Nazarene said zat except you become as little chiltren ... I know it killed him. But it denies ... denies ... and saying now that I'm the killer ... not it. Jew Jew! Und you are a *hayes umbrenger*! It left its daughter ... Jew! She told me the DNA double helix was the intercoiled snake of the *yoga kundalini*? It left her! It says no matter because everything's changing now. Quantum quantum quantum. Everyzink is sub-atomic. Zat is vhere ze real truth lies. Lies! Spies! Vat? Spies! Spies! Who? You. It tells me again it belongs to a mathematical genius. I ask if it's enlightened, like Alienchrist? Do ve not live in ze most enlightened of times? We? You. I say enlightenment is fucking relative. Isn't it? You haf been listening to me after all! Everyzink is relative. I don't trust its logic. Logic, schmogic! Normal! Normal normal normal. Spies! You mean ze sceptics? The spies!

Krechtsene meschugina! I ask what about the normal? Scientistvoice? Normal is relative too. Schmoo! Und any schmuck can know everyzink mit hindsight. I shout don't leave me in the fucking dark! Like it left the girl. And I didn't ask for your fucking company. It says of course I did! Do I think it would come here of its own accord? Don't come, then! Don't come! Don't come! It says I'm ignorant, Shegetz ... and I'm heading for disaster. I shout normal or nothing, Scientistvoice! Don't come back! Can you not see ... your position is deteriorating. You are losing ground already. Soon it vill be too late to do anyzink about it. Programming and misinformation are gaining pace. White lies are now coal black and cynicism is on everybody's lips. Abuse has to be corrected. Normal or nothing! New dogma ... new propaganda.

Don't come back! You are a stupid *naar*. You're a Jew! *Shalom*!

Francis swung his fist and knocked over a lamp. The noise woke Glendora and she sat up in the darkened room.

'Frankie ...'

'It's ok. Go back to sleep.'

'Where are you?'

'I'm over here.'

'What are you doing?'

'I was just getting a drink of water.'

'Come back to me.'

Francis made his way cautiously to the sofa and slipped back under the blanket. He didn't realise how chilly the room had grown and her body was warm and reassuring. They both sighed together and fell asleep and he dreamed of neurotica and normality and divinity and death and his dream met hers in the Dreamtime and they dreamt each other's dream and died each other's death.

It rained next day and the sound of heavy drops beating against the window panes woke Francis. He was alone in the room. The gas fire was alight and artificial flames leaped from the imitation coal. He could hear sounds from the kitchen and Glendora came naked into the lounge, carrying a tray with coffee. She placed the tray on the table and lit a cigarette for Francis.

'Making yourself at home I see.'

'I don't feel at home here, Frankie.'

'Why not?'

'I feel uncomfortable. It's her house.'

'It's my house, Glenny. Our house.'

'I can feel her watching me.'

Who was watching? Francis wondered if Glendora knew. Who was watching. Better not to accuse her. Accuse? Her.

'No, no ... she's watching me. Not you.'

'Give the house back to her.'

'I told you, it's *my* house, Glendora!'

'You can come live with me.'

Francis thought about it. Only for a moment. A split second. He was tempted for a split second. But then the fear took hold again.

'I'm not going anywhere. I'm staying here.'

'You don't belong here any more, Frankie. It's not good for you ...'

'I'm not going to let the witchbitch get away with it.'

'You're only hurting yourself.'

'Enough!'

Francis threw the cigarette at the gas fire. Heart. Flung the blanket away and got to his feet. Glendora was silent as he dressed. Didn't like the new anger in him. She knew he was a violent — could be a violent man. But not with her. He had to mind her — not murder her. Maybe their time had come. She was confused. Afraid. A familiar feeling that had gone away to a large extent since she met Francis. But now was creeping back. Glendora didn't want it back again. Didn't want to lose him but didn't want him to change into something like her father and uncles from that longtime ago. Wondered if she should stay to find out if it was going to get worse or if she should go now. While she could. But the thought of what was waiting out there made her hesitate. She lit a cigarette while he went upstairs to the bathroom and looked in the mirror. The same stranger stared back. Fichte stared back. The before-boy. Laughing. Crazycunt. Windowlicker. Francis pulled away from the image and shouted down the stairs for Glendora to get dressed and he'd take her home.

'I've got my own car, remember?'

'Sure ... of course ...'

'Have you got to go somewhere, Frankie?'

'No ... I don't think so ... I don't really know ...'

'Why don't we spend the day together?'

'What will we do?'

Francis was unsure of the situation. Confused by the proposition. Afraid of the implications. Unable to focus on the ramifications. Perplexed at the idea. Undecided about the inference. He was shaking when he came back downstairs. She held his shoulders until it stopped. He came back to her and smiled. She said ...

'Let's go for a walk in the park.'

chapter eighteen

chapte r eighteen

chapte r eighteen

Francis Page saw a lot of Glendora over the next couple of weeks. They went everywhere together. Restauranting in the East End and shopping in the West End. Walking in the parks and training together at the gymnasium. Drinking in bars on the nights they weren't working and lovemaking at the flat or the house in Leytonstone Road. Glendora preferred the flat and steered him round there whenever she could. He seemed to have recovered from his moody phase and she put all the previous thoughts of leaving him out of her head. She didn't know how she'd do out there without him. In the unknown. And she didn't know how he'd do without her. Especially now his wife had gone. Better to take it day by day. Like everything else.

Francis had mortgage problems. He didn't tell her but the bastards at the building society were getting shitfaced with him. Had a good mind to go down there with a Beretta and blow half the wankers away. Greedy fuckers! All right as long as they got their money. Miss a few months and they were onto you like a fucking rash. Could do without that kind of fuckology right now. Work scarce since the incident with the police and to cap it all the bastards taking him to court for grievous bodily fucking harm.

'Listen, Glenny, I might take you up on your offer.'

'What offer was that, Frankie?'

'To move in.'

This took her by surprise. After all her efforts to get him to make the move before. And now when the little doubts were forming in her mind he takes her up on it. But what could she say? It was what she wanted just a few months ago. It was still what she wanted. As long as he minded her. As long as it wasn't the other way around. She wasn't strong enough to take care of him if it all went bad. But it was a chance she was prepared to take.

'Frankie ... you mean it?'

'I wouldn't say it if I didn't mean it.'

'When, do you think ...'

'The sooner the better really.'

'Whenever you like ...'

A month ago she would have said Now! Right now! But now —

'Why did you change your mind?'

'Something ... probably what you said about me just hurting Angeline ... myself ...'

Glendora leaned across the restaurant table and kissed him. The gesture embarrassed Francis and he looked around to see if anyone was watching. Didn't know about the little misgivings in her mind. If he had he might have hesitated. But he thought that in a way it might not be a bad thing. He reasoned. And logicised. Normalised. Might be better than being alone. Help keep the demons away. And the diabolical doublecrossing pocketsearchers. He and Glendora were closer now than they'd been for a long time. He believed. Living together seemed the next step. Then they'd be out of it all and into a new life. Soon.

Sooner. Soonest. Best. America coming and after that easystreet. In any case, the house was beginning to attract roaches and rats and if Angeline moved back she could clean it up and sort the mortgage out at the same time. He didn't want to please the lovehate woman but he wanted to please the bastards at the building society even less. What would the girls do if the shitbags repossessed the place and sold it off for a fucking song to some foreign fucking huckster at an auction. There were things like negative equity and equality and quality and misinformation and propaganda and he'd still end up owing the bastards money. Fuck it. No!

'Let's have a little celebration then.'

'Glendora ...'

'Champagne!'

'Listen, I think you ought to know ... I've been hearing these kind of, voices ...'

'Haven't we all. Waiter!'

They drank Champagne and Glendora seemed so happy that she lost her instinctual inhibitions and got a little drunk and a little loud and Francis had to take her home to the flat. He put her to bed and she looked up at him and said whenever you like? Had to sort out a few things with Angeline first and that was the way it was. Told her to sleep and he'd see her tomorrow. She sighed and turned over in the bed. Then purred like a cat. He looked down at her. Down. Despite all the pros and cons gone over in his mind — still some nignags. Something saying wait but there was no choice now. Glendora already asleep and her body moved only to the rhythm of her breathing. Francis con tinued to watch her. Fascinated and afraid at the same time. He wanted to reach down and place a pillow gently over her face. Peacefully smother the life out of her so she'd never be disappointed again. But his hands wouldn't move. He felt something hot on his face and was annoyed and surprised when he realised it was a tear.

Outside, the air cool with approaching winter. Francis sat in the Jaguar for a long time and smoked several cigarettes. He realised that meaning wasn't automatically given to life — you had to make your own meaning. Childhood pictures flashed into his head and he knew the boy back then was now a stranger to him. Life itself was becoming increasingly remote. Nothing existed in the abstract any more. Nothing existed until he looked at it — until it came within his perception. Things came into his mind that never had before. Strange things. Sometimes they made sense but mostly they didn't. Contradictions. He noticed odd things — like buildings slipping and the air changing colour. Verbal images like work, truth, guilt, God — had no existence outside his mind. In reality.

Francis started up the car and drove slowly away down Dalston Lane. Turned left into Kingsland Road and headed west towards Paddington. Still early and he wasn't working until ten. But he didn't want to go back to the house and he'd had enough to drink. He stopped the Jaguar at the lights red just before Tottenham Court Road. Waited for the green. Wasn't thinking when they turned. Was thinking — but not about driving. Mind on a million other things. Like the spontaneous occurrence of adrenochrome and how to see others as they see themselves and *sat-chit-ananda* and *istigkeit* and ab-sub as elements in the total awareness and how the sensum is subordinated to the concept. Car horns blaring from behind. And shouts of come on you cunt! Foot on the accelerator and fast along the Marylebone Road towards the Pink Peacock.

I'm Eyeless. I'm Earless. The beginning of life is at the moment of conception and not the moment of birth. Tell that to the anti-abortionists! I'm Christ the interplanetary Alien. And I'm Juliana of the Revelations. Not Jeanne of the Dreaming? Someone said the level of adrenaline in the blood of a baby being born was higher than in a man having a heart attack. Wow! Und you can call me Albert. Scientist. And

I am the great Animal. King of all the Khans. Queen! And most living things do not die. They are killed. You can't possibly say that's logical. Rational. Reasonable. I am vision and I am death and I am normal and *Je suis la pucelle martyre d'Orléans. Jeanne qui a des visions*. The modern psyche is simultaneously liberated and trapped by the power of its own symbols. Says who? Says Sigmund. And Socrates is drunk again in the doss-house. Death is the attainment of equilibrium and we all carry the imprint of our primordial beginnings at the root of our being. And I'm the vampire here to suck the last living drop of blood from your veins.

And who's that always highless? Eyeless!

The Jaguar drove itself to the club and Francis sat for a while in the car park. Not remembering the journey from the flyover at the junction of the Edgware Road. He tossed his cigarette butt through the car window and got out. The Peacock was closed but Francis knew George Dimitrov would be inside. Knocked on the side door and one of the barstaff let him in.

'Francis ... you're early tonight?'

'I love my work, George, you know that.'

'Of course you do. And if I won the lottery I would give it all to the Samaritans.'

'Your place is reserved at the right hand side of God.'

'No more than your own ... on the left, of course.'

'We'll both find our true reward in heaven, George.'

Heaven. Wherever that would be. Maybe some state of congealed lethargy. Somewhere to stare at the sub-atomic spot for ever. Forever. Sounded good.

'I have to make a phone call.'

'Go right ahead, my friend.'

'Confidential.'

'Use the office.'

'Thank you.'

Francis drank a bottle of mineral water before going back to the manager's office. Lit a cigarette and looked at the telephone. This was going to be fucking difficult. But no turning back now. He knew what she'd think. She'd think he was backing down. The witchbitch would think she'd won. And what if she did? He didn't care if she did or not — the hatelove woman. In any case this had to be done now. He told himself several times there was no other way and finally picked up the receiver as if it was red hot. Potato hot. Dialled the number and listened to the ringing tone go on for a fucking hour. He was about to leave it so.

'Hello?'

'Angeline?'

'Who's that?'

'It's me, Francis. Don't hang up!'

'What do you want?'

'I want to see the girls ... on a regular basis.'

'I'm hanging up ...'

'No! Wait ...'

Silence on the other end of the line. Francis thought for a second she'd hung up. But he could still hear her breathing. He waited for her reply. Silence went on.

'You've got some bloody nerve, Francis, after all you've done.'

'I'm entitled to see them, Angeline.'

'Take it to court, see how far you'll get with your record.'

Francis listened to the sounds outside in the club. The rest of the staff reporting for their night's duty. Soon the doors would swing open and he'd be back on the street.

'Look ... I think we can make a deal.'

'What kind of deal?'

'You can have the house.'

'What?'

'You heard. You can have the house if I can see the girls.'

'And where will you live?'

'I'll move out.'

'I see. You'll shack up with miss sooty will you?'

'What the fuck do you care what I do, Angeline?'

'I don't!'

'Well ... d'you want the fucking house or not?'

Angeline didn't reply immediately. He waited. Could see her in his head. Heady. Haughty. She wasn't normally this hesitant. Usually she could make her mind up about something pretty quick.

'I won't bother you, Angeline. I give you my word. I just want to see the girls every couple of weeks.'

'They don't want to see you.'

'They do! Listen to me ... Fiona does ... and Sinéad will come round.'

He wondered where the girls were now. Probably in bed. Dreaming of their own little God in his Trinity with Santa Claus and Toothfairy. Francis wanted to ask Angeline about her God but decided not to. Just waited for her answer.

'How can I trust you, Francis?'

'You have to trust me, Angeline. Look, I'm working. I can't stay on the phone all night ...'

'All right. But this better not be one of your stunts.'

'It's kosher, Angeline ... you won't regret it.'

'And I'll have to ask the girls if they want to see you. I won't force them, Francis.'

'They'll be all right.'

'If they're happy about it, you can see them ... every other Sunday. But don't come near the house. Just phone when you're coming and they'll be ready.'

'Ok, ok. Thanks.'

'But if you come near me, Francis ... all deals are off and I'll get an injunction.'

The office was huge. Limitless. With smooth walls. Official office. Officer. That was another thing. A horse of a different hew. It reminded him — he hadn't forgot. An elephant never knew what hit it. And that Bertie bollocks didn't either.

'There's one other thing ...'

'What's that?'

'Can you get your brother to drop the assault charges?'

'I can't do that!'

'Yes you can. It wouldn't be nice for the girls if their father was put in prison by their mother.'

Another pause. Silence. The office was unreal. Reality was at the other end of the phone line.

'I don't know ...'

'C'mon, Angeline ... it was just a mistake. I shouldn't have gone round there. But a court case is not going to do any good for anyone. All in the witness box ... giving evidence ... think of the girls, for God's sake.'

Silver! Francis hung up the phone. Smiled to himself and left the office. Outside in the club things were busying up. Barstaff making final preparations for the onslaught and the Clubberking polishing his CDs and bouncers limbering up and laughing amongst themselves. Francis approached the group.

'Who's first outside?'

'You and I, Francis.'

'Same as usual, eh Agnes? We always get the shit shift.'

Francis could feel the smile before he saw it. Nightingale's smile. The smartman smile. Waiting with its words.

'That's 'cause you guys are *in omnia paratus*. Ain't you, Francis Page?'

Francis didn't answer. Even though he understood the question.

'I reckon you're just the realest man, Francis Page, *inter alia* ... and all those little hookers outside know it. Ain't that right, Agnes?'

'I do not know what you are saying, *maricón ... quieres morir o qué*?'

'Bolivian ballbuster ... you always gotta stick up for your man ...'

Was he her man? How did the American know? He knew nothing! It wasn't true. Liar!

'I'm not her man ...'

'Come, Francis. We do not need to listen to his *mierda que suelta*!'

'Don't gimme that pachamama stuff, Agnes. It might work with dumb jerks like Francis ... but I ain't just some crazy yank faggot ...'

'Are you not?'

'I'm much more than that, honey. But I guess you already know it ... don't you?'

Dumb jerk! Crazy cunt! Spazo! Looney tunes! Mad! Mad! Mad!

'Why do you not go back to Coca-Cola land where you came from? We have had enough of your *charleta intelectual*. And do not think you are so superior.'

'A dog would be your superior, baby.'

Francis slammed the smartman up against the wall of the club. Both hands round the throat. Smartbeat! Smackbeat! Nightingale's eyes began to pop before the others could prise Francis' fingers away. The smartman coughed and choked and held his neck while Francis gave him the onefinger salute and headed towards the door. Agnes D'Argensola followed, spitting on the floor by Nightingale's feet as she went. The smartman smirked and whispered to himself ...

'*Lex talionis ... et nunc et semper*.'

Agnes flirted outside on the street and kept coming close to Francis and touching him. She thought it was a sign ... the way he stood up for her to John Nightingale. Francis didn't like that. Tried to stop her but only made her worse and he didn't want to be shown up in front of the skagheads and stagnighters. He felt sad for her because he knew she couldn't understand the problem. Why he couldn't jump on her or give her the baby. He was aware she didn't want to marry him or any kind of thing like that. Much more basic. Genetic.

To Agnes. Francis was a big physical man. Handsome in a dark deadly way. It was biological — evolutionary. *Imprescindible*! All she really wanted was his child. She'd provide the intelligent genes and Francis would supply the physical. That's all! Blood simple! Scientific! South American! And maybe even a little bit because her father never forgave her for being a girl. Because he was a *chicha*-drinking half-Indian miner who spoke *Quechua* and *Aymara* as well as Spanish and dug tunnels under the jungle looking for gold missed by the Incas. And he wanted a son to carry on after he was gone to meet *El Tito*. Agnes couldn't take the poverty and corruption and didn't want to join the *campesinos* in the coca fields. But if she ever went back to the valley of the moon and the island of the sun she would have a boy with her that would make the old *mula de mierda* smile. No! She didn't want to keep Francis! Neither did she know about his problem.

What problem? The problem with the world — still in the dark ages of discovery. Psychological philosophy. Sympathy. Simple human humanity. The weak and the lame will lag behind. Kill them! Before they bring us all down. To the level.

Francis and Agnes went through their routine with her teasing and him tutting until they were relieved by the second shift from inside. Agnes sat next to Francis at his table during their break.

'Let's make the baby, Francis.'

'What?'

'Let's make a boy ... a son for you.'

'I don't want a son.'

'Sure you do. Every man wants a son.'

'I don't. I got two daughters, that'll do me.'

'What if I look after it and don't bother you with the details?'

He wasn't the only one who was crazy. If he was crazy. Francis wondered why she wouldn't leave him alone. He wanted to be left alone. Enough problems without this shite.

'You're fucking crazy, Agnes ... leave me alone.'

'No *problema* for you.'

'It'd be my kid. I couldn't just ignore that.'

'Well, you can send it Christmas cards if it makes you feel better.'

'It would *not* make me feel better! And there's no *can* about it!'

Who was this fucking woman? What did she want from him? He knew what she said she wanted, but what did he really want? Francis was getting annoyed. Wished she'd go talk to her *Yatiris* and her *Ekeko* God.

'I want the baby, Francis!'

'Get someone else to give you one!'

'Your baby!'

'Why?'

'I have my own agenda.'

'Everyone has their own agenda ...'

'What about it then?'

'No! It's not part of mine.'

'Come on, what have you got to lose? We can even do the artificial *imseminación*. My Embassy can arrange it all ...'

'Enough!'

Francis threw back his drink and walked away from the table. Christ Allfuckingmighty! Didn't he have enough fucking problems with all the other bastards? Agnes' eyes followed him across the club. She knew there had to be a way of getting him to agree. She'd find it. But it would have to be soon — *tiempos* were ticking.

chapter nineteen

chapte r nineteen

chapte r nineteen

Francis Page moved into Glendora's flat in Dalston Lane on Halloween. He wondered if the date was in some way significant. So did she. Sky lead grey and Winter well on the way. With its ice and snow and snivelling and stagflation. Hostile footsteps in the frost. Night-time nepotism. All safe and sane together. Inside looking out. Francis took very little from the house. Just his clothes and toothbrush and some photographs of Fiona and Sinéad. Whole lot in one large sports-bag. Wednesday late afternoon with the city beginning to rush about itself on the way home. Glendora upbeat about it now. Doubts of the previous days gone. Dissolved away and things back to how they were between her and him. Before. Better even. She was cheerful and bubbling over in a way he hadn't seen from her in a while. Eyes bright and alight and smiling as she helped him put his things away. She'd been preparing dinner before he arrived to surprise him and now insisted he relax with a drink in the studio. As she called it. Until things were finalised in the kitchen.

Francis sat in a black leather chair and lit a cigarette. He looked round the room he knew so well but it was as if he'd never been inside it before. Studied the parquet flooring with its scattering of coloured mats. White walls with contrasting paintings by Lorenzo and La Tour. Art deco furniture and high pink ceiling. All so fucking strange. Was this home now? Was this heaven? Hell? Was this where he wanted to be? Would he die here? The room felt claustrophobic and stiflingly hot. Francis took off his jacket and undid a button on his shirt. Glendora must've had the heat turned up. Didn't want to complain — nittypick. Not yet. But it would have to change. He'd only just got here for fuck's sake! Leave it go! They'd get used to each other after a while. No fucking point in getting on each other's nerves after the first few fucking minutes. Like that with Angeline. Never again! No more lovehate. Or hatelove. Francis could hear her singing in the kitchen. Playing music by Nina Simone and singing along. *Since I fell for you*. Voice soft and musical. Happy. Francis was happy that she was happy. Was he? Nothing outside any more. All gone. Was it? Only what he could see existed. Feel. Touch. Fuck the rest? He felt happy. Although it was difficult to distinguish between different emotions these days. Be easy to believe that everything would be all right. Faith, hope and chastity. For everandeverandeverandever. No more acting the part. Pretension. No more taking it all for granted. But there were new terrors. Of Time and Death and a horror of ultimate meaninglessness.

He was listening to the Voices even though he told himself he wasn't and living each moment on the edge of eternity — paying the awful price, the charge for consciousness. Was there any such thing as never? Was there ever? Forever never. Never forever. Was his fractured perception of Time flawed? Did the past cease to exist as soon as his awareness moved beyond it? Or was it always there — like a ghost in the gloom? Did the present only matter because he was inhabiting it now? Or was today no more real than yesterday? Francis couldn't understand why all these fucking questions kept forming like bubbles in his brain. To burst with little charges of electricity that made him wince. Didn't know what they meant — the questions. Never mind the answers. Maybe they'd always been in his head. Lying dormant like seeds in the desert. Triggered by a shower of rain. What triggered him? Voices? He halfknew the Voices were only himself. All himself. Halfknew. He didn't know. But the questions were coming up fast lately like green shoots of grass. Could be these Voices had come to help him. Out of him. Self. Maybe he shouldn't be so hostile to them. If he listened a bit more he might find the answers and then the questions would go away. No more electric bubbles. No more green shoots. Francis had enough fucking problems without worrying about the meaning of the fucking Universe. It was better the way it had been. Simpler! Simplicity. Stillness.

'Here we are ...'

Glendora carried in a tray and put it down on the black polished dining table in the middle of the studio. Francis got up and walked across. She kissed him and pushed him down onto a chair.

'I hope you like lobster.'

'Lobster?'

'It's a special occasion, Frankie!'

Francis didn't know whether he liked lobster or not. Glendora returned to the kitchen and came back a few minutes later with strawberry sauce and a vegetable cocktail of spinach, beansprouts, peppers, peas and sweet chestnuts. She'd already opened a bottle of Chardonnay and lit a couple of pink candles.

'Very, very salubrious!'

'A very salubrious occasion.'

'I never knew you could cook ...'

'Several things you might not know, Frankie.'

'Is there? What?'

'Don't worry. Now that you're here ... you might find out.'

They ate in silence and listened to the sassy sound of Nina Simone putting a spell on them. The room acquired a strange aroma. At first Francis thought it was the expensive food but then it seemed to be something else. A colour he couldn't think of. Violet. Not warm — but not cool either. A Glendora smell. It belonged to her. The woman. It overpowered his own turquoise smell but he didn't mind. The food tasted unusual but not unappetising and after a while the violet and turquoise mixed to make a vivid terre-verte.

'Any news about America?'

'No.'

'Nothing?'

'Nothing. Mind you ...'

'What?'

'Nothing.'

Francis looked at the food in front of him. It looked back.

'What, Frankie?'

'Well ... I'm not sure if the bastards are holding out on me.'

'Holding out?'

'Hard to explain. Just something in the air ... Matthew said something.'

'What?'

'Nothing.'

'Frankie ...'

'It's nothing, Glenny. Probably me. You know what I'm like.'

She stopped searching. Francis lit a cigarette and picked at his plate. It was strange that he hadn't heard any more about the tour. Somefuckingthing should have been arranged by now. Were the wankers crowding him out? Better fucking not be! He'd fucking kill someone! No more no killing. Thinking about it made Francis feel restless. Anxious. Wanted to go straight over and ask Percy Shillinger what the fuck was going on. Maybe better not to. Now. Now or never. Never?

'Anyway, Frankie ... there's something else ...'

'What else?'

Glendora paused. Hesitated. Afraid to say what she wanted to say.

'What else, Glenny?'

'If this thing falls through, Frankie ...'

'What thing?'

'The American thing ... you know what these tours are like ...'

Did she? How did she?

'What are they like?'

'Unpredictable. These groups ...'

Were they? How did she know that?

'What else?'

'They're very whimsical ...'

'What else?'

'How much do you need?'

'How much what?'

'Money. You know ... for the club ...'

'Twenty ... maybe a bit more. Twenty grand. To begin with. Why?'

'Some people I know are looking for someone ...'

'Some people you know? What people you know?'

'To go abroad and bring back some merchandise for them.'

An atmosphere of unreality began to creep over the room.

'What the fuck are you talking about, Glenny? What fucking people? People at the casino? What kind of fucking merchandise?'

'Yes ... people at the casino.'

'*I* know the people at the casino. *I* know the owners of the casino. If they wanted something they would have come to me, not you.'

'These are ... punters ...'

'Punters? What kind of fucking punters, Glenny?'

She could see him getting angry and she stopped talking. The doubts were back. She'd thought this would be a good time to bring the subject up. Wrong. Wrong time. Wrong thing. Francis stared at her. Straight at her. Eyes on fire. Burning right into hers. Firebeat! Too close for comfort. She was afraid. He'd never hit her but there was always a first. And a last time. And she knew if he started. He wouldn't stop.

'What punters, Glenny?'

'Just these guys, Frankie ... let's forget about it. It's nothing anyway.'

Cold silver silence. Even Nina Simone stopped singing. Francis continued to stare straight into her. Silverbeat! His eyes tore her bones from her body and she felt all limp and loppy. She knew this wasn't going to go away and wished she'd never started it.

'Abroad where?'

'Amsterdam ... I think.'

'And the merchandise?'

'Drugs ... I think.'

'For fuck's sake!'

Francis swiped the dinner things off the table and onto the floor. He stood up, grinding glass and green vegetables under his shoes and Glendora put her hands up to shield her face. Worst case scenario. She wanted the flat back. To herself. He wasn't minding her any more. He was going to murder her.

'Sorry! Sorry, Frankie.'

He didn't speak for a moment. Neither did he move. Just stood there like an angry statue. Angrybeat! Glendora slowly lowered her hands when she realised the inevitable was not inevitable after all. Francis turned away and walked across the room. Lit another cigarette.

'Who are these bastards? Why are they talking to you about these things? I'll cut their fucking balls off and feed them to their fucking whoremothers!'

'I'm sorry, Frankie. Please ...'

Poured himself a large glass of Jack Daniels and drank it down in one. Then poured another and paced the room with fists clenched.

Glendora didn't move. Sat at the dining table and hardly dared to breathe. Too late to breathe. Francis was confused. Didn't know what to do — whether to kick the shit out of her or tell her not to be so fucking naïve. What was she fucking up to? He was always able to count on her. Could always trust her. Nobody else — only her. What the fuck was she up to? Who the fuck was she talking to when he wasn't there? What were the several things he might not know?

'What kind of drugs?'

'I don't know.'

'Don't pretend you don't know, Glendora. You're not fucking naïve. I'm not.'

'It was just a casual conversation ... there were no details.'

Francis felt as if reality was outside himself. As if he was looking out at it but couldn't get to it.

'How much money?'

'Five thousand.'

'That's a fucking detail all right!'

'I only overheard, it Frankie. I wasn't told ... they weren't talking directly to me.'

'Who were they talking to then? Maybe you were meant to overhear ...'

Francis sat in one of the black leather armchairs. Heart. Beat. Glendora sensed she was safe now and moved slowly towards him. Like a small animal senses things. When to lie down and when to stand up. When to stay and when to run. The time to run hadn't come. Yet. She sat on the arm of the chair and kissed the top of his head. Francis put his arm round her waist and pulled her into him. She obviously didn't know what she was doing and it was their first day of living together. Got to be calm. And civilised. Ignore the dogmatisation and propaganda and not let it get to him. Difficult not to let it get to him. Have to warn her to be more careful. Counterfeiters everywhere! She looked pale for a black girl and that worried him. What were the bastards doing to her? The pendulum clock on the studio wall began to tick. It might have been ticking all the time but Francis didn't hear it until now. Sounded like hammer striking anvil. Every strike an exploding second in his life. Tick. Dang. Tock. Dong. His drink hand began to twitch. Then shake. Francis put the glass down on the floor. Felt as if his face was contorting involuntarily. Twisting. Becoming grotesque. Abnormal. Convulsive. Insane. Was it? Glendora ignored his dilemma and was saying how nice it would be now they were together at last. But she was no longer near him. She floated away and he tried to call her back but his mouth was twisted into a horrible shape and no words would emerge. Every finger in the paintings on the wall pointed at him. Shouted something. What? What had he done now? About to get up and slash them into pieces and burn them into ashes — but Glendora came back and took the cigarette butt from his fingers. She stubbed it out in the ashtray.

'Who were those guys, Glenny?'

'I don't know their names, Frankie ... they don't come in very often. I think they're from Manchester.'

'Manchester?'

'Yes, sounded like it ... maybe Moss Side.'

'You'd know that ... what Moss Side sounds like?'

How would she know that? Francis was confused. And his confusion made him afraid. And his fear made him angry. And his anger made him dangerous.

'They're Yardies.'

'Black boys?'

'Yes.'

'Jesus, Glenny ...'

'I don't know them, Frankie.'

'You must know them.'

'Only as punters. They were talking round my table and I told them I might know someone ...'

'Jesus Christ! You told them what?'

'You know ... who might be interested.'

This was getting serious. She was talking to people he didn't know. The Heroingod? And what did she say about him?

'You didn't give them my fucking name?'

'Of course not!'

'Do they know yours?'

'Only the casino name ... on my tag. Countess.'

'Thank fuck for that!'

'I'm sorry, Frankie. I won't mention it again.'

'To who?'

'Anybody.'

Glendora poured him another Jack Daniels and lit him a cigarette. Francis walked to the window while she cleared up the broken dishes from the floor.

He saw the woman in black outside on the street.

Her voice drifts up to me through the glass of the window panes. Telling me not to be afraid of the drug, Jalal al-Din? What drug? No drug's a good drug. It depends ... She says I have my drug ... have I not? Only ganja and speed ... sometimes a little coke. And the other things? What other things? The strength ... the power ... the riches? No. I tell her she's got it wrong ... those are different things. Are they, Jalal al-Din? What's this got to do with you, Khananimal? I thought you were only interested in killing? She says she knows about the drug, Jalal al-Din. So do I. Asks me what I know? That it's bad fucking news? She says every man needs the *thing* that gets him where he wants to go. What about women? Explaining that most people live lives of pain or boredom or poverty and they long to escape ... just as you do. Tells me there are different ways ... The drug is alcohol and gold and love and religion. There are many windows in the wall. Sure ... and hate and killing ... Every man chases his own dragon. That is all it is. She says to transcend the world for even a few minutes is a longing of the soul. The other things don't fucking kill. Do they not? She sneers at me and says men do not follow their drug because they want to be bad, Jalal al-Din. Do women? They do it because they want to be good. They want to escape. Telling me that sanity and sobriety will only take me so far. After that it must be religion ... or war. I must make my choice. Jalal al-Din. God's not a killer. God is the worst killer of all. Don't fucking say that! In the end, death is the only addiction. She says there's nothing I can do to get rid of death. You are death, Jalal al-Din. You came into existence together and you will disappear together. I'm life! I'm everything! I'm conscious ... subconscious ... abconscious ... superconscious. She laughs a low growl and says to me the way to superconscious is through sub conscious and the way to subconscious is through the chemistry of the animal. We are made up of those chemicals. We *are* those chemicals. Do you understand? No I don't! Of course you do. It is just a matter of control. Control and understand. Calling me to come out of the darkness of conscience ... of scruple, Jalal al-Din. She knows I want to. No I don't! Yes you do. Do I? Yes. She knows I've been thinking about it. How does she know? Because you are a man like me! But you're a ... Even though I am a God. She says I need no longer be afraid of the world ... of what the world will do to me. Spit in its eye! I'm no longer a boy. I'm a man so I must stop pretending there's a better side. Accept what *is*! I'm not sure what is ... whether it is or whether it isn't. Physiological fact does not invalidate spiritual experience, Jalal al-Din. Bad ain't fucking good neither, no matter how you phrase it. She says maybe not.

But to be really good ... I have to admit that I'm bad!

Glendora returned from the kitchen with coffee and reclined on the floor. She unlaced Francis' shoes and removed his socks and massaged his feet. Dark outside and she pulled the curtains and switched on a low light in the corner of the studio. The imitation logfire flickered on their faces and cast dancing shadows up the walls. Francis relaxed again and put all the recent shit out of his mind. This was their first day of living together and he wasn't going to let no wiseguy spoil it for his little Glenny. Glenny goodhumour. The bourbon and the heat made him drowsy and he left the coffee untouched. Eyes half-closed in the opaque room. And they said that fifteen billion years ago Space and Time began. What was out there before that? And maybe in another fifteen billion years it would all end. What would come after it? What would fill the space left behind? Outside in the night sky, light from a supernova star that exploded back near the beginning of it all was just becoming visible. Look up there and see the past. And going faster takes more time. Travel to the future? $X^n+Y^n=Z^n$. Did the past, the present and the future exist together or was it all just a figment of his imagination? Did Time flow at all — or did he just need it to? Was it something he himself created when he measured it? Maybe everything really just *was*. That's all! Francis could feel the vibrations of the Universe. $G+\Lambda g=8\pi T$. He could hear it calling out to him and he wanted to go to it. Needed. To dissolve in it. To go back to the spiritual ancestors of the dreamtime — Alcheringa and Tjukurpa. And know that nothing is lived but everything is re-lived. And he saw that, in the same way all events are interlinked with each other — part of each other — become each other — die and reincarnate as other events — he might just have some responsibility in it all.

Glendora shook him gently and he woke. He was disorientated for a moment. Unsure of his surroundings. She looked at him like the silhouette of some ghost. Blue-black in the glimmer-room. Negative. Image. Floating in his imagination. A shining background aura round her whole body. Like in the pictures of saints. Or the Syàmasundara. She took the bourbon glass from his hand, unbuttoned his shirt and said softly.

'Bed.'

chapter twenty

chapte r twenty

chapte r twenty

Francis Page continued to work out at the Hardcore gymnasium. Although his training partner lately was Glendora because Francis had the fuckinghump and as little to do with the other bastards as possible these days. Including Matthew Moore. Glendora helped him with his sets and reps and anyway his workout wasn't as heavy now as it used to be. Higher reps and lighter weights would keep him cut and he wasn't all that bothered about size any more. That was for the fucking poseurs and pricks. Glendora circuit-trained and encouraged Francis to come round with her in a routine that he'd once have regarded as embarrassing in the fucking extreme. Only for fucking squash players and ponces.

John Nightingale and his ironhoof friends down the other end of the weightroom working out with the loose stuff. A voice inside told Francis he and Nightingale should *not* be in the gym at the same time. Somebody got their day wrong. The irons minced and admired themselves in the mirrors and Nightingale watched with a wicked eye as Francis followed Glendora round the circuit. Something in the air.

Francis could sense it. Incidentair! Dangerair! Dangerbeat! Nightingale deliberately talked loudly so he could be heard all over the weight-room. Waving an aeroplane ticket in his hand.

'Yeah, I'm flying back to the Big Apple, you guys. Soon as New Year's over. Home for a tour of the good old USA. Know some dudes down in Sheridan Square who're real swingers and I might not come back once I bounce with those boys. Make some real dough and quit the scene. *Veni, vidi, vici!*'

The smartman knew his words would attract attention and Francis fumed fiercely down the room. Whatwasgoingonbeat? Nightingale blew him a kiss and smiled that dangerous smile. Glendora noticed Francis wasn't following her any more and came back from the hyper-extension to see what was wrong.

'You hear what that pillowbiter said?'

'No.'

'He's got a fucking ticket.'

Francis allowed the shoulder-press stack to slam down onto the apparatus.

'A ticket to what?'

'Ride! Plane ticket to fucking America!'

'Oh ...'

'It's for the tour, Glenny ... the Antichrists' Tour.'

'How can you be sure, Frankie?'

How could she not see? What was going on?

'Because he fucking said it. There's somefuckingthing going on. I knew it. Where's my fucking ticket ... eh?'

'I don't know ...'

'Nobody's even told me when the thing *is* ... never mind anything about fucking plane tickets.'

'Maybe it's just a wind-up, Frankie ...'

'Let's find fucking out!'

Glendora instinctively grabbed his arm but Francis was already on his way down the weightroom. To Nightingale and the musclemen forcing out heavy reps of incline flyes.

'Frankie ... wait ...'

'Not waiting any longer!'

Glendora held onto him — dragged along by momentum.

'Wait ... he wants you to do this. He shouldn't be in here the same time as you anyway. Frankie ... let's leave ...'

Francis ignored her and nosed to nose with the smartman in a matter of seconds. Serious situation developing in fitnessland. Gym instructors stood by after summoning up reinforcements. Nightingale's training crew took a couple of steps back from the bench.

'You should *not* be here same day as me, Francis Page. You badass *brutumfulmen*.'

Francis didn't want to verbalise with the man. But this time there was no way not to.

'What's this shit about aeroplane tickets?'

'Ain't you got yours yet? Obviously an oversight.'

'This is the fucking tour, isn't it?'

'Sure is. Flying on the twenty-fourth of January. *Quo vadis*?'

'Who gave out the tickets?'

Francis knew the answer before he asked the question.

'Who d'you reckon, Francis Page? Percy the *vir princeps* Shillinger.'

'Dirty. Dirty. Dirty fucking bastard!'

Glendora kept pulling at Francis' arm and gradually moved him inch by inch back from John Nightingale. The mustered gym instructors sweated in anticipation and an unusual silence crept round the weightroom. Other users sensed something was going on and stopped what they were doing. Glendora continued to pull Francis backwards — away from the confrontation. While he locked glares with the American's gloat and looked for any reason to attack. Slightest excuse.

Francis was manoeuvred slowly back to where he began. The smartman's voice after him —

'Francis Page ... you losing your memory now? You ain't supposed to be in here. Because you make trouble all the time. *Et emoriar, quam sit tibi copia nostri.*'

Glendora turned Francis round to face her.

'Whose day is it to be in here, Frankie?'

'Mine!'

'Why is he here then?'

'How the fuck do I know?'

'You sure it's your day?'

'Yes! No ... I don't fucking know!'

'Let's go.'

Glendora tried to get Francis to leave the gym.

'I don't give a fuck whose fucking day it is. I just want to know about this tour. What the fuck is happening, Glenny?'

'I don't know, Frankie. You can sort it out at the club.'

'You're right! I'll sort the fucker out with Shillinger.'

Matthew Moore came into the weightroom at that moment. Kitted out and ready to train. Signalled a greeting to John Nightingale before beginning his warm-up routine. Then he saw Francis.

'Francis ... what the fuck are you doing here?'

'Same as you, Matthew. Free country, ain't it?'

'It's not your day ...'

'You can fucking say that. Again. Yes!'

Matthew came across to Francis and lowered his voice.

'You know you and Nightingale shouldn't be here at the same time.'

'Maybe it's not his fucking day?'

'For fuck's sake, Francis ...'

Glendora was still holding onto Francis' arm — trying to pull him towards the changing rooms.

'You've fallen over the fucking fence a bit lately, Matthew.'

'What kind of a fucking remark is that?'

'Have you got a ticket to America?'

'A what?'

'A fucking ticket! You know what I'm talking about.'

Matthew Moore didn't answer immediately. He looked away. His Alpacagod looked back at Francis.

'Well ... it's not that I actually ...'

'You have one as well, haven't you?'

'Francis ...'

'What sort of a fucking friend are you? Jesus ... you can't trust no cunt!'

'Listen ...'

Francis didn't want to listen. Glendora pulled harder on his arm.

'Never mind fucking listen, Matthew. Why don't you just fuck over there with the fucking queers.'

'It's your own fault, Francis.'

'Bound to be. How do you make that out?'

'If you don't know, then ... never mind.'

Matthew Moore walked away. Francis wanted to follow and punch the fucking face off him. Heartbeat! Friend or no fucking friend. Along with all the rest of the pricks in this fucking place.

'Sort it out with Percy Shillinger, Francis.'

Glendora's voice soft and pleading came from somewhere a long way off. Could feel her small hand on his arm as she gently pulled him towards the door. Air in the gym heavy. Oppressive. Purple. Tasted of decay. Francis moved in slomo. Followed Glendora's face walking backwards ahead of him. Her mouth still moving but he could hear no words. Room full of low growls and stripped teeth. Hackles high on the backs of necks. Blood covered the sense cells of the brain. Neurotrans-mitters. Mission impossible. They moved towards the door and it moved away from them. Ugly faces across the gym. Sneering. Sniggering. Francis wanted to smash them to pulp. Fracture skulls. Rupture vital organs. Shatter kneecaps. Gouge out eyes. Bite off ears. But he couldn't get away from Glendora's gentle grip. His feet would only move in her direction — towards the door which shrunk down to the size of a catflap and he knew he'd never get through it. But he had to. Otherwise there would be a killing! Lights in the weightroom grew dim. Couldn't see the leering faces any more. Nightingale or his shirtlifter friends — gym people — Matthew Moore — not even Glendora. But he could still feel her hand leading him. Somewhere. Where? Somewhere he ought to be. Away from where he was. Where he didn't want to be. He felt water.

Something inside my head or maybe not saying that water is so therapeutic, Shegetz. I don't need treatment. You haf been talking about dreams. Saying it knew Freud and why don't I ask what I want to ask? I say I won't leave my daughters and she knows ... It asks who's she? Jeanne. Fiona? Says I should read *Die Traumdeutung*? Or *Studien über Hysterie*? I'm not fucking mad! The voice is the mad one ... and Freud's fucking mad as well! Vat is madness anyway, Shegetz? Don't tell me it's relative. You already told me it's relative. If you tell me it's relative again I'll go fucking mad. No no no ... sniggering and saying of course, it's given many names by ze medical und scientific communities ... paranoia, mania, psychosis, schizophrenia. My son vas schizophrenic. Eduard. Don't want to keep fucking talking about it. Talk. Talk. Talk. Talk. Talk. Says it's merely speculating. I ask who the fuck it is to speculate about anything? A disembodied voice! I haf told you, I knew Freud und he vas ze vorld's most famous neurologist und psychoanalyst. Sigmund shitarse! I say nobody believes all that bollocks any more. Don't you believe it, Shegetz? About wanting to fuck your mother? Except maybe the black cunts ... who keep going on about it. Do you vant to fuck your mozer? No I do not! Vat do you vant zen? I don't know. Vhen vill you know? Soon ... maybe. Be more specific. I don't fucking know ... it should stop asking me fucking questions. It is my job as a scientist. To rationalise. Normalise? Logicise. Asking now if I dream? It knows I do. Sexual dreams? There it fucking goes again ... every fucking thing ain't sexual. It vas to Freud. Isn't it to you? No! Really? Really! Asking me if I've heard of the Super-Ego? Ze Id und Ego? Sometimes I don't know what I hear. Am I hearing things? Sometimes I think I know ... then I don't. Ah ha! Ze concept of introvert und extrovert. You need a psychiatrist, Shegetz! Says maybe I ought to talk to Jung. Who? Carl Gustav. I don't need a doctor. I said a psychiatrist. Leave me alone! Talk to Jung. I'm not going insane! You are already insane. Help me then! Talk to Jung. Where is he? He's dead. Oh Jesus ... You could talk to him. I already have. Then you are definitely insane.

'*Quos Deus vult perdere prius dementat.*'

Francis turned and saw a hazy silhouette through the steam of the shower-room. Moving in slomo. Heartbeat! A highpitched white noise in the air. Going straight through his brain. No other sound in the ghostlike steam-mist. Francis moved closer to the silver shadow.

'*Non mihi, non tibi, sed nobis.*'

The words were away in the distance. But the man was close. Wet. Warm. Whispering. Like the music of Mahler. Francis felt the man touch him. He didn't move. Felt the man's hands on his body. Felt the man's breath on his face. Felt his own desire. Inside himself. Desirebeat! Hardening. Bloodfilled. Aggressive.

'*Contraria non contradictoria sed complementa sunt.*'

Francis felt a continual indefinite tremulous naked pining fear. Of something deep within himself. Something that was unidentifiable and unaddressable and emerging in the humid shower-room.

'*Tange me ...*'

Francis hit the man in the face with his forehead and he fell back against the tiled wall. Blood mingled with water.

'*Sine ira ... sine ira ...*'

Francis hit the man again with his clenched fist. Again and again and again and again. Until he slipped down onto the floor. Crimson coloured steam and the whole room red. Francis turned the limp body over onto its stomach. Reached his arms round the waist. Barelyconscious. Trying to talk. Say his Latin shit. Francis pulled him up into position and entered him from behind. The man groaned and tried to move away from the violence. Francis held him round the waist with one arm and pressed on the back of his neck with the other. Screaming. Screaming. Screambeat!

'You fucking asked for it! You fucking asked for it! You fucking ... fucking ... fucking ...'

Francis threw the man to the floor when he finished and moved back across to his own shower-head. Red steam everywhere and he could see nothing. Nobody. Just the distant words.

'*De profundis* ...'

And Merlin sent Childe Roland to the castle to save Burd Ellen and Childe Roland to the dark tower came and nobody knows what happened to him. The piercing white noise faded gradually away and left behind complete and utter silence. Not even the sound of water. Not even the smell of blood. Not even the taste of violence. All gone. Washed away.

'Let's not fucking fall out, Francis ...'

'Matthew ...'

The water from the shower-head was cold and ran down Francis' body onto the marble floor. He was naked and alone in the place — except for Matthew Moore. No steam and a stream of clear water running away into the channel and disappearing down the drain grille. Francis didn't know how long he'd been there. Could have been minutes. Hours. Days.

'I thought you'd be gone by now.'

'Did you?'

'But I'm glad you're still here. Old friends shouldn't fall out.'

'No ...'

Matthew turned on his shower. Water spilled down his body.

'About America ... It's to do with that Pigg guy.'

'Who?'

'You pissed in his drink.'

'I did?'

'Talk to Shillinger about it. He might be able to sort it out.'

'Ok ... thanks, Matthew. I'll do that. I will.'

Francis dried himself off and got dressed. Glendora was waiting for him in the sportsclub foyer.

'Frankie ... what took you so long?'

'Sorry.'

'I thought you'd gone back in there ...'

'I was talking to Matthew.'

'What about?'

'America.'

Francis and Glendora climbed into the Jaguar — parked around the corner in Ramillies Place. He started the engine and pulled away slowly. Heading east until they stopped outside The Cajun Chicken and Francis parked the car and followed Glendora inside. She'd already ordered coffee and was looking at the menu. Francis felt as if he was waking from a dream and reality returned slowly. Couldn't remember clearly what had happened. If anything had happened. Something to do with the recent moodswings. From love to accusation to love to accusation and he could tell for the first time that Glendora was getting fed up with it. He was getting a bit fed up with her too. All her healthy habits. Found his humour turning resentful at times. Like then. And now.

He wanted something full of saturated fat and carbohydrate and genetically altered ingredients. Like a cheeseburger and chips. Or a ten-topped pizza or even a cardiacfuckingkebab. The fact that Glendora was a health freak seemed more than a bit ironic to him. Considering she was a whore and an addict and probably a lot more besides. But since he saved her she'd started to make decisions for herself and since he moved in she was making decisions for both of them. She decided these days where they went, what they did, what they ate. Watched. Spoke about. Read. Imagined. Believed in. Not again! Had to fucking stop! She had begun for the first time to look for the man behind the man. The man she never needed before. The man who wasn't there. The aesthete. The sophisticate. Beyond the brute. Things were changing again!

Francis let her have her way a lot with the little things because he had so many bigger things on his mind. But it mattered now. Sitting in this restaurant. She was swallowing him up. And all this shit about drugsmuggling and Amsterdam and fucking Yardie bastards!

'I'll have the chicken Maryland with sweetcorn and Frankie will have the fish jambalaya.'

'No I won't!'

'What's that, honey?'

Glendora paused. Looked at Francis.

'I want a cheeseburger.'

'Don't be silly ... you can't get that in here.'

'Why not?'

'It's Cajun and Creole cuisine, Frankie ... better for you.'

'I want a fucking cheeseburger!'

The standingby waitress bent over the table and sniffed.

'We could do the gentleman meatballs and southern mash?'

'I want a cheeseburger ... with chips!'

'Francis ...'

The waitress stepped back a bit from the table. Took out her order pad and pencilled with a small stammer.

'Chicken Maryland and burger with fries.'

Francis called after her as she slipped quickly away.

'A *cheese*burger!'

After dinner they drove in silence back to the flat in Dalston Lane. Glendora climbed briskly upstairs and busied herself inside with this and that. Francis just sat on a chair in the studio and looked out the window into the darkening night. When it was time, they both changed into their working clothes and went their separate ways.

chapter twenty-one

chapte r twenty-one

chapte r twenty-one

Vomen eh. Zey are not normal, Shegetz. I ask what *is* fucking normal these days? It says maybe I think it's all a big joke? I say I'd be happy to understand even that much ... even if everything was pointless. It's the unreality that I can't cope with ... It asks if I want a scientific analysis? Can you give me one, Scientistvoice? Let's see ... normal. Opposite to *ab*normal ... or *sub*normal. Vat most people believe zemselves to be. Who says? Zey says. Ze normal ones. But ze laws of physics haf no in-built asymmetry ... zey work chust as vell goink backvards as forvards. Death und Time are linked togezer. I know that! But there's many times to die ... isn't there, Scientistvoice? Many deaths ... It says Lieserl died of scarlet fever. It vasn't my fault. It was! And asks me why so few *normale mentschen* are near ze door to Nirvana and ze rest of ze rejects still stuck in ze mud of metempsychosis? Don't change the subject. Und when you get zere, vat comes after zat? I say it doesn't make sense. And it's telling me that everything has a scientific explanation. An explanation in science. I shout no fucking thing makes *sense!*

Take it from me, Shegetz, und don't listen to any of zose crazies. You vant to do vat *yourself* says. I say when I listen sometimes it make sense and sometimes Alienchrist makes sense and sometimes Animalkhan makes sense and sometimes Eyeless and Earless make sense but, all together, nothing makes sense. Chust listen to reason. Reason? Reason. Ze *menouvolim* think zey're so damn smart. The fucking smartarses? Ze dopes understand nuzink, Shegetz. Talk about 'ab' and 'sub' all of ze time ... in ze paradox-ridden realms of ze Universe und ze subatomic, ve vill see nozink ve recognise as normal! Ze *schmucks* chust do not understand, so zey get frightened. Saying to me there's no need to get frightened of strange stuff, Shegetz. It is chust stuff zat doesn't yet fit in mit ze *so-called* physical laws. Dark dirty rooms with alcoholics and addicts. That's all! *Toyt des moyekhs*! Tells me sure, science vill explain everyzink eventually, chust need to make ze connections. They're all fucking crazy ... aren't they? Of course zey are! Everybody is crazy. Or nobody's crazy. Everyone or no one. Cold rainstreets at night. Vomen especially. Saying now the thing is, women aren't normal ... in the same sense as men. More *shtoompapa* zan men. Women? Oh for sure, men are senders und vomen are receivers. Ze ladies are darklunar. Invisible und hidden. And you must also know ... zey haf lower levels of activity in ze cortex of ze brain und believe zey can see things clearer zan ze *chochomim*. That definitely explains a fucking lot ... Zere is logic in everyzink. Even in madness I ask? It says nothing is unexplainable. Stinking policecells. Just because there's somethings I can't explain now, don't mean I'll never be able to explain them? Vat you see mit your eyes shut doesn't haf higher significance zan vat you see mit zem open. Shopdoorways. I say it sometimes seems to me that the fantasies are the real things and the rest is just fucking chaos. Are you mad? You already told me I was. Did I? Listen, Shegetz, ze past is not fixed und unalterable. Who wants to talk about the fucking past? I say I have to get back to work now. It says understanding only comes if it's called and in order to explain anything, you have to explain everything! The wiseguy smartarses can't explain everything! Of course zey can't. You just said they could. I *did not* say zey could! I said *in ze future*! In *ze future*! Not now! God doesn't reveal himself in the facts of the world, Scientistvoice! Soupkitchenqueues. You are chust lookink for meaninks zat are palatable ... but not necessarily true, Shegetz. I'm looking for reason. Normality. Sorry. But you are chust like all ze ozer madmen who know ze time ... but not ze day. Like you? Chust like me! But don't you see, Shegetz ... ze *beheymes* call me *genius*!

'What about this crew of *macarras*?'

Agnes D'Argensola stood down in the street. Pointing at a group of young gits falling towards the club. Loud and obviously drunk and intimidating everyone they passed. Straight to the head of the queue. Pushing and shoving.

'Where do you *niños* think you are going?'

'Inside.'

'Oh no you are not.'

'You're a woman! And a dago. She's a dago woman, guys!'

The boys laughed. Agnes swung the handbag with the brick inside — clouted the foremost fucker across the side of his impudent head. He fell back against his friends and shook what he used for brains back into place.

'Jesus ... what the fuck was that?'

'What you'll get again if you do not fuck off!'

'Get her ... the fucking bitch!'

'Francis ...'

Love was a fucking mask for hatred and there was danger in accepting or giving it. No choice sometimes though. No choices. Lovehate. Hatelove. Francis Page snapped out of his inertia just as the mob of midgets surged forward. Put himself between them and Agnes. The queue took a couple of backward steps as the ringleader was picked up bodily and held feetdangling in the air. Pack of rowdy rat-heads stopped in their tracks. Whole crew of them openmouthed and backing into the road to be nearly killed by the kamikaze Paddington traffic. Francis followed them down to the kerbside — still holding their leader at armslength.

'Now ... why don't you lads do like the lady told you and fuck off!'

'It's Francis fucking Page ...'

'Jesus fucking Christ!'

'Sorry, Francis ... we didn't know this was your club.'

'Well you do now.'

'We're on our way ... don't worry ...'

The boys held their hands up to placate the bouncer.

'A very intelligent decision. You're not so stupid as you make out now, are you?'

'Any chance of getting in next week?'

'Any chance of staying sober?'

'Oh ... sure ... 'course, Francis ...'

Francis placed the boy gently on the ground and the likely lads trooped off — making threatening runs at the jeering queue as they went. Agnes came down and took Francis by the arm. Smell her! Smelled of sex. Smelled of life. Love. Lovehate. Hate! Hatelove.

'Thank you *mi héroe*.'

She kissed his cheek. He wiped it with his hand.

'They were harmless enough.'

'We make a good team, do we not Francis?'

'If you say so, Agnes.'

Francis felt guilty for wiping his cheek. He knew it hurt her. And eternal guilt was punishment for feeling guilty in the first place.

'I see your *princesa* is with you again tonight.'

'That's right. She's waiting for me to move inside.'

'Are you fucking her, Francis?'

'What sort of a question is that?'

'A simple enough one.'

'Well, it's none of your bloody business, Agnes!'

That was what always happened — as soon as he felt sorry for her she angered him with her stupid words.

'Give me the baby, Francis.'

'I will not!'

'You can fuck her as well if you want ... as long as it is not true.'

'As long as what's not true?'

'That she has the AIDS.'

'She hasn't got fucking AIDS, Agnes!'

'Would you be prepared to take the test?'

'What test? I haven't got AIDS either! Will you fuck off ... for fuck's sake!'

Francis was getting upset. Agnes was distracting him with her shit about babies and he didn't see the black limousine pulling up down the street. Neither did he notice Percy Shillinger and his minders getting out and sneaking into the Pink Peacock nightclub by the side entrance.

'Come on, Francis ... let us make the child.'

'I'm not making any more children ... with anyone!'

'*Por favor*, Francis?'

'Will you leave me alone, Agnes ...'

'*Bastardo*!'

'Call me what you like.'

Glendora emerged from inside the club. Whispered something into Francis' ear while Agnes eyed her with contempt. Stresstrigger! Francis stormed in through the doors, followed by the black girl. And Agnes left on her own to cope with the queue of airheads and acidhearts.

Percy Shillinger was holding court at a discreet balcony table. Francis took the stairsteps three at a time. Heartbeat! Followed way behind by Glendora. Shillinger sighed loudly when he saw them coming and all eyes turned to follow his. Francis like a mad bull. Madbeat! Bullbeat!

'What's happening, Shillinger?'

'Francis ... I thought you were outside?'

'I was, until I heard you sneaked in through the side door.'

'I don't sneak anywhere, Francis.'

'Is that right? How come I haven't seen you around here lately then?'

'Pressure of business, boy. Who's outside with Agnes?'

'No one now!'

Shillinger straight away dispatched one of his men down to tell George Dimitrov to get cover outside on the steps with Agnes. Before every shitbag in London came through the fucking door. Francis thought they already had!

'Francis, Francis ... what the fuck's eating you tonight?'

'You're reneging on me, Shillinger.'

'Reneging? In what way?'

Francis temporarily forgot what he wanted to say. What the angry words were.

'This American tour ... you promised me. The rest of them have their fucking plane tickets.'

'Ah, so that's it?'

Percy Shillinger took a small gold case from an inside pocket. He lit a cigarette and blew the smoke towards Francis.

'You know fucking well it is.'

'Listen, Francis ... we had so many wanting to come, we decided it would be better to take only single men. Less aggravation from the wives, if you see what I mean.'

'I'm a single fucking man, Percy!'

'No you're not. You're a married man with two children.'

'Angeline left me.'

The witchbitch. Shillinger smirked. Francis saw the smirk. Saw the sly wink of an eye towards the nearest minder.

'She did not? For fuck's sake ... I never knew. Why didn't someone tell me?'

'Everyone fucking knows.'

'I didn't, Francis. Nobody tells me fuck-all.'

'Well you know now, so you can give me back my fucking place.'

Shillinger sipped his drink. Looked up to see Glendora arriving at the table.

'No can do, boy. All the arrangements are made.'

Glendora tugged at Francis from behind.

'Don't worry about them, Frankie ... we don't need them ...'

'And who might this young lady be?'

'Francis' bit of brown sugar, boss.'

'Mind your fucking mouth, you!'

Francis beat the balcony table with his fist. Beatbeat! Knocked over expensive drinks and made Percy Shillinger move back in his chair so's not to get his Armani suit wet. Minders moved closer. Big fists and bulges in their coats. Heart!

'You're fucking me about, aren't you, Percy?'

Shillinger wiped a few specks of liquid off his jacket with a red silk handkerchief.

'Jesus, Francis, you've known me ... how long?'

'Long enough to know you're a two-faced cunt! You brought me down in the first place.'

'How did I do that?'

Francis didn't know. Couldn't remember. But he did. The bastard did — no matter what he said.

'I don't know ... but you did.'

'You brought yourself down, Francis. Did it all on your own, son. You're a dinosaur. Things are done differently these days.'

'I'll kill you, Shillinger. Some fucking day I'll kill you.'

'Ok, ok ... that's enough! I'll tell you the truth, Francis. The reason you're not coming is because you're an arsehole. Is that plain enough for you?'

Beat! Francis struck Shillinger straight in the face. Knocked him backwards off his chair with blood spouting from his nose and a top tooth stuck in a bottom lip. Minders immediately into action. Lead pipes laid across Francis' head and back. Didn't feel a fucking thing. No pain. No sense. No feeling. Not even the hot blood that stained the white collar of his shirt red. He was like a lunatic. Lunbeat! Abeat! Ticbeat! One minder went over the side of the balcony onto the crowd below. George Dimitrov's cue to send up reinforcements. Francis was overpowered among the debris of upturned tables and torn suits and blood and broken glass. Glendora tried to help but she was too slight to make much of an impression. She picked up a heavy ashtray and smashed it across one bastard's head. He punched her in the face as he spun round. Sent her flying across the floor. Crazyfuckingbeat! Francis struggled back to his feet with renewed frenzy. Scattering legs and arms and lead pipes in all directions. A club hammer appeared from nowhere and embedded itself into the back of his head. Dull sound of skullbone on steel. A groan. Francis sank slowly to his knees. When the minders regrouped they grabbed him and Glendora and dragged the pair of them across to a side door. Slung out onto the wet concrete of the alley that ran alongside the club. Galvanized dustbin lids crashing to the ground and frightened cats screamed away from the scene of slaughter. Percy Shillinger appeared behind his men with a bloodstained handkerchief held up to his face. Pushed his way through to the front.

'You're fucking finished, Page! I'll fucking tell you that! You'll never fucking work in this fucking town again!'

Glendora helped Francis over to a wall. Just beginning to regain consciousness. Unconsciousbeat. Semi-consciousbeat. Consciousbeat.

Shillinger out in the alley strutting up and down and pointing his finger at them. Francis saw him through a bloody veil. Saw the demon. Bertie the bollocks. Konrad Fichte. The King of Tangut. The enemy. God's enemy. Francis made a mad run back into the mob. Struck Percy Shillinger a heavy blow to the side of the head which floored the bastard into the garbage on the ground. Francis kicked him in the stomach and a stream of yellow vomit spewed from his lying mouth. Mixing with the blood and bullshit. Baseball bats hummed a sick little tune in the early morning air and Francis was beaten back across the alley and onto the ground. Blood poured from his face and ears and hands and head. Heeaarrtt. Blows kept coming in — even after he relapsed into unconsciousness. Beeaatt.

Glendora crouched over Francis and only when the minders couldn't hit him without hitting her did they let up. She screamed at them to leave him alone. He'd had enough. They were going to kill him. That was the idea. They cursed and swore and moved menacingly back across the alley. Giving Francis a few kicks for good measure and calling him a cunt and spitting on Glendora. Percy Shillinger was helped away and the side door of the Pink Peacock slammed shut and all silent again. Except for Glendora's sobs and whispers from the queue-crowd that gathered at a safe distance to see what lunatic was getting himself killed.

Where am I? Flying, man. Flying where? Through omneity. Where's that shithead Shillinger? He says not to worry about anyone else, because I'm with him, Chela. Jesus fucking Christ ... You got it. What's happening? Tells me I'm fireflame. Pureflame. Set free in a metamorphosis of matter. Watch out for the UFOs! They're FOs up here. Fucking Outofthisworlds? We know what they are. Do we? Do you? Well ... as far as anyone can know what anything is. Or where they are. I ask him if we're in or out? Out or in? He asks me if I know the difference, Chela? What's to say we aren't in the innerspace ... y'know, like inside the subatomic Universe? He asks who's been talking to me now? Zillions of fucking germs flying about. Cells. Microbes and amoebas and protozoa and other dinky little duodecimo shit. Maybe we're just something the same ... flying inside the belly of an enormous fucking cow. Tells me I'm losing touch, man. And he's Christofthe-coalmines. That was Earless. I'm the Christ of the Cosmos. I ask him where he's been? Busy. Doing what ... your father's business? Tells me I ain't the only schizophrenic in the world. I'm not a schizophrenic! Saying it's nothing to be ashamed of, Chela. Get me back down ... or back out. But he won't. Until I tell him. What? That I'll fight myself to find myself. I can't! You gotta! Just get me down ... out. Say the word! What word? Love, Chela. Love! No. I won't. It's too neat for me ... two dimensional ... obvious to the point of being null and void. Tells me I'm confused, man ... scared. I was. But I'll be ok. Better. Be better. Better be. He reckons I must clear my perceptions of the *tsatsa* ... blow away the clouds of smallself. Break the chains of language. Destroy the ladder, Chela. Destroy the ladder. If I don't, I might climb back down again. I think he wants too much from me ... something I never was and never can be ... You can, Chela! They won't let me. Who? Konrad. Annie. You ain't them. I am. I'm them. They're me. No! He says I don't have to go back to being them again. If I find the stillness ... then I'll find the answers I want without going nowhere at all. That's easy for him to say. He's shouting now ... just listen will you! Don't shout at me! You just won't listen! If you listen you'll hear what I hear. See what I see. Be easy for you to say what I say. There ... there's the coloured dream. There's the still landscape with no dramas and no symbols. D'you see it, Chela? I see it. Listen. What do you hear? Nothing! For sure! D'you know why? Why? Because there's nothing to hear, man. He says everything that's heard is the static of want. Want? Sure, want want want want want. Want what? Everything! You want this you want that and when you get what you want you don't want it no more ... you want something else. All your time spent wanting. Listening to the want static. I mean ...

ain't it obvious? I want to go back down ... out. Does it scare you, Chela? Yes! Ain't it beautiful ... and appalling at the same time ... the meaning? Yes! I want to get back down. It's driving me insane ... being here. Don't go back! I want to. Stay! No! Telling me to think about the transience of what I want to go back to, Chela. The total futility. What I want is only good when I don't have it. Once you get it ... it immediately loses its value. Desire destroys! Says I should just let the *mysterium tremendum* overwhelm me, Chela. The fireflame will purge all ego and self into divine purity. Don't keep fighting it, man. Embrace the pureflame of *le pays d'eclairement* and you'll be free. Forever!

'Frankie ...'

'Jesus ...'

'Frankie ... speak to me.'

'Am I back down? Am I out?'

Francis was still out there. Half out there. With Francis. Coming back into a body that was independent of — yet linked to — himself. And he struggled to find the person within the person.

'It's me, Glendora. You're raving ...'

'Glenny? There's a gun in the car ...'

'No, Frankie!'

'Get it for me. Get me the fucking gun!'

'An ambulance is on its way.'

'No! No ambulance! No fucking police!'

'Frankie ... you're hurt.'

'I'm ok. No ambulance! Get me up.'

Glendora helped him to his feet and they staggered down the alley and out into Eastbourne Terrace at the back of the Pink Peacock nightclub. Heeaarrt. Sirens could be heard through the thickness of the night and Glendora pleaded with Francis to get himself checked into the hospital. Beeaat. But he was in enough fucking trouble with the police — what with a court case for assault pending and all the rest of the shit that was going down in his life at that moment in time. And now this on top of it fucking all. No American tour. The bastards! Thank you very fucking much God!

A long painful struggle to the Jaguar. She eased him in onto the back seat and climbed behind the wheel. The engine shuddered as if in fear, then purred away down Praed Street towards the flyover. Francis lay flat on his back. Head on fire and clothes torn and covered in blood. Glendora drove slowly and carefully so as not to attract unwanted attention. The lights of the city shone down into his face as they flashed past in the early of the morning. He tried to block them out but his head hurt even worse when he closed his eyes. Tried to sit up. Couldn't. The left wrist was broke for sure and maybe his skull as well. Several ribs certainly shattered. Long as they hadn't punctured anything vital. He'd call Doctor Drummond once he got back to the flat. Drummond was used by all the villains who were out on the edge. Stabbings and gunshot wounds and all sorts of other illegal injuries. He was expensive but he kept his fucking mouth shut.

The Jaguar finally found its way to Dalston Lane and Glendora had difficulty getting Francis up the stairs. Had to rest on the steps several times and blood oozed from the wounds with even the slightest exertion. She thought he wasn't going to make it and she cried. For a while he thought he wasn't either. And he laughed.

chapter twenty-two

chapter twenty-two

chapter twenty-two

Christmas only round the corner and Francis Page feeling furious. Betrayed again. Denied again. Sold out and shit on. Doctor Drummond patched him up after an 'I can't be held responsible' argument about going into hospital. Francis wouldn't go and Doctor Drummond wasn't held responsible. The injuries were serious enough but Francis was a fast healer and a couple of weeks under Glendora's intensive care made him good as newgold.

But the fact remained that Percy Shillinger was now seeing to it that every club in the city gave him the coldshoulder. No fucking work from nofuckingwhere. Money too tight to talk about and Francis didn't like the idea of having to depend on Glendora for everything. Anything! She'd soon get fed up with that. Probably fed up already. No matter how much she thought of him. Things were bad. Bad bad bad fucking bad. Angeline sorted something out with the girls and they waited on the previous Sunday for their father to show up. But he didn't. How the fuck could he? The state he was in and with fuck-all money? The pain might have been receding — but not the ragebeat heart!

Dark evening. Sleet falling on the street outside the window. Glendora getting ready to go to work and Francis sitting back in one of the black studio chairs watching some blatant liar on the television. What was he going to do? The fucking bastards! Francis was feeling out on the edge. Despair down. Down. Was it only him? Or were there others in the world that life had it in for in a big way? Maybe the things some of the Voices told him were right! That he'd done something really diabolical in a previous life — apart from what he'd done in this one. And now paying the karmic price for it all. Could it be he was guilty? Of everyfuckingthing. That his mother and father and teachers and screws and other bastards who controlled him were right all along and he really was a fucking worthless wanker after all? And that's why things never worked out. Worth fuck-all! Fuckworth! Unlike all the other wideboys in the world who'd some little saving grace to recommend them. Some small minuscule thing that said they weren't pure shit altogether. Some *thing* — no matter how small. He had fuck-all! Francis was sure it was all over now. Couldn't see any comeback from here. No more dreaming and planning and believing like a complete cunt that every fucking thing would turn out all right in the end.

Believed now it wouldn't! Maybe time to throw in the white towel. Call the whole fucking thing a day? Get the gun from the glove compartment of the Jaguar and turn all the lights out. No more dreaming or drowning. Death. Animalkhan said it wasn't so bad — as long as you were prepared. Couldn't be more fucking prepared than this. A man had to know how to die to know how to live? Death was life? Death was growth? Death is the beginning! Dying preceeded death — and he was dying now. Who the fuck would miss him? Not Angeline — and the girls would soon forget he ever existed. Glendora would learn to live without him. She was doing that already. Strange how, when you got what you wanted, being without it didn't seem to be that desperate any more. Like Alienchrist said. Anyway — women like her always found someone to mind them. If it wasn't him it would be someone else. Agnes D'Argensola would have to find another stud to start a baby with and that was it. That was the sum fucking total of it all. The meaning of *his* life!

Glendora came into the studio wearing her black and gold croupier outfit. She looked down at Francis and smiled. Worst-case scenario. She was no nurse, but she knew she had to get him back to himself — or she'd go back to herself. One or the other.

'Ok?'

'Oh, sure. I'm fine.'

'This is not the end of the world, Frankie.'

'No ...'

'Listen, I thought you were a tough man.'

Was a tough man. Was he? Ever? Or was it all just a pretence? Francis didn't know. And he didn't care any more. And he didn't want to talk about it to Glendora. Argue with her about it. But he knew he had to. Otherwise —

'This sounds fucking ominous. Tough? It's being kicked out of me.'

'If you are, then get up and fight! Don't allow these people to see you down and out.'

'The thing is, Glenny ... I *am* down and out.'

'You're not! Show them you don't need them, Frankie.'

'The thing is, Glenny ... I *do* need them.'

'You don't!'

'What else is there? I can't even fucking work!'

'You'll think of something, Frankie ... I know you.'

But that was just it — she didn't know him. He didn't know himself. How could she know him when he didn't know himself? How could anyone know him? Had anyone ever known him? The known and unknown boy — man.

'Will I? Do you?'

'You'll have the last laugh on them. The smiles will be on the other side of their ugly faces by the time you're through.'

Glendora came and sat on his lap and hugged him. Get him back. He got her back when it was all over. Now it was her turn to repay him. She had to do it even if it put a strain on her. There was no alternative. There was — but she didn't want to think about it. The lifelight in her eyes made something stir inside Francis. It might have been spirit. It might have been spite. Didn't like being beaten. Maybe she was right. He *was* a fighter — Khananimal said so. A man was made to fight! If he didn't he was a woman! Heart! Heart! Heart was everything! Fuck the bastards! Them all! Glendora saw his expression change. She stood up and put on her coat. Blew back a kiss from the door. Francis turned away from the televisionliar.

'Listen, honey ...'

'Yes?'

'Find out a bit more about that thing.'

'What thing, Frankie?'

'You know ... the Amsterdam thing.'

Francis slept fitfully that night. Waking several times in a sweat and calling out for Glendora. Voices came into his head and went out again. Only to be replaced by others. New voices and old voices. Some making sense and others so disorganised and confusing that he couldn't trust them. Eventually he got up and went into the studio where he turned on the television and immediately turned it off again. 4.00 a.m. Glendora would be home in a couple of hours. He sat there in the dark and looked at the December sky through the window. Stars shining in the blackskyness of space and Francis wondered what else could be out there. If there was a Beginning — was there a Beginner? *Ex nihilo*.

Genesis. Big Bang or Moment of Creation? $E = mc^2$. Ratio of matter/energy to volume/space at moment of bang/creation = one quadrillionth of one percent of ideal. Miraculous? A little matter — a lot of energy. Awesome energy. The whole fucking thing. The full fucking monticule. Or was it all just an elaborate practical joke and he was the only complexchemical creature? All the rest airwave aliens. Scientistein said the Cosmos was expanding and spaces between galaxies getting bigger and bigger — moving further and further apart. End up as one great cold dead graveyard when all the stars burned themselves out? Or maybe the force of gravity would reverse it and start the whole thing contracting in on itself until everything was about as big as a fucking tennis ball — so dense and hot that it would implode into the ultimate black hole? Either way, Francis wondered what would be there then. In the space left behind. Big question. Too big for him as he sat there in the black chair. Too big and too small. Too complex and too simple. Obscure in the extreme and so obvious it was fucking ludicrous.

A more pressing problem was why he couldn't sleep at night any more. And why he couldn't stay awake during the day. At first he thought it was the nature of the work he'd been doing all his adult life. But lately it was becoming chronic. He wondered who these Yardies were and how Glendora had come to know them. Didn't quite believe her explanation and suspicion racked his mind. All these things. Watching and listening. Allthetime. Bugs. Videos. CCT. Internet. Satellites. Harassment. Stalking. Retina scans. Handgeometry. Fingerprints. Voicerecognition. Digitalisation. Telepathy. Genetic mapping. Were the bastards supplying her? With junk? Francis rose from the chair and systematically searched through the flat for signs of heroin use. But after an hour he found nothing incriminating and went to the kitchen and made coffee. He smoked a cigarette and listened to the sound of Northeast London waking up. At 6.45 a.m. he heard Glendora climbing the stairs. She came into the kitchen and kissed him.

'Couldn't sleep again?'

'How was the club?'

'Busy.'

'Must be a lot of loose money in London these days.'

'Most of them don't live in London.'

'Where then?'

'All over. Come from all over, Frankie ... especially coming up to Christmas.'

Glendora slipped her shoes off and poured herself a coffee. She moved into the studio and sat down. He followed. Sat opposite and stared curiously at her. She knew what he wanted her to say but she didn't say it. He would have to ask. It would have to be his own idea. Not her place to initiate things. Let him be the man. Let him believe he was controlling the situation.

'Anyone in?'

'Like who?'

'You know ... black boys ... Yardies.'

'No. But I spoke to a guy who has dealings with them ...'

'Who?'

'You know him, Frankie ... James Greenwood, does the door for Shoeless Sadies's on The Strand.'

'That wanker? Mouthallfuckingmighty!'

'He said he would make contact.'

Francis began to wonder just how many people she knew. All these strangers. Not strangers. Unreal people. For-real people. Too-real people.

'What's it got to do with him? How do you know that bollocks?'

'I told you ... lots of people get in the casino ...'

'I suppose ... maybe ... what happens next then?'

'We'll have to have a meet.'

'*We'll*? Who's *we'll*?'

'They know me, Frankie. They trust me. It won't happen otherwise.'

She was taking over. And Francis didn't like it. It confused him. And they both knew what happened when he got confused.

'How can you be sure of that? Did they tell you that?'

'I know it. Nobody told me ... look, d'you want this or not? You don't have to, Frankie.'

'I don't want you getting involved.'

'I'm already involved. Just for asking.'

'I don't like it. I don't like it.'

'It'll be ok, Frankie. Don't worry. Come to bed.'

Glendora put down her coffee cup and crossed the room. She pulled at his arm until he rose from the black chair and followed her to the bedroom. Stepped out of her croupier clothes and then slipped off his dressing gown. Down on the big bed her small dark hands touched his skin and her lips moved over his scarred body like a light warm breeze. Francis forgot about all his little doubts and frets. Glendora hummed a silver tune as she hovered over him. He didn't know what the tune was and neither did he care. Its sound inside his soul told him there was nothing in the world to worry about. Nothing else except that moment. The Universe had imploded and *they* were what came after. Them. Just *them*. Him and the big bed that was floating in Space-Time and the black woman who was so close that she was part of both of them. The three were one. Him, the bed and her. Trinity of touch! Eternal in that eternal hour of early morning. Sweat between their bodies sealed them together and in the essential moment of orgasm everything was understood and their minds fused into the unified roundness of man and woman. The circle was completed. The half made whole. The old Universe was dead. And a new one born!

Eyeless in Erdenet! And legless in Leicester Square! Uncle John gone. Stoned at the stake. Far out and away! And junkie sadfuckers with nothing else in their pathetic lives? And shaky babies going turkey in the fucking womb? Withdrawal symptoms at birth ... twitching into delirium at ten minutes old? And brutality and parasitical poverty and sleepinginyourownshit ignorance?

Francis dreamed of the woman in black.

Even in the dream her voice comes floating at me ... massaging my mind. Saying forget sentiment, Jalal al-Din. Telling me the drug is power. And power is good. Power is right, Jalal al-Din. That's her word ... and there are other things. I know ... I know ... I know ... Understanding. Understanding everything they tell me? Understanding what? Whatever it is to be understood. I say I don't think these fucking Yardie shitheads have the fucking good of humanity in mind. But she says if it was legal, Jalal al-Din, the Emperors of Wall Street would be trading it. For fuck's sake ... horse trading on the international stock markets and rock indexed on the FTSI and the Dow Jones and Hang Seng selling snow. Selfstyled highpriests setting themselves up as guardians of the healthy world. Ordinary people. She asks me who they are, Jalal al-Din? The cunts are plotting to kill me. Is it only that they are imaginationless? Or something more sinister? Have they something to fear? Apart from the fucking obvious? She says these people are twosided, Jalal al-Din ... they have darting eyes. Like the snake. Who can I trust, Genghiskhan? Tell me what to do? I'm to trust the power, Jalal al-Din. Because it's honest. Get rid of the curse of contrition. And she's right ... fuck the browbeating. Rise up like a phoenix out of the ashes of my own sins. Leave all the guilt behind. Wouldn't it be ... lovely? Who am I, Genghis? You are Jalal al-Din. But am I the *sum* of what I am? She says I'm a man like her, Jalal al-Din. And she's a God. As well as a ... I'm God too. I got to get more fucking guns. For protection. The ordinary is not the only way to live, Jalal al-Din. Warns me to keep away from ordinary cowards and sober women. And a man must never surrender. I must find my own power. Do not ask anyone for it. Find it and take it! Find my own window in the wall. Take it if someone else has it. Take it from them. It's mine through birthright. Is it? You know it is! I nearly had it! I still want it! I want it back because it's mine! Fuck all that other bullshit? Fuck stillness and fuck stateofmind! But then there's doubt again and I ask her what if she's wrong, Genghiskhan ... what if she's just as naïve as the ordinarys she's killed? Do not doubt she screams at me! Doubt and I'm lost! Shouts I can have what I want, Jalal al-Din. When? Just as I once had it. It's still there ... for me to take. Do you not understand? They took it away from me. Who are they? Sure ... they. Them. You know them ... they're plotting to kill me. I ask her, Khananimal, what if I kill and get caught and put into prison again? I'll go crazy again! I must find another fucking way. If they get me again I'm finished. I know she thinks I'm finished now, don't you? I know what you're fucking thinking! No! It's just not just not just not. Right! It was there once. I had it. But the fuckers took it all away. It was stopped. There's right and there's fucking wrong! It was stopped.

And the most dangerous drug of all. Is money!

Loud banging on the front door woke Francis and Glendora. She was immediately afraid and wrapped her arms around him. Held onto him. Still half-asleep and fearful it was the nightmare come back again. To lie on her and hurt her.

'Frankie ...'

'It's all right, Glenny ... don't worry.'

'Who is it, Frankie?'

'I'll brain the bastard, whoever it is.'

'Oh God ...'

'It's all right. Don't be afraid ...'

Glendora wasn't sure. She clung onto him until he had to release her fingers from around his arms and hold her trembling hands. He told her it was ok and his words were strong again and took her fear away. Francis slipped out of bed and she asked him with her eyes to be careful. He lifted the window and looked down into the street below.

'It's Matthew fucking Moore!'

She breathed a small sigh of relief and turned over in the big bed. Reassuring kiss on the forehead and he said go back to sleep. Then dressed and let Matthew in. The two men went to the kitchen and Francis poured coffee.

'What time d'you call this?'

'Half nine.'

'A bit on the early side for you, Matthew.'

'I'll have to be getting up every morning at the crack of fucking dawn to look after the alpacas.'

'Be a fucking culture shock for you.'

'Don't fucking worry about that, Francis. I'll do it all right. My family were farmers.'

'Were? When? Once?'

'Grandfather. Ould fella left the land and came to town. Never mind all that ... listen, I was over this way so I thought I'd call in.'

'Why? Changed your mind about the club?'

Suspicious. Francis wondered what he really wanted. But he played it cool.

'No. I heard about the episode at the Peacock.'

'When ... just now?'

'No ... course not. A few days ago ...'

'Took your time, then.'

'Sorry ... you know how things are, Francis. There's a lot going on in my life at the moment.'

That was also suspicious. What was going on? How much did he know? About what?

'Sure. Doesn't matter to me one way or the other.'

'Jesus, Francis ... I'm sorry this had to happen.'

'Not your fucking fault, is it?'

'Are you getting any work?'

Francis lit a cigarette. Offered one to Matthew.

'No problems. Plenty of things in the pipeline.'

'Only I know a few lads if you like ...'

'There's no one you know in London that I don't, Matthew.'

'I suppose ... listen, I've told Shillinger he can stick the tour up his arse as far as I'm concerned.'

'Don't fucking do that!'

'What?'

'Don't throw away good money on my account, Matthew.'

'It's not on your account.'

'What is it then?'

'Principle.'

Fuck principle. The Animal just told him. Fuck conscience! Fuck genuflecting ! Francis was still distrustful of this man who was once his friend. Once. And now?

'Principle won't buy you the fucking farm you want, will it? I appreciate the gesture, Matthew, but don't be a fucking mug all your life. You need the dough and I've got something sorted.'

'What is it?'

Why did he want to know? Who did he want to tell? Francis found it so hard to figure people out. Even the ones he knew well.

'Can't tell you.'

'Well, whatever it is I hope it works out, Francis.'

'It will.'

'Good man. Listen ... what I really want to say is ... you know where I am. If I can do anything ... I mean *anything*, Francis ... at any time.'

'Appreciate it, boy.'

'Ok?'

'Ok.'

Matthew Moore finished his coffee and they shook hands before he left the flat. Francis stood at the front door and watched him drive away. Then came back upstairs and slipped into the big bed beside Glendora. She stirred sleepily.

'What did Matthew want?'

'To say he was sorry.'

'Sorry for what?'

'For everything. And to say he'd do anything for me.'

'That was nice of him.'

'Wasn't it?'

chapter twenty-three

chapte r twenty-three

chapte r twenty-three

The British Midlands flight landed at Manchester Airport to the south of the city in the afternoon before Christmas Eve. Glendora accompanied Francis Page. Dressed in a black coat with fur-trimmed hood that hid her face completely. She looked like a famous actress or a pop star with her minder. Light snow fell from a greywhite afternoon sky and the wind blew down a north-easterly direction and cut through their clothes and into their flesh. Short taxi-ride to the Post House Hotel in Heald Green and they only had an overnight bag each. Upstairs in their room, Francis lit a cigarette and looked for the coffee pot. Glendora collapsed with fatigue onto the bed. Snow fell faster and heavier and the light was fading in a coppercoloured sky. Francis poured coffee into a cup and sat opposite the bed. Christmas traffic outside tried to make it home with tinselly gifts and shopping and all sorts of other seasonal stuff before the weather caused further chaos.

'Funny kind of night for this meeting.'

Francis spoke to no one in particular. He watched Glendora as she lay motionless with legs dangling over the edge of the bed.

'There's a lot going on this time of year, Frankie. People coming and going everywhere ... buying presents and visiting families. Less suspicious.'

'Is that what they said?'

'Something like that.'

'What time is it?'

'Now, or the meeting?'

'Both!'

'3.30 p.m. now. 8.00 p.m. the meeting.'

Francis sighed. Still unhappy about all this. Suspected double-crosses and treblecrosses and ambushes and conspiracies everywhere all around him. Another mouthful of black coffee. Stubbed his cigarette butt into an ashtray and checked out the room for hidden microphones and other surveillance equipment. Gave a suspicious glance to the black girl. Glendora was back close to her world again. Old world. And it made him uncomfortable. She wanted to tell him to relax but decided against it and lay back down on the bed. When Francis found nothing he returned to his chair.

'You hungry?'

'Tired.'

'Not hungry?'

'No.'

'I am.'

He picked up the phone and asked room service for a cheese-burger with chips. Glendora said she wanted to get a couple of hours sleep before they set off uptown. Francis wondered how she could be so cool about this. He lit another cigarette and waited for the food. Eating a lot of junk stuff lately. Also stopped training — putting on weight. Wasn't something deliberate. Didn't seem any point to all that bollocks he'd carried on with before. What was the point of training if he didn't need it. To bounce with. And he never was into eating healthy shit in any case. But always dressed well and proud of his appearance. This past couple of weeks he was turning into a bit of a tramp. Moping round the flat all night and sleeping all day and not showering or even shampooing his fucking hair. Glendora passed a couple of remarks but he took no notice.

He'd also started economising. Turning off the heat at night when Glendora was at work and insisting on only the cheapest specialoffer foods from the supermarkets and walking on his short excursions outside the flat instead of using the Jaguar. He cancelled the cable television and refused to make outgoing telephone calls. Even to look for work. Glendora found this new frugality hard to take. It intruded on her personality. Infringed on the woman she believed she was becoming. Brought up on fuck-all and she liked the little extravagances she worked hard for. Liked eating out and going to a show every now and then and new clothes and good wine. She snorted cocaine to keep off the heroin and puffed a bit of Moroccan to get up with and took a little speed to stay on her feet.

Francis was frowning on all this expense and insisting she cut back. Things had to change. She was going to say something to him about it. Tell him she'd moved away from the girl she was when he saved her. Tell him she was still frightened like when strange knocks came to the door at night and still needed him but was getting stronger every day and didn't know where she would be. Eventually. When she found herself. Her real self. The her who never was. The little lost girl was gone and she waited to meet the woman she was going to be. Decided not to say anything. Once they'd scored this deal and he had walking about money again he'd turn back into the man he really was. The man behind the man.

Francis studied himself in the mirror. Belly getting bigger and face growing thinner. Sunken. Dark circles round the eyes. *If* that was him looking back. Could be someone else. The snow was a blizzard now.

Francis could hear the noise of it falling — could smell the whiteness of it. Feel its cold texture drifting on the shivering ground. Creeping into every corner and spreading all over this city. Covering up the dirt. He looked round the room. It felt strange. Alien. Anonymous. All the colours were grey although Francis knew they were not. Walls blended into the floor and ceiling and furniture barely perceivable in the greyness. Even Glendora was absorbed into the room — into the bed. Francis looked down and saw his feet blending into the floor. Dissolving into the ambience of the hotel room.

'Where is this meeting?'

Glendora didn't answer. She was gone. Swallowed up. Invisible in the greyness which was now spreading to the outside world.

'Glenny!'

'Whaaat ... what?'

'Where's the meeting?'

'Oh, Frankie ... you know ...'

'I've forgotten.'

'At a club called the Crazy Horse ... Claremont Road ... Moss Side South.'

'Don't know if we'll be able to make it in this weather.'

'Don't worry ... the taxi will get us there.'

Glendora turned over on the bed and closed her eyes once more. But it didn't matter now. Colour had returned to the room. The carpet was red and the curtains a bluish turquoise. To match the bed and furniture coverings. Ceiling white and walls pink above the dado rail and dark blue below. A few pictures spoke to him in a language he didn't understand and he was reassured.

'Dis be de mon?'

'Yes.'

'Hope him be reliable ... Countess.'

'He is.'

Glendora stood in front of Francis in a discreet corner of the Crazy Horse Club. Three black men wearing darkclothes and shades sat round a table. Francis didn't like the place. Every bastard in it was fucking black. He was uptight. Suspicious. Hello darkness my old friend. He wished he had a fucking gun. One of the men motioned for them to sit.

'Yo ah passport be seen, spar?'

I've come to meet with you again. The black man spoke directly to Francis. Francis didn't reply because he wasn't listening. Glendora touched his arm.

'He wants to know if your passport is in order.'

'Would I be fucking here if it wasn't?'

'Yo ah know seh Amsterdam atall?'

Francis lit up a cigarette. Blew smoke into the frightened air.

'Sure I do. Been there loads of times. I thought drugs were legal over there.'

'Hear wha ... not de stuff us runnin, mon. Rotterdam once be de place, but it too hot dere now seh. Sure yo knows Amsterdam?'

'I'm no fucking tourist, if that's what you're thinking.'

'Hey ... chill, mon. Easy now. Wha fi yo ah gettin vex?'

These bastards were black. But they talked differently to Glendora and it confused Francis. He wondered if they knew each other better than she let on. Seemed too much of a fucking coincidence — them being in London at the casino and the American tour being shot out at the same time and him needing a way out of the shit and every fucker being black in here even though some of them talked different. Maybe it was all a big fucking set-up. Francis couldn't figure out the logic behind it — the reason — normality — nor what the outcome was meant to be. If it was. Harmful to him. For fucking sure. How well did Glendora know these people? The question kept on asking itself. Over and over. Was there some conspiracy she was in on? She was the same fucking colour!

'Will we fly over from here?'

That's what he meant. *She* was asking the questions. And she assumed she was fucking going. Why did she assume that without consulting him? She was taking too much fucking control lately. Things definitely had to change.

'Where be *yah*, gel seh?'

'Here ... Manchester.'

'No. London. Be ah cool from deh, special if yo spar him seh tidy hisself up some.'

Francis didn't like that last remark. Arrogant blackbastards! Whole situation was trouble. Could smell it. From start to fucking finish. No alternative now. Francis had the feeling that him and her might not get back out through the door if these fuckers smelled any kind of hesitation. Reluctance. Crisis. Christ is.

'When do we leave?'

Francis asked the question this time. Wanted some control here. You had to control the situation and not let the situation control you. One of the first rules of the door. Applied to all aspects of life. He couldn't have Glendora and these fucking smackheads sorting everything out and him sitting to one side like a fucking lemon. Meringue. Merlin. Merlingo.

'Day after tomorrow seh, mon.'

'That's Christmas Day!'

'Seen? We ah idrin ain't got no holiday seh ... not lik yo bouncer doghearts dem.'

Francis didn't get all the strangewords but he knew some of them were disrespectful.

'Hey hey hey ... listen, you bastard ... less of the sarcastic stuff!'

'Wha ah gwan? Yo mon him be out o manners, Countess.'

'Let's just get this sorted, can we?'

Glendora intervened in the darkening situation between Francis and the Yardies. Black. Beat. Faced each other sullenly across the table for a moment. Blackbeat! One of the men suddenly laughed out loud and sat back in his seat.

'Yo be some boldfaced youthman, spar!'

'Him haf some nerve seh. May be him ah do.'

Black sniggers amongst themselves. Francis didn't laugh with them. Beat. One Yardie pushed a package across the table. Black!

'Dis be ah tickets dem ... same de address. Also two thousand in ah cash seh. Yo gets de rest when yo ah come back.'

Francis picked up the package without taking his eyes off the men across the table. Neither did he open it — just slipped it inside his coat. Smirking smileheads!

'And when is that scheduled to be?'

'Same day mon. We doan want yo ah hangin over dere seh with de merchandise. Yo ah mek be mugged.'

Laughed again and gave each other fists. Francis scowled and called them shitblackbags under his breath. The black man slid another package across the table.

'Dis be de money fi ah merchandise.'

'How much?'

'Why yo ah needs to know?'

'I need to know if I'm going to be fucking responsible for it!'

This was an insult. Francis didn't know it but Glendora did. No trust. Silence crept round the floor and climbed up and sat on the table in front of them. The black men looked at each other until the one who was in charge finally nodded.

'Thirty thousand.'

Francis took the package and passed it to Glendora. She put it into her bag.

'How do I get the stuff to you?'

'Yo ah doan, spar. We ah cum fi yo ... thru de gel yah.'

'Doan yo ah want know what be de merchandise?'

'No. I don't give a fuck!'

Another silence. Air inside the club full of fear. Francis could taste it. Ferociousness. Savage. Selfish. Better to be outside in the open. Business seemed to be over and Francis saw no point in hanging around any longer. Certainly no intention of socialising with these fuckers. Stood up from his chair. Glendora remained seated.

'Yo ah haf nuff money dere, mon. How many doors dem yo ah do fi dat kine o cash, tough guy?'

Francis didn't reply. Fucking people really beginning to get on his fuckingnervesbeat! Arrogant wankers. And he wondered if all black people were like this or was it just they had their fair share of shitholes — same as the whites? Maybe Konrad Fichte and his fucking Efrikaners weren't so stupid. Or was it just him. Was he being overcautious? Oversuspicious? Over overthetop? With his lowtrust. Notrust. The men across the table looked up at him and shrugged their shoulders.

'Any question, Countess?'

Francis placed both hands on the table and leaned forward. Fuckthembeat!

'One. Why me?'

'Yo ah gel dat vouch fi yo.'

'No. I mean ... you guys must have experienced couriers? Punks who do this kind of thing all the fucking time.'

'Sure us do. But yo be a new face spar. Yo be clean. An doan forget mon, yo ah come to we. If yo doan want ah work seh ...'

Francis slowly took his hands off the table and reluctantly accepted their explanation. Nothing else he could do. Now. If this was a set-up he'd have to go along with it — play it by ear. He tapped Glendora on the shoulder and motioned her to her feet. One of the black men grabbed her arm and held it. Stresstrigger! Francis made a move towards him but Glendora shook her head.

'Yo ah vouch fi dis mon, sista?'

'Yes, of course. I told you ...'

The man let go of her arm and looked up at Francis.

'Doan fuck up, spar. If yo ah does ... de gel ha fi pay us back seh.'

Heartbeat! Francis leaned across and took the man by the coat-collar. Pulled him out of his chair and onto his feet. Black hands inside jackets. Glendora held her arms in the air. Panicstricken and waving desperately.

'He's not armed! He's not armed!'

Faces close by in the club looked on. But didn't intervene. Moved away from the danger. Out of the line of fire. Black hands stayed inside dark jackets. Air cuttable. Tense. Sour. Francis leaned over and put his face up close to the man standing.

'I'll do the job and there'll be no fuck-ups. Only don't threaten me or her, you cunt!'

Francis held the man for a moment, then let go of his lapels and took Glendora by the arm. Moved slowly away from the table. Her first and him backwardwalking to the door.

'And have the rest of my fucking money ready when I get back!'

The Post House Hotel was friendly and welcoming after the Crazy Horse Club. Francis and Glendora tried to sort out the logistics of the trip. Had to fly back to London in the morning and out to Amsterdam on Christmas Day. Rendezvous near the Bijlmer area of that city and then back again the same night? That's what those blockhead black-heads thought! Fucking Christmas and if Francis was going to be abroad he wanted to relax for a couple of hours and have a few drinks. Glendora was against it. Said stick to the plan. As if she knew all about this kind of thing. And maybe she did. But he made up his mind to stay over until Boxing Day. Wankers weren't going to collect their merchandise that fucking quick and anyway they could say they missed the flight and in any case. Who fucking cared!

A few drinks at the bar after dinner and then an early bed. They didn't make love but Glendora lay on his shoulder and he felt that she felt safe for the moment and if they did die — at least they would be together. The snow settled and the sky was ebony clear with a full moon that shone silver light through the curtains and into the hotel room. Filling the space with a ghostly luminescence. Francis couldn't sleep. As usual. Even though he'd been awake most of the previous day. Reckoned his body clock was all fucked up and didn't know night from morning or when it was right to be awake or asleep or any fucking thing else.

Looked down into Glendora's face. Eyelids darker than the rest of her and closed now with long black lashes sealing them to the tops of her cheekbones. Her body moved to the rhythm of the breath that swam out through white teeth in a slightly open mouth. Could he trust her? Yes. No? Yes? No. Forgot to ask her why she decided to come along on the pickup. Or maybe he hadn't. Did she say that a couple would be less conspicuous than a man on his own? And did he say not a couple like them? Big hardface bouncer and a beautiful young black girl. And did she tell him they looked for inconspicuous people? The customscrowd. And the more ostentatious you were the better chance you had of getting through? And did he want to know how she knew all this? Forgot to give her a lecture for not discussing the thing with him in the first place. Looked bad in front of the black bastards. No wonder they thought they could threaten him. She said she *had* discussed it with him. But he was sure she hadn't.

Moonlight crawled around the hotel room and spread across the walls and ceiling. Despite the urge inside him to move on, Francis didn't like being away from London. Been all over the place of course back in the days when he minded the pop stars and politicians. Didn't worry about it then. These days he felt uncomfortable in unfamiliar places. Demons behind every fucking door. Wearing mad Annie's make-up and his father's frown. Talking like school teachers. Demons with Angeline's shrill scream — telling him that the whole world was a great fucking cannibal. Words floated on the silver moonlight in front of his face and gradually decayed and turned to a ball of squirming maggots that fell onto the bed. Francis brushed them off and they struggled away across the carpet and hid behind the furniture. The silver moonlight was cold even though the rest of the room was warm. Francis closed his eyes and tried to sleep. But images appeared in his head of mental hospitals and his mother's sedated eyes and the other kids pointing and calling out. Mad! Mad! Mad! The darkness behind his closed eyelids was overpowering. So he opened them again to the sickly smell of the maggots. Crawling closer to the bed and squirming away again as soon as he looked in their direction.

Glendora stirred beside him but didn't wake. She whimpered softly like a small animal that was hurt in some way. He wanted to wake her. Find out what was wrong. What was troubling her. Decided not to because he wasn't sure he wanted to know. Lit a cigarette and watched the blue smoke curl upwards through the silver room. It moved in slow motion and enveloped the lightshade that hung from the night-shade ceiling. Francis watched the smokething. It was alive and it made patterns that had some significance. Even though he wasn't quite sure what that was. He watched it for hours and days and weeks and months and years. The silverness gradually grew more gilded as the sun came up outside the hotel window. Dawn broke and he fell asleep.

chapter twenty-four

chapte r twenty-four

chapte r twenty-four

'Where are we going to get accommodation in Amsterdam on Christmas Day?'

'Don't worry, it's all sorted. I've got a contact.'

'You've been here before, Frankie?'

'You heard me telling those Yardie bastards I was, Glenny.'

'When were you here?'

'Long time ago, honey ... when I was minding.'

'Doesn't seem quite like your kind of town ...'

'Maybe not. But pop stars used to come here to get stoned and politicians came here to get shagged.'

'And what about you, Frankie?'

'I just made sure they didn't get caught.'

Francis Page wanted to ask her if *she'd* ever been here before. In the bad old days before he met her. On the junk or on the game. If she had, their paths never crossed. If that's why she was asking. He wanted to reassure her. But left it so. There was enough tension.

They made their way towards the arrivals gate at Schiphol Airport. The place was practically deserted and Christmas carols played musakly over the loudspeakers in all the lounges. Snowing outside and no taxis at the rank. Cold white world. Clean and clear. Of cuntology.

'What are we to do now?'

'You worry too much, Glenny.'

They waited a few minutes and Francis lit up a cigarette. Contrary to the signs on all the walls. From away in the halflight a silver Mercedes made its way slowly in their direction. Seemed to be a mirage at first. Coming out of the whiteness. Snow mirage. Clearer as it came closer and stopped at the taxi rank. Tall wellbuilt blond man in his midforties emerged and shook hands with Francis.

'Julien ...'

'Francis. *Hoi*. It has been a long time.'

'Yes. My fiancée, Glendora.'

'Beautiful. Charmed, Mademoiselle.'

'You have somewhere for us?'

'Yes, my brother runs a little place on Van Woustraat. It is small, but very comfortable. He has kept you a double room.'

'Thanks, Julien ... one I owe you.'

'It is I who owe you, Francis. Now we are square, as you say. Yes?'

'Sure.'

Francis and Glendora climbed into the back of the Mercedes and Julien drove off north from the airport and then east along the expressway. Towards the city. Nobody spoke during the twenty-minute journey and Glendora looked out the window at the snow scenery while Francis stared straight ahead. Directly behind the driver. Looking through him and out past the windscreen and white world to a distant point of concentration. Preoccupied. Lost in the penumbra of midwinter. Concentrating. On something specific but nothing in particular.

Amsterdam was a small synchronised city. Densely packed buildings and narrow streets and old canals running like arteries through its heart. Van Woustraat was just to the south of the city centre and the car came to a halt outside a small hotel called the Black Tulip. Francis reached over and touched Julien on the shoulder.

'What do you know about the Bijlmer district?'

'Class A! Hard stuff! So ... that is why you are here? Be careful.'

Francis paused before getting out of the car. Glendora waited near the hotel entrance for him.

'Listen, Julien ... I need a gun.'

'I am sorry, Francis my friend. I am legitimate now and I don't want any trouble with the gendarmerie.'

'For old times' sake?'

'My friend ... I would not know where to find a gun these days. After the muscle game I put my savings into wine. That is what I am now ... an importer and exporter of wine.'

Francis wondered if he was telling the truth. There was no way of knowing for sure. And routine comforts calmed anxiety. Like the feel of a semi-automatic against the skin.

'Ok. Don't worry about it.'

'I can get you a hotel room, Francis, or give you advice on a good vintage. Nothing else. You should be out of all this yourself by now. Chances are for young men to take.'

'You're right, Julien. I'll be out of it soon enough.'

'I hope so, Francis ... and I wish you well in your venture. *Tot ziens!*'

The Merc pulled away north-westwards along Leidsedwarsstraat. Left Francis and Glendora standing on the snow-covered pavement. They waited. Watched the silver car disappear into the silver afternoon and even then Francis waited some more. As if he expected Julien to turn round and come back and toss a silver handgun through the window. Glendora shivered and pulled him across the pavement to the golden entrance of the Black Tulip Hotel.

Julien's brother was a *gezellig* type of guy and every courtesy was extended. Hotel full of tourists and ambience excessively Christmassy. Too much for Francis. Hated all the fucking fuss at this time of the year. Too much tinsel and togetherness. Sycophancy and shite. Kissing and cuddling and hugging and handshaking. Reminded him of smalldays gone when all these things — these childtypethings — were not for the Fichte family. Fuck the arseholes! *Lekker* smells of game and pancakes floated out from the dining room as they made their way to the double-room Julien's brother laid on. It was spacious with a kingsized bed and antique furniture. Oriental rugs spread over the wooden floor and this made Francis feel more at home. They threw their bags into a corner and he flopped onto the bed while Glendora freshened her face in the en-suite bathroom. Pictures on the walls by Rembrandt and Vermeer and van Ruisdael and Hals and other homegrown artists. Dutch portraits dramatically lit. Stared at Francis. Knew him. What he was here for. And they frowned. Silver flecks of snow blew against the silver window and down in his silver wine cellar, Julien drank a bottle of silver Sauvignon and laughed and laughed and laughed.

Rendezvous on a small street called Daniel Defoe Laan off Gooise Weg just to the north of the Bijlmer area of the city set for 21.00 hours — and now only 14.00. Seven hours to go. Glendora wanted to come along but Francis drew the line there. Women could be a serious fucking handicap in dangerous situations and a man could get himself killed trying to mind them. Francis rose from the bed and took the Yardies' package from his bag and placed it carefully into a drawer. He locked the drawer and put the key into his top pocket. Glendora finished freshening up and they went down to a late lunch.

Deeper into the evening the hotel ordered a taxi and Francis travelled south-east towards the Zuidoost suburbs of the city. Alone. Away from the beaten track and the holiday revellers and the lights of the centre. He was nervous about this arrangement. Would have preferred Julien to drive him. Someone he could trust. But the old friend wouldn't do any more. Couldn't. Because he was now an honest man. With a reputation.

The further out they went, the more surreal the landscape became. Quiet white area of town disguising the danger and he told his taxi driver to wait as he walked down along Gooise Weg and turned right into the lane. Checking the piece of paper in his hand for the correct address. The money package bulky inside his coat and looked like the bulge of a shoulderholster. Francis came to a dark door with the barely readable number twenty-two. Hesitated. Looked up and down the lane. Then knocked four times in slow succession. As instructed. No response. Francis was told not to knock twice. So he waited. The taxi also waited down on Gooise Weg and Francis saw the driver glance at his watch. Door opened suddenly and a young man with an ear-ring through his eyebrow stood looking out. Mediterranean. Greek or Turkish or Cypriot or some fucking thing.

'*O sen misin*?'

'What?'

'*Parayı tasıyan adam sen misin*?'

'Speak fucking English!'

The man waved Francis inside and made him raise his arms. Frisked him and found the package. The man smiled and led the way up steep narrow stairs. Bare room at the top — except for a wooden table and one wooden chair. Another young man sat on the chair. Also Mediterranean, with shoulderlength hair tied back in a ponytail and a large tattoo on his neck that came up from under the collar of his shirt and looked like some kind of black snake. A plastic bag in the middle of the table. The man took four packets of heroin from it and motioned to Francis to test the merchandise. Francis picked one and looked at the powder. It was coarse brown but that didn't matter. Dealers and junkies would refine it to white skag and cut it with washing powder or warfarin or some other fucking rat-poison shit. Francis mentally weighed the bag in his hand — several kilos. The first man placed the money package beside the drugs and the seated man smiled.

'*Otuz bin mi*?'

'English, for fuck's sake!'

The seated man tore open the package and began counting the notes inside. Francis took a narrow test-tube from his pocket and slit one of the packets with a penknife. A small amount of horse into the glass phial. Francis shook it until the chemical solution turned light blue. Looked highquality. Maybe sixty per cent pure. Litmus test for junkie lightfingers. He tested the other bags in turn.

'*Sadece yirmi*!'

'What the fuck are you going on about now?'

'*Sadece yirmi bin*!'

The man rose from his chair and smashed his fist against the table. The second man pulled out a Heckler and Koch P7 automatic pistol and pointed it at Francis.

'*Gerisi nerede*?'

'I can't understand what you're fucking talking about.'

Snakeneck struck Francis across the face with the back of the his hand. Snakefuckingbeat! Francis grabbed him by the throat and swung him round into the gunman's line of fire. Then sunk teeth into the cunt's neck. A fine spray of blood erupted from the snake and spread over the room. Red. Alive. Francis saw his own life in the blood. Ebbing away. And all the evil he'd done. Evil on a grand scale. And now was the time to pay the final price. The gunman tried to get a clear shot but the blood was on his face and in his eyes. The slight hesitation was long enough. Francis twisted snakeneck's arm up behind his back. Dislocating it at the shoulder. The man screamed and tried to hold in the spraying blood with his good hand. Gunman took a shot.

Hit snakeneck in the face.

The bullet came out through the back of his head. Francis felt it pass him by. Close. In the deathroom. Snakeneck stopped screaming and struggling. Gunman trying to get off another shot. Francis flung the dead body across the room. Knocked the gunman off balance and the automatic flew from his hand. They both reached the weapon at the same time and each man held onto the other's grip on the gun. In a struggle for life. Francis was stronger and a left cross sent the younger man flying backwards towards the door. He pointed the automatic and the man scrambled through the exit and down the stairs and away along the silver street. Leaving the money and drugs and a red stain spreading across the floor from the head and snake neck. Francis sat looking at the blood for a long time.

Wondering if he was still alive.

Then he stuffed the heroin and the money back into the plastic bag and put the gun into his coat pocket. Walked carefully downstairs. Gunman gone. Leaving a trail of footprints in the snow which led towards the taxi. Taxi gone as well.

Francis looked around. Everywhere white and silent in the stillness of the Christmas night. He scooped up some snow and tried to wipe the blood from his face and hands, then walked east out of Daniel Defoe Laan and north along Gooise Weg and under the expressway. No sign of life. Except for a remote head-shop or two selling black hashish and blond cannabis to dopeheads who didn't know it was Christmas. Stickies and pipes and bongs blowing ganja fumes out into the silver air. And the East-European and Asian women on eight-hour shifts in their redlight windows. In exile out here away from the more respectable local pros in the centre. Everyone else in the bars and clubs or at home for the holiday. No vehicles of any sort ploughed through the virgin snow in this part of town and only distant sounds of music and laughter audible in the cold faroff air. As if the whole fucking world was inside hibernating — safe in the warmth of its den and afraid to move out amongst the junkjugglers and jugularbiters.

Francis didn't know which direction took him back to the Black Tulip Hotel. He touched the handle of the gun in his pocket — for reassurance. If he got picked up now he'd be fucked completely. Never see the light of fucking day again. Knew the cab came down here in a south-easterly direction. So he kept going north-west along Gooise Weg until he came to the intersection with Kruis Laan. Buildings loomed and the sky lowered itself to street level and snow stuck to his shoes like quicksand and tried to pull him back. Each step an effort and his breath hard and rasping up from burning lungs. Shadows round every corner. Dead men's shadows. Faceless shadows. Trying to grab him and hold him along with the snow until the fucking ghouls came to rip all the bones from his body and leave the rest of him in a bloody heap on the ground. Silver-red. Like a shed snakeskin. Staining the whiteness and a pair of black holes looking up like eyeballs in the snow. Francis tightened his finger round the trigger. Thought he heard something behind and pulled the gun from his pocket.

Did I tell you my son vas schizophrenic, Shegetz. Christ! No no ... not him. Eduard. Don't fucking do that! I'm fucking jumpy enough already. It tells me I need to relax. How can I ... I'm fucking lost? Are not ve all? I mean zat in a scientific sense. I mean it in a real fucking sense. It asks me what's real? And I don't have the answer. I ask if it knows where the Black Tulip Hotel is? Of course. It is on ze Van Woustraat. And where's that? Keep goink to Hugo De Vries und zen take a left. Across ze Amstel und turn north at Rijnstraat ... zen across ze Amstelkanaal und keep goink north into Van Woustraat. Thanks. My pleasure. Do you mind if I accompany you? No ... just keep an eye out for cops or crooks. How can I tell ze difference? You can't! It turns my head towards the clearing sky and says, Shegetz ... look up. Vat can you see? I say stars. Silver stars. And I ask what's out there beyond them? Scientistvoice? It says nothing. But I know there must be something. A vacuum. That's something, ain't it? It is nozink. It's space surely? No, it is nozink. What's nothing? No thing. Und only by livink can ve escape from ze non-time of nothinknes. Non-time, Shegetz. No time. Haven't got time. Now. Haf I not explained it already? Maybe. I can't remember. Memory poor. Poor memory. Telling me time is what stops everything from happening at once. And says we invented time ... it didn't exist before us humans. It is a feature of neuropsychology ... not physics. I don't want a lecture but it's too late to stop it from saying that from ze standpoint of physics, zere is no observable entity called Time. Only Space-Time. You're losing me, Albertstein. No, look ... get off ze Vrijheidslaan here und turn north into Rijnstraat. No no ... not the bloody directions ... Oh, I see ... vell, ze speed of light is ze only absolute constant. Only? Only! Everyzink else is variable, Shegetz ... Space und Time included. Normality? Insanity? Zey are not rigid frameworks. Zey can be stretched ... like elastic. Und any change in consciousness weakens ze link between man and ze natural order from which he sprang ... I say forget it! I just want to get back to the hotel. Tells me I'm already there. But I know I'm not ... I'm here in the fucking snow. Zat too. You're fucking mad. So are you. And I shouldn't be listening. I know it's wrong, but it won't stop. It says what I hear is subjective, Shegetz ... like sin und evil. Und subjectivity does not exist in science. Therefore madness does not neither. No? I ask what about the cold? The fucking cold exists, doesn't it? The snow? Vat you see is chust an illusion. No ... I know I'm conscious. Albertstein! I know I'm fucking conscious! Sometimes. And that makes a difference. The difference. How do you know? I know! How do you know you know?

I can feel myself. Freezing! *Narrischkeit*!

Francis saw the bright sign outside the Black Tulip. Shining like a silver star to guide him. It was only a hundred metres away now and he quickened his steps through the snow. Reception was closed and laughter drifted out from the bar and dining-room areas. Francis careful not to be seen as he hurried to his room. Glendora frantic. Waiting for him.

'Oh my God! What happened?'

'Don't panic ...'

'There's blood all over you.'

'One of the bastards had a gun. I nearly got fucking killed.'

'Jesus Christ, Frankie ... are you hurt?'

'No. But there's a dead body back there.'

'Oh no ... why?'

'They didn't speak English, but I think the fucking money's short.'

'It can't be ...'

Francis emptied the bag onto a table in the room. Took the automatic out of his pocket and threw his bloodstained coat onto the bathroom floor.

'I've got to get cleaned up.'

Francis went to wash the rest of the gore off his hands and face and change his clothes. He asked Glendora to count the money. All sticky with blood. There were three of them in the room now. She, he and the old boyfriend. Back. Beautiful as ever. She touched him lightly with her fingers and the desperate longing filled every cell in her body. She turned away. Turned back again. He was smiling. Saying how much he missed her. He knew how much she missed him. Wanted him. Longed for him. Glendora looked at the gun and listened to Francis making sounds in the bathroom. She touched the metal barrel — felt the trigger. It was there. It could be done. She turned away again and walked to the bed. Sat on it for a single instant and then came back to the table. When Francis returned she'd counted the money and was watching the skag. Staring at it. Just staring. With pain in her face. Like someone waiting to die. Wanting to die.

'How much?'

'Twenty thousand ...'

'Bastards!'

'What's going on, Frankie?'

Francis didn't know what was going on. Only that he nearly died an hour ago and there had to be some reason for that.

'Your fucking friends left the package ten fucking grand light!'

'They're not my friends ...'

'Whatever. The package was still ten fucking grand light.'

'What does it mean?'

He didn't know what it meant either. It was meaningless. Like a lot of things lately. Only everything that went wrong was related in some way to everything else that was wrong.

'Something ... I don't know. I'm not sure ... it was either a set-up ... or someone is on the fucking fiddle. And it ain't me! Do you know ... what's going on?'

'Of course I don't, Frankie. You still got the merchandise ...'

'Sure I got it, but that's not the fucking point ...'

Francis started to cough and spit up blood. Didn't know whether it was his own or the blood from Snakeneck. Glendora got him a glass of water.

'Here, take a sip of glo ...'

Rinsed his mouth out and combed his hair.

'We've got to get going ... now!'

'They'll kill us ...'

'Who'll kill us? They won't fucking kill us, Glendora. I'll fucking kill them!'

Whoever they were. Whatever they were.

'You don't know them, Frankie ...'

'Do you? What do you know?'

'I know *of* them ...'

Did she? Did she? Did she? Francis realised for the first time that he was shaking. Glendora steadied him.

'Listen, it's their fucking fault I nearly got my fucking head blown off. Now, there's a fucking dead man in a building across town and another bastard on the loose who can identify me.'

'What are we going to do?'

'Get the fuck out of here right now!'

'We told the hotel we were staying overnight ...'

'Well, it's back to the original fucking plan.'

'What will they think?'

'Who?'

'The hotel people ...'

Julien's brother greatly upset at the early departure. Enquiring if the room was not to their liking or was it the food or the service? Said Julien would be disappointed and refused to take any payment whatsoever. But return tickets produced and explanations given that some booking error must have been made and it was fuck-all to do with his esteemed establishment. And yes, they'd be happy to accept his offer of a long weekend's free accommodation later in the year. Maybe in Summertime when Amsterdam was at her most beautiful best and the flowers were in bloom and the canals shining like silver and the galleries all open and *bedankt bedankt* but we have to go. Now!

A taxi south along the deserted expressway and made their midnight flight with only minutes to spare. Francis discarded the gun as they drove over the Singel-gracht bridge and heard it hitting the ice-water. Then he rolled the rear window back up to keep out the silver cold. Glendora carried the money in her bag and he had the heroin taped around his stomach. Taking a big fucking chance. No time to think of alternatives. But no problem either at Schiphol because it was Christmas night and everybody'd had a *jenever* or two and they were late and the plane was waiting. Rushed through passport control and boarded with their hand-luggage only which was stashed in the over-head baggage rack and they settled down for the fortyminute flight.

Decided to exit separately at Heathrow Airport. In case of complications. The atmosphere was relaxed and seasonal for Glendora but for Francis there were eyes everywhere. Accusing eyes. Faces. Disembodied voices. Without warmth or colour. Metallic. Suspicious. He was filled with a sense of foreboding and knew something terrible was about to happen. At any moment. They walked forever. Forever. Down neverending corridors. Until at last he saw Glendora move safely through the customs gate up ahead of him. But he knew he was going to be stopped. He knew it. Deserved to be stopped.

Then he was through. Suddenly. Without knowing how.

Francis drove the Jaguar in silence back to the flat. Studied the money and the heroin for a long time. What if he decided to keep it all? And fuck the Yardies? What could they do about him? Who did they know in this city that he didn't? Couldn't touch him. He knew it and he knew they knew it. But then there was Glendora.

chapter twenty-five

chapte r twenty-five

chapte r twenty-five

Francis Page slept for a change that night. No demons in the room with him. All in Manchester or over in Amsterdam. Glendora the restless one — tossing and turning and talking in her sleep about Lady Godiva riding a brownhorse and purepethidine and doublediconal and methadone and palfium and temegesic and dihydrocodeine. She cried and tears rolled down her brown cheekbones and stained the pillow a transparent colour. If Francis had been awake he might have comforted her. Or maybe her restlessness would have raised new doubts in his mind. But he slept the sleep of death and woke to a blustery Boxing Day. A few winterbird songs floated south from the trees on Hackney Downs. Francis rose quietly and cooked a quick fried bread and coffee breakfast. Brought a tray back to Glendora and woke her with a gentle shake.

'Frankie ...'

'It's ok. We're home.'

'It went wrong.'

'Maybe not.'

'What do you mean?'

Wasn't sure what he meant. Yet. But plans were forming in his head. Secret plans. For only himself to know. In case —

'Just leave everything to me. When are you due back at the casino?'

'Tomorrow night.'

'Call in sick.'

'Why?'

'Just call in sick! Tell them you got to take a few days off.'

Glendora wiped the sleep from her eyes and sipped the coffee. Not yet fully awake but aware that something serious had happened.

'Frankie, you're not going to do anything dangerous?'

'I'm not doing *anything*. Nothing at all. All or nothing.'

She didn't understand what he was saying.

'We'll get hurt. I'm afraid.'

'No one's going to hurt you. I won't allow no one to hurt you. I told you that!'

'*They will* ...'

'Not if you're here with me.'

'We can't stay in here forever.'

'I'll sort it out. Don't worry ... I'll sort it out. Just do as I tell you for the time being.'

Glendora always believed Francis when he told her he wouldn't let anyone hurt her. Believed him now. Even though this was different. He was different. She was different. This was dangerous. She knew the Yardies would try to get to him through her. She believed him but already decided there had to be a back door. An escape hatch. After breakfast he counted the money again and weighed the heroin on the bathroom scales. She watched him and watched the junk and felt the conflict inside her. A deadly struggle was going on between what she felt for Francis and the old addiction. There was always temptation around — at parties and at the casino and she managed to resist it up to now. But now it was so close. It was so easy. It whispered to her and called her softly and promised her something that Francis couldn't provide. Smiled seductively. Lustfully. Rakishly.

'What d'you want to do, honey?'

'What do you mean? When?'

'Tonight. You're not working and we're in the money.'

'I thought we were going to lay low.'

'This is London ... not Manchester or Amsterdam. This is my city. I'm not laying low here for nobody!'

Glendora became frightened again. Concentration broken. Afraid. Even though she believed him. Francis thought he was the toughest man in the world and maybe he was. But he wasn't the cleverest — or the most ruthless. But she still believed him. And he wouldn't take no for an answer.

'What say we go over to the Pink Peacock and throw some cash around?'

'Frankie ... we're barred.'

'Are we?'

'Yes.'

He wondered when. And why. But it was a small thing and there were plenty other clubs.

'Ok ... the Streetwalker then ... up in Soho.'

'Percy Shillinger controls that too.'

'Fuck the bastard! What about the Barenaked in Bayswater?'

'Should be safe enough ... but do you really think we ought to, Frankie?'

'Listen, Glenny, I've been going stirfuckingcrazy in this flat lately with no money and nothing to do. We took the fucking chances, not the Yardie bastards nor Percy fucking Shillinger nor any other shitbag.

We're entitled to go out and celebrate. We have it coming to us. Let me tell you this, if anyone tries to interfere ... I'll fucking kill him!'

Lot of talk about killing lately. Glendora didn't resist any further. Francis made up his mind and that was fucking that! And anyway. She backdoor believed him.

Spent the rest of the day kidding about and drinking the Champagne that Francis went to the off-licence for and laughing and making love. Like in the old days. In the simpledays. In the stillnessdays. He hid the heroin away where she wouldn't find it. Just in case it might be too much temptation. Francis knew he had to move the skag as soon as it was safe or else come to some kind of compromise with the dealers. But for now he didn't give a shit. Time to have a good time. Scientistein came back briefly during the day to go on about normalogicness. And Alienchrist whispered softly about love and immortality but Francis didn't care. He didn't care about reincarnation nor relativity nor the fact that life was ludicrous. And he didn't care whether he was crazy or not or whether his mother was mad or if the entire fucking Universe was in total fucking flux or if the only real meaning of life was the influence he had on that process. Things were beginning to go the right way.

Francis could see the future approaching. It was silver. Singing. A song he'd heard before. Long time ago. A happysong. Sanesong. He made reservations for dinner at the Moodyblue restaurant in Mayfair and Glendora looked sophisticated and a lot older when she put on her long black evening dress. Francis wore a tux and hired a limousine to take them there at eight o'clock and then on to the Barenaked night-club. Life was lightening up. At last. And the poor and fucking penniless had only themselves to blame and if he really was everybody else he didn't care because tonight he was himself. Francis Page. And tomorrow could take care of the rest.

The limo pulled up at the head of the queue outside the Barenaked nightspot. Francis and Glendora emerged from its plush interior. The crowd strained to see — thinking it must be some beautiful young film star and her bodyguard. Francis told the driver to go get himself something to eat and then wait for them outside. The man tipped his peaked cap and pulled slowly away. Glendora already walking towards the door and Francis knew the bouncers so there was no bother getting in. He also knew the manager who gave them a secluded table — near the bar but away from the lights and with its back to the wall. A bottle of complimentary Champagne arrived and a big cigar for Francis.

The Barenaked in Bayswater was much more *haut marché* than the Pink Peacock even though both clubs were closely located. And the clientele tended to be well matured and better heeled. Suited Francis tonight. He was carrying and preferred to rub shoulders with the macaroni than slum it across the tracks with the sorry little slagbags.

Francis sat back with his drink and watched Glendora. She looked like a picture painted by someone really famous. Worth money. Latent and daring. But there was also a nervousness about her. Eyes darting at every sudden movement and her smile not quite meaning what it said. Still wondering how well she knew the black Yardies from Manchester and formulating a plan to test her. Test her loyalty. Test her love. Test her life! During the day he thought of the word 'glo'. She said it — it was one of their words. A Yardie word. In the Black Tulip room. He thought about the word all day. Wrote it down when she was showering — to see what it looked like. It looked like a lie!

Agnes D'Argensola over at the bar with a couple of girlfriends and saw Francis before he saw her. Came across to the table.

'Francis ... *buenas noches*!'

'Agnes ... not working?'

'Cannot work every night. A girl has to have some little pleasures in life. Mind if I join you?'

Agnes looked directly at Glendora, even though she was speaking to Francis. Sat at the table before either of them had time to object.

'Don't worry, I will not stay long. I am out with the *chicas* tonight.'

'You their minder then?'

'Very funny, Francis. No, I just came across to say I am really sorry about what happened at the Peacock.'

'Not your fault. Why should you be sorry?'

'You know what I mean. We were good together.'

'We were never together, Agnes. The only way we'd be together is if we got locked in a lift.'

Francis meant it as a joke. For Glendora's sake. Even laughed. But he was sorry as soon as he said it. Agnes was fairly drunk and the remark stung her. Wasn't enough that he refused her offers of carnality and paternity but now he was making little of the professional bond between them. Francis wanted to take the words back. But didn't know how.

'I meant we were a good team, Francis. What are you doing now?'

'None of your business.'

Again. Didn't mean to be so fucking rude. The words just came out that way. Against his will. His tongue taking on a volition of its own. Not in conjunction with his brain. He wished Agnes would go away. Before things got worse.

'I heard a rumour about drugs.'

'What fucking rumour? What drugs? What are you fucking saying, Agnes?'

Agnes ignored his question and turned to Glendora.

'How is your condition, *señora negra*?'

'My condition? Frankie ...?'

'Shut the fuck up, Agnes!'

Agnes wasn't going to shut the fuck up.

'*Perdón ... ha sido de mal gusto*, especially in a posh place like this.'

'Why don't you fuck back up to your friends at the bar?'

'How is Angeline?'

Francis wondered what she knew about the witchbitch.

'How the fuck would I know?'

'She found out, did she not?'

'What? What d'you mean by that, Agnes? How d'you know about that?'

'Do you not wonder who telephoned and told her?'

'You Southamerican bitch ...'

Getoutofmyfuckingfacebeat! Francis swung his fist across the table and knocked Agnes off her chair. Blood spurted from her nose and dribbled from her mouth as she staggered back to her feet. Bouncers across the floor quickly along with the manager. While the high-class clientele scattered to a safer distance.

'She started it! That bitch wants to keep her big mouth shut!'

'I know her, boss. She's got a thing for Francis.'

'Throw the whore out!'

Agnes dragged towards the door. Swinging her handbag at the bouncers who tried to escort her. She hung onto the bar-rail and screamed obscenities in Spanish as they tried to prise her fingers loose.

'She is a drug-pusher! That *puta negra* is a drug-pusher!'

'Get her fucking out of here!'

Agnes' sister-friends came to her aid and pandemonium broke out between themselves and the door staff. Reinforcements called and the excitable women eventually fucked out. With Agnes continuing to scream at the top of her voice ...

'You think you are a big *hombre* now, Francis Page ... with your drugmoney. The rest of us are not good enough for you? Your old *amigos ... Bastardo! Malvado! Puto maricón*!'

Hanging onto the door jambs and howling across the club.

'I know her ... *puta negra*! I know where the money has come from. She is a drug dealer and she is making *el ridicúlo* out of you, Francis. And she has the AIDS!'

Doormen finally flung Agnes and friends out into the night. Francis formed a mental picture of her in the street — kicking the flamenco fuck out of the limousine. Driver pulling his hair out. Manager across to their table.

'Jesuschrist, Francis, what can I say? I knew she was one of Percy Shillinger's ... that's why I let her in. She'll never set fucking foot in here again. Nor any of the others. It's ok now folks ... please resume your seats. Security have dealt with that little problem ...'

Manager shiteing on himself and sent complimentary drinks to his more favoured clients. Fawned all over the wellheeled, upmarket moochers and hoped the little disturbance hadn't spoiled their evening. Free Champagne flew and the tension subsided with anxious laughter and nervous repartee.

Two sinister sorts in plainclothes up at the bar went unnoticed in all the commotion. Now they began to take an interest in Glendora and her escort ...

'I know that one all right, Inspector. Only too fucking well.'

Francis over the next couple of days called up his contacts at the Cosa Nostra Casino in Gloucester Place. Scouts posted for sight of any Yardies showing an interest in the whereabouts of Glendora and express instructions given that he was to be notified as soon as the bastards showed up. No sign of James fucking Greenwood and Francis made a mental note to go over and see that tosser at Shoeless Sadie's. In the meantime he recruited a few bodies from the Manor Park council estate south of the river in the Woolwich Docks area. Mad bastards who'd murder their own mothers for a fiver and anyone else for a lot less. Firearms sorted and a waiting game began.

New Year's Eve when Francis got the call. Couple of black guys with the Yardie-speak enquiring about The Countess. And when they were told she wasn't working that night they asked for her home address. Francis made the pre-arranged call to Manor Park and the trap was set. Also the test for Glendora. Just a small piece of simple surveillance equipment from a friend in the business. He hid a couple of microphones in the flat without her knowing. One in the studio and another in the bedroom. Reassured her he had things under control. She was frightened out of her wits and wanted to know why he had to leave her on her own. Told her it was necessary and she'd be ok and to stay cool and he'd be just outside the door. She didn't want him to leave her and hung onto him until he had to shout at her to get her under control. Across the street in a deserted cycle shop the Manor Park crew checked their weapons. Two in the morning before Francis heard the soft tell-tale sound of a door being forced downstairs. Put his finger up to Glendora's lips and signalled for her to pretend she was asleep on the sofa. Then silently left the flat. Francis moved across the landing and hid inside a storage cupboard. Switched his earphones on. Cautious steps on the stairs and three black figures cased their way up quietly. Others in the street outside. The flat door quickly and easily forced and they closed it behind them when they moved silently inside. Francis heard them approaching Glendora and shaking her with a hand over her frightened mouth.

'Which part yo ah mon, gel?'

'Gone!'

'Gone where seh?'

'I don't know.'

'Which part be de merchandise?'

'I got it.'

'Show!'

Sounds in the earphones of Glendora getting up and opening a drawer. Yardies whispering amongst themselves and the horse being tested.

'Look ok, gel. Where be ah money?'

'I don't know.'

'Yo mon haf dem?'

'I suppose so.'

'Which part him be now deh?'

'I told you ... I don't know.'

'How be it me breddahs jook it out of yo?'

'He left me! I don't know!'

Glendora's voice reached a higher pitch. Frightened. About to scream his name. Francis heard all he needed. She wasn't in with the bastards. Trust restored. He flung the flat door open and pointed a mini Uzi machine pistol at the black men. Glendora flew to him and hid behind his back. Francis cautiously signalled down from the window.

'Let's go!'

'Wha yo ah want seh mash up our runnins, mon?'

'Across the street, boys!'

Yardies shuffled towards the door. Eyeing Glendora threateningly. Shoulders swinging. She moved in a circle round Francis and held onto him for her life. And soul.

'Be back soon, honey. Lock the door.'

'I want to go with you ...'

'I'll be back soon. Lock the fucking door!'

Two of the Manor Park boys already on the landing outside the flat. Guns covering the situation. Four others downstairs with the drop on the Yardies who stayed in ambush outside in case anything went wrong. Jaws falling on the black men upstairs when they realised what they'd walked into. Should have been smarter in a strange city.

'Welcome to London, boys.'

Francis and his team frisked them and confiscated several Sig Sauer P228 military police pistols before escorting them downstairs and across the street to the empty cycle shop. Bastards well tooled up and Francis wondered if they brought the guns down from Manchester with them of if someone in London supplied the hardware. Who? Plenty of Yardies in this city but they were usually at war with the northern crews. Maybe that cunt Greenwood? No time to worry about it now. Francis sat the black men down and the Manor Park boys stood over them.

'My woman's on her own. She gets nervous when she's on her own, so let's get this over with.'

'Ouno ah gonna dus us, mon?'

'What gave you that fucking idea? We're civilised people down here.'

Francis lit a cigarette.

'What yo ah want den?'

'I want to make a deal.'

'What deal be dat seh?'

Blew smoke at the Yardies.

'Ok, look ... you fuckers nearly got me killed in Amsterdam so I reckon you owe me.'

'Yo de rank dat shot de Turkmon, spar ...'

'His fucking partner shot him trying to shoot me. Because your fucking money package was light.'

'Hear wha ... how be light?'

'Ten fucking grand!'

'Rass!'

Francis liked having the upper hand. For a change.

'Now, either you fuckers were setting me up to get killed, or there's a serious flaw in your organisation. Which is it?'

'Doan know. Us haf ah straighten dat out seh. Wha be yo deal, spar?'

'You keep your merchandise, I keep the cash.'

'Cyan do dat, mon ...'

'Why not?'

'Us still haf fi mek a livin. Us do business with Amsterdam all ah time, mon. One Turkmon dussed an it got seh be seen.'

Francis felt the room grow large. But he was doing his best to stay with it here. Until things were sorted.

'What about the missing money?'

'Us ah deal with dat, mon. It doan be ah yo concern seh.'

'It be my fucking concern all right! I want to know if you bastards were setting me up.'

'Why us ah do dat, spar? Us businessmen. Doan even know yo ...'

Francis thought about it for a moment and gradually came to the conclusion that the bastards were probably telling the truth and the flaw must be inside their organisation. The Manor Park boys getting restless.

'Let's just kill the cunts, Francis, then we can keep the whole fucking lot.'

Fingers twitched on triggers and adrenaline flew around the fucking hugeroom. The black men stayed stum. Francis gave them their due. No fucking cry-babies. He put his hands up in the air.

'Don't be fucking thick!'

'Why the fuck not?'

Why the fuck not? Francis had to think of a reason. While he still could.

'No killing! Because I got a woman over there who's nervous enough already. I don't want her looking at ... over her fucking shoulder for the rest of her life. And you boys all got wives and children too.'

'You ok, Francis? This is London ... you just said so.'

'Plenty of these fuckers down here ... you guys know that. Especially up here in Hackney. And these Jamaicans might fight amongst each other, but they join forces when the fuckers are threatened from outside. D'you boys want a war? I fucking don't! No killing!'

'Me kin see yo be an iree starman, breddah.'

'Shut the fuck up!'

Francis discharged his gun into the plasterboard of the wall and everybody shut up. Stresstrigger!

'I don't suppose you'd like to tell us who your contacts are down here in London?'

'Us be ded if us ah spill. Yo knows dat, mon.'

They didn't know how close they were to being dead now. Or maybe they did. Francis stayed cool. With effort.

'You black buggers ain't in no position to bargain here. But, like I said ... I know there's more fucking knotheads where you lot came from. So I'll compromise. Half each!'

'Us already give yo ah two grand seh.'

'And I got fucking overheads. You think these boys work for nothing. Half each! Take it! I'm telling, not asking.'

'Mus gwan tek it den mon. But doan tek us simple.'

Francis counted ten thousand from the money package and threw the rest on the floor — along with the horse. The black men picked it all up.

'Wha seh bout us weapons, spar?'

'You tell me where you got them and you can have them back.'

The black men shook their heads and filed out through the front door of the cycle shop. Francis watched them shouldershuffle away down the road to a dark vehicle parked on a corner near the railway station. He called out after them ...

'Nice to do business with you, boys. Call again ... sometime.'

chapter twenty-six

chapte r twenty-six

chapte r twenty-six

Francis Page waited in the Jaguar outside his ex-house in Leytonstone Road. Sunday morning churchgoers hurried to their cars and pulled their collars up against the early February weather. Francis had been waiting for a while and he looked at his watch. 11.20 a.m. Going to go up to the door but Angeline warned him not to come near her and he didn't want to fuck things up. Genetically. Genetics. Genesis. Genetic factors in the girls' favour? How many bad genes? Cut all the dirty scumthings out!

Bertie dropped the assault charges which was another good thing and for some unknown reason the police decided to let things go as well. In the clear now — so it was best to stay cool. Third time he had the girls for Sunday. That part wasn't going as well as Francis thought it would. Fiona was fine — but Sinéad seemed to go into herself when she was with him. He wondered what the bastards were saying to her. Calling him? Toerags! If he found — The door opened and Angeline stuck her head out. Looked across the road to make sure the car was there, then led her two daughters out onto the driveway. Fiona ran to the Jaguar and jumped in alongside Francis on the front seat. Angeline had to carry Sinéad reluctantly across the road. The younger girl clung to her mother's neck and looked at her father as if he was some sort of gargoyle out of a Grimms' fairytale.

'She doesn't want to go, Francis.'

'Aw c'mon, Sinéad. Angeline ...'

'We said only if they wanted to.'

'They *do* want to. C'mon, baby, get in the car and we'll go get a McDonald's.'

Sinéad didn't respond and Angeline shivered in the dying winter-wind. She waited while her ex-husband pleaded with his youngest daughter to get into the car. Francis was looking a bit better. Better than when she left him at least. And she saw something of the old Francis in his face. Like hope or belief — and even a little confidence. Maybe things would turn out ok for him. Maybe the blackwoman was good for him. Angeline felt a little twinge in her stomach when she thought that thought. It wasn't jealousy but it still twisted her gut. Made her angry for a splitsecond, but she didn't want to wish any harm on Francis. Now she had the complete independence she'd always wanted for herself and the girls were growing up it was getting better by the day. So, there was no real need for animosity. Yet it tore her just a little to think of him and her as they were for that brief period all those years ago and of him and *her* maybe being the same way now. No matter!

'She told me she doesn't want to go, Francis.'

'Or did you tell her?'

'Of course I didn't!'

'Sorry. C'mon, baby. Let's try this one last time. If you still don't want to come next time ... then we'll leave it so.'

Sinéad looked at her mother and Angeline nodded. The girl climbed slowly in onto the back seat of the car. They drove east through Stratford Town and past the shuttle and Eurostar terminals and the open spaces of playing fields and football grounds. Fiona tuned the radio and Sinéad looked forlornly out the back window at the evaporated image of her mother. As if it was the last and final time they would ever see each other again.

Francis decided it was time the girls were introduced to Glendora. Found it hard going with Sinéad on his own and so far wasn't able to get a single word out of her. Thought maybe the company of an adult female might put the girl a bit more at ease. They continued across the motorway and the Jaguar came to a halt outside the flat in Dalston Lane. Francis sounded the horn. Glendora emerged after a minute and approached the car. She was against this. Never been good with children and it was only because Francis got angry she finally agreed. The girls watched her suspiciously as she moved in onto the back seat beside Sinéad. Younger girl moved immediately away and pressed herself up against the inside of the car door.

'This is Glendora, girls.'

'She's black.'

'No, Fiona ... what you say is: "Hello Glendora, how are you?"'

'Hello, Glendora ... how are you?'

'I'm fine thank you, Fiona. And who is this?'

'This is Sinéad.'

'Hello. Sinéad ... what a lovely name.'

No response. Francis shook his head at Glendora and she didn't push things. He had an emerald ring in his pocket engraved with the letter G. Passed it on to Fiona and whispered for the girl to give the ring to Glendora. A gift from his two lovely daughters. To her. For the occasion. Symbolic. Hoping it would break the ice. Fiona's eyes were wide and she said it was beautiful. Glendora said thanks and kissed all the cheeks. Sinéad said nothing.

'Where to first, girls?'

'McDonald's!'

'That suit you, Sinéad?'

No response.

'McDonald's it is then.'

Francis was in the money. Bit like the old times when he was well respected in this town. Felt good to be back. Even if the circumstances were different. Junk would get onto the streets whether he was part of the fucking thing or not. So he might as well make what he could like all the other bastards. Some of the Voices contradicted themselves about it but he didn't give a fuck what they said. Anyway, after the total cock-up that was made of the whole fucking thing by the Yardie bastards he knew he wanted no further part of it. Even if they *did* come back to him. Which was highly fucking unlikely.

Made a point of going round to Shoeless Sadie's on the Strand and catching James fucking Greenwood by the neck. Prick nearly shit on himself and promised Francis there'd be no comebacks. And anyway he didn't know the Manchester men all that well and he was just a fucking fixer. Putting people in touch with other people so to speak. Francis never liked the bollocks and didn't believe him. Greenwood was immature. Shavehead shoulderthrower on the up. So he thought. Wanted to be with the big boys. Have the money and cars and women and drugs and didn't care how he got there. Knew everybody and into everything that was going. Talked a mile to the minute. Too much. For Francis' liking. Tosser had some sort of connection somewhere. With the Yardies. Or someone else.

But the girls were all that mattered on this little Sunday and he wanted Sinéad to love him. Like Fiona did. And it hurt him when she didn't. More deeply than it showed. Wanted to be a good father to *both* his daughters — not like that arsehole Konrad. And forget about the past and start afresh and for everyone to be happy. Ever. After. A few more minutes driving and they parked the car just off Trafalgar Square and headed for the chainburger house. Fiona hung onto Francis' arm and chattered away while Glendora and Sinéad followed silently and reluctantly behind.

'Are you and Glendora getting married, Dad?'

'I'm still married to your mother.'

'After the divorce.'

'What divorce?'

Fiona didn't mean to upset her father. But she'd said it now. So there was no use trying to take it back.

'Mum says she's getting the divorce she should have got years ago.'

'Who told her that?'

'Nobody. She decided it for herself. You'll be my stepmother then, Glendora.'

'I'm not so sure about that, Fiona ...'

'You will of course! She'll be our stepmother, Sinéad.'

Sinéad said nothing. She didn't want to talk to her sister because then she'd have to talk to her father.

'And who'll be your step*father*?'

'Nobody, Dad!'

'Ain't your mother getting married again?'

'She said only mad people get married ... and she's sane now.'

Glendora laughed. Francis looked at her with a frown and she put her hand over her mouth.

'Eat your burger and chips, Sinéad.'

'Fries!'

'What?'

'Burger and *fries*. You're a dinosaur, Dad!'

'Don't call me that! Sorry. Sorry ... did you hear what that Fiona called me, Glenny?

'I heard. I don't think she meant ...'

'Don't you start as well. Are you going to stick up for me, Sinéad?'

No response. The younger girl picked at her meal and took an odd sip from her banana-flavoured milkshake.

'Is she all *right*?'

'Course she is. You're all right, ain't you, Sinéad?'

Sinéad said nothing. Her father intimidated her. Even though he didn't do it intentionally and didn't know he was doing it at all.

'No ... I mean, is she "all right"?'

'What?'

'She *can* speak, can't she?'

'Of course she can speak! What the fuck are you saying, Glendora?'

'Nothing, Frankie. It's just that she hasn't said a word ...'

'Are you insinuating she's fucking retarded?'

'Of course I'm not ...'

'There's fuck-all wrong with either of my daughters!'

Francis brought his fist down hard on the table. Stresstrigger! Genebeat! Glendora and Fiona fell silent. Sinéad began to cry. Other eaters around them went quiet. Serving staff said nothing. People looked away and pretended. Pizzicato phrases behind their hands. And Sinéad's small sobs.

'Now look what you've done.'

'You did it, Frankie, not me. I'm sorry, girls ...'

'Let's get out of here. We're finished anyway.'

Fiona pushed the remaining fries into her mouth. Sinéad stood up and wiped her eyes.

'I know what we'll do ... let's go up to Oxford Street and buy something.'

'Clothes?'

'I was thinking about some toys.'

'I'm too old for toys, Dad!'

'She is not. Is she, Sinéad?'

No response. They left the restaurant with Fiona pleading with her father to buy her some CDs if she couldn't have clothes and him smiling and saying that he'd have to see what kind of music was on them and Glendora and Sinéad walked silently behind all the way to the Jaguar and reluctantly climbed inside. Francis didn't see the car that pulled out after him as he drove away up the Haymarket towards Piccadilly Circus.

Deoxyribonucleic acid! A self-replicating material present in all living organisms as a constituent of chromosomes and the carrier of genetic information. Francis didn't know where the fuck *that* came from. Just appeared in his head. As he was driving. From out of the blue. Maybe he read it somewhere or saw it on the television? Fuck it! Forget it. Strange to think that part of him was in the girls. Part of what made him what he was. Part of Angeline also. What made her what she was. He was what his father and mother made. Annie and Konrad. They made him. He was them. And somefuckingthing it was as well! He only hoped whatever good they gave him was passed on to the girls. Might be ok. Delusions and hallucinations were secondary symptoms rather than part of the primary process — maybe due to lifestyle and cell deflection stops infection. Nutrition? Drugs. Alcohol. There was a good side to him too. From now on the good side was going to take preference over the other thing. Maybe that would rub off. Course they also had the holierthanthous in them and Angeline's shitdontstink syndrome. What a fucking mixture. God help the poor dolls!

The Jaguar drove itself round the Circus and into Shaftsbury Avenue. Fiona's chattering voice blurred into the noise of the West End and the silence from the back seat became cerulean. Like the sky beyond the car window. Francis glanced up and saw clearly the Universe expanding. The space beyond the interior of the Jaguar growing steadily towards its destiny. What was really out there? The Voices told him things but mostly he didn't believe them. Most of the time he realised they were imaginary. Some of the time of course they weren't. Some of the time they were real. What about when they became real all the time? When reality became a vacuum and all there would be was the Voices? Francis knew they were steadily becoming a physical part of him. Like his nose. Or his arm. He was *listening* now to the things they told him. Not like before. Arguing with them. Debating. Turning their messages over in his mind and making nonsense of his previous understanding of the world. Heat goes to hydrogen goes to helium goes to carbon goes to oxygen goes to heavyelements goes to ninetytwo goes to nature. Again! Atoms to molecules to bases to amino acids to proteins to cells to amoebas to fish to amphibians to animals to man to murder! Concentrate on the fucking driving! Keep your mind on the fucking road! In the end death. Or in the beginning death. Whatever way you wanted to look at it. Death! The thing no one could look full in the face. Only Animalkhan. Institutionalised death. Invisible death. Denied death. Alwaystheredeath. Always. Still there. Waiting. Escapeless. No matter how you tried to hide it. At least until the cryonics and genetics and eugenics and bionics. Or else believe in Alienchrist. Francis swerved to avoid a bus and Fiona shouted watch out dad and Glendora gasped in the back seat and no response from Sinéad.

He lit up a cigarette and Fiona coughed like her mother and waved the smoke away. Rolled down the window and threw the butt out into the street. The car made its way slowly north along Windmill and Lexington and Poland Street. Parked up in Dufours Place and out to stretch the legs. Early afternoon and a fair crowd in Oxford Street — for the time of year. They moved through the shops that were Sundayopen with Fiona wanting this and that and the other and Francis shook his head but bought them for her all the same. And Glendora walked silently behind and Sinéad reluctantly accepted the gifts from her father. Began to rain. They hurried back to the Jaguar. Francis suggested the cinema and Fiona said the name of some new film but Glendora had developed a headache and Sinéad made no response at all. So he decided to drop Glendora back at the flat. Kissed her but she drew away. Cold. Shoulder. And went inside without saying goodbye to anyone.

Francis decided to take the girls for tea to the Cybercookie Café in Bethnal Green and bought them lemonade and cakes and black coffee for himself. Wanted a cigarette badly but was determined to show the girls his good side and didn't have one. Cigarette. *Had* a good side. He had! Hadn't he? Wouldn't fucking kill him for an hour or two. To do without a fag. Then he took them back to his ex-house out in Leytonstone Road. Francis sounded the horn and Angeline came to the door. Sinéad jumped immediately from the back of the car and ran to her mother without a goodbye kiss or anything. She left her presents on the seat and Fiona had to carry them across the road. After giving her father a big hug and telling him thanks and she loved him a lot and would look forward to their next outing. In a fortnight's time. Sinéad already inside the house. And Angeline shrugged her shoulders at him while she waited for Fiona to finish waving.

Francis sat in the car for a while and smoked a cigarette. He felt uneasy. A smell of danger in the air. The girls were in danger. Who said that? Were they ? From who? What? He'd kill anything that came near them. Kill. It was becoming an easy word to say. He was a drug-courier now and they spoke like that. Words like that. Kill. And crucify. And every tosser was twofaced. Couldn't believe a word out of any of their fucking mouths. As long as he knew *that* he'd be on his guard and everything would be all right and so would his daughters. No fucking fear!

The Sunday evening street was deserted. All the wankers back inside for their tea. Watching pornography on the television sets and running down every other fucker in the near neighbourhood. Or complaining about their jobs or shiteing on about what a lovely little family they were and this other one was a fucking whore with half the town up her and that one was a queer and the foreigners were all clever lazycunts. Did they think they were? Who? Right? Maybe Annie was right. Maybe Konrad — bastard that he was. Back in South Africa or downinthedustdead? Who the fuck cared in any case?

Almost dark and silence along the street unsettling. Two stray dogs padded towards him. The closer they came the bigger they grew. Alongside the car they looked like fucking horses. Who owned them and did the bastard send them out to get him? Growled outside the window and Francis could smell the dampness off them. Like decay. Could smell the animalness of them and the hatred on their breath. Thought of Genghiskhan. They growled and stood on their hind legs and looked in at him. Francis noticed curtains being moved and rat-eyes peering out. From all sides. Evil eyes. Ignorant eyes. He started the engine and stretched away down the street. Hoping he'd run over and killed the dirty mongrels.

chapter twenty-seven

chapte r twenty-seven

chapte r twenty-seven

Sinéad didn't come out any more Sundays. Neither did Glendora. Just Fiona and Francis Page from then on. Also a while since Amsterdam and the money beginning to feel a bit thin. Rest of the doormen had already fucked off on the American tour and Francis feeling a bit blown away. On his own. Alone. Feeling a bit dejected and left out. Feeling a deeper kind of dread than the one he was used to. A jerky feverish fear. He could see evidence of the deception all around him. In the way clouds were arranged in the sky. Or how a tree cast its shadow. Or the alignment of glasses on a bar. Or a sinister street name. The caricature of himself that passed for his personality was regressing further into a self-obsessed limbo. A parallel world. A dimension outside the ones he already knew. Or thought he knew. He began to observe people more closely than ever before. From a distance. From inside himself. Particularly people he believed might be on the edge — like him. Not like him. You could see the fuckers every day. Walking around. Just walking aimlessly around. Not knowing where they'd come from or where the fuck they wanted to go. Francis could tell they were gone when he saw them on the street in flared trousers up around their ankles and red stripy socks and sports coats a couple of sizes too small fastened across their bellies by a middle button. Or a safety pin. People lost to the world. Disappeared into disregard and deadpan indifference. I'm gone, Uncle John — don't you know I'm gone.

Francis began to train again — this time at The Ironman Gym over near West Ham. Alone. Barred from the Hardcore — along with a lot of other fucking places. Glendora was tired and wanted to stay in bed. More listless than usual lately and he wondered if this was the beginning of a deterioration in her condition. Maybe it was time for the AIDS to come? He asked her to go see the doctor but she said her regular check-up was due soon and she wanted to wait. Wanted to be on her own a lot these days. Feeling blue. Feeling let down a little because of what he did to her. That time. When he left her alone in the flat with the Yardies. Even if it was only for a minute. Even if he was right outside the door. For a moment she thought he'd gone and she was dead. And the letdown feeling in the bottom of her stomach just wouldn't go away. No matter how she tried or what she said or where she went. Francis believed it was something to do with the virus. He considered she might be afraid. Might not want to know. What was wrong. Not yet. Not for a day or two more. A week or two more.

Vomen, Shegetz. Zey are not nor.... You told me! *Oy vey ... lechayim, shomer shabbat*! You know everyzink now? I didn't say that ... Do not get too clever, Shegetz. Ignorance is a safety mechanism. Ve vould go mad if ve knew everyzink. I'm already mad. Are you? You told me! You told me what's normal and it doesn't fit me. What fits you, Shegetz? Nothing. Anything anything anything anyfuckingthing. The thing in my head or maybe not says evolution is continuing and maybe my condition is part of the process? Vat do you think? Don't know don't know. Maybe in ze future you vill be considered a genius. Like me. I say I can see the future. Can you, Shegetz? I can see the whole fucking lot. It says no one can see the whole lot. I know I can. It's impossible. I ask how so you say, Scientist? Because of ze choices ozer people make. Decisions. It says to see ze whole caboodle you vould haf to see through all ze eyes on ze planet. I *am* all the eyes on the planet ... and the Universe. Alienchrist told me. And all the parallel worlds as well. Oy vey ... you are some crazy *meshugina*. Don't don't don't! And zey say scientists is mad ... why do you think you know everyzink, Shegetz? God told me. Things. I say, like ... how we sometimes step into the parallel worlds. We sometimes fall through the gateway. Accidentally. Inadvertently. Step over to find ourselves there ... on the other side. In a strange place that only looks familiar. I ask if that's normal? It says sure it is. Maybe not right now ... but everyzink is normal in ze long run. It is all down to perception. Some people haf a reduced perception of things und zey believe zat reduced perception is normality. Normality. Reasonability. Logicality. Rationality. My vord! Ve know it is not ... you und I, Shegetz. To ze rest of ze *naares* everyzink else is 'ab' or 'sub'. Some can by-pass ze filter. Accommodate more. Zat's all! Zere is no more 'ab' or 'sub' in ze bigger vallvindow. How many times, Shegetz, haf you been scheduled to go someplace, but you get a strange feelink to stay home? I shout never! Sure you haf. Modern life, Shegetz. Modern life blocks out ze sixthsense. Somezink gets past ze filter zat ve are not ready for yet. Routine und schedules und rushink all over ze place und clichés like quality time und ozer *schmooze* make you ignorant. What kind of a scientist are you? It says a reasonable one. It is reasonable. Normalable. Logicable. Rationalable. Tells me to reason it out for myself if I still have doubts. You book a flight und get ze feelink about it. You haf already paid for ze ticket, so you say ... vat ze hell, it's chust a crazy feelink. Ze plane crashes. Nobody ever knows about ze feelink. Huh?

Sein und Zeit!

'Francis Page?'

'Who wants to know?'

'I'm Detective Inspector Dunne and this is Detective Sergeant Spencer ... drug squad.'

Two men in tracksuits stood over Francis as he pumped out a ten-rep set on the bench press. With smirks across their slagfaces as wide as the Thames. Francis sat up. Only a couple of other lifters in the gym and the two men pulled up a bench and sat facing him. Didn't speak for a long time.

'What the fuck d'you people want?'

'We've been watching you, Francis.'

Francis continued with another set on the apparatus.

'I know you've been watching me. You didn't think I knew? I did!'

'You and your girlfriend.'

'And we know you had a little trip to Amsterdam over the Christmas.'

'So fucking what?'

'Holiday?'

'Did you bastards pay for it?'

'No ...'

Francis sat up and faced them.

'Then it's none of your bloody business.'

'We know why you were over there, Francis.'

'Then you know I was visiting an old friend.'

'Oh yes ... Julien. We know all about him too.'

What did they know about Julien? Nothing! Nothing!

'He's a fucking wine merchant ...'

'Bit of a connoisseur are you, Francis?'

'All this is very interesting I'm fucking sure. But I'd like to get on with my work-out if you don't fucking mind.'

'Like to keep in shape, don't you?'

It was none of their business what he liked. But Francis wanted to be cool. Stay cool.

'I'm trying to get back into it. You two could do with losing a few pounds. Are those tracksuits supposed to be camouflage or what? If they are then it ain't working. Spot you a fucking mile off. And I don't want to be seen talking to you.'

'No one in here to see us, Francis.'

'We've been careful. We could have come up to you before now, but the last thing we want is to arouse suspicion.'

Suspicion. The word detached itself from the rest and repeated itself over and over. Until it became absurd.

'What fucking suspicion? What are you talking about?'

'We wouldn't want people to think you're a grass, Francis ... a copper's nark.'

'I'm *not* a fucking grass! Nor a nark! Not me! Never!'

'Precisely.'

'What are you afraid of, Francis?'

'I got nothing to be afraid of! Who told you that? Nothing!'

Francis rose from the bench-press and began to walk away. D.I. Dunne grabbed his arm. Beat! Francis could feel the heat rising. But he knew he wouldn't win against these bastards. They got you every time — whether you were in the fucking frame or not. It didn't matter. All the same, there was a limit to what he'd put up with. Francis beatglared at D.I. Dunne. The detective released his grip.

'What about Amsterdam, Francis?'

'I thought you said you knew all about it?'

'Tell us your story.'

The whole story. Sad story. Sad sad sad sad. Come back!

'Nice place. Plenty of perverts. Suit you two down to the fucking ground.'

'What about heroin?'

'Filthy fucking stuff. A disease on the face of the planet.'

'Why are you running it then?'

They knew! Be cool. Cool cool cool cool.

'How dare you even suggest such a thing! I'll be calling my fucking brief.'

'Your little schwartzer knows all about it, doesn't she?'

Beatbeatbeatbeat! Francis clenched his fists. Near the point. Getting to the point where he didn't care if this cunt was the chief fucking constable. He'd still kill him. With his bare fucking hands.

'Let's get to the point here. We know you're bringing in the skag, Francis, so don't bother us with your fucking fairy stories.'

'Bringing in what?'

'H, heaven, horse, smack, brown, stage, skag ... whatever you want to call it.'

'We're not interested in you, Francis.'

'We know you're only the messenger boy.'

'We want to know who you're working for.'

'Simple as that!'

Francis walked to the pec-dec. The men followed.

'It's as simple as ... I don't know what the fuck you pair of fucking comedians are talking about.'

'We can do this the easy way, Francis ...'

'Or the fucking hard way!'

'So don't be a thick arsehole all your life.'

'Do yourself a favour, Francis ...'

'Do yourself a fucking favour ...'

He started a set. They waited until he finished.

'Look ... these are pennyboys you're working for. Only bringing in a bit at a time. Haven't got the money or infrastructure to bring a ton or two through in containers ... direct. Straight from Spain or Portugal.'

'Or maybe they're new boys on the block trying to cut some territory. Bringing in a few Ks at first, before going on to bigger things.'

'If they're not killed first.'

'So they rely on arseholes like you, Francis, to bring the stuff in via the airports.'

'Very risky. Couriers take all the risks. For peanuts.'

'Balloons inside their bellies ... or bottled up their arses ... or fannies for that matter.'

'While the dealers sit back and count the cash. These are the bastards we want, Francis. These guys will sing when we get them.'

'Not big enough to buy their way out and worried about going inside because of who they've crossed to get where they are ... you see what we mean?'

He saw what they meant all right. They were trying to trick him. With their soft words. Their marshmallow words.

'I know what you're saying ... I just don't know what the fuck it's got to do with me.'

'We just want you to set up another little trip.'

'Only this time let us in on it.'

'We're waiting at the drop ...'

'We arrest the main men ... the dealers, and send them off to jail where they belong ...'

'We're not interested in small fry like you, Francis.'

'You help us and we'll help you.'

The men were becoming remote. Outside the reality of the gym. Which had itself grown larger than it was. He knew it was time to leave.

'How would you do that? What would I get out of this little hypothetical arrangement?'

'You, Francis, would get to keep your little bitch nigger ...'

Stresstrigger! Francis jumped up and hit D.S. Spencer in the face before he'd even finished speaking. Cuntbeat! The man's eyes crossed in his head and he fell backwards off the bench onto the floor. D.I. Dunne grabbed Francis to prevent him from doing more damage. Francis shook the man off and turned to face him. But he didn't hit the inspector. D.S. Spencer shook the spinning stars out of his head and tried to crawl back to the bench.

'Francis, Francis ... you could get yourself arrested for smacking a detective sergeant in the face.'

'Fuck him ... and you.'

'I know he can have a bit of a bad mouth on him, Francis, but basically ... you don't want to cross him. He can do things ... not above doing things, if you know what I mean.'

'What things?'

'Spencer is a bit of a villain himself, Francis ... not above fitting someone up if he wants to. You know how these things work ... you've been around the block.'

D.S. Spencer on his knees over the bench and spitting blood onto the floor. D.I. Dunne put his arm round Francis' shoulder and took him over to one side. Voice low so the D.S. couldn't hear him.

'Spencer knows you got your girlfriend off the shit, Francis, and how she depends on you. Depends on you a lot from all accounts.'

'You leave her alone or I'll kill the fucking pair of you!'

'Jesus, Francis ... I'm on your side. I'm trying to fucking help you out here. Everyone knows she gets frightened when you're not with her ...'

'Everyone ...? I'm with her all the time now.'

'But you wouldn't be with her, would you, Francis?'

'What?'

'In Holloway. If someone fits her up for a fall. Some people on the force are racists, it's inevitable and no matter how hard we try, we can't keep them all out. And they don't allow minders into the women's prison. Look ... I'm talking straight, Francis, but everyone else is not like me. It might be out of my hands ...'

Francis tried to listen. But all he could see was Glendora in a cell and all he could hear was her heartbreaking sobs. And the sound of her smallvoice calling his name. D.I. Dunne patted Francis on the back and returned to help D.S. Spencer to his feet. The Detective Sergeant glared at Francis with contempt before being led from the weightroom by his superior. Francis sat back down on the bench. He wondered where the fuck that pair of bastards had come from. How much did they know? And who the fuck told them?

Whatever else happened — Francis was lucid enough to know he couldn't allow Glendora to go to prison. That was one thing that couldn't happen. No matter what else did. That was one thing that wouldn't happen. Would not happen! Wouldnot. Happen. She'd die in there. He found it hard enough himself when he was inside and if he found it hard — what the fuck would it do to Glendora? All the slags would be onto her. Every fucking screw and con and junkie and psycho and lesbian. It would not fucking happen! Another pick-up for the pushers? That was going to be impossible to arrange. Francis doubted if they'd come within fifty fucking miles of him after Amsterdam. But it had to be done. Somehow. Some. Way. There might be others. Glenny might know. Or James fucking Greenwood. Although he wasn't a grass, Francis didn't care what fucker he crucified when it came down to Glendora.

Over in a corner the woman in black watched him from an exercise bicycle.

She's not looking my way but I know she's watching me. I can hear her saying know your enemy! Jalal al-Din! Study him. Be close to him. I say I know these slags all right ... but they have me by the bollocks at the moment. She says I should have been prepared. For whatever comes. Even if it is death. Asks if I've been listening to her at all? I tell her I'll work some fucking thing out ... just need to think. She tells me not to take anything for granted. Everything for granted. I won't.

I won't. She says anything can occur in the turmoil of battle ... that every warrior believes death will visit the next man. Not him. Otherwise he would be afraid. And many die unprepared. I should use my time wisely. If you have done nothing with today, it is because you believe you have many more days. You believe you can spare one. Or two. A month. A year. You waste this time on nothing. On things that do not matter. She tells me to ask the question ... what if tomorrow were to be the final day of my life? Would I waste today? She says many pretend they are preparing. Yet few are ever prepared. I say I'm not worried about myself, Khangeng ... but she depends on me. The woman ... you know how you are. She tells me my destiny is the woman's destiny. And there are dangers around every bend in the river. Behind every tree in the forest. In every man's eyes. In every woman's smile. I myself was killed by Korbelin as I lay with her in an embrace. Lesbians? It was at Yinchuan ... or perhaps Gansu. Or crossing the Wei river. Or outside Ejin Hor Qi. I cannot be certain. It could have been at any of these places. Or a thousand others. The danger is everywhere. It is constant. And no matter how careful a man, it will kill him in the end. Even a warrior like you.

And a God like me.

Francis left The Ironman Gym near West Ham and picked up the Jaguar from the car park. He sat behind the wheel for a while. Trying to think. D.I. Dunne and D.S. Spencer would be back. Especially Spencer — slags like him would keep coming back until they were sorted out. One way or the other. Could be a strain minding Glendora sometimes. She made him vulnerable to all sorts of shitbags. That's why he didn't want to move in with her. Better to keep a bit of distance. But it was too late now. Sometimes Francis kind of half-wished the AIDS would finally do its work. But not really. Yes — sometimes. Then he felt guilty for the feeling. Knew enough about it to know it wasn't nice. A cold — the flu at first. He was always watching out for signs. Skin cancer. Internal infection. Thrush. Herpes. Brain damage. Worse things — and finally a hard fucking death. No!

No no fucking no! Not for Glenny. He'd shoot her in the head with the fucking Glock first. Put her out of her misery. Why the fuck wasn't there a cure? By now? He'd sort it out for her if he could. Whatever she needed. He'd make sure she got anything — AZT, enzymes, protease inhibitors, combination therapy, any kind of drug cocktail — no matter howthefuck much it cost. Too late for a vaccine — even if they found one. Maybe it would never come to it. Francis heard or read or saw something about prostitutes in Africa who were immune to the virus. High levels of T cells. Whatever the fuck they were. He'd buy her some if he could. Steal her some. Glendora knew what might be facing her. Knew about the drug side effects — depressions, sickness, diarrhoea, numbness, tuberculosis and the fucking rest. Knew about kemokinds and virus mutations and coat proteins and canary pox and antivirals and loads of other shit. Knowing wasn't enough. Horse bolted and the damage done. No going back. No use being sorry now. No penance. No absolution. No mercy. It. The thing. The problem. The *problem*. No solution to the *problem*. One of two things — stabilisation or shooting. One or the other. And now there was D.I. Dunne and D.S. Spencer. Shite!

chapter twenty-eight

chapte r twenty-eight

chapte r twenty-eight

Shoeless Sadie's was swinging to the laidback jazz sound that was its trademark. Francis Page didn't like the noise. Glendora did. The music brought something back to life in her because she'd been a bit down for a few weeks now — and while Francis believed it was probably nothing, in her condition everything was something. Francis knew the manager who found them a table away from the weirdos and ordered a couple of complimentary drinks. Talked about the bouncers away on the American tour and asked Francis if he heard Jack Black was dead. Died while out there. In a place called Detroit. Rest of the boys bringing the body home with them when the tour ended in a week or so. Francis wasn't interested and James Greenwood was supposed to be working that evening but the manager had seen no sign of the young bollocks yet. Probably fucked off if he copped Francis coming in. Glendora looked pale. Francis said nothing to her. Better to say fuck-all under the circumstances.

He watched round the room for any sign of his man. With-it people everywhere. Intheknow types and chic sorts with werepartofthisscene attitudes. A multi-visaged kaleidoscope laughed back at him. Told him it knew something he didn't. Swirled round and came right up close and grinned into his face. Then shrunk back before he could get a good fucking smack at the smugness. One minute the place seemed as big as a football pitch and the next the whole crowd of derniercriclients were on top of his table. Francis tried to brush them away but Glendora caught hold of his arm and sat him back down on the seat. Her small hands felt like skeleton fingers on him. Her words swirled in the prismatic air. Bumping into him like flies. In a desert. Flies in the madness. Madness was a desert. It was selfcontained. Barren. Clean. Untouchable. Yet touching things outside itself. Francis wondered when it was that life began to change. Was it yesterday? Or ten years ago? Or had it always been changing and he just hadn't noticed until now? Had the changes accelerated lately? So much so that they were becoming obvious to everybody. How could he stabilise his life? How could he make it slow down? It was going too fast and he was likely to lose control. He needed to do something — but he didn't know what. Somebody knew. Glendora? Angeline? James Greenwood?

'James Greenwood ...'

'Where?'

'Over there, near the door.'

Glendora pointed and Francis flew across the floor before the shavehead saw him and did a bodyswerve.

'James ...'

'Francis? Christ, you frightened the life out of me. What d'you want, Francis? What's wrong now, eh?'

'Nothing's wrong. How're things, James?'

'All the better for not seeing you. Fuck it, Francis ... I never see you unless it's trouble ...'

'Listen, James, all that other thing was just a misunderstanding.'

'What thing? Oh ... that thing. Glad to hear it, Francis. Everything's ok then?'

Everything wasn't ok. Nothing was ok. Was ever ok. Would ever be ok.

'Listen ... I need a small favour from you ...'

'Jesus, I hope you're not going to say what I think you're going to say ...'

'What d'you think I'm going to say?'

'Say it first, then I'll tell you.'

The little rat was talking in riddles. Francis didn't want to get confused. Had to keep a clear head.

'Bringing in some junk?'

'You're fucking clairvoyant! Jesus Christ Almighty ... I don't fucking believe it ...'

Francis wondered if he was taking the piss. If he was —

'Last time was just a bit of a breakdown in communications.'

'I'll say! No way, Francis! Those Yardie bastards came after me ... after you were finished with them. As if it was all my fault. I barely escaped with my fucking ears.'

'It was *their* fault, James, not yours nor mine.'

'They won't trust me again, Francis. They won't trust anyone. And certainly not you!'

Francis didn't care whether they trusted him or not. Business was business. Nobody trusted anybody in business.

'How can I get in touch with them?'

'How the fuck would I know? I don't know fucking everything, y'know ...'

'You knew before.'

'I used to know, Francis. Those boys move about. I don't know where they've gone. They could be anywhere.'

'They live in fucking Manchester, James ... unless they've fucked back to Jamaica?'

Greenwood was winding him up. Francis clenched his fists.

'All right, all fucking right! I've got a telephone number ... that's all. There's nothing else I can do for you, Francis. Honest!'

'In Manchester?'

'Sure, it's in Manchester ... where else? Of course ... Manchester.'

'It'll have to fucking do.'

'Just don't involve me, Francis. I've had enough of all that crap to last me.'

'Ok, ok ... you're not fucking involved.'

Francis ripped the piece of paper from James Greenwood's fingers and stalked back across the floor to Glendora. Noticed Greenwood shortly afterwards whispering an excuse in the club manager's ear and disappearing. Maybe he was afraid Francis would come back — looking for more beans to be spilled. Or blood. Unstable. Unpredictable. Both of them. Better to be gone. In either direction. Francis showed the piece of paper to Glendora.

'That's all the prick's got ... or says he's got.'

'I think you should leave it, Frankie.'

'I can't leave it!'

'You got twelve thousand last time. That was enough to go to the bank with.'

'I had expenses, Glendora.'

'What expenses?'

Questions. He didn't like her asking questions. As if she didn't trust him or something. Maybe she didn't trust him. Like he didn't trust her.

'The Manor Park crew took five grand. And we ain't exactly been living a quiet life since then. Bought a lot of stuff for the girls and lost a bit on the horses and in a few clubs.'

'How much left?'

More fucking questions.

'Two grand.'

'Oh, Frankie ...'

'Never mind the "Oh, Frankie!" Got to do one more. A big one.'

'And you think they'll do business with you, after the last time?'

'I can only fucking ask.'

'And they can only tell you where to go.'

Francis wondered who the fuck's side she was on.

'If they do, they do.'

'What about getting a job?'

'A what?'

'You know ... a job.'

'Like ... straight work?'

'Yes.'

'You're fucking crazier than me!'

Early morning when Francis and Glendora got back to the flat in Dalston Lane. She went straight to bed. Because she said she was extremely tired. He sat in the kitchen for a while with a cup of coffee and a cigarette. Eyeless and Earless came and sat with him and told him not to get too far down on the drug thing. Told him to stay cool and off the guilt trips and it was just a matter of relativity. That's all. Told him he had to give up his bad habits for better ones and then laughed in his face and it was all just a matter of respectability. That's all. A matter of each to his own. That's all. And it was all a matter of who had the right to go about saying who should do what. That was all. But Francis knew there had to be some fucking control somewhere. And he kept remembering the kids. And they said it was all to do with sedentary cloning. Much more dangerous than drugs. Man. And happiness was synonymous with subordination. Keep 'em amused and they'd control themselves. But it wasn't enough. Everyone wanted to escape. The urge to escape was in everyone all the time. It was just a matter of the way we were. That's all. Nothing else. The human condition. Francis didn't give a flying fuck who took drugs and who didn't. Long as it wasn't Glendora. Yes he did! No he didn't! They told him in the only way he could acknowledge that ancient civilisations took the poppy for religious purposes. For medicine and enlightenment. And what about normality? And there were many windows in the wall. Seeing beyond the limit of vision. That was the problem. People saw too much and became troublesome. Understood too much. Began to take liberties. Couldn't be allowed. Had to be stopped. Whole of civilisation could come to a halt. Maybe it fucking should! No more. No more. No more!

The sky outside the flat lit up with an instant brightness. Then faded back to black. Francis wondered what it was. A comet? A UFO? An exploding star? Maybe an angel falling from heaven. Too late now to know. Gone. Melatonin began to secrete from the pineal gland in the stem of his brain. Francis could see for a brief moment through his third eye. The beta waves of his brain accelerated and excited him — sitting there with his coffee and cigarettes. And he knew that he didn't need to move to be active and he saw that the Almighty was made in his image ... Matthew, Mark, Luke and John ... $E = mc^2/X^n+Y^n=Z^n/G+\Lambda g=8\pi T$. He saw that money and beauty and health led to the inevitable next step — God. Preservation. Conservation.

The Cosmological Constant. $S=K\log W$.

The first faint fingers of dawn began to lighten the sky out over the Thames estuary. Francis felt tired. Hardly touched the coffee and several cigarettes burned away in the ashtray. Glendora stirred in the bedroom and made a little moaning sound. He listened for a moment and the sound stopped. Earlyspring birds whistled in the trees around Dalston Hospital and the ghost of a moon laughed down at the sad logistics of a sick earth — unexceptional little planet circling round a middle-aged sun in an ordinary galaxy out in the arsehole of the Universe. Francis stood up and walked to the bedroom. Glendora looked like a spectre lying there. Skin almost transparent and her eyes dark holes in a small brown face. He undressed and climbed into bed beside her. She turned over and her arm fell across his chest. He could feel the fever running from her and into him. And he knew she would be all right. Hoped. She. Could.

'Doan know why us ah doin bizness, bwoy.'

'I told you on the phone, I'm giving you men a chance to get back what you lost on the last job.'

'How yo ah do dat, mon?'

'A big run. The biggest you've got. I'll go anywhere and bring back as much as I can fucking carry. You pay me twenty grand and that's it. A fixed fee. No percentages or nothing else. Anything you make is your own fucking business.'

Blondin's Bar in Covent Garden was quiet in the early justafter-openingtime morning. Francis sat with two of the previous Manchester Yardies in a corner of the room. He sipped a Jack Daniels and soda and the coloured men drank mineral water. They'd wanted the meet to take place in Manchester like before. But Francis reckoned that was a recipe for a bullet in the back of his head. So he convinced them with a lot of difficulty and duckdiving that Central London would be safer and made them an offer he knew they wouldn't refuse. The men whispered between themselves for a moment or two and then turned back to Francis.

'America.'

'What?'

'Dat be where ah big money at, mon.'

'Tink yo ah bring in twenty kilos?'

'Fuck off!'

'Dat be a yes or no seh?'

'How the fuck am I supposed to carry in twenty kilos?'

'Dat yo bizness, bwoy. But us no smalltime rudies, mon. Doan get youths dem swallow balloons no more. Too many accident and loose end seh. It be in special packaging.'

Francis already didn't like the sound of this thing. But he had to listen.

'What kind of special packaging?'

'New ting, mon. Dis stuff be ah undetectable under seh airport security equipment.'

'I never heard of anything like that before ...'

'Yo ain't in the game, mon. Dis stuff designed fi de Space-Station ting.'

'Only available in America. Anti-photosens'tive ... anti-magnet an no video frequency nor lightsens'tive electromagnet radiation stuff see thru it seh.'

Francis didn't know what they were talking about. But he pretended he did.

'What the fuck is this stuff called?'

'On the street it be known as "surestuff". Be like clingfilm dat ... transparent an flexible ... only wi same property lik lead dem.'

'Even so ... it's too much weight. No way I could get that much through.'

'Us cyan do ah bizness den, spar.'

The black men began to stand up.

'Wait. Look ... be realistic for fuck's sake.'

'Shouldn't trust yo atall, mon. Doan know wha yo worry bout. We ah done dis before seh.'

'With twenty kilos?'

'Maybe not dat much ...'

'Be cool y'know dat. No danger.'

'It's still a lot of fucking weight ...'

'Us hear yo ah mash up wit de mon an cyan get no work seh ah breakin heads. Dat be straight?'

'So yo gotta tek wha yo ah get.'

'Yo ah wants it or not then, spar?'

How did they know he was out of work? Somebody was fucking talking. Somewhere.

'I don't know ...'

'Yo cum fi we, mon. Us shouldn't be doin bizness dem wit yo atall pon wha yo dun by us before.'

'You fuckers nearly got me killed with your fucking cock-ups. I'm the one shouldn't be doing business with you. If Amsterdam's anything to go by, I'm sticking my head in a fucking noose.'

Francis reckoned fuck them. He knew they needed him as much as. As much as. As?

'Us doan find no ranks tek dat missin ten grand. But yo haf ah point, mon. Dis time dere be ah no money fi handle seh.'

'How so?'

'Dat all be ah seen in advance. Yo just pick up de snow an bring ah back.'

'Snow?'

'Sure, mon. Cum from Yardman in Florida. Us connection dere.'

'Not heroin?'

'Heroin be from east seh. Charlie be west, spar.'

'Where in America?'

'New York.'

'De idrin dem bring ah coke up from Jamdown an yo seh bring ah back yah.'

'To London or Manchester?'

'London ... lik before. Only dis time us meet at ah airport.'

Cunts! They didn't trust him. But he didn't care. Business was business.

'And my money?'

'Half now, half later.'

'It's still a lot of fucking weight.'

'Hear wha ... yo wan fi mek money or not?'

'Ok, ok. I'm in!'

'De woman be ah wid yo agin.'

No. Francis didn't want Glendora going. Not after the last time.

'Too dangerous for her.'

'Look better seh mon ... us explain all dat before.'

'I don't want her involved.'

Both of the black men stood up and put on their coats.

'Wait ...'

They hesitated while Francis made up his mind. But his mind was already made up.

'All fucking right! You bastards. On one condition.'

'Wha be dat, mon?'

'We travel next week.'

'Doan know if us cin set itall up dat fast.'

'Next week or not at all.'

The Yardies whispered again between themselves.

'How fi seh nex week special?'

'I'm going away after that.'

'What part deh, spar?'

'None of your fucking business ... but it's for a long time.'

'Me doan lik dis seh ...'

'Look, you fuckers are putting the pressure on me to run twenty kilos. Next week's the only time I can do it.'

The black men whispered together again. For a long while. One for, the other against. The one for won the argument in the end and turned back to Francis and made a fist. Francis shrugged his shoulders. The one against leaned across the table and looked straight into Francis' eyes.

'No double-cross dis time, dogheart.'

Both Yardies turned and walked away from the table. Francis shouted after them.

'Tickets?'

'Be in de post, mon.'

The dealers left the bar. And it was as if they'd never been there. It was as if a kind of breeze had blown through the place. Blackbreeze. Moving the curtains and disturbing the beer mats and making Francis shiver. Somebody walking on his grave. Then everything returned to normal. Francis ordered another Jack Daniels and soda and sat at the table for a long time. Head full of sparks and quarks and helium and helicopters. He remembered D.I. Dunne, and the smug racist face of D.S. Spencer floated in the boozy air before his eyes. Francis didn't really know what to do now. Twenty kilos was a lot of weight and if he got caught he'd definitely do at least a ten stretch. If he doublecrossed the dealers any fucking thing could happen and if he didn't the fucking scumsucking squad would fit up Glendora. Needed more thought. Been in rough situations before but they were screwing the lid down tight on him this time. Unless. A fucking long shot but there was just a glimmer. Something flew across his mind when he was talking to the Yardies. When they mentioned America. A spark that lit up in the back of his brain. Igniting and growing into a small blaze. The fire of salvation. The manager of Shoeless Sadie's told Francis the Antichrist tour was coming to a close in New York sometime the following week. Matthew Moore would be there. Needed thinking about.

Three days later Francis received a package in the post. It contained ten thousand pounds, two airline tickets to New York and a three-day double room reservation at Morgan's of Madison Avenue. For discretion. Also a photocopy of a street map of Stratford — with the ex-house in Leytonstone Road where Angeline now lived highlighted in red. And the names 'Fiona' and 'Sinéad' written underneath.

chapter twenty-nine

chapte r twenty-nine

chapte r twenty-nine

New York City was a madbad crazy place. Francis Page had never been there before but he knew all about it. Didn't everybody? It was a dreamscape. The image in everyone's eye. That thing that made people want to go there. For the first time in a long while, Francis wasn't uneasy about being outside London and wished he'd come here many years ago. Things would be different now. Things would be good-bad. Or bad-good. But better. Definitely better. Because this city was everything that was off in the world. And everything that was on. A schizophrenic city. Diseased. Genetically flawed. But beautiful. Everything that was goodbad and badgood.

Their plane touched down at JFK around midday and Francis immediately felt a surge of adrenaline. Took a cab northwards along the freeway into Queens and then west through Brooklyn and across the East River into Manhattan. Up through Chinatown, Little Italy and the Lower East Side. Madison Avenue was in Midtown — that area of the city which was immediately and unmistakably the New York of

Francis' imagination. Skyscrapers reeling and traffic cops rolling and yellow cabs clicking and clacking and honking and swearing like swarming insects and vents belching steam from ancient underground heating systems. Just like in the movies. Madison was sandwiched between Fifth and Park and didn't quite have the same sense of glamour as its more famous neighbours. But it was still impressive. With coffee bars and delis and big strutting buildings and streetcred and superiority complexes.

Morgan's Hotel was selfconsciously chic. A flophouse inhabited by hasbeens and wannabees and handsomestaff in designer uniforms and an air of low profile about the whole place. Francis felt it was the kind of hotel that could be slipped in and out of without too much attention being paid to whatever it was you were doing. A mixture of multiplex and monochrome decor just a little past its bedtime and lizards lounging and girls calling. But their room was big and had a jacuzzi and a coffee bar and two hundred complimentary Camel cigarettes so Francis decided it was good enough. In the lobby he spotted a poster proclaiming that the Antichrists were performing a onenightonlyendoftourgig at the Radio City Music Hall. While outside on the street he caught quick glimpses of himself. Spectres wandering in the wilderness. Poor relations of psychiatry. Prescription fodder. Dull and uninteresting dramatis personae with unsociable habits and unfashionable clothes and undesirable odours. Amongst the big colourful cast.

Glendora unpacked up in the room. But Francis was restless. He paced up and down for a while smoking the Camels. Until he began to get on her nerves and she told him to go for a drink or something and settle down. He took the lift from the fourteenth floor and strode across the lobby and out into the city's early March afternoon. Francis stood on the sidewalk for a moment, wondering where to go and trying to keep out of the resolute crowd's route. Opted to head south for a while and then right past the Sony Building into West 55th Street. Plenty of bars and dives of all declensions. Shebeens and speakeasys and swelljoints. After a bit of indecision, Francis stepped inside a place called Shorty's on Fifth Avenue and ordered a Jack Daniels and soda. Mid-afternoon and happyhour crowds yet to pour in from the shops and offices. One or two other customers sat along the bar and an odd couple held a serious and psychologically demanding conversation with some arm waving and shoulder shrugging and feigned oblivion to the rest of the world. Francis found a quiet corner table with its back to the wall and sat down. He stared out through the curtained window at the street scene. A colourful tableau of sight, sound and smell. Forget them other fuckers! He could feel the ambience. Sense it. Touch it. Taste it. The rich vein of electricity that ran through this place. It suited him. Even more than London. He believed at that particular moment this city was his soulspace. His homeland. He thought he could feel something in the air and hear it in the streetmusic and smell it in the unique perfume of prosperity.

That thing that's sometimes inside my head or maybe not asks me what I think of the Big Apple? I say I love it. I hated it. Why? It is a ghetto ... ze whole place. One big *schmutzy* ghetto. And ze people ... chust look at ze screwballs. I say I can see fuck-all wrong with them. Sure you can, Shegetz. Zey are all hafink nervous breakdowns. Not zat a neurosis would do most of zem any harm. Jolt a few of ze *groysshalterischers* out of zeir complacent comatoses. That's only your opinion! An opinion! Opinions ain't facts! It tells me I couldn't survive here, Shegetz. I ask why the fuck not? It says I'm too naïve. I'm not fucking naïve! Compared to zese *halb-naares* you are. I'm not bad! I'm as good as any other person! Not bad. Not bad. At all. All bad. Not me. I could make a go of it here. Zere you go again already ... you are finally satisfied mit ze mystery? You think you know it all now? I know what I know. Listen to me, you are better off back home. I ask what's home done for me so fucking far? Here ... zere ... what is ze difference? You vould be ze same you. No I wouldn't! I'd be a different me. A normal you? Don't start with all that normality crap again, I shout! It's more normal here than anywhere I've ever been before. You think zis is normality? Chust stand back und take a look, Shegetz. Take a look at society in a straitjacket. Did anyone ever tell you that you're the one that's touched, Scientistein? Of course zey did. Then why should I be listening? Because it vas *klutzes* like zese who said it. I vas touched mit genius ... not madness. Tells me madness is a social creation ... and this kind of society created it. Chust look around you, Shegetz ... who is really crazy? Sometimes ... sometimes ... sometimes ... I am. If you think you are, zen you damn-well *are*. But I know I'm not. Zen you're not. They've been telling me to kill myself. Who haf? Some. Just some. Und haf you tried? Not yet. You vill if you stay here. I'm only here for two days. Two days long or two days short? Ve'll haf to vait und see. I say I hope I'll come back again ... if I get the chance. Give it a go here. Don't! You can't tell me what to do. I scream out that I'll make my own decisions. Vill you? And I won't leave my daughters. You vill! You know vat my vord is, Shegetz ... so vhy don't you listen? I complain that everyone's telling me to listen to them. I can't listen to everyfuckingone! Telling me what to do all the fucking time! Do this do that dotheother. Do what? Die? Death is the meaningbeginning? It says I'll die if I stay here. Maybe I'll die if I don't. It vill get to you, chust like it got to me. What? Ze craziness of zis place. Vonce, in Stuyvesant Square, I saw two dogs. So big zey vere horses. You'll see zem too. Maybe you already haf? I haven't! You are lyink, Shegetz. I can see ze big lie all around you. Holdink onto your arm.

Hangink onto your heels. Like static.

Someone sat at the next table. Middle-aged man in a business suit and a younger woman. They glanced uneasily at Francis — not meeting his eyes. Sipped Martinis and whispered secrets to each other.

Francis got up and walked across to a call-box at the end of the bar. He searched for change and dialled a number from a piece of paper.

'Millennium Hilton.'

'Hello. Hi ... I'd like to speak to one of your guests ...'

They shook hands when Matthew Moore arrived and Francis ordered two drinks. Lit a cigarette and looked directly at his friend. Exfriend. Oldfriend. Sizing him up and weighing the question in his mind to establish whether he could trust this man. He decided not to. Outside on the street the dogs were gathering.

'Well ...'

'How's the tour going?'

'Hard work. We're earning our fucking money, Francis. Too many fucking firearms in this country.'

'That what happened to Jack Black? Did he get shot?'

'No no ... the bollix died of a heart attack from eating too much fucking fat meat.'

At least that's what the autopsy revealed when they opened him up. Francis smiled.

'Where's his body?'

'Downtown ... in the city morgue. We're taking it home with us tomorrow.'

'Can I go see him?'

'What? Jesus, Francis, why would you want to do that?'

'Jack and I were friends. Just to pay my respects ... that's all.'

'Don't know if they'll let you in ...'

'No? They'd let you in though, Matthew, wouldn't they?'

Matthew Moore was uneasy. Wondering what Francis was doing here. In New York. Something was going on.

'I suppose so ... we all got these passes ...'

'Your picture on it ... the pass?'

'Of course it is.'

'You could get me in to see him.'

'You can see him when he gets back to London. Go to the funeral.'

'I'd prefer to see him sooner than that, Matthew ...'

Francis was acting calmly. But a little twitch of his left eye told Matthew he was in trouble.

'C'mon, Francis ... it's me you're talking to. What's going on?'

'Nothing ...'

'You're in some sort of lumber!'

Matthew knew Francis was never all that thick with Jack Black. Now he wanted to go see his dead body. There had to be an angle.

'You're trying to bring something back in the coffin ... aren't you?'

'Well ... ok, you're too smart for me, Matthew ...'

'What is it?'

'Just a piece of jewellery. I'll cut you a share of the money ...'

'For fuck's sake, Francis ... how did you know where to get hold of me?'

'Got a number back in London.'

'From who?'

'I still have a few contacts, Matthew.'

Francis continued to watch Matthew Moore. The younger man was ill at ease. Nervous. Eyes scanned the bar and then returned to the table. He grinned awkwardly at Francis and raised his glass to his mouth. Francis continued to stare, trying to see inside the man's head. Trying to read his thoughts. Understand his soul. Wondered if Nightingale had told. Their secret. If there was a secret to tell. Maybe Matthew knew but was saying nothing about it. Couldn't trust any bastard. Couldn't couldn't couldn't. Had to be careful. All the time.

'Nightingale with your lot?'

'You know he is.'

'Has he said anything about me?'

'What would he be saying about you, Francis?'

'Nothing ...'

'Has he got something to do with this? Is he in on this, Francis?'

Why would Matthew think John Nightingale was in on it? Francis was cagey. Careful. Everyone was an enemy.

'Are you kidding? I wouldn't do business with that cunt. Listen, Matthew, remember when you came round the flat?'

'What flat, Francis?'

'Our flat ... in Dalston Lane. Glenny's ...'

'When was that?'

'Back before Christmas.'

'Oh ... aye.'

'I remembered what you said.'

Matthew tried to remember what he said. Whatever it was then — it was trouble now.

'What was that?'

'Don't tell me you forgot already?'

'No, no ... I haven't forgot, Francis.'

He was lying. But Francis didn't care. Business was business.

'You said, if you could do anything ...'

'I did? Sure ... yes, I did.'

'You said *anything*, Matthew.'

'Sure ...'

'At any time.'

'I remember.'

'Now's the time, son.'

Francis told Matthew Moore he was being watched because of some trouble over in Amsterdam and needed a bit of a hand to get the merchandise back.

'Just how much jewellery, Francis?'

'Just one or two small pieces. Bottle it up Jack's arse ... no problem.'

Francis laughed. Jack would have seen the funny side of this. Matthew didn't. Frowned. Francis stopped laughing.

'Look, Francis, I don't really want to get mixed up in anything dodgy at the moment ...'

'Just get me into the morgue, Matthew ... and keep watch. That's all.'

'I don't know ...'

'Easy as anyfuckingthing, man. Look, even if it's picked up going through ... who's going to blame you? There's a load of you in the fucking party ... could be anybody.'

'I suppose so.'

Matthew didn't want to do this. But he felt he owed Francis. For something. He didn't know what.

'That's it, boy. I'll make sure you're looked after.'

'For fuck's sake, Francis ... how did you get yourself mixed up in this kind of stuff?'

'It's a long fucking story. Will you help me?'

'Jesus, I'd like to, Francis ... but I don't know ...'

Francis wanted to punch him in the side of the head. For being so fucking shitearsed. But he kept control.

'Ok, forget it.'

'There must be another fucking way?'

'No other way, Matthew.'

'I don't really want to get involved in dodgy ...'

'You already said that!'

'For fuck's sake, Francis ...'

Matthew Moore threw off the rest of the drink in his glass and Francis called for two more. Shorty's beginning to fill up as happy hour approached. Place full of Bronx and Brooklyn and huggys from

Harlem and freebasers from Flatbush and queens from Queens and sharks from Staten Island. Martinis mixed and Bourbons rocked and Budweisers and Miller Lights and Rolling Rocks and pitchers of Anchor Steam and Wicked and Samuel Adams and Molsons and Dos Equis and Dubonnets straight. The two men drank and talked some more and friendship tentatively re-established itself and extra money offered for the alpacas and there couldn't be too much of that. Until Matthew Moore had to go and then they stood up and shook hands and Francis watched as the boy pushed his way through the crowd and out onto Fifth Avenue.

A coloured man came and sat down on the chair just vacated by Matthew. Francis eyed him suspiciously.

'You ain't with the man?'

'You talking to me?'

'I'm talkin' to you, whitey. You ain't with the man?'

'What?'

'The man ... you ain't with the man?'

'I don't know the fuck what you're on about, mate!'

Francis attempted to get up from the table and found the muzzle of a semi-automatic Beretta model 92F sticking into his stomach. He sat back in his chair.

'Who you talkin' to there?'

'A friend of mine.'

'You got friends in New York?'

'He's Irish ... a minder, like me ... on the Antichrists tour.'

'The who tour?'

Francis wondered who this bastard was. CIA? FBI? And did he know? What did he know? Who did he know? Was he real? Or another robot?

'Antichrists! Don't you read the fucking posters? At the Radio City Music Hall.'

'That so?'

'Not that it's any of your fucking business.'

'I'm makin' it my business!'

Sort the problem to survive. Sort the problem and survive. Sort the problem. Survive. Problem to survive.

'Listen, I don't know who the fuck you are, but you better fucking shoot me or get that fucking gun out of my stomach.'

'Or what?'

'Or you'll be retrieving the barrel from your arsehole.'

The coloured man looked at Francis with a frown. Long frown. Finger twitched on the trigger. He began to laugh. Loudly. Put the gun back in a holster inside his coat and stood up. The frown returned momentarily to his face and he seemed as if he was about to say something. Then he laughed again. Even louder than before. And left the bar shaking his head.

chapter thirty

chapte r thirty

chapte r thirty

'Where have you been, Frankie?'

'Out. You told me to go get a drink.'

'I meant in the hotel. This is New York. Out where?'

'In a bar. You told me to go chill out.'

'I didn't mean for this long. I was getting worried, Frankie.'

'Worried? About me or you? No ... nothing to worry about, honey. Let's eat. I'm hungry. Where do you want to go?'

'I'm not sure we should go out ...'

'Fuck that! We're in New York and I'm going out!'

Francis Page chose the Tavern on the Green for its view and Glendora was glad to be out of the hotel room. Despite her earlier fears. Wished she had some snow. Or even speed. Something to get her up and out of the depression that was dogging her. She hoped everything would go ok this time. It was important. Maybe when Francis got back on his feet and when he had his club to amuse him they might consider seeing a bit less of each other. It was funny, she couldn't wait to get him to come live with her and now — it was changing. Glendora ordered grilled chicken with Caesar salad while Francis had a heavily garnished burger with fries and black coffee. Footpaths meandered outside the restaurant in Central Park — like snailtrails through the trees. Evening falling and the lamps gave the place a still, quiet feel. Even though Francis knew it was full of murderers and muggers. A few horsedrawn buggies ignored the danger and carried romantic couples for a view of the night-time skyline. To the music of Manhattan.

All the joggers and rollerbladers and streetperformers gone home. In case someone stole everything from them. Everything they had. In the whole world. And even maybe their very souls as well. Snook up and took them at knifepoint. When they were enjoying themselves and at their most vulnerable. One or two brave locals walked fiercelooking hounds out among the ponds and pavilions. While sounds of zoo animals drifted across on the still air above the noise of the peripheral traffic. The Carousel was quiet — organ safely locked away for the night and statues of Robert Burns and Sir Walter Scott and Hans Christian Andersen and Alice and the Angel of the Waters closed their eyes to the rapes and robberies and their ears to the screams of the innocent and naïve. Away to the north, the reservoir hid the grinning skulls of those wearing concrete boots and Latino locals fished the Meer. And around it all the clear starfilled sky was a canopy of crystal hope that would never again become black and lifeless.

After eating they decided to walk back to the hotel, across Fifth Avenue. Glendora was impressed by the sheer consumerheaven of the superstore windows and Francis had to pull her away several times. East along 67th Street and then south on Madison. An early Spring breeze blew across Manhattan from the Hudson River and city smells and sounds filled Francis with a kind of longing. For lost years. Or for another chance to shine on the sequined stage of life. Without handicap. Or heavy boots to hold him back. Without the Alienchrist or the

Khananimal or the Scientistein or Saint Joanofdreams. Anyone. Just himself. Whole. Hearted.

Back in the hotel room, Francis began to systematically empty the mini-bar. Glendora was nervous. Didn't like his irresponsibility and wondered what was eating him. Same thing that was eating her? Wondering for some time. Aware for some time that she wasn't the only one who was changing. Saw something creep over him. Gradually. Like a sickness. A disease. Something was wrong with him but she didn't know what. He was changing from the inside. Being microwaved. Maybe his disease was the same as hers? Could he have caught it? They'd been careful. She wanted to ask him but knew he wouldn't tell her if she did. Shouldn't be like this. Not now. Should be keeping cool heads because they didn't know yet where and when the contact would be made. Could be anytime. Day or night. Anywhere.

'Please don't drink too much.'

'Why not?'

'Because we're here on business, Frankie ... you know that.'

'It's all taken care of. Let's just relax.'

'Not yet ... we haven't made contact.'

'I've made contact.'

'When? Where?'

Questions again. She wanted to know too much. For her own good. Maybe she knew the answers already?

'Today ... In Shorty's bar.'

'Frankie ... you should have told me.'

'It don't concern you, Glenny. This is my show.'

'There are two lives here, Frankie. And where's the stuff?'

'Don't know.'

'When will it be delivered?'

'Don't know.'

'Well, what did this contact have to say?'

Fucking fucking fucking questions! Francis was trying desperately to keep control. But she wasn't making it easy for him.

'Asked me if I was with the man. Didn't make any fucking sense.'

'For God's sake, Frankie ...'

'He laughed a lot, this guy.'

'Jesus, Frankie ... have you blown it?'

'I haven't blown it, Glenny.'

'Jesus ... you've blown it again ... what do we do now?'

'Shut up!'

Glendora was about to say something else but Francis put his finger up to her lips. Shhh. Already finished off the Bourbon and started on the Scotch. Asked if she wanted a drink but she didn't so he told her to suit herself. Glendora made coffee and turned on the TV. Flicked through the cable channels until she found a film to take her mind off the mess that her life was becoming. Again. After all the expectations and all the optimism. She settled back on the bed to watch and wait. For whatever was to come.

Morning brought a hangover for Francis and empty miniatures all over the floor. At least the booze made him sleep and kept the dirtyfucking-dogs at bay. He rose quietly from the chair where he'd passed out and checked Glendora in the big bed. Still asleep and he left her there because he didn't want to listen to her whinging — while he made coffee and smoked a cigarette. Midtown Manhattan was already alive outside the hotel window and singing its morning song. Hysterical traffic crawled along Madison and people poured across the gridwork of streets. Francis felt lightheaded and wasn't sure whether it was looking down from the fourteenth floor that made him dizzy. Or the effects of the booze. He turned back into the room and sat down with his cigarette and coffee cup. No contact yet. Or maybe someone came in the middle of the night while he was plastered. Chance gone forever of making big money and the dealers and detectives queuing up to kill him when he got back. Glendora stirred and he brought her a cappuccino. Maybe she was still up when the call came?

'Did I miss anything?'

'When?'

'Last night.'

'Just a couple of old films ... you know the sort I like. And you hate.'

'I didn't mean that ...'

'What then?'

The room was reeking. Of booze and bewilderment. Francis found it hard to breathe. What had he done wrong now?

'Any contact? I got a bit Brahms.'

'No contact. I stayed up 'til three ... only slept lightly after that.'

'Ah well ... we'll just have to wait some more then.'

'You sure you haven't blown it, Frankie?'

'I haven't blown it, Glenny!'

Francis called room service and ordered a baconandegg breakfast with coffee and toast and they ate in silence. Glendora ate. Francis drank lots of coffee and watched TV until it began to frighten him — which didn't take long. Turned it off and tried to read the newspapers which were delivered to the room — with compliments. All the headlines were encrypted messages and he hadn't figured out the code yet. And all the disaster stories were connected in some way with him and all the pictures pointed. The fucking finger. How the fuck did they know he was here? Francis threw the papers across the floor and lay on the bed for a while. But soon got up and started pacing the room. Getting on Glendora's nerves again.

'Let's go out and see some of the sights.'

'We can't, Frankie!'

'Why the fuck not?'

'They might come.'

'Well, they'll have to come fucking back!'

'They expect us to be here.'

'Not all the time ...'

'*All* the time!'

Francis wondered how she knew so much. Or thought she knew so much. But the room was closing in and he had to get out before it crushed him.

'That's going to look a bit suspicious, isn't it? If we don't go out at all?'

'I think it's better to stay here.'

'Well, *I'm* going out, Glenny. *You* can stay here.'

He brushed his teeth and pulled on his shoes and jacket but she didn't want to be left alone by him in a dangerous place again and was ready before he got to the door.

Day bright and unseasonably warm. Francis hailed a cab on Madison and they set off downtown. He wanted to see Wall Street and Chinatown and the Brooklyn Bridge and everything else there was to see in this city of dreams. She was again glad to get out despite the same reservations as she had the day before. The taxi drove south past the Square Garden complex. Posters shouted Knicksbaseball and Rangershockey and Glendora insisted on getting out at Macy's and having a look round that All-American superdupermegastarstore where they stayed for lunch. She shopped for cosmetics and clothes and Francis bought a few things in the hardware department that he said he wanted for souvenirs.

Outside on Broadway, they mooched round the shows and Glendora wished they were staying long enough for her to see a revival of Showboat. Then caught another cab's attention and travelled further south into the Village. She commented on the quaintness there which seemed genuine enough although the Bohemians were passé to the point of being trippers. And the brownstones and camp copy-writers passed them by into Soho with its continentals and castiron buildings. Francis wanted to get out in Little Italy and walk south along the Bowery to Confucius Plaza in Chinatown. But Glendora was afraid of the place and as much as he and the cabby tried to convince her the Godfather was only a work of fiction she wouldn't be persuaded. So they carried on to City Hall and walked from there down to Wall Street. For Francis — this was where it was really at. The centre of civilisation. The capital of capitalism. He could smell the money. Like a narcotic. Latent on the heady air. Intoxicating him. This little potofgold place. He could stay here forever. Sleep on the street. Eat off it. Become absorbed by it. Part of it. Flesh and blood and concrete and sinew and steel. But Glendora got bored quickly and they headed back north to Nick & Eddies in TriBeca for a traditional homecooked dinner in the late-afternoon garden. And afterwards the hotel bar for a few drinks and up again to the room before ten o'clock. Still no contact. Glendora was tired after her day in the city. Looked tired. Was a tired colour. Went to bed. But Francis couldn't sleep. Drank coffee and stayed away from the mini-bar.

It's an obsession, Chela. No it isn't! An obsession with being young and sexy and rich and violent. What's wrong with that? There's no compassion. Don't show them anything old ... or decaying. Ignore experience, wisdom ... the knowledge of the Kahunas. Fuck the Kahunas! These humans have learned to hide death. Pretend it doesn't exist. Don't! Don't talk crap, Alien. They see death every day on these fucking streets. Bastards getting clipped all over the place. But they ignore it, Chela ... like it's a computer game. Virtual reality. Do they fuck! Then why do they discard their elderly? Ignore their sick and disabled? Jesus! My earthname. You're such a bleedingheart! If there was no dying ... I know, I know ... there'd be no change! Death is the fucking beginning! I'm tired hearing it! Not just change, Chela ... no learning. No enlightenment. No achievement. No evolution. No reaching the mindstate of immortality. Crapfuckingcrap fucking crap crap fuckingcrap. What's the matter with you, Christalien? Why don't you tell me something I want to know? Because you can't! When I evolve in a million fucking years to be like you ... then I'll know. But now I'm not interested. If you're not interested, you'll never evolve to be like me. Then I'll be fucking happy in my ignorance. No you won't! No? And am I going to be all that better off? If I do? For all the change? And learning? And enlightenment? And achievement? And evolution? Change change fucking change! What's changed all that much? What's changed since time began? You don't know! You're just as confused as I am. It's all bollocks and none of it matters a fuck. Look out there, Alienchrist ... onto those streets and tell me things have fucking changed. Tell me! Tell me something! Tell me something I want to know. I need to know. I have to know. Tell me the truth. Some bastard tell me the real honestofuckingod truth! Stateofmind. State of mine. Stateofmine. State. Of. Mind!

'Who are you talking to?'

Glendora climbed off the bed yawning.

'Nobody, honey.'

'I thought it was them.'

'No. Nobody yet.'

'We're going back tomorrow, Frankie. Where are these people? I think you might have blown it in that bar.'

'I told you, Glenny, I *haven't* fucking blown it!'

Triggerbeat. She was pushing him too far. Could see it in his eyes. Time to back off a bit. Poured some coffee and came up close beside him on the sofa.

'In a way I hope you have. I wish we could go back to the way it was. So simple.'

'You wanted me to move in!'

'I know ... I'm not talking about that. You know ... it was uncomplicated.'

'It'll be all right. Once this is over.'

He stroked her hair like silk and she kissed his chest. Her woman-smell drove all the dogs from his head and they slipped slowly down onto the carpet. Stars winked at them from outside the high window. She caressed his thighs and kissed behind his ear. Her fragrance overpowered and dominated everything else in the room. In his life. In the Universe. She was the Universe. The Universe was black and silky and smelled of almond and sadalwood and tasted a slightly salty lifetaste and made little faroff noises that couldn't be understood but could be recognised as the meaning of everything. For the time. Being.

About to enter her when he heard a light knock on the hotel-room door. Francis listened. Glendora lay still under him. They waited. Nothing. Waited. No more knocking. Waited. Silence returned to the night. Francis got up and went to the door. He listened. Nothing. Looked through the spyhole. Nothing. Opened the door a hairsbreadth. Nobody. Francis didn't notice the room door opposite also open a hairsbreadth — nor the eye looking through the spyhole. The corridor outside their room was empty. Except for a leather suitcase directly outside the door. Francis carried it into the room and kicked the door closed. Heavy. With a brass lock. The lock key taped to the top of the trunk. Glendora came across and took the key. Opened it. Full of cocaine. Snow. Charlie. Pure. Silver. Uncut and uncontaminated. In blocks wrapped first in the Yardies' new space-age cellophane and covered over with silver paper. Francis hoped the stuff worked — but if it didn't his contingency plan would.

Whole twenty kilos worth maybe a couple of million on the street. Or more. In snort bags or as rock. Cut with horsetranqs or castorsugar or bakingpowder. Or worse. Francis was glad it wasn't skag. Didn't like running that bastard stuff. And he remembered her face in Amsterdam. The black girl's face. When she saw the four bags of horse. Remembered the thing that reared up inside her. An old flame. An undead need. An addiction that could only be controlled — never eliminated.

Francis closed the leather case. Turned the key in the lock and put it inside a wardrobe. Snow wasn't her bigthing so he didn't worry. But wondered if she was truly still off the skag. Maybe she was back on it — unknown to him. Showing a lot of interest in the scene lately. Looking lethargic. And all this mixing with pusherpunters. But Glendora already back in bed. Glad contact had been made at last and she could relax. He made more coffee and waited for her to fall asleep. Seemed to take a long time. Maybe she was waiting for him to do the same. Eyelids finally fell over the little lost windows of her psyche and he waited just a while longer to make sure. Then Francis transferred the cocaine into the army kit-bag he'd bought at Macy's. Filled the suitcase with newspapers and magazines and books for the weight. Then re-locked it and put the key into a pocket of his coat. Francis poured another coffee and smoked another cigarette. Then got into bed and lay awake beside the woman.

Their return flight from JFK was scheduled for midday. Francis was tired as dawn broke over the city and wanted to sleep. Had to force himself to stay awake. An extreme effort of will not to stay in bed beside Glendora. But he remembered something was at stake and dressed quickly before she woke. Kissed her gently and whispered in her sleeping ear that he was just stepping out for some cigarettes. Glendora didn't answer as he took the kit-bag from the cupboard and silently slipped out of the room. He waited in Rosen's Deli on East 51st Street. Francis was nervous. Early morning people looked at him suspiciously. Could be FBI or CIA or DEA or IRS or FAG for all he knew. The whole huge art-deco delicatessen frowned at him. Walls laughing. Knew what he had in the kit-bag. Wasn't fooling anyone.

Smells of the street mingled with the deli odours of sausage and eggs and waffles and pancakes and maple syrup and coffee. Francis had eggs over easy with toast just for appearances' sake. He stared at the food without touching it and sipped a cup of Colombian. The smell was overpowering. The smell of New York at this time of the morning. A just-wokenup smell of staleness from the night before covered over with a blanket of breakfast. Beginning to get to him. Francis waited. In the smell.

Earless said he liked it ... and prostitutes. That it reminded him of sunflowers. Cornfields. How could it? It was the smell of shit! Cunt high on absinthe. Strange. Mad. Maybe Scientistein was right afterall. Mad-know mad-be! Had to be careful of the cuisine in places like this. Because genetically modified food stunted organgrowth and damaged immune systems. Taking enough risks with Glenny. Self-mutilation ... not syphilis. And the trees made the wind by waving their arms. Stop changing the fucking subject! Earless? And things disappear when they're out of sight. And big things float and small things sink. And if you say what use is the Mayfly you might as well say what use is the earth. And all the life on it. What use is the Universe? Who discovered the Universe? How did they know it was there? Did someone tell them? Black holes. Quasars. Pulsars. Nebulae. Cepheids. Theorems. Axioms. Loops. Metasystems. Integers. Primes. Recursive functions. A compulsive paranoid and a friend of Freud. Who? Him. He found a hole in the centre of mathematics. And then starved himself to death. Me? No, me. Me!

'Francis ...'

'Matthew. Everything ok?'

'So far so good.'

'You took your fucking time.'

'Had a bit of an end-of-tour bash and it was hard to get away without looking suspicious.'

'I was worried maybe you might be having second thoughts?'

'I'm still not happy about this, Francis ... what's the kit-bag for?'

Matthew looked jumpy. And Francis didn't like him asking questions. He wanted to tell him nothing. But he knew he'd have to tell him something.

'A man asked me to drop off some stuff for him while I was over here. You know, Matthew ... got to make the trip pay ... bring something over, bring something back.'

'It ain't drugs, Francis? Tell me it ain't drugs. I'm having fuck-all to do with drugs!'

'Jesus, Matthew, you know how I feel about drugs ... it's chocolate.'

'Chocolate?'

Francis really hadn't thought this through and it was the first thing came into his head. Moore looked even more nervous.

'You want to take a look?'

'No ... it's ok, Francis.'

'Go on, Matthew ... take a quick peek.'

Matthew looked briefly into the kit-bag. Saw the packages wrapped in silver paper.

'Special chocolate, Matthew. There's money in it.'

'Ok, Francis ... say you're serious ... it can't be illegal to transport chocolate?'

'This stuff ain't allowed out of England ... if you get my meaning.'

'No ... I don't get your meaning.'

'For fuck's sake ... it's fucking *hot*, boy!'

'Hot? Hot chocolate? Hot fucking chocolate?'

Francis laughed at the idea of smuggling hot chocolate. Matthew didn't laugh with him.

'It's industrial stuff, you cunt! Nowhere else has the ingredients yet.'

'Jesus! Fucking hell, Francis ... it's just dawned on me. It's genetically engineered. The shite's genetically engineered!'

'You've hit the nail on the head, son. I didn't want to tell you, but you've sussed it.'

'For God's sake, Francis, what're you getting yourself mixed up in? It's one thing shoving a few diamonds up some stiff's arse ... but that stuff's fucking political. You'll end up in trouble!'

They arrived at the city morgue and Matthew Moore showed his pass to the attendant and kept the man busy and slipped him five twenty-dollar bills to allow Francis to be alone with the body and pay his last respects. Seeing as how the two of them were great friends and the attendant's mother came from Ireland originally and maybe Matthew had heard of her. Back in the old country.

Jack Black's body had been prepared the night before and was in a small room off the main morgue. A kind of jumping-off stage where he waited to be flown back to England. He lay in a wooden box that was a cross between a coffin and a tea-chest and he looked happy. Died the way he loved to live. Eating. Francis put on a pair of rubber gloves and unbuttoned the dead man's shirt. The autopsy cut down the stomach was still fresh and Francis took a small butchering knife from the kit-bag and re-opened it. The stench of formaldehyde almost made him vomit but he knew he had to be quick. Francis stacked the twenty kilos of cocaine on a bench and then reached inside Jack Black and removed the contents of the dead man's stomach. He stuffed the intestines into the kit-bag and replaced them with the cocaine. Francis sewed the autopsy cut back up with a sack needle and synthetic thread. Then he cleaned up the mess as best he could, hoped no one would notice anything, and said thanks Jack. For dying.

Matthew asked what took him so long and Francis shrugged his shoulders. Back outside on the street, he deposited the kit-bag containing the intestines of Jack Black and the instruments of operation into a rubbish skip. And told Matthew Moore it was the pick-up point for the hot chocolate. The Irishman looked at him sceptically, but decided to take his word for it. Matthew took a cab to the Millennium Hilton Hotel and Francis hurried back up Midtown before Glendora woke up and got panicky again. Finicky. Feisty. Like she was getting a lot lately.

chapter thirty-one

chapter thirty-one

chapter thirty-one

Heathrow Airport rose up out of mist as the New York plane approached across the Berkshire countryside. Sucked the silver flying machine down onto its concrete runway. Like Mercury the messenger bringing his clientele of rogues, vagabonds and thieves. Engines went into reverse to slow the jumbo jet down then it taxied lazily in towards the terminal. Francis Page looked through the cabin porthole and let out a low kind of moan. He wasn't glad to be home. Would have been happy to stay in New York. But the girls were here and he knew he couldn't leave them. Mixed feelings. Mixedupmind. Aboutitall. Francis hoped that he'd be able to go back again to the Big Apple. Something told him he wouldn't. New York. Some intuition. An entity inside him that said this would be the one and only time he'd traverse the Atlantic Ocean. Frantic motion. And it was becoming increasingly clear that some aminoacid derivative was close to the scene of the crime. A breakdown product of protein. Glendora touched his shoulder and startled him. People disembarking from the plane. She said they should go through with a group. Safer. One of the several things he didn't know? But was learning.

Inside the baggage hall. Leather suitcase placed carefully onto a trolley and other baggage piled on top. No problems at passport control or customs or anywhere else and they sauntered safely through to the arrivals lounge. Glendora nervous and tried not to show it but Francis remarkably cool and didn't seem to be worried at all. She sighed heavily when they were finally out in the car park and held onto his arm as if she was going to collapse. Then she laughed and straightened up and there was a little skip to her step. For the first time in ages.

Francis knew the bouncers would be back in London that night from the Antichrists tour. Should be! A later flight and he hoped Matthew Moore would be able to get the charlie through. In Jack Black's body. A Spring sun shone down on Heathrow. Seemed to say everything was ok. Would be well. Could be. Welcome back. Wellbeing. Being well. Being human. Humanbeing. Francis felt optimistic. Good. Good as gold. Solid as silver. Silverpaper. Silver stars in his mother's eyes. Turning to quicksilver and running like molten tears down. Down. Down. Annie with her gun. Annie with her crazy eyes. He could see her eyes across the car park. Waiting for him to come home. Could feel them watching his footsteps in slomo as he approached the two black men standing beside the Jaguar.

'Wha yo ah seh, star?'

'For fuck's sake ... you bastards are making it a bit too fucking obvious.'

'We jus cruisin us criss car dis way, mon. You be through ok?'

'Sure we are, but anyone could be watching. There's security cameras all over the fucking place.'

'Be cool, mon. New face seh. Beas dem doan ah know yo.'

'I'm not fucking happy. Not happy. Not fucking happy at all.'

The Yardies didn't care whether Francis was happy or not. He forgot they told him they'd be waiting at the airport. Because they'd been stung by him before.

'Jus ah gi we de suitcase, mon. Us haf wheels yah seh.'

'What about the rest of my money?'

'Us haf it yah.'

'Give it to me then.'

'First seh us check de merchandise dem.'

'What? Here?'

'Look, spar, us doan want no mash-up lik last time.'

'You're fucking crazy. You fuckers'll get us done up good and proper.'

'Doan be ah jumpy, mon. No one here but us Yardman.'

One of the coloured men pushed the bags off the top of the leather case and lifted it into the boot of a black Mercedes parked alongside the Jaguar. Held his hand out to Francis for the key. Francis hesitated and the coloured men exchanged nervous glances and fingers hovered round coat openings. Francis shrugged his shoulders and pulled the key from an inside pocket. He looked at it for a moment. Then at Glendora. One of the Yardies snatched it from his hand and stuck it into the lock.

Screeching of tyres tore up the car park and blue flashing sirens appeared out of everywhere. Detective Inspector Dunne's voice bawled from a loudspeaker for the four of them to lie face down on the ground with their hands behind their heads. The Yardies saw they were surrounded by armed uniforms and decided it would be suicide to try and shoot it out. Glendora was already in the position and Francis followed slowly.

'Wha be ah dis, mon? Yo touch we, dogheart?'

'It's your own fucking faults. I told you it was too fucking dangerous out here.'

'Beas dem bin waitin fi yo, mon. Dis be no accident seh.'

'You black fuck! You saying I set this up?'

'Look lik it, mon!'

The uniforms advanced cautiously on the four and handcuffs fastened behind their backs. Pulled to their feet to face D.I. Dunne and Detective Sergeant Spencer of the drugs squad. The rest were Armed Response Team with Heckler and Koch SD3-A3 sub-machine guns. The uniforms carried the leather case and the rest of the luggage across to a waiting Maria.

'Francis Page ... we meet again.'

'Don't know you.'

'You don't? Of course you don't. That's right! But we know you.'

'And who have we here?'

'Some black scum, Inspector.'

'Careful with your language, Sergeant!'

'Two pimps and a pro.'

Beatheart! Francis tried to headbutt D.S. Spencer. Grabbed by the uniforms and beaten down onto his knees with the butts of their weapons. D.S. Spencer shouted, 'Right lads, load 'em up,' and they were dragged across the car park and slung into the back of a separate Maria. Two Armed Response Team climbed in after them — H & Ks like lazy lethal blackcats cradled in their arms. Two others took away the Jaguar and the Mercedes for closer examination. The rest followed in bluelights eastwards through Hounslow and Hammersmith towards Paddington Green police station.

Nobody spoke in the back of the wagon. Francis sat next to Glendora. She shivered and he thought he heard her sob to herself. Kissed her on the cheek and winked but it made no difference and she sent him a little perplexed youfuckeditupagainfrancis look before laying her head on his shoulder. Across the van the Yardies were even blacker than before. Eyes fixed and firing bullets straight at him and their mouths twisted into ugly revenge. Francis looked back at the uniforms. Grinning at him. Dogfaces. Could smell their dogbreath. Taste their doghate. See their dogness. One second they were sitting at the back of the van, then they were directly opposite with the Yardies. Then beside him and Glendora. They skipped round the small enclosed space and even up onto the roof. Francis growled at them. A dog-growl. And they settled down again at the back of the Maria.

All put into separate cells at Paddington Green. Francis shouted to Glendora not to be afraid — they'd be out soon enough. Her eyes full of panic. Pleaded with him not to leave her alone. Again. With the dogfaces. Nothing he could do about it. Shouted to her as they dragged them apart that everything would be ok. Not to worry. There was nothing to worry about. The cell door slammed behind Francis and he found himself alone in the steel silence. Dogbeat! Paced up and down and headbutted the walls and kicked at the door in sheer frustration. Nothing he could do. But waitbeat! He settled back down a bit and sat on the bunk. Head in hands.

They bore him barefaced on the bier: Hey non nonny, nonny, hey nonny: Nothing I can do about it! And in his grave rain'd many a tear ... Jeanne? Not Joan good sir. Not Jeanne? Not Joan. Genghis? Do you not know? No I don't. Have I not remembrances of yours that I have longed long to re-deliver? We'll be out of here soon. Can you talk to her and tell her? You do not know? I told you I don't know! Nothing! I am Ophelia. Daughter to Polonius. Is he a good brief? Send him down to Glendora. He is Lord Chamberlain, good sir. Of Denmark! I don't know any Danes ... except Danny the Dane who drives sometimes for Percy Shillinger. But you know me, good sir. I do not! Oh indeed. I do not! Then you know, sir, my affliction. My madness. My torment. You're my mother? You're Annie. There's rosemary, that's for remembrance: pray you, love, remember. I remember. And there is pansies, that's for thoughts. There's fennel for you, and columbines: there's rue for you:

and here's some for me: we call it herb of grace o'Sundays. O, you must wear your rue with a difference. There's a daisy: I would give you some violets, but they withered all when your father died. He died? Konrad died? They say a' made a good end. The bastard is dead! Long live Judas! God help me ... God help me! What the fuck is all this? It is the false steward, that stole his master's daughter. I loved you, mother. Ophelia. Annie. Ophelia. I loved you.

And bonnie sweet robin was all my joy.

The cell door opened and D.I. Dunne entered on his own. Studied Francis carefully without speaking. Then lit up a cigarette.

'Where's Tweedlefuckingdee?'

'With your girlfriend.'

'Keep that cunt away from her ...'

'Where's the coke, Francis?'

'In the suitcase.'

D.I. Dunne sighed and walked up the cell.

'You know what's in the suitcase, Francis.'

'Cocaine.'

'No, Paper.'

Francis looked surprised. Even though he wasn't.

'You're fucking having me on ...'

'No I'm not, Francis. You know I'm not having you on.'

'The bastards ... they must have pulled a fucking flanker ...'

'And why the fuck would they do that?'

'It's your own fucking fault, Mr Dunne. They must have seen you people talking to me ... following me around.'

'No one saw us, Francis.'

'Then why did I have a fucking gun stuck in my stomach in New York fucking City?'

D.I. Dunne's turn to look surprised. Maybe they had been a bit obvious.

'What gun?'

'I was approached in Manhattan by a black man who kept on about "the man". I assumed by that he meant you people.'

'What did you tell him?'

'Fuck-all!'

'Come on, Francis ...'

'I told the bastard fuck-all, Mr Dunne! Your own strategy's fucked this one up, not me. And my life won't be worth a shit after this.'

D.I. Dunne's face furious. Pointed his finger at Francis and was about to speak. Then turned and left the cell with a slam of the steel door behind him.

Francis waited and wondered what that slag D.S. Spencer was doing to Glendora. Dogs dogs dogs! Beat! Beatdog! He'd kill every fucking bastard one of them if they as much as laid a fucking finger on her. D.S. Spencer was a dead man. No killing! Deadman. No killer. Yes! Dead. Man. Killer. Be killed. A uniform opened the cell door about an hour later. And he was released. Glendora waited for him at reception and the uniforms handed over the keys of the Jaguar and told them they were free to go. Good job he'd left the Glock at Glendora's flat. No sign of D.I. Dunne or D.S. Spencer. The car obviously gone over good and fucking proper and needed to be left into a garage to be put back together again. But it was driveable and as they left by a rear exit, they saw the Yardie men emerging from the station and heading in the direction of their black Mercedes.

'What's going on, Frankie?'

'I don't know, Glenny. They let us out too easy. Did any of the slags touch you?'

'I was searched by a policewoman and asked a few questions about New York, that's all.'

Glendora was confused. Suspicious. Do her good for a change instead of it always being him.

'What kind of questions?'

'About the drugs. I said I knew nothing, that I was just tagging along with you for a break.'

'Good girl. And what did they say about that?'

'They asked what you were doing in New York and I told them you were having a bit of a re-union with a few friends.'

'What friends, Glenny?'

'You know ... the bouncers. Matthew and the others.'

'You mentioned Matthew?'

'Yes. I thought it was as good a story as any. It checked out. Why, did I do something wrong?'

This made Francis nervous. For some reason. It was probably nothing. Baseless. Faceless. Fuck it.

'No, no ... it's ok. I don't think so.'

'What happened to the coke, Frankie?'

'I switched it.'

'Christ, Frankie! Where is it?'

'Safe.'

'But, how? Where?'

'Never mind. What you don't know won't hurt you.'

Glendora was going to ask him again where the snow was. And why didn't he tell her? Didn't he trust her? Any more. She decided to leave well enough alone. She'd have to know sooner or later.

'W'happ'n, mon ... start talkin.'

Francis was cool. Sipping a JD and soda. In control. Again. And the black cunts knew it.

'Don't worry, the charlie is safe.'

'How yo ah do dat?'

'Never mind. It's just a good fucking job I took care of it.'

'Which part it be now, spar?'

'I can't tell you that. I need a bit of time.'

The Yardies were worried. In case they got shafted again. Spooked. Sullen. Unpredictable in this state.

'Two days us give yo, mon.'

'Two days will be fine.'

'Two days it better be here! Dem be all, spar.'

'Ok, ok. It'll be here, don't fucking worry.'

'An dere better be no juggle pon de corner seh!'

'You still got the rest of my money?'

'De breddahs mek fi yo be seen.'

Arrangements made for a further meeting to hand over the cocaine and the rest of the cash. Francis rose to go. Then turned back to the dealers.

'Just one thing. I'll overlook it this time, but don't go threatening my family again. If anyone goes near my children, I'll kill you bastards and everybody belonging to you.'

He smiled but they didn't smile back. Francis waited for a response that didn't come. He was satisfied. Made his point. Let them know. They couldn't fuck with him or they'd find out. Find out! Left The Musketeer on Starcross Street and picked up the Jaguar from the Euston Station car park.

Midnight fell on the city and the sky dull and starless. Aliens crossed the streets in front of his headlights. Didn't know he knew. Maybe they didn't care. Maybe they knew the Theory of Everything. Like he did. And how temperature was radiation and radiation was energy and energy was matter and matter was man. And that each question answered spawned another. And that empty Space wasn't empty at all. And that Merlin was baptised by Blaise and beguiled by Nimue and entangled in a thorn bush by the Lady of the Lake where he still slept. To this very day. And his voice could sometimes be heard. On still starlit nights.

Glendora was asleep when Francis got back to the flat. She looked so innocent. Vulnerable. Heaven wouldn't melt in her mouth. Would it? He felt an urge to pick up the pillow again. But walked away from the bed before it got the better of him. Wasn't all that tired himself despite the drama of the day. So he made coffee and sat looking out the window at the raging scene of substantiality.

chapter thirty-two

chapte r thirty-two

chapte r thirty-two

Francis Page drove west through the city to the Wellbeloved funeral home in Willesden. Night dark and dense. Everyone asleep and unaware of his mission. Didn't know where Jack Black was lying at rest before his cremation and Matthew Moore agreed to meet him and take him to the place. Francis would have preferred to let things lie a bit longer. Just in case. Let the dust settle some more before approaching the cocaine. But he had to be quick before the twenty kilos went up in smoke with Jack in the crematorium.

Turned the car into Leighton Gardens near the sports centre and waited. 2.30 a.m. A few minutes later Matthew Moore's car pulled up down the street. The two men waited some more before signalling with their headlights. Matthew got out of his car and approached Francis. They walked in silence a short distance to the back of the Wellbeloved on Chamberlayne and climbed a low brick wall. Then made their way to the rear entrance where Francis forced the lock. Matthew took him by torchlight to Jack Black's coffin and he signalled silently for the boy to go back outside and keep watch.

Francis unscrewed the coffin lid and looked down at Jack. Still smiling. He covered his mouth and nose and cut the stitches in the dead man's stomach. Gave it a minute to accustom himself to the stench, then reached inside and removed the packages of cocaine. He placed the charlie into a sports bag. But the smell of the place grew more powerful. Getting the better of him. Overpowered him. Like a living thing. Crawling on his skin. He tried to brush it off. Smell of death. Death the beginning or death the end? Something was happening inside his head and Jack's features detached themselves from the rest of his body and became entities in themselves. Nose and ears and eyes. Had to concentrate. Slow down. Wait!

Francis looked about. Everything dull and colourless. A sad colour. Colour of melancholy. Monochrome. Twodimensional. He began to shake. Convulsing and dropping his torch and the sports bag onto the floor. He bent over and everything went black. Like the night. Like death. Francis tried blindly to find the exit but the entire funeral home had become one thing. One entity. A live thing. Dead thing. Livedead. Swallowed him like Jonah and he couldn't find his way out. Everything shimmering and alivedead. Carpets and furniture and floors and ceilings. Almost transparent. Nonexistent. Ghostlike. Hypothetical. Panicbeat! He felt his way around the soft fleshlike walls until the crematorium furnace opened up in front of him and he fell inside. Francis felt the jets of pure flame hit him from all sides. Singe him. The flamespray became a swarm of redhot needles — biting into his skin — blinding him — ripping him to pieces. He turned black and brittle and the flamejets went off. Francis waited. Skin burned away and black bones glowing with hellight. But he was still alive.

Wait! Slow down! Francis waited until he could see the hazy outline of the room. He waited. The smell of burnedoff skin overpowered him. Sickened him. Francis vomited onto the floor and waited. Waited. Oppressiveheat. Oppressivesmell. He felt claustrophobic. But he waited. And the disease of schizophrenia was analogous to phenyletonuria and would eventually be dietetically treated. Should be. Could be. But he had to slow down. Wait! For something in the future.

He calls out to me, Chela ... wait. Says he was the son of *Yidam* and waited thirty years. My message is love, man. My message is love. And who are you now? Really. Still Alien. A long long long long time. The *yogin* ... the son of *Garuda*. Can you tell me how to get free, Christalien? I see a dark shadow ... spitting and shouting. Do not listen to that woman! Which woman? Animal? It is I. Can you tell me, Animalkhan? How to get free? Don't listen to the hate! I will kill you, Jesus of Nazareth. I'm already dead, Temujin of Deligun Bulduk. Listen to me, Chela ... ain't I told you to love your enemy? Have I not told you to know your enemy, Jalal al-Din? You have. You have. Fear that which can destroy the soul ... Matthew, 10:28. Fear nothing and live like a man. Beware the animal ... Mark, 32:18. Kill all those who would oppose you. You'll be perishing and dying forever ... Luke, 12:8. To die is to live. Destroy his power ... John, 16:11. The woman in you will betray you, Jalal al-Din. The hate will take you down, Chela ... into the quicksand ... the *samsara*. Discard her and escape. You might never escape. Know yourself, Jalal al-Din. Know love, Chela. Death can only destroy the weakness. Once a part of evil dies it can't be born again. To be near death is to be near life. End of body is beginning of soul, man. It will be a profound experience. I died for love. They killed me for revenge. Death was the meaning. Death was the beginning. Know it! Live with it! The real meaning of life is death! The real meaning of death is life! Don't listen! Listen! Don't listen! Listen! Don't listen! Listen! I'm listening, Goth. Don't listen! Listen! I'm listening, God. I was a God. I was God.

I am God!

His eyes cleared after a while and he could see the outline of Jack Black's coffin above him. Francis got to his feet and tried to brush the burned blood from his skin and the vomit from his clothes. Didn't know how long he'd been lying there. Found the torch and looked at his watch. 3.30 a.m. He got to his feet and looked into the coffin. Then stuffed a couple of cushions from the funeral parlour into the body and tidied the deadman up as best he could. Out of respect. Sorry, Jack. And thanks again.

No sign of Matthew outside and the streets all unnaturally quiet. Even for that time of morning. No people up and down and cars stationary in the road. Spring birds all flown away and the wind lay quietly behind Willesden Junction. As if it was hiding. Francis walked slowly and silently back to the Jaguar. Something wrong. He could sense it. Taste the tension. Feel the apprehension. Matthew Moore's car was gone. Maybe he'd found out what Jack was carrying back inside his stomach. And decided on retribution. About to ambush Francis and cut him down in a hail of flying bullets. Dead. And no famous last words. Just a gasp of air and a death rattle in the throat.

He stowed the sports bag in the boot of the Jaguar and sat in onto the driving seat. Still no sight nor sound of any living human being. As if the world had come to an end. Hit by a comet while he was out cold inside and him the last man standing. No women or children left neither. So quiet the sound of the engine kicking over startled him. Some fucking thing wrong. All right! A police car pulled across the bottom of Leighton Gardens and another screeched to a halt behind the Jaguar. Not fucking again! The Armed Response slags pointed their sub-machine guns at him for the second time in one week. And D.I. Dunne called for him to climb out of the car. With his hands over his head.

Francis thought about the Glock in the glove compartment for a moment. Then the faces of Fiona and Sinéad said no daddy no!

Assumed the facedown position on the floor of the car park and he was handcuffed again and hauled up to see the grinning dogface. Of D.S. Spencer. D.I. Dunne already retrieving the sports bag from the boot. The inspector ripped it open and looked inside. Then smiled and gave the thumbs up sign to his sergeant.

'Got you this time, Francis.'

'What d'you mean? We had a fucking deal.'

'But you tried to stiff us, didn't you. All deals are off now.'

'Cunt!'

Francis tried to struggle away from the uniforms behind him so he could bite several lumps out of D.S. Spencer's face. Again he felt the butt of a gun on the side of his head and saw the ground coming up to meet him.

They kept talking. Talking talking talking. That light and laughter were the flowers and dreamscapes at the moment of expiration. Yes. And the exploration of space would lead to the most stubborn of primary facts. And a rogue Alien was the root cause of all the love and hate on the planet. And amphetamine addicts with no eyes and no ears and no home to go to and no possessions other than an understanding of everything and no life apart from living. And God! God who was the supreme fascist! AnimalGod! AlienGod! And materialistic explanations for all phenomena. Adenine, thymine, guanine, cytosine. Fourbasealphabet. DNA. Five deathstages. Denial, anger, bargaining, depression, acceptance. Australopithecus. Zinjanthropus. Olduvai Gorge. Lake Turkana. Laetoli. Hadar. And it wasn't enough to say the earth went round the sun. He had to ask why. The more he knew — the more he didn't know. Angeline! Glendora! Annie! Ophelia!

'Francis ...'

'Ophelia ...'

'Francis ...'

'Ophelia?'

Francis was in the back of the Maria again with Matthew Moore trying to pick him up off the floor. Two armed uniforms sitting grinning down at him. Dogface déjà vu!

'What are you doing here, Matthew?'

'The bastards jumped me outside the funeral parlour.'

'I thought ...'

'You thought I shopped you?'

'No ...'

'Yes you fucking did, Francis.'

Yes he did! Of course he did. What else was he to think?

'Slags!'

'Did they get the stuff?'

'The bastards got it.'

'Fuck! We're well in the shite now.'

'Say fucking nothing, Matthew.'

'Say nothing ... there's nothing to be fucking said, Francis.'

Matthew Moore wished now he'd never got himself into this. Never let Francis get him into this. Never met Francis. Page.

'I mean ... don't implicate anyone else.'

'Like who? I know fuck-all about this ... and what can they do to us for a few fucking gemstones? Eh? It's not as if it's fucking cocaine or anything, is it?'

Francis looked away as a deep feeling of guilt came over him. Like he was responsible for every fucking evil thing in the world.

'It's best you know fuck-all, Matthew. Listen, I think I can swing a deal here. I know those two slags Dunne and Spencer.'

'How d'you know them?'

'Long story. But listen, the point is ... we'll be ok. I'll make sure of that.'

Matthew wanted to believe him. Had to believe him. There was no other option.

'I trust you to get me clear of this, Francis. I've got me stash now and I'm ready to hit the road.'

'You're leaving London?'

'Sure am ... hope to be, anyway. Next week. It's all set.'

Matthew's words meant nothing. Now. Lost in the shambles of the situation. And because it was so serious, Francis sent it away. And concentrated on the surreal.

'You're not still going ahead with that fucking alpaca farm shit?'

'And why not? They're on the way as we speak. Six cows and two bulls in transit.'

'Well, you know I think you're making a mistake ... but good fucking luck to you!'

'You sure you can get me out, Francis? Even bail will do.'

'Guaranteed!'

The wagon pulled up again at the back of Paddington Green police station and Francis and Matthew Moore manhandled into separate cells and left to stew for several hours before anyone bothered to come near them. Francis' mind somersaulted. Might have convinced Matthew everything would be fine — but he couldn't convince himself. And what about Glendora? And what about Fiona and Sinéad when he didn't turn up with the drugs. Tonight! For fuck's sake! Francis began to panic. Panicbeat! Kicked at the steel door and shouted for D.I. Dunne. No one came. Francis tried to calm himself by lying on the bunk but it didn't work and images came into his head — kept coming into his mind even though he tried to keep them out. Blood images. Faces. Fretting. Pleading. Gun images. Fire. Screaming. Angeline images. Scolding. Annie images. Falling. Konrad images. Laughing. Glendora images. Glendora images. Glenny images. Crying images. Sighing images. Dying images.

Eventually D.I. Dunne and D.S. Spencer entered the cell. Dunne sat on the bunk while Spencer stood by the door. D.I. Dunne took out a packet of cigarettes and offered one to Francis. Took it.

'Well, Francis, this is a right turn-up.'

'What's going on, Mr Dunne?'

'You tell me. You tried to pull a little flanker on us, didn't you?'

'It wasn't like that. I told you the bastards were onto something.'

'Well ... whatever. It all turned out for the best in the end.'

'Not for me and Matthew Moore it fucking didn't.'

'Someone has to suffer, Francis, that's the way of the world. But we got the drugs ... and the drug smugglers. Didn't we?'

An uneasy feeling was creeping over Francis. He didn't like the tone of D.I. Dunne's voice. The smugness of it. The somewherebeforeness of it.

'What about the dealers? The fucking Yardies? They're the ones you really wanted.'

'What Yardies? Those two we nabbed the first time made it clear to us they had no connection with any drugs and they were merely foreign nationals having a holiday in our lovely country. Probably back in Jamaica by now.'

'That's a load of fucking bullshit!'

D.I. Dunne motioned for D.S. Spencer to leave them alone. The sergeant left the cell with a sinister scowl and D.I. Dunne closed over the door.

'Sorry about that, Francis. Don't know who you can trust these days. Listen ... I know it's a load of bullshit. But proving it's a load of bullshit is another matter altogether. Unless you can give us something solid, maybe an address for our friends up in Manchester. Or would there be anyone else involved?'

Francis knew what he meant. You couldn't trust no fucker. No hooker. No dealaway stealaway shite detectives. After all.

'Like who?'

'People we know. Who'd be easier to put away. Take the rap for you and your Irish friend if you cooperate. Maybe like Percy Shillinger?

Big shots like him who think they're above the law. Now, if you were to give me something like that ...'

'The bastards have already threatened my family!'

'All the more reason to get them behind bars as soon as possible, Francis. Don't you think?'

'Not *those* bastards ... the fucking Yardies!'

'C'mon, Francis, you know the game. I want to help you. But I can't help you if you don't help me. If not about this little caper then something else. You must know something for fuck's sake. You've been around a long time. Not much nor many you don't know about.'

Francis didn't like Percy Shillinger — but he wasn't going to stitch him up. Even if he could. It wasn't the way. And this D.I. Dunne was turning out to be a fucking robot like the rest. Silence was safety.

'You're some kind of naïve fucker, Mr Dunne, if you think I'm a grass. If that's what you think.'

'What do you mean, Francis?'

'I'm beginning to believe that keeping my fucking mouth shut might be the only fucking insurance I've got.'

D.I. Dunne moved away from Francis. He shrugged his shoulders and little metallic robot words came out of his mouth.

'Ok, Francis ... have it your way. I'll try to do what I can ... you know that. But it's going to be difficult. What about your Irish friend?'

'Matthew Moore has fuck-all to do with this!'

'Oh no? Are you telling me he *didn't* bring the stuff through for you?'

'I'm saying he didn't know what it was.'

'What? I might believe you there, Francis ... just might. But the court certainly won't.'

'It's the fucking truth. He knows fuck-all.'

D.I. Dunne's Justicegod looked towards the ceiling. Blindgod. Windupgod. And what about the promise? Francis Page made to

Matthew Moore? What would happen to it. Would it cry and cry? And die and die?

'Look ... if neither of you can give me anything, then it's going to be difficult ...'

'What about my family, Mr Dunne?'

'What about Jack Black's family, when they find out how you pair of fuckers desecrated his body? And what can I do, Francis? You're giving me nothing.'

'I gave you the fucking drugs.'

'No you didn't! You tried to pull a flanker and it didn't work.'

'Jesus fucking Christ! Just send someone round to protect my girls!'

'I'll see what I can do. I'll do what I can, Francis.'

Would he? Francis didn't think so. He'd have to get someone else to sort it. Maybe the Manor Park boys. When the bastards let him get to a phone.

'Tell me one thing, Mr Dunne ... how did you find out?'

'Powers of deduction. We're not called detectives for nothing, Francis.'

'Fuck fuck fuck fuck fuck!'

Francis headbutted the wall. D.S. Spencer heard the noise and came back into the cell. Francis flew at him. Six uniforms followed and kicked him around until he was subdued enough to be formally charged. While D.I. Dunne just shrugged his shoulders in a helpless gesture and told Francis there would be a hearing in the morning where it was likely that he and Matthew would both be remanded until the case came to trial.

'What about bail?'

D.S. Spencer laughed out loud and shook his head. Then left the cell with the rest of the sniggering slagheads. D.I. Dunne waited behind and put a finger up to his lips as if saying he'd sort something out. Francis didn't know whether to trust him or not. Seemed all right for a slimeslag and anyway he had no choice. Nothing he could do. Nothing!

Something had changed again. How? Why? Who made it change? Someone was controlling things. Pulling strings behind the scenes. Some bastard! Or bastards! Who? He had to warn Glendora. And Angeline. When they eventually allowed him his statutory rights to a few telephone calls. No reply from the flat and where the fuck was Glenny? Angeline reluctant to listen at first but she eventually saw the seriousness of the situation and promised Francis she'd take the girls to Bertie's for a few days and also that she'd get in touch with a solicitor. Who came down to the station later that night but unable to offer any crumbs of consolation. Bang to rights! *Corpus delicti*! Tosser! He did promise one thing. To go round to the flat in Dalston Lane and check on Glendora. Get her to a safe house. The Manor Park boys would keep an eye on her and his little family as well. Until things blew over. Calmed down. Sorted themselves out.

Next morning Francis and Matthew Moore were remanded to Pentonville Prison until a trial date could be set. Kept segregated from each other and both pleaded not guilty and claimed the evidence was planted by a corrupt police force on account of previous grievances. Two days later Angeline visited Francis to tell him a message had been delivered to her. By a man with a black accent. And how did the bastards know where Bertie lived? Was nofuckingwhere safe? The note said the girls wouldn't be touched. As long as mouths remained shut and Francis and Matthew Moore took the time on their own. And didn't try to implicate anyone else.

So that was it. No choice! Nothing he could do about it. Glendora or the girls. If he sang they'd kill his family — even if he could trust the slags in narcotics to do a deal. Which he couldn't. Do nothing they'd be safe — if he could trust the black men. Catchfuckingthirtythree! But no fucking choice. The detectives had what they wanted so they should leave Glenny alone. Nothing to link her with the run. She'd done fuck-all. Couldn't touch her — except for a frame-up. The bastards! They wouldn't do that now he hoped. Fucked goodandproper. Him. And what about Matthew Moore?

The solicitor could find no sign of Glendora. Despite several visits to the flat and a few of the clubs and another to the Cosa Nostra Casino in Gloucester Place where he was told she hadn't reported to work for nearly a month and they weren't running a fucking rest home for retired fucking heroin addicts. Whether she was with Francis Page or not! And her job had been filled by another croupier. Who they hoped would prove more reliable. Francis just hoped she'd gone to ground somewhere and she'd get in touch with him soon. But he wasn't convinced and climbed the fucking walls for a while. With frustration. And fear!

chapter thirty-three

chapter thirty-three

chapter thirty-three

The trial took place twelve months later at the Old Bailey. And the jury listened while the barristers of Francis Page and Matthew Moore repeated allegations of police planting twenty kilos of cocaine in a case of blatant entrapment. But photographs of Jack Black's disembowelled body were produced and the whole trial only lasted two days. The jury were shocked at the sacrilegious outrage and took only twenty minutes to return a guilty verdict. Beyond any reasonable doubt! Was anyone? Didn't they realise the whole fucking human race was really only an accident and once it extinguished itself it wouldn't be back again. Evolution wouldn't be repeated! But they were sure. Certain. No fucking doubt about it.

Angeline and Fiona were in court for the proceedings. Sinéad wasn't. Neither was Glendora. Francis heard nothing at all from her since the arrest. Nothing! Not a fucking syllable! Went up the fucking wall at first. Kicking and punching prison warders and having to be forcibly restrained and slung into solitary and eventually sedated in the prison hospital. They gave him anti-depressants and sedatives to calm him down. Clopixol and clozaril and depixol and dolmatil. Then neuroleptics to knock the shit out of him. Chorpromazine and phenothiazine and olanzapine. Followed up by orphenadrine and proclyclidine to counteract the side effects of twitching and hand tremors and pillrolling and a protruding tongue. And when they were sure he was no longer a danger to himself or any other bastard they allowed him back onto the remand wing of the prison. Just as long as the regimen of tranquilliser taking was maintained.

Francis lived a mirage through remand. Sometimes a nightmare and sometimes a noddyland. Sometimes fidgety and sometimes catatonic. Voices didn't come and he felt completely alone. Nobody to talk to. Nobody to tell him what to do. Try to tell him. A numbness in his mind like a thick woollen blanket that stifled all thought processes in a heavy, sicklywarm cyclonic depression that lay on top of him and forced his face down into a sea of inertia.

Now the judge was whining on in his summing up of the situation. Words about the shocking circumstances of this case and the large amount of Class A drug involved. Not to mention mutilation. And Francis could feel his mind returning. Slowly. Slipping in under the door of neuroleptic passivity. His old self. Backagain.

Welcome back! Molière? Muhammad? How are you after your sleep, Chela? Fuzzy. Wuzzy. Woozey. Try to hang onto your mind. They took it away with their tablets. You gotta keep it with you, man ... no matter what they do. Says he'll come if he can and make the routine meaningful and the pain bearable. I can't fight any more. Simplicity, Chela. Simplicity or sinecure? Simplify your life, man. Eliminate excess baggage. You'll have more room to be cool. Looks like I'll have no choice from now on. Listen to that judgeslag up there. He'd like to fucking hang me. Don't worry about it, you're only unhappy now ...

you'll be happy forever. Just live in the moment ... in the *chang chok*. And don't look for it back again once it's past. Maybe I won't want it back again. Maybe it wasn't worth having in the fucking first place. What you do with it gives worth. Not what you could have done with it! What choices have I got left, Christalien? Life! Life is your choice, man. And death is only the beginning.

Live. How? Simply. Live?

Judge looking down at Francis with fury on his face and asking if the prisoner wished to say something. Defence team suggested he'd been suffering from psychosis recently and was on medication. Tried to offer the fact that he wasn't responsible for his actions in mitigation. But the judge decided it was no excuse for smuggling drugs in a dead body and certainly not for disrupting his court. Sentenced them both to six years' imprisonment. Which was the maximum the law would allow. And he was only sorry it couldn't be twenty-six. Or the guillotine. Or even garrotting. For such outrageous crimes against a young, vulnerable and deceased society.

Francis wasn't listening. He was back again. Talking to Alienchrist about *garuda* and the *bardos* and being everybody. And seeing the future. Because it was really only his fragmented egoism which denied him that insight. Begin as nothing and end as nothing. And what about the in-between bit? Life? Life! Being? Being! And Being couldn't be separated from Becoming. Capable at any moment of seeing all and being all. Brain and senses and nervous system blocking it out. Selecting. Sifting. To save sanity. Sanity? The narrowsafe perception of a blinkered existence? He had to escape! Had he already? Had to find an escape mechanism from the world of small self and trepidatious time! Get away from the moral and technical and opinionated and assertive! He could see the great canvas of the larger Self. The bigger picture! How small he was ... how minute and insignificant was the ego against the backdrop of *everything*. Fly? Yes!

The screws pulled Francis out of the dock. Matthew Moore shouted at him but he couldn't hear the words. Swearing. Accusations. Liferuined. Matthew spat at Francis and kicked out at him. But Francis remained calm and the screws kept the two men apart. He looked up at the public gallery and saw Angeline's expressionless face. Saying I knew this would happen. I knew it would end up like this. I always knew. And beside her the slender figure of Fiona. Wiping away a tear. Francis tried to remember how old she was. Fiona. Fourteen. She was fourteen. Must be by now. Ought to be. As far as he knew. Growing up. God help her. God!

Francis was sent back to Pentonville and Matthew Moore taken away to Strangeways prison up in Manchester. For some time Francis could hear Matthew's silent screams. Life in ruins and he'd get even. Some day. If he had to wait forever. Francis didn't care. Didn't give a shit. Hoped he would. Wanted him to. Back at the prison, he was no longer on remand wing and that made things a little better. Conditionswise. Banged up in a peter with a muppet called Ingrams from the County of Cambridgeshire who'd held up a local post office van with a sawn-off. But the fucking idiot was caught when he decided to deliver the letters addressed to people he knew. Out of some kind of misguided fucking code of conscience. Ingrams was a crackhead and Francis didn't like the prick. Ignored all attempts to make friends and be like kindred spirits. The camaraderie of crooks.

Ingrams soon got the message and made other friends. Telling them Francis was a weird fucker and was on tablets and shouldn't be in prison at all. But a fucking psychiatric hospital. Francis didn't want to take the tranqs because he didn't believe there was anything wrong with him and it was all part of the same fucking conspiracy from outside that had him here in the first fucking place. But they kept him calm and he didn't have to think much about anything and sometimes that suited him. Under some circumstances. Pentonville was full of schizos who committed crimes to get in out of the cold. Same people he saw outside the New York window. Wandering about. Nowhere else for them to go. Shunned by society. Misunderstood fucking misfits. Despised. Discriminated against. Pissed on and persecuted. Francis wondered if they saw *him* like that. He was different though. He was! Best part of the fucking prison population was mentally ill. And that included those in charge. Unsupervised fucking psychiatric hospital. Because nobody could be bothered with the bastards. No psychiatrist nor politician nor policeman nor judge nor jury. On their own in a nightmare fucking world of nonentity.

Most of the other prisoners avoided Francis and some knew his reputation from the outside and rumours ran around the closed and cloistered society that was prison life. Where whispers were lived off. Fed on. Permeated the atmosphere. Were absorbed into and constituted the lifeblood that ran through the veins of the place. Francis was considered too dangerous and too unstable to fuck with. Fuck-wit! Even the screws wary and there were always three or four of them to make sure he took his medicine. And always watched closely during association.

Nobody visited and the months moped by. Voices few and far between when he was taking the tablets. Sometimes pretended to swallow and tucked them under his tongue and spat them back out when the screws were gone. Then some of the Voices came back. But they were confusing and incoherent and negative and nasty. Normally he could understand — no matter what the language. But with the drugs in his system he could make sense or meaning of very little. And then he went berserk and beat the bollocks off Ingrams for coming back one day from court with a crack packet bottled up his arse and pulling it out of the shitsoiled toilet bowl. They sent him down the block to a private peter and no more mistakes after that.

Sometimes when he could think, he remembered Glendora and wondered what happened to her. And who grassed him to that fucking slag D.S. Spencer? And what happened to D.I. Dunne? Why didn't he do something? Like he promised. Where was the missing piece of the jigsaw? But he wasn't able to concentrate for long and a kind of apathy soon took hold of him again and held him in a grey-iron grip which he couldn't be bothered to break out of.

Six months into his sentence and Francis called to the visiting room. Half-wondered who'd come to see him and only half-cared. The screws sat him at a table and a young woman came and sat opposite. Francis didn't recognise her and it was obvious from her expression that she was shocked by the sight of him.

'*Madre de Cristo*! Francis ...'

'Hello.'

'Francis ... what have they done to you?'

'Who?'

'These *bastardos*. You look terrible.'

'Sorry.'

Agnes D'Argensola lit two cigarettes and passed one across to Francis. He took it absently without thanking her.

'What has your solicitor to say about this?'

'Whose solicitor?'

'Never mind, I will find out.'

'Who are you?'

'Agnes.'

'Agnes?'

'Agnes D'Argensola. *Joder*, do not say you don't even know me?'

'Sorry.'

'Are you on drugs?'

'Tranquillisers ... neuroleptics ... anti-depressants ... sedatives ... stuff. Other stuff ...'

'*Jesús*! Someone must pay for this ...'

'Sorry.'

Agnes looked at the man she once knew. The big strong *hombre* who used to look after her on the London doors. And she felt like crying.

'Don't be sorry. I am the sorry one, Francis. Most of this is my fault for shouting my big *puta boca* off that time.'

'Was it? Did you do that?'

'Do not worry. I am going to get this sorted out.'

'There's fuck-all wrong with me, you know.'

'I know that, Francis. *Lo sé, cielo.*'

Agnes tried to smile even though she was crying and they smoked and she held his hand and he smiled back at her. He told her they'd implanted a device which was eating his brain away and soon he'd be a cabbage. Or a cauliflower. And it sent signals to the Internet which then broadcast his thoughts and misdemeanours to the entire world. She said again she'd sort things out and he was sorry to see her leave. Such a short fucking stay. And he had such a long time to go. That night in the cell he tried to remember her. See her face. It was white. Then black. Young. Then old. Familiar feelings returned. Came and went. Despair. Disgust. Hatred. Apathy. Love. Life. Death. All came very close in the darkness. And he knew he would dream the end of the dream he'd begun all that ancient time ago. All through the long minutes and days and years. And he pretended for a while — until it all fell away and he was alone.

Two months later Francis had another visitor. This time one of the solicitors who'd defended his case at the trial. Tosser brought a silly doctor with him who gave Francis an independent medical and psychiatric examination and diagnosed that he should no longer be kept on the tranqs. Heated argument in the Governor's office. While Francis sat outside with a screw on either side of him and threats made on both sides and exposure in the newspapers mentioned and the Governor would not be held responsible like Doctor Drummond and it was said that if Francis was psychotic he ought to be in a secure hospital and not in a mainstream prison. Agreement in the end that the medication would be terminated for a trial period only and the solicitor slapped Francis on the back when he came out of the Governor's office and told him that everything, old pal, would be all right now.

The chlorpromazine and clozapine and phenothiazine and olanzapine and ritanserin and risperidone and sertindole and zotepine and ziprasidone and lithium carbonate all stopped abruptly the following day. Francis continued to feel the effects for some time though. In his blood. In his being. The haze only gradually cleared from his mind. Allowing in a little clarity at a time. Increasing. Growing sharper. Focusing. Bringing the pain. Unbearable fucking pain and agony of perception. The Voices came back. Garbled at first. All talking at once. All wanting to communicate their conflicting contradicting messages at the same time. Head felt as if it would fall off and he pleaded with the screws to put him back on the drugs. But they wouldn't. He got what he'd wanted. No. It was what he told the woman who came to visit. No. She told his solicitor and the solicitor told the doctor and the doctor told the Governor. No!

But then his mind began to sort itself out again. Get back to its old self. And the headaches weren't so bad. Old friends spoke to him. Like Jesus and Genghis. Reassured him. Held him together. As the long seconds passed into minutes and hours and days and months. Francis spent a lot of time alone in his cell. Out of harm's way. Didn't even go down to association because the rec yard was full of shit parcels thrown out the windows by cons who didn't want to stink up their cells. Preferred his own company to the bullbollocks of all the slags around him. Fuckers with heroin hid in their foreskins and jellies in the burnbags and E-men and cunts clucking and mullerings and screams in the night and all sorts of other fucking shite. He began to keep a diary. Hoped to write his memoirs some day. Pages of private words that he allowed nobody else to look at. Found the writing to be therapeutic and the screws happy to let him have extra paper and pens if it kept him quiet and off their backs. He wasn't short of ideas — all the names that were coming to him. In his head. Blake with his visions and Juliana with divine love. Swedenborg with his journal of dreams and Browning with spiritual insight and Alighieri brought hell and Elohim brought heaven and Nostradamus and Donne and Rasputin and Bayazid of Bistun. Francis became increasingly bewildered by the array — disorientated — confused. Didn't know where the fuck they came from. But he couldn't stop them without the tablets and didn't want to once he got used to them.

Agnes D'Argensola visited regularly and brought him cigarettes and the fast food that he liked and she said she'd had an extension to her visa from her friend at the Embassy and she'd wait for him to get out and give her the son she always wanted. The little Che Guevara kid who'd be a genius and play the zampõnas for her and fight the world like his father. He didn't disagree because it was nice to see a face from the outside every once in a while. The world he'd forgot. Had forgot him. And he began to remember Glendora. Glenny. Slight brown body so delicate and dangerous. Spicescent and tonguetaste. Saw her face in his head and wanted her to speak to him. But she couldn't. Or wouldn't. She wasn't a Voice. She was a vision. They were different things. Her mouth opened and closed but no words came out. As if she was drowning. He was going to ask Agnes to try and find out something about her. But he thought it might rock the boat. So he left it so. And the face kept coming back into his head and the mouth opening and closing and eyes pleading and soft soul crying. Its little heart out.

chapter thirty-four

chapter thirty-four

chapter thirty-four

Two years of his sentence down the line with Francis Page having alternate periods of prescribed drugs and tabletfree lucidity. Most times he volunteered to go back onto the tranqs when things got too difficult to handle on his own and he felt his heart beating too fast and the heartbeatpanicviolence welling up inside and he knew it wouldn't be long until he damaged someone. Then Agnes would come and convince him he was all right and he'd go cold turkey again for a while. Drugfree periods becoming increasingly frequent and more prolonged and he felt he was getting back to his beginnings. Even if he wasn't.

Francis was now forty-five but looked older. Hair going grey and skin the same colour. He wasn't working out. Though every day he promised himself he'd start again tomorrow. Never comes. And he didn't like the prison gym. Too many tossers in there talking through their arses and he knew it would only be a matter of time before he got into trouble. Neither did Francis want to lose any remission. No matter how apathetic he got. Or crazy.

Apart from a few kicking and boxing matches with the screws in the beginning and that little episode in the cell with Ingrams — been behaving himself for the most part with the help of the tablets. What with the year he spent on remand and the rest of it, there was a chance he could be out in another eighteen months. Francis didn't want nobody to fuck that up. So he continued to keep to himself.

July and the atmosphere inside Pentonville humid and oppressive. Cons walked around in their shorts and the smell of sweat and shit everywhere. Stinking up the place. As if it wasn't bad enough already. Choking him. Crawling on his skin. The voices in Francis' head becoming more belligerent. Baiting and goading him to go and cripple some cunt. Maybe because he was trying to come off the neuroleptics completely. Maybe it was all part of the plot. Sometimes he felt like giving in to them and getting a crowbar from the engineering shop and laying into the whole fucking lot of the freaks. Left and fucking right. Kill at least halfadozen of the bastards before they got him under control. Or shot him stone dead. Through the fucking head.

Then he thought of his girls. And Glendora. And the outside. No killing. Not if he wanted to see the outsidelight again. He realised if he killed someone he would be kept in prison forever. Ever. Never. Never was. A killer. Before. Francis also tried to find out how Matthew Moore was coping up in Strangeways. At least it was easier for his relatives to visit him there and maybe some old friends and family came over to see him sometimes. Bring him an alpacaburger. Francis wrote a couple of letters but never got no reply. Matthew was obviously still angry. What could he do about it? Apart from the regret? Maybe make it up when they got out.

As well as July it was Sunday and family day. Francis wasn't expecting Agnes D'Argensola because she came only a week ago. So he was surprised when a screw called him to the visiting room. Agnes nowhere in sight. But a slim girl of about sixteen sitting at his usual table.

'Who are you?'

'Don't you know me?'

'No. Wait ... you're Glendora? Glenny?'

'No, Dad ... Fiona!'

'Fiona?'

'It's me.'

'Oh fuck! Oh for fuck's sake ...'

Francis jumped to his feet. Sending the chair flying back behind him and nearly knocking over the table. He threw his arms around the girl. Lifting her off her feet and swinging her round the room. Other visitors moved out of the way and screws came quickly to calm him down. Before he started a fucking fight. Francis and Fiona sat back down on the chairs. He felt such elation. Like a rush. Hadn't felt anything like it for a long time. He grinned at Fiona over the table and held tightly onto her hand. The screws moved back to their positions when they were satisfied everything was safe. Fiona smiled back shyly and tried to avoid her father's eyes.

'What are you doing here ... in this place? After all this time, baby?'

'I wanted to come before, Dad. Mother wouldn't let me.'

'Mother? Angeline? The lovehate woman? Did she change her mind?'

'Not exactly ...'

'How come ... you don't want to be here, honey ... you're here then?'

He was strange to her. Not the father she knew. Remembered. Wasn't the memory in her head. He was sadder. Pathetic almost. But she loved him just as much.

'I've left home.'

'No, no ... you can't ... when?'

'It's ok, Dad. I'm studying. I've moved in with a couple of friends down in Holborn ... Brooks Court.'

'Friends? What friends?'

'Girlfriends, Dad. Don't worry.'

The realisation of her made him come back a bit. To himself. His old self. What was himself. And he couldn't help worrying.

'What about money? How do you live, baby?'

'I've got a grant ... and a student loan. And Mother doesn't see me short. She's very good like that. Kind of like ... what would the neighbours say?'

'I'm surprised at her ... that she agreed at all ... Bertieschmertiwoman ...'

'She doesn't like it. But I'm going on seventeen and I've had enough of home.'

'Seventeen? Are you seventeen already, baby?'

'Next birthday.'

'Next birthday? D'you know, I've forgotten ... in the name of Jesus Christ. Where did all the time go to? The years? Like my own ... once upon a time ago.'

She wanted to be close to him. Lean across and hug him like before. When she was younger. And he was older.

'It's ok, Dad. I'm going to come every visiting day from now on.'

'Does your mother know you're here?'

'I told you, Dad ... it's none of her bloody business.'

'It is! It will be ... until you're eighteen.'

'What she doesn't know won't hurt her.'

'I used to say that ...'

'Like father like daughter, eh?'

'What she doesn't know won't hurt her. I always said that.'

'And it's true.'

'No ... it's not true!'

What she didn't know did hurt her. When she found out.

'Anyway, I didn't come here to talk about Mother ...'

'How's Sinéad?'

'A stuck-up little cow!'

Little silent Sinéad. Francis tried to remember her face. He couldn't. Only the abstract of what he thought her face ought to look like.

'My other daughter. Your sister, Fiona ... don't talk about your sister ... little Sinéad, eh?'

'Well, she is, Dad.'

'Just like Angeline ...'

'You and I are two of a kind, Dad. So are they.'

'You're not like me, honey. Oh God no ... don't be like me.'

'I want to be like you, Dad.'

'No! Just be yourself, baby.'

Francis fell silent as a powerful sense of melancholy swept over him. Fiona's face twisted before his eyes. Like some grotesque fairground mirrorimage. He wanted to hold it. Stop it from contorting. Straighten it out. Straighten her out. What could he do? Stuck in this fucking shithole. Heartbeat! Francis was getting angry. He could hear the laughing scowl of D.S. Spencer and silently vowed revenge. He would have his vengeance. Rightful revenge on the heads of all fucking Philistines. And Pharisees. And Sadducees. And Sanhedrin. And Sicarii. I am vengeance. I am intolerance. I am the God that made me. I am Gammadion. I am Lambeg. I am Inquisition. There will be blood. Righteous blood! Killing! No killing. Kill them! Spill their entrails! Genghis! Gehenna!

'Dad ... Dad ...'

'Fiona ...'

'You're frightening me.'

'I'm sorry, baby. I wouldn't do that deliberately. You know that.'

Fiona wanted to leave now. It was enough — for the first time. She'd be back. And the strangeness between them would disappear and it would be like it was before.

'I know, Dad. I think the time's up anyway.'

'Listen, honey ... you remember the woman who came out with us on one of our Sunday trips?'

'What woman?'

'We went to McDonald's first ... then up to Oxford Street. Sinéad was being sulky and we had tea together afterwards at the Cybercookie ...'

'The coloured woman?'

Was she coloured? She must have been. Francis wasn't sure — but he remembered her name.

'Yes. Glendora. Glenny. You remember.'

'She was nice. I liked her.'

'I need you to do something ... to contact her for me.'

'Doesn't she visit?'

'No. Well ... there's a reason ...'

'Why not, Dad?'

'It's a long story. Listen ... you remember the flat she and I lived in ... where I picked her up and dropped her back off that day?'

'Somewhere in Hackney ...?'

Francis searched for the name of the street. It was in his head. He knew it was there.

'Dalton's ... Dalton's Lane? Dalston Lane ... I'm sure that's it ...'

'I remember, Dad.'

'You remember? Good girl ... you remember ...'

'It was near a school ...'

'Was it? Would you go round there for me? Please.'

'Of course I will. What if she's not there?'

'Tell them you owe her money. Something like that. Try to find out where she's gone ... what's happened to her ... get a forwarding address. Or a phone number ... anything.'

'I'll do my best.'

'Good girl. Good girl. Just be careful ... be very very careful. Ok?'

They kissed goodbye and Fiona left with the other visitors. Francis watched her go. He was proud. A proud man. A proud father. A great daughter.

I was a daughter once. But what now? What now? You have broken my heart, Heathcliff. I'm Dad. Your father. I shall not pity you, not I. You have killed me. No no no, Fiona ... I've killed nobody. How strong are you? Not as strong as I was. But sometimes better. How many years do you mean to live after I am gone? Annie? I wish I could hold you 'til we were both dead. Glendora? Will you forget me ... will you be happy when I am in the earth? I'll never forget you. I'll never forget you. Twenty years hence will you say ... that's the grave of Catherine Earnshaw. I loved her long ago. My children are dearer to me than she was and at death I shall not rejoice that I am going to her. Will you say so, Heathcliff? No! I'll come to you. I'll come to find you, Glenny. I shall not be at peace. I'll come as soon as I can. I'm tired of being enclosed here. I'm wearying to escape into that glorious world and to be always there; not seeing it dimly through tears and yearning for it through the walls of an aching heart; but really with it and in it. Are you my Glenny ... or are you Annie? I forgive you. Are you my Glendora? Forgive me! Annie? Mother? I've dreamt in my life dreams that have gone through and through me like wine through water and altered the colour of my mind. Me too, Mother. Me too. Heaven did not seem to be my home and I broke my heart with weeping to come back to earth and the angels were so angry that they flung me out. Where are you now? Are you here? Whatever our souls are made of, yours and mine are the same. Are you with me, Mother? If all else perished and you remained, I should still continue to be and if all else remained and you were annihilated, the Universe would turn to a mighty stranger. I should not seem part of it. You're part of me, Mother ... we're both part of each other. We are each other! You and me. Me and you. We've braved the ghosts together and dared each other to stand among the graves and ask them to come. They come to me. And now you too. Come. They may bury me twelve feet deep and throw the church down over me, but I won't rest 'til you are with me ... I never will! I'll be with you soon. But I need help now, Annie. I need to get out of here. Will you help me? Let me in! Let me out! Let me in! Mother ... Annie ... I've come home!

Francis found himself lying on the bunk in his private cell. The door was open these days, so he could come and go as he pleased. As long as he was no trouble the screws were happy to let him wander about. An odd figure. Eccentric. Spazo. Windowlicker. And he never went far. Preferred his own company and the Voices who visited him in solitude. Different today. Happy after Fiona's visit. Felt alive again. Straightened out. Sociable. Wanted to get out of the little cell and do something. Now maybe was the time to get back into training. He was motivated at long last. The gym. Get fit again. Back into hardbody shape. Ready for the out. Get Agnes to bring in some vitamins and protein powder and desiccated liver and other stuff. No drugsteroids. Something for his skin. Come out fighting. Hit the ground in good condition. Show all the shitbags.

The man who ran the gym in Pentonville prison was called Hatchet Harry Kane. Francis knew of him but they'd never met on the outside. Harry ran a few things over the river in the Lambeth area and even as far south as Lewisham. He heard of Francis Page of course and there were whispers in the prison that when the two met up there'd be fucking fireworks. Francis kept away from the man up to now but needed to get himself good again and if Kane was in the way — well. He'd soon be fucking out of it. Two screws followed Francis into the changing-room and kept asking if he was sure he wanted to do this. Wouldn't it be better to leave well enough alone? They were worried and wanted no wars in their wellrun institution. Francis wanted no trouble neither but was entitled to work out like every other wanker in the place because he'd been behaving himself and was on full privileges and they could come and supervise the fucking proceedings if they liked.

Heads turned when he walked into the weightroom. Followed by the screws. Kane and a few other fuckwits down the end on the hack-squat machine. Hatchet Harry pushing out four hundred pounds on a hundred and fifteen degree angle. Good going for a man of his age. Stopped in mid-squat and looked down the room at Francis. Francis took no notice and made his way to the multigym where he began to pump out a fifty-kilo warm-up set of military presses. Hum of excited voices in the air and Hatchet Harry Kane started a measured walk down the room. Followed by the wankers and shitheads and brownoses and pillowbiters who hung round him. The screws watched nervously. Fingering their batons and one on the radio just in case reinforcements might be needed. But made no move to intervene. Francis continued with a hundred-kilo ten-rep set and Hatchet Harry gave him a little clap.

'Not bad, for a fortysomething.'

'I hear you're no spring chicken yourself, Harry.'

'We're from the same schoolyear all right, Francis.'

'Things are a bit different these days. Y'know ... than what they were.'

'Do tell. I'm glad you came down, Francis. I was going to go up and see you. Be sociable. Costs nothing, does it. Mind if I jump in?'

'Be my guest.'

'The rest of you prats fuck back to whatever you were doing. I want to have a private chat with Francis here.'

The others sloped away and the screws breathed a sigh of relief when the forecast fireworks didn't ignite. After all the shite. Just showed what prison whispers were like. A load of bollocks. Most of the time. But the screws stayed close by — just in case. Kane and Francis did a few stations of the multigym together.

'I hear you had a bit of bad luck, Francis.'

'You could say it might have been my own fault, Harry. For trusting people. What are you in for?'

'A five. Cut some little fart's ears off for not minding his own. Prick nearly bled to death and I was a bit pissed and the toerag's claret all over my clothes. Convicted on circumstantial and forensic fucking evidence.'

'Hard break. Should have been more careful.'

'Like yourself.'

'True enough. What d'you know, Harry?'

'I'll be out in a few weeks, Francis. Good behaviour and all that crap.'

'That why I'm getting the old welcome wagon? They said you were going to try to kill me.'

'Try? Trouble in here is a mug's game, Francis. Do your stir and get the fuck out.'

Was it as simple as that? Maybe. Maybe not. Francis decided to try again.

'What else do you know, Harry?'

Harry didn't tell Francis what he knew. Wasn't going to. But Francis reckoned he knew something. Otherwise —

'What else could I know, Francis?'

'Who grassed me ...'

The words surprised Harry Kane. His mood darkened a bit as he hammered out a hard set on the bicep curl.

'This town's full of fucking narks and nonces, boy. Shit on their own mothers for half a fucking nicker. Especially the black fuckers.'

'Somebody stitched me. If you know anything, Harry ... I'd be obliged.'

'Then I'd be a grass myself, Francis. No better than the rest of the cunts.'

Francis put the weight up and pumped out a heavier set than Harry. Mind games.

'There's no protection for a grass, Harry. You know that. You know the score ... the business.'

'I don't know anything.'

'Then, why are we having this little chinwag?'

'You're in my gym.'

'It ain't your gym, Harry. It's the prison's.'

'I run it. And I'm just welcoming you, Francis. It's been a while since I had a decent training partner.'

Harry put the weight up again and pumped out an even heavier set for the benefit of onlookers.

'What say we go round together a few more times before I do the off?'

'I'm happy to train with you, Harry. Any time.'

'Good man. Oh, one other thing ... there's a rumour about a room-full of coke.'

'What? You talking about the stuff I was given the six for? Confiscated.'

'Was it now?'

Hatchet Harry Kane broke away from the routine and went back to his hangerson. Leaving Francis to finish the work-out on his own. Harry knew something. Wanted something. Francis was awake enough to know that. Harry knew something. Harry had let him know. Wanted him to know. Wanted something for what he knew. He'd tell Francis what that was when he was ready. When it was right. All Francis had to do was wait. In the meantime he showered and changed and went back to his cell where he continued to write down more of his memoirs. Until the lights went out and he lay there alone in the dark. Waiting for the wooden horse.

chapter thirty-five

chapte r thirty-five

chapte r thirty-five

Bodyandsoul. Singerandsong. GodandDevil. Spaceandtime. Being-andbecoming. Alienchrist! Animalkhan! Where are you? Live. Die. I am evolution made conscious of itself. Part of Gaia. I am Gaia! Hydrogenhuman! Scientistein! Tell me more about your theories. Gravitydrives. Gateways. Foldingtime. Pharelia. Don't desert me! Everyone I knew is gone and I'm left here with the strangers. Hostilestrangers. Get me out! Get me out! Get me out! Get me out! Public responsibility was only a mathematical equation of majorityrule that left differentpeople vulnerable to discrimination. Losing touch with language. And love. And logic. And life. The paradiselost of ignorance against the pain of developing intelligence was the widening breach between alien and animal. And the psychotic wall was getting higher. Higher. Higher. So high it would be impossible to ever break out. The terminal isolation of insanity looked over — the wall — in through the cell door. And said suicide. Carve your failure in stone. No more change. No more choice. The final fate. The ultimate hell of a singular reality — a doomed frozen Universe from which there's no escape. Get me out! Let me out! Jeanne! Jeanne! *Je suis toujours là,* Dauphin.

Francis Page sat in the visiting room opposite his daughter. Fiona waited for him to come back to her before she spoke. Knew her father was off the medication at the moment, so he was likely to say any thing at any time. Or to wander off in the middle of an otherwise lucid and intelligent conversation. She was also beginning — just beginning — to get used to the continual upanddown of emotions. Some unnaturally intense. Particularly his expounded love for her since she began to visit. One minute she'd find his views of a given situation distorted and unreal — swinging back the next minute to a clear view of reality. She realised his memory had twisted the events of time and he remembered her childhood differently than she did herself.

She remembered that her mother resented her when she was young. Because she took away some imagined thing called freedom. And sealed Angeline to Francis against her will. Kept her in the limbo which she'd walked into of her own volition and Angeline couldn't help resenting her eldest daughter because she reminded her of her own lapse of judgement. There was no violence or anything like that. She wasn't deprived of anything. Just love. Just a coldness which Francis warmed with his fatherimage. The big man who loved his little girls. By the time Sinéad came along, Angeline had largely gotten over her pique and the younger girl wasn't subjected to the same resentment. But the damage was done for Fiona. Francis didn't remember this. If he ever knew it at all. He talked to his daughter as if those times were some quiet, coloured, fairytale landscape. Remote. Then he'd engage in questionandanswer exchanges with his Voices before realising she was still there and take varying periods of time to come back to her — his demeanour often swinging between high spirits and severe depression.

Fiona's fifth visit. Every time she came he asked her about Glendora and every time she had to disappoint him. This time it was different.

'Listen, Dad ... I've got some bad news.'

'Bad news? Don't tell me any bad news. I've had enough bad news in my life.'

'You asked me to find out. You keep asking me.'

'Find out what?'

Francis couldn't remember — maybe who was making the robots? No. Something else.

'Glendora, Dad.'

'She's dead ...'

'How do you know?

'... drowned.'

'Shot. She was shot, Dad.'

Fiona was surprised when Francis didn't react. At least not in the way she expected him to. She'd been afraid to tell him since she found the article in a back issue of a local Southend newspaper at the college library. And now there was no reaction. Nothing. Or what appeared to be nothing.

'It couldn't have been her. Could it have been her?'

Fiona handed her father an emerald ring. Engraved with the letter G. Francis looked at it. For a long time. Remembered its significance and held it as if it was still on Glendora's finger.

'Somebody could have stolen it ...'

'No. I claimed her things, Dad. From the police. They were glad to get rid of them. There's a memorial plaque ... near the sea. It's nice ...'

'Who killed her, Fiona?'

'It was drugs, Dad ... she was full of heroin.'

'Then it wasn't her. She was off it ... did you see the body?'

'There was no body. She was cremated.'

'It wasn't her ...'

Fiona reached across and touched her father's face. Just like Glendora used to do.

'There were pictures ... photographs ...'

'Did you see the face?'

'Well ... not exactly ...'

'What exactly?'

'Well ... the bullet went in from behind and came out ... I'm so sorry, Dad.'

Stresstrigger! Francis was quiet for a while. Heartbeat! Saying nothing. Heartbeat! Looking at the emerald ring. Heartbeat! Then he started to shake. A gradual kind of thing. Fingers first, then feet and finally his whole body. Fiona watched uneasily. Other visitors and even the inmates began to notice. He jumped to his feet. Glendora! Knocked the chair backwards and threw the table over onto the floor. Fiona backed away as he produced a highpitched noise from his throat. Like a doghowl.

Visiting room cleared back from him and he stood in the centre. Like a crazy man. Screws running. Francis upended the first one and stamped on his face. Stamp. Stamp. Stampbeat! Two others grabbed his arms and he swung them round, banging their heads together with the strength of a superhuman. The three screws struggled to get up from the floor. But Francis was berserk — kicking them back down to the ground. Blood splattered over people nearest to the mêlée and women and children screamed and tried to get out of the room. The panic-stricken crowd jammed the exit and hindered other screws trying to get through to Francis and their three colleagues being wiped about the floor. Began to baton their way in out of frustration and a fullscale riot soon erupted. Convicts saw their wives and girlfriends being hit and retaliated with fists and chairs. Sirens were sounding in a matter of seconds and whistles blowing and the air full of shouts and screams and the smell of blood.

Reinforcements mustered and a way cleared through the hysterical visiting room. Cons dragged away to their cells and howling women and children taken out of the danger area. Consoled with a little traumatreatment and cups of strong coffee. By the time they got to Francis he'd killed one of the screws and halfcrippled the other two. Took about ten of them to overpower him and even then a hypodermic full of a haldol-sparine cocktail was needed to finish the job. Injected straight into the straining jugular. Fiona watched from behind an upturned table in her crouched corner. The screws saw her. Heard her gasp and hurried her away. She kept looking back as they fitted a strait-jacket onto the unconscious Francis and medics examined the men on the bloody floor. She was shown through a door at the end of the corridor which took her back to reception and eventually out onto Caledonian Road. Stratford was only seven stops on the tube from King's Cross and she thought she might call over and ask Angeline to please go see if Francis was all right. But she knew her mother wouldn't do it so it was a waste of time. She caught the bus back instead to the city centre.

Francis was falling. Down. Down. Back into the quicksand. Was this the present? Or the past or the future? He didn't know. He was aware that the present didn't exist — so it couldn't be now. It could only be then. The present never *was*. Only anticipated or remembered. Never actually *being*. An illusion. So everything else was an illusion as well. What was the point? Of anything? Whose imagination was he a figment of? Who was his Creator? Creat. Or. Mother. Father. Madness. Genius. What did any of it matter? Earless had a brother. Vincentvincent. Dead child. Perfect child. Vincent! Vincent! How could that be? It was. And Sien was beautiful. Sien was beautiful. Despite the syphilis. Poor children. *Poor* children. Ate the paint. Drank it. It was life. Heard voices and was locked up. Mad? But was he? Was *he*? No. No. Better dead than mad. Dead. At the meeting point between sanity and surreality. The beginning? Where was Ghengisthegreatkhan? And Aliensonof-abdallâh? There was more he needed to ask them. Things they hadn't explained. But they were gone.

For good. Life wasn't so sacred afterall. It was quick. Ignominious. Brutal for some. Misunderstood by all. Yet had to be lived. Threemillionyearold microbes resurrected from perma-frost. Masters of timetravel. Stop it! Stop fucking it! What? It! It! It! Stop stop stop it! It was enough with these slagsofscrews kicking the shit out of him without all this grief as well. Sorry. Sorry, sorry, sorry. Only a certain amount of time allocated at birth. X many days, months, years. Time pressing down on him ... driving him down. Pushing him down. Chiding him like Angeline for wasting so many days. Throwing them away chasing shadows. Following illusions. He was the creator of his own time and he wore it like a ball and chain. Measured it and carried it around with him. But it was an illusion. Illusion! Stumbling round in a dark age. Mutilating himself and others ... mentally, physically and emotionally. To love is to lose! Life and death didn't exist. He was nothing. Nothing! Had to go back to nothing. To oblivion. To the beginning. To really exist?

'Enough ... that's enough.'

'Where am I?'

'You're in the prison hospital. You had a breakdown, Francis.'

Break. Down. Francis. Breakfrancisdown. Something was wrong-again!

'I can't move.'

Francis strained against the straps that held him. Along with the sedatives.

'It's for safety, your own as well as everybody else's.'

Francis tried to remember what happened. He was talking to Fiona. About? About —

'Where's my daughter?'

'You've done something very bad, Francis.'

'What have I done now? What have I done now?'

What. Have. I. Done. Whathaveidone. Now?

'I'm afraid your daughter won't be visiting again for some time.'

'What's happened ... happening to me?'

His words drifted off and dissolved into the expanse of the room. Pulled Francis after them. Dissolving him. But the other words pulled him back.

'You're going to Broadmoor, Francis.'

'Broad ... moor? Broadmoor? A fucking mental hospital? Fuck that fucking place!'

'It's a secure mental unit. You'd be better off there, Francis. They have the facilities ...'

'I'm not fucking going there, doctor!'

'You're psychotic, Francis. Dangerously delusional. I'm afraid you have to.'

'I'm not fucking mad, doctor!'

Madfuckingbeat! Francis began to struggle. Strange sounds came up from inside him and he raged against the restraint. The bed shook and the room reverberated to his roars. Doctor hastily prepared a hypodermic and Francis tried to bite him as he inserted the needle into a vein. Then Francis fell back into oblivion.

In the beginning God came out of the void. And the spirit of God moved upon the face of the Universe. Ordinary matter was made of energyatoms held together by electromagnetism to form molecules which in turn formed solids, liquids and gases and very large objects were bound together by gravity. Atoms were made of a dense nucleus surrounded by a cloud of electrons and the electromagnetic force held the nucleus and electrons together. The nucleus was made of protons and neutrons bound to each other by the strong nuclear force. Protons and neutrons were made of quarks which were also held together by the strong nuclear force. The cosmos expanded from the size of an atom to the size of a grapefruit in a millisecond. The Universe was a seething hot soup of electrons quarks and particles. The cooling cosmos permitted quarks to clump together into protons and neutrons. The Universe was a superhot fog because charged electrons and protons prevented light from shining. Electrons combined with protons and neutrons to form hydrogen and helium atoms and the light shone. Gravity made hydrogen and helium gas coalesce to form giant clouds that became galaxies and smaller clumps of gas collapsed to form the first stars. Galaxies clustered together under gravity and the first stars died and spewed heavy elements into space which formed into planets. You know the rest!

chapter thirty-six

chapte r thirty-six

chapte r thirty-six

Anonymity was the greatest weapon of all. Anonymity was invisibility and what couldn't be seen couldn't be defeated. Francis Page sat outside Paddington Green police station in the black Citroën. 2.00 a.m. in the New Year morning. And a full year on since he moved into the little Brooks Court flat with Fiona. Slags inside making a lot of noise and he could hear them shouting and singing. Francis waited. Wiped the 9mm Browning automatic with a chamois cloth that he took from the Church of St Eduard the Martyr and made sure there were fourteen bullets in the magazine and one in the chamber.

New Year revellers celebrating all over the city and taxis busy with the clubbers. Francis concentrated on the drunken carry-on of the slimescum inside the police station. Knew Detective Sergeant Spencer was in there with his crew. Watching confiscated paedophileporn and encouraging them to piss in each other's whisky and slobber all over the WPCs who had no respect for themselves in any case. Smartshit innuendoes and slyness and absolute crap pouring out from all their filthy mouths. Francis waited. New Year, New Year. So good he said it twice.

D.S. Spencer fell out into the car park about forty minutes later. Laughing loudly and shouting back obscenities at the crowd of goat-gobblers still inside. Slags pissing out the windows and throwing women's underwear down into the station car park. The D.S. found his vehicle and fumbled with the keys. Francis cruised the Citroën up alongside. Got out and opened the boot. Then came up behind D.S. Spencer with the Browning.

'Need a hand, Mr Spencer?'

'Naw, naw ... I'll be all right. Who the fuck's going to nick a detective inspector on New Year's Day, eh?'

'I am.'

Spencer turned and looked at Francis through squinting inebriated eyes.

'And who the fuck are you?'

'Don't you know?'

'Rasfuckingputin?'

Francis struck D.I. Spencer two sharp blows on the side of the head with the butt of the Browning. The detective crumpled onto the bonnet of his car. Francis quickly turned him over on his face and dragged his hands behind his back. Slipped a plastic bag-tie over the wrists and pulled it tight. Then threw the D.I. into the boot of the Citroën and drove away.

Thirty minutes later Francis turned the car down a muddy track and stopped outside a remote country house in Essex. He listened for a minute or two before pulling round the back and switching the engine off. Listened again. No sound. No light. Everything dark and quiet. Francis felt he was home. Back with the house that had shielded him from the confusion. And would again. Nothing seemed to have changed since he was there last. Best to make sure. He climbed slowly out of the Citroën and advanced undercover towards the back door. Gunhand outstretched in front of him. But it was ok.

The house was still his friend. Just the same as he left it. Cold and gravelike. With a powdering of dust covering the sheet that covered the blood that covered the floor. Francis went back and dragged the semiconscious D.I. Spencer out of the boot and into the house. He threw the detective into a chair and shot him through the right kneecap. Francis knew the D.I. wouldn't be able to take the pain. The way he had. D.I. Spencer was fully conscious now. And screaming.

'Shut up, you woman!'

'Who the fuck are you? You'll pay for this ... whoever you fucking are.'

'Not before your dues are settled, Mr Spencer.'

'Who *are* you?'

'I am retribution. Take a closer look.'

Francis came over and pushed his face up close and wiped some blood out of D.I. Spencer's eyes.

'Francis ... Page?'

'There ... now you know. What a fucking mess you're in.'

'Jesus Christ!'

'Alien can't save you now, Mr Spencer. And how come you're a detective inspector already? Nothing but a fucking gruntsergeant last time. When you were in my shoes.'

D.I. Spencer didn't reply. But Francis could still put two and two together. It was obvious —

'And what about the cocaine? What about the *twenty kilos?*'

'What about it?'

'Where the fuck is it? They told me it was somewhere. Out!'

'It's fucking destroyed, Francis. Burned.'

Francis walked unevenly away and stood at the door for a moment. Turned and came quickly back. He stood in front of D.I. Spencer and shot the man through the left kneecap. The detective screamed and writhed round in the chair with blood pouring down the legs of his trousers and soaking into the dust on the sheetcovered floor.

'Where's the cocaine, Mr Spencer?'

'It was destroyed ... down at the Yard. For fuck's sake ...'

D.I. Spencer's voice was full of pain. Words came in small, gasping syllables.

'Don't give me that, Mr Spencer ... somebody switched it.'

'Not me! I had nothing to fucking do with it after Dunne took it from your car ...'

Dunne? Dunne? The good guy? This was the bad guy. Francis was sure of it.

'... he was in charge of it before it was destroyed.'

Francis tried to think. Maybe Spencer was lying. Maybe he wasn't. He didn't know how he could be sure. D.I. Spencer saw the doubt on Francis' face. Saw the confusion. A chance.

'Listen, Francis ... you know I don't like you ... didn't like you. I won't lie about it. I don't like pushers or dealers and I don't like blacks. But I'm up front about it. What you see is what you get. I don't put drugs back on the streets ... you can believe that or not.'

The bastard sounded convincing. And Francis was confused. Because he'd been fooled before.

'I'll kill you if you're lying to me, Mr Spencer ...'

'I'm not fucking lying. Page, you bastard ... sorry, Francis ... look, I'm fucking dying here. If I knew any fucking thing don't you think I'd tell you ... to save my life?'

'I don't know. I don't know. I don't know.'

'Talk to Dunne ... he'll tell you the cocaine was destroyed. You trust him, Francis ... don't you?'

'I don't know. Yes. I don't know ...'

'Take me to him, Francis. I'll get him to tell you the truth ... then you'll know ...'

Francis paced up and down the floor. Didn't know what to do now. Didn't believe D.I. Spencer because he knew the man was the devil. The devil. And the devil always lied. Tried to trick people. Especially Francis Page. Not this time though.

'I'll let you live if you tell me where I can find him.'

'Sure, sure ... whatever you want to know. He's a fucking desk-jockey now, Francis ... ever since they made him a fucking D.C.I. He has an office at Scotland Yard. Don't see much of him myself ...'

'Where does he live?'

'Out by Canvey Island ... near Southend. Big house called Heavensgate in Chislehurst Avenue ... near the sea.'

Southend. The name meant something to Francis but he couldn't remember what. Something to do with drowning. He pulled D.I. Spencer up out of the chair by his hair. The detective immediately fell to the floor and groaned — about to pass out again from the pain. Francis dragged him by the legs to the back door. Down along the garden through the weeds to the derelict shed. He opened the door and was hit full on by the dreadful stench from inside. Flies swarmed. Even at that unnatural time of year. And rats scurried away from the intrusion. The smell brought D.I. Spencer back to his senses and he saw two badly decomposed bodies over in a corner. Pieces of rotten flesh still hung like dirty bandages from bones and eyeless sockets stared and teeth laughed out of an open mouth. The other had no head.

'Jesus Christ! Don't leave me here ...'

'I'll come back for you, Mr Spencer.'

'When ... for fuck's sake ... who the fuck are they ...?'

'Soon. If you're telling the truth.'

'I'll bleed to death ...'

'No you won't, Mr Spencer. I didn't.'

Francis fixed the detective's wrists to one of the iron posts that held up what remained of the shed roof. With another plastic bag-tie. Then he locked the door. D.I. Spencer screamed after him. To come back. That he was telling the truth. And Francis would come back. If he was telling the truth. But first he drove back to the city.

Francis sat in the Citroën outside D.C.I. Dunne's house in Canvey Island just before 3.00 a.m. in the morning. He smoked a cigarette and waited. Chislehurst Avenue dark and quiet. A hard frost falling from the clear moonsky and little or no wind. Francis got out of the car and walked up the driveway of the big house called Heavensgate. Stood outside the front door and listened. Quiet as the grave. Front door locked. So he walked round the house looking for an open window or some other way in. Any way in. Francis carried a crowbar with him in case something had to be forced. But he didn't want to use it unless he had to. Probably alarms all over the place. Careful!

The loaded 9mm Browning crouched inside his coat pocket. Francis looked carefully. Everywhere locked. Tight. Not a chink nor a niche nor an unguarded opening. He realised he'd have to chance it and listened for a minute at the back of the house. Then rammed the crowbar into a door-jamb and pulled gently. Muffled sound of timber splintering and a grating of metal on metal. Francis stopped and listened. Lucky. No alarm. The door opened an inch or two. He re-set the crowbar and pulled again. This time the lock gave way and the door swung into a large kitchen. Francis entered the house and listened again. No sound. No dogs. Hoped he had the right house. Either that or D.C.I. Dunne thought he was untouchable. Unaccountable. Unforgivable!

He advanced slowly through the place. Checking every room for cats or booby traps or CCT cameras or satellite receivers. So far so good. Ground floor of the house clean. No sign of life. He slowly climbed the stairs. Five doors along the landing. All closed. Francis moved silently. Opened the first to find a bathroom. Second showed him a young boy of about ten or eleven. Fastasleep. Third contained D.C.I. Dunne and his wife. Also asleep and snoring in a kingsized bed. Francis opened the fourth door as a precaution and found a spare room. And the fifth was the bedroom of a teenage girl — probably about Sinéad's age. Empty. Francis went back to the third room and silently approached the bed. Hooked the crowbar into his belt and carried the Browning at arm's length. D.C.I. Dunne's wife stirred and Francis stopped. Waited a moment for her to settle and then moved forward again.

Francis woke D.C.I. Dunne with a hand over the detective's mouth and the gun to his head. But the Chief Inspector panicked and started to struggle. His wife woke up and screamed. Francis hit her in the face with the crowbar and she fell back onto the pillow. Then he dragged D.C.I. Dunne out of the bed and flung him across the floor.

'Jesus, my wife ... what have you fucking done ...?'

'Shut the fuck up!'

'Who are you? What do you want? You didn't have to do that ... the money's downstairs in the safe. D'you know who I am? I'm a detective chief inspector!'

The chief inspector made an attempt to get to his bloody and unconscious wife. Francis flung him back against the wall.

'Let me see her, please ... she's hurt bad ...'

'It's me, Mr Dunne. Don't you remember me? You never came back to help me ... to let me look after my woman.'

'What the fuck are you talking about? Are you an escaped lunatic or what?'

'You could say that. You can call me that. I don't mind that now.'

D.C.I. Dunne looked at Francis. Close as the dim light would allow. Recognition dawned as the boy came to the door from the next bedroom — rubbing his eyes.

'Daddy ... I heard a noise ...'

Francis beckoned the boy into the room and told him to sit down on the floor beside his father. The woman in the bed began to come to with a low moaning noise. The boy started to cry. D.C.I. Dunne hugged him.

'Francis fucking Page! Jesus, Francis ... don't hurt my son. He's done nothing to you.'

'I won't hurt him, Mr Dunne. I just want to know what happened.'

'What happened about what?'

Francis knew he knew. Because everything was known to some people. The people who knew everything. But he played the game. For now.

'The cocaine. Glendora. Everything. You know ... Mr Spencer told me to come see you. He gave me your address. I want to know the truth, Mr Dunne. If I know the truth, then he won't get hurt.'

'You promise? Promise me, Francis. If I tell you everything ... you won't hurt him?'

'I already told him. If I know the truth ... I'll come back.'

'Back where? Look, Francis ... just don't hurt him ... ok?'

'Tell me the truth, Mr Dunne. And don't forget ... God is listening.'

D.C.I. Dunne was very frightened. Francis Page — of all people. Talking about God.

'We switched it ... I switched it. For Bicarbonate. The plods at the Yard didn't know what the fuck they were burning ... and I supervised it all anyway.'

'We? You said we first. You said we ... you and Mr Spencer?'

'No ... Spencer had nothing to do with it, Francis. He's strictly by-the-book. We ... me and your girlfriend. The black woman ... and her old boyfriend.'

'Boyfriend? No! No! What are you telling me? Lies? God is fucking listening!'

Heartbeat! Francis didn't believe him. Heartfuckingbeat! How could the man lie like that? Had he no God? Who was his God? Cocaine God. Noname God.

'You wanted the truth, Francis ... you said you wouldn't hurt him if I told you the truth. This is the truth! I didn't have the set-up to push the charlie myself. You know ... lab houses and chemists and security teams for the distribution ... collectors ... pushers ... too many people. Too much hassle with local London dealers.'

'Glendora? Glendora?'

'She made the contact ... but my name couldn't be mentioned. She put it out that you and Moore had switched most of the snow before you got nabbed and now you wanted to deal from inside.'

Francis grabbed the boy by the hair and pulled him away from his father. D.C.I. Dunne tried to grab him back but Francis kicked the chief inspector away.

'James Greenwood? What about Greenwood and Hatchet Harry?'

'After the deal was done, the Yardies didn't want it on the streets that they had to pay twice for their stuff ... have every two-bit pusher trying to double-cross them. So they just put it about that the deal fell through and the coke was still out there. Somewhere ... just sitting ... nobody knew where it was. Except you and Moore.'

'That made us ...'

'Sure sure ... a target for every wideboy and bandit this side of Aberdeen. But that wasn't my idea, Francis. That was down to the woman ... she didn't want any comebacks ...'

Francis didn't want him talking about the woman. Lying about the woman. Him and his lying nogood nogod. But he listened. Because —

'Comebacks?'

'Yes ... y'know, from you if you got wind of what happened.'

'You mean she wanted me dead?'

'Of course ... said you'd do away with her boyfriend ... like you did before! But I don't want to know anything about that. What d'you think happened to Moore? He got done for in Strangeways because he wouldn't say where the stuff was. Of course ... he couldn't say, could he? Because he didn't know.'

Heartbeat! He was lying! Was he lying? Who was telling the fucking truth? Was this the truth? The truth was more confusing than the confusion. Francis couldn't be sure. What old boyfriend? He was the only boyfriend. There was no other boyfriend. Was there?

'Where is she now?'

'Who? Your girlfriend? Who knows, Francis ... out of the country, I'd say ... with her share of the money. The Yardies drowned some whore and I put a bullet in the poor cow's head. Blew her face off ... so no one would know it wasn't her. They had to make an example of somebody. There was no investigation to speak of and to all intents and purposes, Glendora's dead. She's a dead woman, Francis ... her name's on a crematorium plaque here in Southend. Jesus, but you were stupid to trust her. We made the deal just after you were lifted at the airport. How the fuck d'you think we knew where you and Moore were meeting up?'

Bastardbeat! Francis hit D.C.I. Dunne in the face with his gun. The man fell back onto the floor with blood coming from his face. Now it was unravelling. The whole conspiracy was unravelling. The truth at last! The final truth. Only Francis couldn't understand the truth. It was alien. It was incomprehensible. It was a lie!

'Ok, Francis ... that's ok ... I deserve it. Only don't hurt my son. You said you wouldn't hurt my son. You promised, Francis.'

'You hurt my daughter.'

'I did no such thing, Francis. I don't even know your daughter.'

'Don't lie, Mr Dunne! You killed her and drugged Glendora. You got Glenny back on the drug and my daughter is dead!'

D.C.I. Dunne was on his knees. Pleading. Praying.

'I killed nobody, Francis. I told you ... the Yardies stiffed some stupid junkie and I messed up her face and took care of the investigation. It was nobody you knew. Nothing to do with you ...'

'Now God knows the truth!'

'Look ... I've still got a lot of the money. My share ... you can have it, Francis.'

Francis didn't want the money. Money was no good to him now.

'How much have you got left, Mr Dunne? Money.'

'Ten grand maybe ... I can get more ... as much as you want.'

'For my life? For Matthew's life? For my daughter's life? Why would I want your blood money, Mr Dunne?'

'That's what you fucking did it for in the first place, wasn't it? The fucking money? That's why you were the fucking courier, Francis. Don't get all pious about it now.'

'Things were much different then ...'

'You can always use money, Francis ... everyone wants money.'

'God doesn't!'

'Oh fuck ...'

The woman came to and saw blood all over the bed and became hysterical. Francis pointed the gun and shot her straight through the forehead. She was silent. The boy began to cry again.

'You stupid fucking bastard, Page! You've killed my wife!'

'You killed my woman ...'

'She came to me. I protected her when you couldn't! From Spencer and all the rest of the scum. You're a stupid crazy bastard and I'll fucking kill you!'

D.C.I. Dunne made a lunge from the floor. Francis side-stepped the attack and struck him across the side of the head with the crowbar as he rushed past. D.C.I. Dunne fell to the floor again and lay still and facedown. Francis walked across and put the 9mm to the back of his head and pulled the trigger. The boy stopped crying and came up onto his knees. Shivered. Head bowed and hands joined and lips moved in silent prayer. To his God. Who came to him. Eyes watched Francis' feet move back across the bedroom floor and stop right in front of him. A movement. There was someone else in the room. Francis hesitated and glanced sideways to catch a glimpse of his own image in the dressing-table mirror. He pointed his gun at the Fichteboy who looked back at him. Shoot! The boy was doomed. Shoot him! Done for. The eyes in the mirror pleaded with Francis to pull the trigger. Put him out of his misery. Francis looked away and noticed something on the floor in front of him. Looked down and saw himself kneeling on the floor. Praying. As he had prayed before. Had to do the right thing. The humane thing. The boy didn't look up as the muzzle of the automatic pressed against the top of his skull and he felt nothing after that.

Francis went back downstairs. Listened and looked out through the windows to see if any noseyparker was coming to investigate the gun-shots. No lights nor movement in the secluded street. All heavy sleepers or on the Mogadon or Valium or Zopiclone and doubleglazing of only the highest quality. Wouldn't hear a fucking nuclear bomb go off. Price to pay for salubrity. He made himself black coffee in the kitchen and lit a cigarette. Then carried the cup back upstairs and went into the girl's room. Francis looked around. Full of female things. He wondered where she was — when she would be coming back. Computer in the bedroom and Francis switched it on. Music came out. Soft and gentle. A girl's music. Francis didn't know what the tune was — but he liked it. It reminded him of some time in the past. Some time he'd forgotten about now. But the music brought a sense of it back. The time. A sense of time. Whenever it was. He lay down on the soft bed and blew smoke from his cigarette up into the faint perfume air. Music filled the house and he floated away on its sea of sentiment. Colours changed and kalei-doscoped and danced for him in the moonlight room. Heart weightless and felt like singing. The song on the computer. Didn't know it.

Hummed instead. Smoked his cigarette with one hand and waved the gun like a conductor's baton with the other. Francis lay on the bed for a long time. Until light from the new day filtered through the night and made its way into the girlroom. Several holes burned in the carpet with cigarette butts and the computer long since stopped playing.

Francis felt tired but knew he couldn't fall asleep. Not there. In that place. Got up and searched through the house. Wasn't sure what he was looking for. Clues. Information. Something to go on. Found nothing. Just some money and a packet of cocaine. Which he put into his pocket. Then left the house by the same door he'd come in through and drove away in the Citroën.

City already alive as he made his way in along the Thames and across Docklands. Winter people all around. Coats and hats and boots and brollies. All looking growley and glum while he was happy and light for the first time in fucking ages. He went into the Church of St Eduard the Martyr and prayed, before going back to the flat in Brooks Court. I am not yet born; provide me. With water to dandle me, grass to grow for me, trees to talk to me, sky to sing to me, birds and a white light in the back of my mind to guide me.

Francis saw that Glendora was asleep in the bedroom. Close and remote at the same time. From what was inside him. Whatever was him. Once. She didn't wake and he knew she was in some sort of drug-trance. He looked at her arms. A fresh needle mark with blood around it. Some bastard got to her. Again! His good mood left him and he became furious. Heartbeat! Junkiebeat! Kicked things around the flat and smashed chairs and the coffee table. But he was tired and it didn't take long for the frenzy to wear itself out. Work itself out. Fury! Fuckbeat! Then he came and lay beside her on the bed. Put his arms around her fragile body. Like a drowning man clinging to a lifebelt. And she subconsciously moved towards him for protection. From the wild world.

chapter thirty-seven

chapte r thirty-seven

chapte r thirty-seven

Francis Page woke later that day. Darklate. Fiona beside him on the bed. Asleep or dead? He checked her pulse and found she was still breathing. So he rose gently and went to the kitchen for coffee and a cigarette. Francis had to go to work at ten and he was hungry. Also worried about the girl. Been out for a long time. Wondered if she'd been taking anything. Knew she was! Remembered! Francis had a look around to see if he could find any drugs. But he couldn't concentrate for long and gave up the search after a minute or two. Made beans on toast and took some through to her. She woke and smiled weakly up at him. Kissed her forehead and offered her the food and coffee on a tray. She sipped from the cup and picked at the plate. Then lit a cigarette. Francis could hear winterbirds over in Lincoln's Inn. Blown up on the January wind. Sounds of nighttraffic and the cold city. In the room. With him. And her.

'What happened to the rehab?'

'I didn't manage to get over there today, Dad.'

'I can see that.'

'I'm sorry. I tried ... I really and truly tried.'

'You got to give it up. You've been out for a long time, honey. This stuff ain't any good. It'll kill you.'

'It's all I can afford ...'

Francis felt helpless. There was a time when he'd have known what to do. But now it was all obsession and repression and repetition and robots and he couldn't communicate with other people. Unless they met him on his own level. And nobody did. Except the girl.

'Who got you back onto this, baby? You were so clean ... for so long. I've been trying to find out who did it and no one will tell me.'

'I got myself onto it, Dad.'

'No! Some bastard gave it to you. Who was it?'

'I don't know ... it was long ago. Some bouncer. I can't remember.'

'Remember! Remember!'

'I think ... when I was looking for that woman ... the black woman. Someone told me to try a club over in Paddington.'

'What club?'

'The purple something ...'

But he could kill. That was one thing he could do. He was a killer and only someone who had lost reality and lived in a land of fear could understand why. He could kill for her. If nothing else.

'The Pink Peacock?'

'I think that was it. One of the doormen said he knew you ... and the woman. Said he could find her for me.'

'Which doorman? Can you remember his name?'

'No ... he invited me to a party. Told me she might be there ...'

'Fuck! Fuck the bastard!'

'He had an American accent ...'

Fuckingnightingalebeat! Francis threw the food tray across the room and began to make the animal noises that came up from somewhere deep inside him. Nightingale! Beat! Nightingale! Beat! He stalked quickly from wall to wall, punching out at the furniture and pulling at his hair. Dribbles of froth formed at the corners of his mouth and a trickle of blood ran down out of his left nostril. Fiona was afraid and drew back along the bed. Francis saw her shaking and pulling the bedclothes up round her head. The anger dissipated and he came back and sat beside her again.

'How did he do it, baby? How did the bastard get you back on it?'

'I told you ... a party. I was already smoking a bit of hash and taking some E ... student stuff ... nothing serious ...'

'Don't worry about that, honey. Tell me what the fucker did.'

'Nothing. Really, Dad. Everyone was doing it, so I did it as well.'

'The fucking fucking fucking bastard!'

'It was my own fault.'

'It wasn't your fault. You were off it. I kept you off it.'

'I was never "on it", Dad. What are you talking about ...?'

'Then they took me away. That's what happened. I promised I'd always take care of you ... and I didn't because they took me away.'

'It's not your fault ...'

'It is! I couldn't keep my fucking promise. The bastards took me away.'

Francis buried his head in his hands and sobbed. Shaking. Shoulders. He felt Fiona put her arms round him and hold him until the spasms stopped. She stroked his hair and hummed a tune that he'd heard somewhere before. Maybe his mother? Annie. Anniemother. When she was all right. They stayed there in that position for ever and ever. Hardly moving. Humming. High on mutual tragedy.

Sorrow is a goatsong. Sorrow? *Samsara*. The brute. The coarse. Compassion! There is no compassion. Never again! I'm reconciled! There's only something called the human condition with silhouettes for which there's no responsibility and senses for which there's no adequate control ... to move on is to move away ... become less human.

Inhuman? Voices hissed in his head. Unfamiliar. Goading him. Calling him a coward and a fool and worthless and witless. A herd of them. Legion. Horde. Asmosdeus and Bloodmonkey and Hyenaman and Lilith and Seirizzin and many more. Fiona? She's dead. Glendora? She's doing it again. Fuck all the others.

'I'm here, Dad ...'

Those who languish in darkness. Reconciliation of the brute with the beauty. Some fuckers will never see ... Shine. Shine. In their darkness. Never be any fucking different! No matter what anyone says. Or does. Whispers crept round the room. Accusing. Blaming. Warning. Spreading like a virus in the air. Savagery and selfishness. Nothing will wash away the stain. So fucking hard to forgive. Can't do it! And there's a price for revenge. Can it be paid? They hurt my babies ... my children. I am my children and I store up my suffering for their future. I must kill! God told me. God spoke to me. I spoke to God. I am God. They hurt me! Hurt my daughters!

'I'm here, Dad ...'

'Glenny?'

'Fiona.'

'Glenny.'

You will be the last man alive on this planet. I am. Already! What you do with your life will make you what you are when you die. Everything counts! And must be accounted for. I am Kamikaze. I am Karttikeya. I am Khan. I am Killer. I must kill! Myself.

'He told me the woman had AIDS.'

'Who?'

'The bouncer. Did she? Was it true?'

'No.'

'He said you had it too.'

'I wish I had. Would've taken it away from you ... if I could. Would've freed you.'

Francis could hear the angels. In the parks around Holborn. The Seraphim. And Cherubim. And Moloch calling him from Hell. And God above them all. Above all. The Voices. Vices. Vicious. Time to go to work. Francis cleaned himself up and left Fiona watching television. Pretending to watch television. She seemed a little agitated. He wondered what she did at night — when he was away from the flat. Didn't work and slept like him during the day. Hardly ever went out when he was there — apart from collecting her benefit and doing a few chores round the flat when she wasn't sleeping.

Francis knew cocaine was regarded as a social drug and the prices were fairly stable because of the high demand. Supply. According to supply. Demand was always there. Stable. Normal. Standard. Average. But it was at least fifty quid a gram and her benefit money wouldn't pay for it. Couldn't pay. Somebody was supporting her. Something. The habit. How? Why? Just didn't make sense to Francis. Nothing made sense for long. Things could be clear for a while. Then confused again.

Sometimes he wished he could get hold of a few tranqs. A few sedatives. Some benzhexol or stelazine. Something to give him a break. Pimozide. Or piportil. A little largactil. Veractil. Something to stop the psychosis. Anything. He took Fiona's painkillers and they helped a little bit but not much. He even thought of breaking into some chemist shop but didn't want to take the chance of being caught. They had all this surveillance equipment these days. Maybe he could go somewhere and ask for something? A hospital or group home or voluntary organisation or day centre or drop-in or sheltered sanctuary. Couldn't take the chance. No matter how much he wanted. Only find out who he was and send him back to Broadmoor. What would happen to Glendora then? She'd surely die. Like Fiona. From the fucking drugs.

He listened to the Voices to see if they could give him practical advice. But they puked up a load of profanity these days and never said anything helpful about anything. He missed the Alien and the Animal and the Scientist and didn't like the nowdevils in his head. They cursed everything — but ask the bastards a simple question like where could he get a few fluperthixol tablets. And they were no fucking use at all.

Francis drove up-town next morning after work and had his hair styled back in a pony-tail. Also his beard trimmed to a fashionable shape and bought a pair of shades. Then went shopping for a jacket and trousers of the latest style and a shirt and a pair of chic shoes. Back at the flat he took a shower and trimmed his nails and sprayed some deodorant under his arms. Ready.

The Pink Peacock over in Paddington was busy enough for a Thursday night. Francis sat in a secluded corner of the bar and sipped Jack Daniels and soda. New people on the door who didn't recognise him and once he told them he was in the game himself and dropped a few names and took a few of theirs — as he was opening a new club near St Giles in Charing Cross and would be hiring soon at a good rate — there was no trouble getting in without a search. Most of the inside staff were also new and very young and hardly a familiar face in the whole fucking place. Except for George Dimitrov.

'George!'

'Hello. Who is that? Do I know you?'

'Sure you do, George.'

'Can't see you too well over there in the corner. Give me a clue.'

'Life is a joke that's just begun, that's what I always say, George.'

The *Mafiozniki* man scratched his big Russian head. Then he remembered.

'So you do ... Francis? Is it Francis Page?'

'Keep your voice down a bit.'

'Jesus Christ! I thought you were out of the country, Francis. Away in Mexico or somewhere with all that cocaine. What are you doing back here?'

'Looking for someone.'

'Who?'

'Not you, George. Don't worry. Where's Percy Shillinger?'

'Not in tonight. What do you want with the boss, Francis?'

'I want to ask him about my daughter.'

'Does he know your daughter? What about your daughter, Francis?'

Francis didn't want to say too much. Because George said he shouldn't. A long long time ago.

'Does John Nightingale still work here?'

'Maybe I can pass on a message for you, Francis ... to the boss?'

'Does John Nightingale still work here, George?'

'Sometimes.'

'Is he here tonight?'

'Jesus, Francis, you are a wanted man. Any trouble and you are back inside. Straightaway!'

'There'll be no trouble in here, George. Don't you worry your big Russian head. Is he here? Why don't you tell him I've come to say hello.'

The clubmanager didn't like the look of Francis. Bigbouncer always a bit strange — but looked even crazier tonight.

'Ok ... ok. But you were not talking to me, Francis. I mean ... when they catch you.'

'One more thing, George ... Is Matthew on tonight?'

'What is that?'

'Matthew Moore ... is he on tonight?'

'Did you not hear? He hung himself.'

'Hung himself? No he didn't, George. Someone killed him!'

'Sure they did, Francis.'

Dimitrov decided to humour the madman. Gabbed on a bit about how Matthew changed when he went inside. Went stir-crazy. Then the Irish Department of Agriculture shot all his animals. Should have known better than to get mixed up in drug smuggling. Sorry.

'You know some bastard killed him, George. Are you in this along with the rest of them? Don't think I don't know everything. I've been told the full fucking story.'

'He left a note ... for you. Matthew. They found it in his cell and someone sent it here.'

'For me? Where is it?'

'Here. In the office. I will go and get it for you.'

George Dimitrov slid off his stool before Francis could stop him. Disappeared into the crowd. Francis moved back away from the bar. Behind a pillar. Hand automatically inside his jacket and felt the reassuring texture of the gun. Waited. Someone beside him in the shadows. A ghost. Someone he couldn't see. Just sense. Quiet. Not saying anything. Not even breathing. Just there. Beside him. Someone who wasn't a killer. Like him. Time didn't move! Only he, by his own choice, moved through the infinite worlds of a future that already existed. The language of his Voices replaced the external world with a world of symbolic equivalents. The bulk of life on earth was microscopic. And noise was the emblem of anarchy and the fingerprint of entropy. And truth was not absolute — it was multiple and contradictory — either known or not known. Only. But he didn't want these things flying through his head. Not at this fucking moment. Nor did he need anyone to be beside him. Ghost of Francis past. Not now. Had to concentrate. If he tried to get out of the club he'd be caught. Killed. Concenfucking-trate! Cool! Not crazy. Killer! Animals have no sense of guilt. And the human brain consists of three components. Reptilian. Surrounded by paleomammalian. Surrounded by neomammalian. Fuck off!

Coolbeat! John Nightingale emerged from the office at the far side of the floor. Held a small envelope in his hand and looked towards the corner of the bar where Francis had been sitting. Then came across slowly — weaving his way through the crowd. Francis moved back behind the pillar. Where he couldn't be seen. Nightingale looked up and down the length of the bar.

'I remember you, Francis Page. *Quae nocent docent*. Where you at?' Francis kept his cover. Took the gun from his pocket and held it up by the side of his head.

'C'mon out! You want to know about your daughter? I can tell you. I got a letter for you ... from your old pal. Who you screwed and sold down the river. *Requiescat in pace*.'

Francis emerged from behind the pillar. Nightingale looked at the Browning.

'You gonna shoot me, Francis Page?'

'That depends ...'

'I remember the shower-room. Do you? *Nosce te ipsum*. But I ain't the only one got fucked. Am I?'

'Give me the letter and tell me where Glenny's getting the junk from.'

'Don't know about no Glenny, Francis Page. Only know about your little daughter.'

'She's dead.'

'Might as well be. She came looking for the other broad ... with the AIDS.'

'You'll be dead too, devilman. Soon. I'm your assassin.'

Cool! Beat! Coolbeat! Beat! Beat! Francis raised the gun and pointed it directly at John Nightingale's head. About to pull the trigger. Smartman's eyes looked straight into his. Defiant. Not afraid. Anymore. Francis hesitated.

'Go ahead, Francis Page ... pull the trigger.'

Coolman waited. Smileman. Francis hesitated. Vileman. Looked for words that wouldn't come. Something to square things with.

'You can't kill me, can you? You kill me ... you kill yourself. Right?'

'Why didn't you leave her alone?'

'You raped me, Francis Page.'

'You asked me to. You wouldn't stop until I had to do it. To stop you. She was off it. You didn't have to put her back.'

'She was a *virgin*, Francis Page. I lost the bimbo her virginity.'

Francis felt his finger closing round the trigger. Beat! Smarteyes stared into his and he was confused again. Looked confused. Why?

'I did it because of you. So really, *you* did it. You fucked me and I fucked your little girl. Sure enough. She came back and back to me ... more crack. Then smack. Speedballing. Paranoia. Course, she gotta pay for what she's using, Francis Page.'

'Just give me the letter.'

'When I'm good and ready. I gave her to Percy Shillinger ... for his string. So she could pay. She's out there most nights. Probably trick you for a fix. Maybe she already has? *Quod avetat Deus*!'

Francis looked at the man. Wondered who his God was. Queergod. Feargod. Deargod. And why he hated Francis Page so much. The man read his thoughts.

'I'm like you, Francis Page. I should be gone but I can't get outta here. I am you and will become you ... nothing I can do about it. *Mea culpa*. Thing is, I guess I always knew it. You reminded me of that every time I saw you and I hated you for it. Guess you knew it too.'

Everybody is everybody!

'Give me the letter ... or I'll kill you.'

'If you were gonna do it, you'd have done it by now.'

The man smiled his smile. Sinister. Sensing the air. Like a spider.

'You're gone, Francis Page. Washed up. A crazy fucking nobody. *Acta est fabula*. I'm walking away now.'

The smile grew and filled the room. Francis heard it say some words in slow motion. That as well as everything else — Agnes never made the phone call. To Angeline. The smile did it. The devilsmile.

The American tore the letter into four pieces and threw it on the floor. Turned and walked towards the office. Some of the spaced-out clubbers sensed what was going on and moved out of the line of fire. Francis watched him move away in slow motion. Mincing across the floor. Arrogant. Exotic. Dangerous. Dead. *Ad patres*.

'Nightingale!'

The smartman turned. Smile broad across his face and made a fucking motion with his arm. Francis pulled the trigger and the automatic kicked out the whole clip in under three seconds. John Nightingale stood in the middle of the club for a brief moment — bloody pulp where his chest was just an instant ago. Such a short time ago. Disbelief in the dead eyes and still a smile across the mouth as if he'd had the last laugh. After all. The American's body took a long time to fall over onto the floor and brought screams from the hushed crowd. People ran in all directions. Bouncers in from the door. Throwing clubbers out of their way. George Dimitrov screamed into a mobile phone and Francis picked up the pieces of torn paper from the floor. Slipped away in the confusion. *Sic transit gloria mundi*!

Outside in the car he fitted the paper together long enough to read its message.

FRANCIS, WATCH OUT!

YOU'RE STILL A BASTARD AND ALL THAT FOR WHAT YOU DID, BUT THERE'S SOMETHING GOING ON. DON'T KNOW WHAT IT IS YET. GOT YOUR LETTERS BUT COULDN'T MAKE SENSE OF THEM. KEEP YOUR EYES PEELED. BE OUT SOON.

YOUR FRIEND, MATTHEW.

Matthew got even. By dying. By being killed. And for a brief moment Francis felt the acute pain of it. The searing religious agony of it. A separate thing. Self-encompassing. Apart from everything else. Simple things happened. Even though their consequences could be catastrophic. Straightforward things. And normal people got hurt. Reasonable people. Plainandsimple people. Like the ripple thing. Like the stone in the pond. Complicated by conspiracies. And hidden agendas. And ulterior motives. Everyone was in danger from everything. Especially the innocent. Ordinarypeople? Death was the beginning. And killing was an easy thing now. Straightforward. Rational. Reasonable. Normal. And friendship was something shining. He said — 'Your friend, Matthew'. Francis realised he knew more and more about less and less and wondered why it should be that he alone existed and why the Universe was nothing more than a part of his subconscious soul. Then the confusion came back.

chapter thirty-eight

chapte r thirty-eight
chapte r thirty-eight

Old familiar feelings returned to Francis Page when he opened the door of the flat in Brooks Court. Something wrong. Knew it. Instinct. Like an animal would. And hackles up on the back of his neck. Francis pulled the gun from his pocket and pushed in a fresh clip of bullets. Edged along the hall without turning on any lights. Dropped down on his good knee before checking the kitchen. Nothing. Sittingroom. Nobody. Francis sighed. But the feeling wouldn't go away. Somefucking-thing was wrong! Edged along towards the bedroom. 3.00 a.m. Too quiet. Like death. And cold. Freezing. Maybe the bastards got here before him. The dreamkillers! Fiona should be in the flat. If they harmed her there'd be more death. Killing! The Thames would run fucking red. Peered round the door of the bedroom. Francis saw Glendora on the bed. Still. Moved cautiously across the room. Eyes open. Staring up at him. He smiled down and put the gun away. She kept staring. He touched her and she was cold. As the dead room. As the icy air. His fingers hurt where they came into contact with her dead body. Pain shot up them and into his arm. To his heart. Beeaatt. Francis grew cold himself. To match his surroundings. To match the woman on the bed.

His blood thickened and everything went at slowspeed. Heeaarrtt. Minutes moved as he turned his eyes towards the woman's arm. Syringe still protruding from a vein and on the floor a lighter, spoon and length of rubber tube. Francis withdrew the needle in slomo. Threw it against the wall and watched a little bubble of dead blood emerge from the vein. He tried to think but logic wouldn't come. Only laughter. Manic. Mad. Deep echoes round and round the flat. Moving away to other rooms and coming back to burst his eardrums and he could feel its cold spit on his face. What the fuck? Overdose? Smack for the crack. Bad shit? Accident? Suicide? Murder? Who would the killer have to kill for this?

The blood in his own veins began to warm again. Heart! Boilbeat! Left alone again! Betrayed again! Francis pulled the body from the bed. Shook it. Slapped it. Threw it down and picked it back up again. Threw it onto the floor and kicked it. Come back! You bitch! Screamed and pulled at his hair. But the anger didn't last long and soon he was crying and kneeling beside Fiona and covering her body with kisses. Held her gently and brushed her hair with his fingers. But she was gone. He returned her to the bed and started to systematically smash up what was left of the flat. Bedroom first. Then the rest. Carried the woman's body out to the Citroën and strapped it into the passenger seat. Then returned with a can of petrol and set the flat on fire. Back to the car and Francis sat in the driver's seat smoking a cigarette until he saw flames licking at the windows.

Then he drove away. Down past the Viaduct and south across Blackfriars Bridge and the river. Didn't know where he was going or what he wanted to do next. Thought of driving back up to the house in Essex. Lie low. Live the quiet life. But exhaustion was creeping up on him. A pale lethargy. Like pain. So he headed west instead through a maze of streets towards Hyde Park. To the birds. The angels. God. Drove down along past the Serpentine to a secluded piece of copse-land he knew from when he was a boy. Where he could hide out when the whole world was after him with big sticks to break his fucking neck. After him again.

Wintertime and during the day not many visitors to the Park. A few kids playing hideandseek came and looked in the car window at the two sleeping people. Her with eyes open and him with the scars and the scary face. Nobody woke them while they waited in hibernation for the covering darkness to come. Nobody but Mazikeen and Shedeem. Who enchanted them with magic. And Eurydice who told the dead woman how to come back to life again. And Kwan Yin who came in white robes with a child in her arms. And shadows. Touching the wind-screen with their smokefingers. Trying to get in.

Francis woke around seven and looked across at Fiona. She seemed to have turned her head and was staring out at the evening mist. He touched her. Still cold. Still dead. Started up the engine and drove eastwards out of the Park and north across the river towards the West End.

The Cosa Nostra Casino in Gloucester Place was quiet for a Friday. Francis had a drink at the bar and surveyed the clientele. Then walked through the tables and looked at the croupiers to see if Glendora was amongst them. A couple of black men played the roulette wheel and Francis stood behind them for a few minutes. Couldn't tell if they were the ones from before. Yardies. So long ago he couldn't remember. Looked like Yardies. Even though he couldn't remember what Yardies looked like. But he could remember what Yardies spoke like. The lingo. The speak. He knew it. Could understand it.

'Wha fi we ah go someplace else seh?'

'Dis place be ok, mon ... seh ah why yo wan go?'

'No atmosphere bwoy. Dis yah lik de morgue dat.'

'Nah breddah, it be fine seh.'

Francis came up behind the two men.

'You boys know Glendora?'

'Who ah yo, whitey, seh?'

'I think I might have done business with you guys before.'

'Doan tink so, mon. Us member if yo did.'

'Maybe four or five years ago ... New York?'

'Nah mon ... not we. Yo be tinkin bout some other Yardman.'

'It was you! All you guys is supposed to be brothers ain't you? Where you from?'

The men looked at each other, wary of this sukunyah stranger.

'Manchester.'

'There! See, I knew it.'

'Plenty Yardman in Manchester, spar.'

'But you guys all know each other. You must have seen Glendora.'

'Us ah seh, mon. Doan know any Glendora!'

'You must! You come in here all the time. The Cosa Nostra. The Countess.'

'De Countess?'

'Yes. Yes.'

'Me remember ah Countess. Long time back. Black gel dat. Nice lookin. Why yo ask, mon?'

Francis could see it in their eyes. They knew. Something. Enough. For him.

'Have you seen her?'

'Cyan be tellin yo tings renky. Who yo be anyways?'

'Her partner. I got the twenty kilos of snow.'

'Twenty kilos? Dat be a lot o crack, mon.'

'I got it and I'm looking to trade.'

The black men were interested now. They began to circle round Francis — looking him up and down.

'Wha kinda trade dat seh?'

'Straight sell. I ain't got the organisation to move it.'

'Us hear de Countess her partner be Anansi. Him deh ah mad-house.'

'I got out.'

The breddahs whispered to each other for a few seconds. Turned back to Francis.

'If us deal, yo show ah snow first.'

'No ... first you tell me what happened to the Countess.'

'Her be ded, mon.'

'Dead? She's not dead.'

'Sure, spar. Dussed. Her jook some Yardman few years ago. Them ah drown her.'

Drown? Drown? No. No no no. That wasn't what Francis wanted to hear.

'No no ... that was someone else. Not Glendora!'

'Them drown her in ah bath to mek example ... yo know de ting, spar.'

'Mr Dunne told me it wasn't her. Where the fuck is she? You boys must know ... tell me.'

'Us hear she tek some dunseye ... from a deal. Ten thousand. Amsterdam deh ah seh. Her a junkie. Tek de money fi skag, mon.'

'Den some bea put a bullet in her. Blow ah face away.'

'No no no no no ... not her! I told you. Tell me where she went!'

The men were getting twitchy. Nervous of Francis. He was strange. Vacillating. Jumby. But if he had twenty kilos of charlie —

'Doan know, mon. Us doan know any ting bout all dat. Look ... you show we ah snow dem.'

'Outside. In my car. Come on ...'

Francis led the Yardies out of the Cosa Nostra and down an alley that ran along by the side of the Casino. Citroën parked under the trees near Portman Square. Alongside a black limousine. The black men pulled a couple of 44 Automags from their belts as they walked behind Francis. He stopped just before reaching the car. Black men stopped behind him.

'Wha be ah matter, spar, seh?'

'There's a dead woman in that car.'

'Hear wha ...?'

'There! See!'

'Go tek a look, Beebee.'

One Yardie moved cautiously across to the Citroën. The other kept Francis covered.

'Deh be a gel in yah ok, Danto.'

'Who her be seh?'

'Dunno, mon, but her sure ded as Diablesse.'

'You don't know? It's Glendora, you bastard. It's the Countess!'

'Her a white gel dat. Ain't be ah Countess seh.'

'Course it is. Look closer.'

Yardie next to the Citroën put his face up to the window and shielded his eyes from the glare of streetlamps. The other kept his Automag on Francis.

'Her a white gel, mon. Look like she ah junk herself out.'

Other man getting jumpy. Kept the gun pointed at Francis but started to circle round toward his companion.

'Which part ah cocaine, mon?'

'In the boot.'

'Show we.'

'Wait, Danto seh ... him maybe haf a gun in dere.'

'Givvus de keys dem ...'

Beebee opened the boot of the Citroën and Danto took his eyes off Francis for half a second. Long enough. Francis wasn't there when he looked back. Nothing in the boot neither. The black men backed away up the alley, towards Baker Street. She took the ten grand? For skag? Didn't believe it. Would've told him she was in trouble. Even though he knew anyway. And the bastards killed her for it? No — not her. Someone else. Some innocent? No one was innocent. Any more. Everybody was guilty. He dropped Beebee first with a clear hit to the stomach. But the man wasn't dead. Rolled around the ground swearing and calling to his spar. Soon attract attention. Needed a closerange bullet to the head to shut the cunt up. Francis stepped out into the open and shot at Danto. Missed. Danto shot back and hit Francis in the side of the head, taking away most of his left ear. Now he'd be like Earless. Francis was also hit in the neck and shoulder by the automatic bullets and fell against the alley wall. Danto fumbled for another clip and Francis used the opportunity. Unloaded the magazine of the 9mm Browning up the alley. Just as a man and a woman emerged through the side door of the Cosa Nostra Casino and headed towards their limousine. Bullets from the Browning already in the air. Hitting the woman in the chest. She fell in slow motion to the ground and tried to catch on to her escort. Lay there moving her head to and fro while the rest of the world ceased to be. Stopped. For an instant.

Danto grabbed Beebee and carried him away up the street. Out of the danger area. Francis re-loaded and walked towards the woman. The alley fell silent. No noise. Not even the sound of his slowmotion footsteps. Francis looked down at the pool of blood spreading across the ground from the woman. He looked at the man who was with her. A face he recognised. From somewhere in the past. In another world.

'Don't kill me ...'

The man handed his wallet to Francis. Francis looked inside. It contained about a thousand pounds in cash and a lot of credit cards. The cards carried the name Shillinger. He let the money fall from his fingers and it settled on the damp ground of the alley. Then he threw the plastic cards away. The man had backed off slowly, almost unnoticed — towards the casino. Francis bent down to look at the woman. He saw she was heavily pregnant. She was shot in the chest and blood pumped out from an artery onto her neck and face. She looked up at him with her dying eyes.

'Francis ... is it you, Francis?'

'Who are you?'

'They said you were *muerto* ... so I had to find another *padre. Perdóname*, Francis ...'

Francis knew this woman. From somewhere in the past. He remembered her face — and her voice. And the cigarette she gave him when he was down down down —

'You came to see me ...'

'Who shot me, Francis? Who killed *mi niño*?'

'I've killed the whole world ...'

'*Dame un besito* ...'

He bent down and tasted her warm blood on his lips. An arm went up round his neck and she held onto him for as long as she could. As long as there was life in her. Blood gurgled from her mouth and into his and he saw the soul leave her. Slip away. Heard it. Hiss away. Tasted it in his mouth as it left hers. Something appeared up in the night sky. It was Christ. And he was crying. Had a gun in his hand and put it to his head and pulled the trigger. Starlight speckled the street. Francis saw many corpses around him. Géricault's raftpicture. Bodies of dead and dying. All with bullets in their brains and smoking guns in their hands. All killers. Like him. All silent now. No more talking. No words. No more words. God silent now! Nothing left to say.

Francis heard sirens approaching. He stood up and walked back to the Citroën. Pulled out of the alley at speed with blood pumping from his wounds and clothes covered in scarlet. Like an adulteress. He felt faint and needed to get somewhere safe. Fast!

Francis knew the police would be on to him after killing John Nightingale. Slags would put all the pieces together and realise it was him who shot D.C.I. Dunne and his family. The flat was gutted so they wouldn't find anything there. He thought about Manor Park but the fucking plods would be swarming all over the place there too. The boys didn't know where he was so they couldn't grass him. Not that they would. Because no one was inherently bad. Not even an imbecile. Or a lunatic. Or a psycho. Or a spazo. Or a schizo. Or a windowlicker. Or a killer. But Francis couldn't be too careful. Drove north-east and onto the M11. Into Essex.

Parked round the back again when he got to the house and careful to sus the place out before going inside. Carried Fiona's body in and laid it on the floor in front of the fireplace. She felt so very cold and he decided to build a little blaze to warm her up.

Whispers spitting in his ear. Now you know. What? The consequences. What will I do now? How will it end? In a split second. End? End! I want it to fucking end. Death is an end. Not a beginning? And a beginning. That's what I need ... a new beginning. Choose death now. Death is the mirror in which life is reflected. I'll do it! I'll choose death. Like Jesus. Like Genghis. And Earless. And *d'Orléan*. I will choose death!

Francis realised that all his previous longings for immortality made him the complete fool he was. Everybody was dying. What was a few more fucking days here or there? A few more fucking years? No point in being outraged. Raging against it. Or pretending it wasn't there. Waiting. Sanitising it. Hiding the victims. He'd seen enough recently to know. No difference between all those he'd killed and himself. No difference between Glendora and himself. Fiona. Except they were dead and he was still alive. Such a small thing. Such an insignificance.

Microbe to man. The evolutionary law of upward cosmic growth? Or entropic law of downward cosmic decay? Francis had watched the fall from Eden. And he knew now the real trauma of that forgotten moment when man stepped out of the quantumwave and into Time.

Night was metamorphosing into day and he was getting tired. Like the Vampyre. From night into day. Vlad of Wallichia. Countess Báthori. Dracul. Now that he'd made up his mind to die — he was already dead. Undead. Could see in the dark. Taste the air. Hear a heartbeat. Smell the snowcaps of Cotopaxi and Chimborazo. And for the first time he didn't feel guilty about dying. Wanting to die. He slid from his chair down onto the floor and lay beside the body of Fiona. In front of the fire. Knew his wounds were serious and he'd lost a lot of blood and would probably die in a growing delirium. Francis floated away to Sheol where he met Sakuntala the daughter of Viswamita and Menaka. And she sang the song of the *amitabha* for him and showed him that her music was the purest form of emotion and the essence of all spirit.

Dark again when Francis woke. Not dead! Fire gone out and congealed blood stuck his hair and clothes to the floor. Thought he heard a noise coming from the shed but knew it would only be rats. Fiona's body lay beside him in the moonglow. He pulled himself away from the bloodtreacle and checked the outside of the house. All quiet. Had to finish it. Now. Now was the time. Francis went back inside and knelt down beside the woman. Took the safety catch off the Browning and placed the muzzle to his right eye. Finger slowly tightened on the trigger.

And an overwhelming of Voices screeched round the room. A deafening sound of Babel with some shouting yes and some shouting no and some laughing and others crying and all accusing him of everything. Screeching at him through venomous teeth. He hesitated. It should be symbolic. An appropriate setting. Better than this place. This place of dustdecay. Purgatoryplace. He wanted the symbolism of final freedom. When everything else has failed. As it must fail. Francis really wanted to do it now. Immediately. Needed to do it now. But also wanted an Avalon. Where could it be found? Where it began. Where what began ... the life or the limbo? He *wanted* to do it! Wanted to do it! Had to do it. There was no choice. The only choice was where. Not here. In the friendhouse? Make it a masterpiece. A fitting *coup de pinceau final*. There was no place else. The bastards were all after him and he had nowhere to go. Nowhere to take the girl. If he went back into London they'd get him and then he wouldn't be able to do it at all because they'd send him down with the drugs again. Into the quicksand. And he was afraid. Of what? If he didn't do it now he might not do it at all. He was halfdead already. Undead? Already dead.

Francis saw Fiona move on the floor in front of him. He dropped the gun and lifted her into his arms. Examined her face for signs of life. Willed her dead eyes to laugh up at him. Talk to him.

'Glenny ...'

But they didn't. Nothing left. The movement was some involuntary reaction to rigor mortis. Or the effect of the fire on the body. He sobbed softly and laid her back down onto the floor. Then picked up the gun and put it into his pocket. He lit a cigarette and sat in the silent chair for some time. Forever. Everandever. This was the Black Hole of his existence. The collapsed star. The point of infinite density and zero size surrounded by the event horizon — the region of no return. Francis stood up and went out to the Citroën. Climbed inside and drove away. There was only one other place.

chapter thirty-nine

chapte r thirty-nine

chapte r thirty-nine

Francis Page parked the car behind some trees in Baldwins Gardens. Then walked through to the Church of St Eduard the Martyr. Carefully checked the area as he went. Very late and no one about. No priests that he could see. Francis had his own keys and could go where he liked. He stood in the nave and looked up towards the altar. I am not yet born; O fill me. With strength against those who would freeze my humanity, would dragoon me into a lethal automaton, would make me a cog in a machine, a thing with one face, a thing, and against all those who would dissipate my entirety, would blow me like thistledown hither and thither or hither and thither like water held in the hands would spill me.

'Francis ...'

'Father?'

'Are you all right?'

'I'm fine, Father.'

'You look pale.'

'I'm ok.'

'There's blood on your clothes ...'

'Just a small cut, Father ... you know how these things bleed ...'

'You should go down to the hospital. You look quite badly injured to me ... what happened?'

'I'll go down in a while. I'm just saying a prayer first, Father.'

The priest left him alone. He tried to remember his prayer. Broken concentration. Took him a while to get it back. Let them not make me a stone and let them not spill me. Otherwise kill me.

Francis took the gun from his pocket and checked the magazine. Released the safety catch. Sudden crackle of a radio set disturbed him and he ducked out of sight into the shadows along the aisles. Francis could see some movement towards the rear of the church. Heads popping up and then down again. The priest. With the fucking police. Maybe he might take a few of them with him. Kill six or seven and then top himself with the last fucking bullet. But that wouldn't be right. Not a *coup de pinceau final*. Francis made his way to a small side door and slipped out — as the figures came closer in the gloom of the old church. Radios crackled and hushed voices high on adrenaline.

He locked the door behind him so the bastards couldn't follow. That way. Then crept along quickly to the Citroën. All clear. Back to the house in Essex. Do it there like he intended in the first place. Avafuckinglon! Do it in the early early hours. In the pearly hours. The diamond drops of misty morningtime. Do it with dignity. Kill himself with kudos.

Francis drove east into the City and continued up through Finsbury and Bethnal Green. He was confused again and wanted to get it over and done with. No more bullshit. No more fucking mockery. He drove erratically to confuse any slags that might be following him. Sure he could see a plainclothes car in the rearview. First a red Honda. Then a blue Opal. Then a dark green Jaguar. The bastards were driving his old car. Stole it. The fucking thieves! Francis tried to throw them off the trail. Put his foot down and the Citroën sped through the latenight streets. Up along the A107 and across through Hackney and Dalston Lane. Stopped suddenly. Could remember this street. A small dark memory at the back of his mind. Delicate. Skindeep. But the bastards were after him so he couldn't stay long enough to think about it. Back south along the A10 and Kingsland Road. Turned in towards the City at Bishopsgate and up West along Shaftsbury Avenue. The traffic round Leicester Square swallowed him up and he decided he must have lost anyone who might be following. He parked up and waited to see who was acting suspiciously. Anyone? Nothing. Nobody. Francis got out of the car and walked down through Soho.

He was in New York. Knew he'd be back. No? Somesunnyday. Swimming. Drowning in humanity. Being dragged down and drowned in the sea of slouching people and the swirl of affluence and allrightness. Shinypersons and slovenlyslobs in their own private worlds of pathos and piety. Greek Street was Greenwich Avenue and Beak Street was Broadway. He was back in the Big Apple again. Like he wanted to be. Francis wandered around like a ball in a pin machine. Bounced about. Forgot where he was going and where he was coming from. He meandered down along Dean Street and found his way to Soho Square. Went into the park and sat on a wooden bench. He felt safe in there. Behind the iron railings. Looking out at the scene of gaiety and grundge all around him. A colourful tableau of sight sound and smell.

He could feel the fear. Mistrust. He could taste the turbulence — like a vein of high electricity running through the place. Sense it. Touch it. Taste it. Murder! It tasted like death and smelled like murder. He witnessed crimes of violence in the bloodair and heard screams in the streetmusic and smelled decay in the unique perfume of purgatory. Francis sat on the bench with his head in his hands. He sobbed and tears fell from his eyes onto the short wintergrass.

He sat for a long time. Dawn was breaking to the east — out over Stratford. Before he forced himself to make a move. Stratford. He knew he had to get home. He'd been out all night and Angeline would be angry again. Francis wandered back out of the little park in the middle of Soho Square and looked for his Jaguar. Nowhere to be seen. He knew he left it in Charing Cross — outside the Centrefold Club. Or the Phoenix. Or Wyndhams? Couldn't be sure. Fucking thing was gone now and some bastard had stolen it. Insurancejob. He headed north and took the tube at Tottenham Court Road. Central Line east. Straight to Stratford. Eight stops. Francis hadn't been underground for a long time. Many years. Murky. Darky. Dangerous. Strange sorts staring at him with deadly eyes. Opposite. Got up and changed seats. Several times. Eyes still followed him. Everywhere. Knew he was a killer. Murderer! Schizo! Windowlicker!

Francis cowered at the door and couldn't wait to get out at Great Eastern Road. He walked up The Grove in the pale earlylight and crossed the Maryland roundabout at Forest Lane into Leytonstone Road. Morning people out and about. Going to work or school. North past the college and a group of teenage girls came towards him. Laughing. Excited. About something teenagegirly. Shining in the softness *du matin*. One of them he knew. From somewhere. Once. Before. Sulky face on the back seat of a bottlegreen car and no words. Silent. Sour. Not like now. Bright and beautiful.

'Sinéad ...?'

The group looked at him with a mixture of fear and bemusement and stepped out into the road to get past. Hysterical giggling behind hands. Glanced back over their shoulders. He called out after them.

'Sinéad!'

They stopped and turned to stare at him. One of them pointed a frightened finger. Looked at him with nervous eyes. Knowing but not wanting to know. Denying.

'How do you know my name? Who are you?'

'I'm ...'

'You're a dirty tramp! Don't you come near me!'

'I'm ...'

'You're disgusting ... covered in filth and blood. If you come near me I'll scream. I'll call the police. If you come near me ... I'll have you arrested.'

Denied. Like Christ. The girl turned and rejoined her friends. They continued on their way with words like bloodybeggar and did you see the stateofhim and they should all be taken off the streets and locked away. From normal people. Dirtytramp. Mad! Loony! Windowlicker! Maniac! Murderer! Francis felt his heart beat faster. Heart! Beat! But this time the blood didn't flood his brain and control stayed with him. No anger this time. Just a deep sadness came. A deep deep deep deep sadness. Like black velvet. Wrapping itself round him. And he remembered what it was he had to do.

Francis found himself in a familiar part of Leytonstone Road. He staggered up the drive of a familiar house and fumbled for familiar keys that weren't in his pocket. Any more. Banged on the familiar front door. A light went on in the familiar hallway and a familiar voice asked.

'Who's there?'

'Open the door, Angeline. I'm home!'

'Who is it?'

'Just open the door please!'

'Francis? I'll call the police ...'

'I want to talk to you about Sinéad ...'

'Oh my God ... what's happened to Sinéad?'

The front door opened and a familiar lovehate woman stood in front of him. He tried to kiss her but she pulled back away from him — down the hall.

'Francis ... Jesus, Mary and Joseph ... what are you doing here? Look at the state of you. What's going on? What's happened to Sinéad?'

'Nothing's happened to her, Angeline. I just met her on the street and she didn't recognise me. Her own father! What have you been telling her ... you and that brother of yours?'

Angeline was paralysed with surprise. Wanted to scream but was unable to. Backed away down the hall. Francis followed her into the lounge.

'What are you doing here, Francis? Where have you been? You're hurt ...'

'It hurt me, Angeline. I always just wanted to love her. Like Fiona. That's all.'

'Have you seen Fiona? Do you know where she is?'

'She's in the country ...'

'In the country? Where in the country?'

'She'll be going back to college soon. She told me she'd go back and finish her studies.'

What was left of his ear began to bleed again. Francis put his hand up to the side of his head. Blood seeped through his fingers.

'Fiona loves me, Angeline ... why doesn't Sinéad?'

'Francis, look ... you're hurt. God, you're bleeding!. Let me get you some help ...'

Angeline was trying hard not to scream. Decided it would be better to play whatever game this was. This time. Hoped he wouldn't hurt her. He looked mad. Talked crazy. Even more than before. She had her new life now — with Sinéad. He wasn't in it. And her career and her control and her space and her family when she wanted them and her privacy when she didn't. Serenity. Sophistry. Selfreliance. Strabismity. This man was a stranger. She didn't know him any more. Maybe never knew him. He never really knew her. What happened to *his* new life?

With the blackwoman. What happened to his neck and ear? Bloody. Ugly. Was that what he was now? Bloodier? Uglier? Then she remembered he killed a prison guard and seriously injured several others and the panic welled up inside her. Could he kill her? Would he kill her? Angeline wasn't sure. There was a time when he wouldn't. When she knew him. Believed she knew him. Hoped she knew him. After their fourteen years. But now? Francis pulled the 9mm Browning from his pocket and held the gun to her head. Her eyes widened with the silence that came out through her mouth. Tried to speak normally. But the words shook.

'It's all right, Francis ... don't hurt me. Tell me what's going on.'

'I need a bit of help. A little bit of help. That's all.'

'What do you want?'

'I want a bit of help, Angeline. A bit of help.'

'How? What can I do?'

'I don't know ... just a little bit of help ...'

Angeline suddenly realised he wasn't there to harm her. He was there because he had nowhere else to go. Nobody else to go to. Only her. She could do one of two things —

'Listen ... Francis ... why don't you sit down in the armchair ... like you used to ... and I'll make you a cup of coffee.'

'Have you got a cigarette?'

'No ... no ... I don't smoke, Francis.'

'Fuck!'

'But ... I'll go get you some ... if you like ...'

'You can't go out there, Fiona ...'

'Who? I'm not ... I'm ... why not? You need cigarettes.'

'*They're* out there.'

'Who?'

'Those bastards! You know ... they want to hurt you. They said they'd hurt you and Sinéad if I fucked up.'

'Jesus! Is it the black people? What's happening ...?'

Angeline made her mind up what to do.

'You won't go out there when I'm not looking, will you?'

'I won't. I won't.'

'Promise?'

'I promise.'

'You'll only get hurt if you do.'

Angeline ran out of the house when Francis wasn't looking and straight to a neighbour. Where she telephoned the police. Able to tell them he was alone and armed and asked them not to hurt him if they could help it and could they please find her daughters. Immediately!

Francis remembered why he was here. Where it began. He moved upstairs when he heard the blue sirens arriving in the road.Went to the back of the house and into a bedroom which belonged to a teenage girl. Full of young female things. And Francis remembered being in there before. Not so long ago. He wondered where the girl was. When she would be coming back. A computer by the bed and he pressed a switch. Music emerged. Girl's music. Francis didn't know what it was. But he liked it. He'd heard it before. But forgot where. Lay down on the soft bed and listened in the faintperfume air. Music filled the house and he floated on its changing colours. Heart light again and sirens sang for him in the dreamlight room. Halfwomen, halfbirds flew round his head and made him forget everything. Parthenope and Ligea and Leucosia and Melpomene and Sterope and Terpsichore. A song of death. To accompany his soul on its journey to Heaven. Or to Hades.

The time for your final dream is now. *La pucelle? La pucelle d'Orléans*? I thought everyone was gone. Deserted me. We have not spoken for *éternité*. Where've you been? Here. Waiting *pour vous*. And the others? There is now only *moi*. Is this your room? Is this your girl-room, Jeanne? They said I was mad because they wanted to kill me. Like you, Dauphin. They said I was violent ... *tueuse*! Evil. Full of evil.

But I was only a dreamer. Like you, Dauphin. You were like me, Jeanne ... you had a direct link to God. We just cut out the middleman and went direct. That's all. Those people out there wouldn't understand. None of them. That is because *ils ne rêvent pas*. The flames set me free, Dauphin. The bullet will the same do for you. Yes. But what do I kill, Jeanne? What is me? I know now I wasn't made in the image of God — but evolutionary expediency. If I didn't need my legs I wouldn't have them. They wouldn't have evolved. Or arms or ego. Or anything else. What brain cells can I do without, Jeanne? Put a bullet in and still be alive? Me? What is *me*? How do I kill me? Is this your room, Jeanne? Is this your bed? *Non* ... it is your *lit de morte*. Is it a *coup de pinceau final*? *Oui ... ce dernier coup de pinceau est excellent*. But you must the last dream now allow to come. Do not resist it like *ces gens-là* outside. The dream will be clear and you will understand it. You will know as I know what the images mean. I am your angel voice and without *moi* you cannot live. And by their wanting to take me away from you, their counsel is *du Diable*. And yours is of *du Dieu*.

Francis was back at the beginning and nothing had changed. He was a child again and it was all still the same. He lay on the bed in his room and listened to the other children outside in the street. Calling him. Crazymadschizospazo! The girls on their way to school. Nothing would change. Ever. Tears rolled down his cheeks. He couldn't go through it all again. Wouldn't. But he knew now there was another dimension. Because death is the beginning!

The front door was suddenly battered in and footsteps came creeping through the house and up the stairs. Francis Page put the muzzle of the gun up to his right eye and pulled the trigger.

God. A word common, in slightly varying forms, to all Germanic languages and coming from a root word related to old Irish *Guth*. It is in no way connected with English *good*. Voltaire said: *Si Dieu n'existait pas, il faudrait l'inventer*. Greek and Roman gods were divided into *Dii Majores* and *Dii Minores*. Their blood was *ichor*, their food was *ambrosia*, their drink *nectar*. The Greeks observed a feast of the Unknown Gods, lest any be neglected. Romans and Cyreneans offered sacrifice to the Lord of the Flies and the Philistines had *Ba'alzebúl*, who was covered in blood. Muhammad saw an angel with seventy thousand heads, each head had seventy thousand faces, each face had seventy thousand mouths, each mouth had seventy thousand tongues and each tongue spoke seventy thousand languages. All were employed in singing God's praises. *Allah il Allah*. *Al-Hayy al-Qayyum*. And the *trimurti* of *Brahma*, *Vishnu* and *Siva*. JHVH — the *Tetragrammaton* was too ineffable and too sacred to use. *Kami-no-Michi* saw God in trees and stones and water and caves and emperors who were the descendants of the Sun-Goddess *Amaterasu-Omikami*. And in the Dreamtime the *Quinkan* and *Wandjina* journeyed far and the *Ungambikula* created themselves out of nothingness. And God said unto Moses : I AM THAT I AM.

And now that I move along the Noble Enlightened Path — I know what it is. It is *Shango* and *Olokun* and *Rangi* and *Hina* and *Nidhogg* and *Kuanyin* and *Hapy* and *Ishtar* and *Janus* and *Kali*, and *Thor* and *Tezcatlipoca* and *Gaia* and *Nüwa* and *Xiuhtecuhtli* and *Neith* and *Chandra* and *Tara* and *Quetzalcoatl* and *Eros* and *Anubis* and *Ra-Atum* and *Yomi* and *Kagutsuchi* and *Athene* and *Zeus* and *Pan* and *Venus* and *Mars* and *Odin* and *Väinämöinen* and *Ilmarinen* and *Perun* and *Yarilo* and *Belanus* and *Epona* and *Lugh* and *Pinga* and *Tirawa* and *Tsohanoai* and *Itzamna* and *Chac* and *Viracocha*.

I KNOW WHAT IT IS! Know what it is. Know what it is. Know. What. IT. is!